Anders de la
MOTTE
RITES of
SPRING

Anders de la Motte is the bestselling author of the Seasons Quartet; the first three books of which – *End of Summer*, *Deeds of Autumn* and *Dead of Winter* – have all been number one bestsellers in Sweden and have been shortlisted for the Swedish Academy of Crime Writers' Award for Best Crime Novel of the Year. Anders, a former police officer, has already won a Swedish Academy Crime Award for his debut, *Game*, in 2010 and his second standalone, *The Silenced*, in 2015.

To date, the first three books in the Seasons Quartet have published over half a million copies. Set in southern Sweden, all four books can be read as standalones.

Anders de la MOTTE

RITES of SPRING

Translated by Marlaine Delargy

ZAFFRE

Originally published in Sweden by Bokförlaget Forum in 2020

First published in the UK in 2021 by
ZAFFRE
An imprint of Bonnier Books UK
80–81 Wimpole St, London W1G 9RE
Owned by Bonnier Books
Sveavägen 56, Stockholm, Sweden

A CIP catalogue record for this book is
available from the British Library.

ISBN: 978–1–78576–948–1

Also available as an ebook and an audiobook

1 3 5 7 9 10 8 6 4 2

Typeset by IDSUK (Data Connection) Ltd
Printed and bound in Great Britain by Clays Ltd, Elcograf S.p.A.

Zaffre is an imprint of Bonnier Books UK
www.bonnierbooks.co.uk

To all my readers,
because you allow me to have the best job in the world

April is the cruellest month, breeding
Lilacs out of the dead land, mixing
Memory and desire, stirring
Dull roots with spring rain.

T S Eliot: 'The Waste Land'

Prologue
19 May 1986

As soon as Little Stefan drove onto the marsh, he began to think about the dead girl. It was impossible not to. The game of Chinese whispers that had started on the morning of May the first had already travelled around the area several times. Filled his head with horrific images from which there was no escape.

Her lifeless body on the sacrificial stone in the centre of the stone circle. Her white dress, her hair loose around her head. Her hands folded over her chest, two antlers clasped in her stiff fingers. Her once beautiful face covered by a bloodstained handkerchief, as if whoever had taken her life had been unable to look her in the eye afterwards.

Most Tornaby residents were already absolutely certain that they knew who'd killed her, that the whole thing was a dreadful but simple story. A family tragedy. However, there were those who quietly maintained that something else entirely had happened during Walpurgis Night. That maybe it was the Green Man himself who had claimed his spring sacrifice.

It had been a long time since Little Stefan had believed in ghost stories, but he couldn't help shuddering. The marshy forest closed in around the dirt track, scraping at the paintwork with long, green fingers. This was the part of the castle estate he disliked most of all. The dampness, the smell of decay. The sodden ground that at one moment felt solid, at the next sucked your boots so deep into the mud that it was a real struggle to escape without help. *The marsh belongs to the Green Man*, his grandfather used to say. *People ought to stay away.* At least the superstitious old misery guts had been partly right.

The track led deep into the marsh, to Svartgården, where the girl had lived. Only a month or so ago he'd given her a lift to the bus stop. She'd sat right next to him in the front seat of the pick-up. She hadn't said much; she'd seemed lost in her own thoughts. He'd stolen glances at her from time to time, watching her face, her movements, and out of nowhere he'd been overwhelmed by a feeling he couldn't explain.

He was married, he had two young daughters, a house, a car, a good job. Things he usually valued, but at that moment, sitting beside that beautiful girl, they had felt like a burden. His whole life was already mapped out, one long, predictable journey without an ounce of the tempting, forbidden pleasures that emanated from her. He could smell it on her – sweet and sharp like newly opened lilac blossom. A perfume that evoked yearning. Desire.

At one point when she looked away, he'd almost reached out to touch her, as if that would enable him to access everything he didn't have. He'd stopped himself at the last second, but the sense of loss had lingered for several days.

He had to concentrate in order to avoid the deepest potholes the further on he drove. Lasse Svart was supposed to maintain the track, according to his lease, but needless to say he didn't bother. For years Lasse Svart had relied on the fact that the count would never be able to find another tenant; nobody was interested in a dozen or so acres of sodden forest, so he more or less did what he liked out at Svartgården. His own little kingdom, far away from laws, rules, and curious eyes.

But that was before Walpurgis Night. Before Lasse's sixteen-year-old daughter was found dead on the sacrificial stone, the ground all around ploughed up by hooves.

During Walpurgis Night the veil between life and death is at its thinnest. Things are on the move, nature is hungry and the Green Man rides through the forest.

Little Stefan suppressed another shudder.

The forest opened out as he reached the muddy yard surrounding Svartgården. Three dilapidated buildings huddled in the gloom beneath the trees, as if they were trying to hide. Rusty agricultural tools and machinery lay among the nettles.

He'd been here many times before, usually with Erik Nyberg, the castle administrator, and they'd always been met by a pack of yapping terriers before he'd even switched off the engine. Today there wasn't a dog in sight. The place was quiet; even the birds weren't making much noise on this spring morning. A strange, oppressive silence filled the air.

Little Stefan remained standing by his truck for a minute or so as he tucked a plug of tobacco beneath his top lip and waited for Lasse or one of his women to poke their head out of the door and ask what the fuck he wanted, but nothing happened. Lasse's red pick-up was nowhere to be seen, nor was the battered old Ford the women usually drove. He glanced at his watch: seven thirty. Who went out at this early hour?

He caught a movement out of the corner of his eye. A small dog was peering around the corner of the smithy; it was little more than a puppy.

'Hello! Come on then,' Little Stefan said, without really knowing why. The dog took a couple of cautious steps, keeping its belly low, tail tucked between its legs. Then it suddenly stopped and stiffened, as if it had heard something.

Little Stefan turned his head, but the house was still in darkness. When he looked back, the dog was gone.

He set off up the concrete steps leading to the front door; halfway up he realised it was ajar. He paused, unsure of what to do. On the wall next to the door he saw a half-metre-tall figure woven from fresh green branches. His grandfather had made one every spring and hung it on the front door.

So that the Green Man will ride on through the night. So that he won't stop at our house.

'Hello? Anyone home?'

The words bounced off the walls and came back like a distorted echo, as if it were someone else's voice. Someone who was watching him from the darkness. Imitating him, mocking him.

Little Stefan looked at the creepy figure again, and for a second he was ready to run back down the steps, jump in his truck and get out of there. Tell Erik Nyberg that no one had been home, and reading the water meter would have to wait. However, he was a grown man with a job to do, not some little kid who was scared of ghosts.

He knocked on the door frame.

'Hello?' he shouted again. 'Anyone home? It's Little Stefan, from the castle.'

No response.

The silence from inside the house was making him increasingly uncomfortable. His shirt was sticking to his back. He took a deep breath and knocked once more, harder this time. Pushed the door open and stepped into the porch. There was a weird smell, a stale odour that reminded him of animals – but what was it?

'Hello?'

He checked out the kitchen. The table was littered with dirty plates, glasses and cutlery for three people. Several flies were buzzing around among the remains of the food. One of the chairs had been knocked over. Through a doorway on the other side of the porch he could just see a neatly made bed.

'Hello!' This time he yelled up the stairs.

Still nothing. He was feeling very uneasy now, but he pulled himself together and made his way up the creaking wooden staircase.

The upper floor was in darkness. On the left was a bedroom with a double bed, also neatly made. The door on the right was closed. It took him a few seconds to realise that it wasn't simply a uniform green, but was covered in a carefully painted pattern of leaves. Almost a work of art, in fact.

Elita's Room, someone had written in attractive, ornate lettering at eye level.

So this was her room. This was where she had lived her life.

Elita Svart. The spring sacrifice.

Little Stefan reached for the handle; his heartbeat seemed to be reverberating throughout the house. He was on the point of doing something forbidden, stepping into a world to which he was not permitted access. An uninvited guest, an intruder.

Then he saw another message on the door. Small, distorted words that almost blended in with the artwork, but became clearer as his eyes grew used to the darkness.

Nature is hungry and the Green Man is riding through the forests.

At the same time he spotted something else. Hidden among the leaves there was a large, terrifying male face.

The realisation was sudden, and chilled his blood. He didn't know where it had come from or why, but the sensation was so strong that it made the hairs on the back of his neck stand on end. Something had happened in this house. Something evil that had made Lasse Svart and his women leap to their feet in the middle of their supper, run out to their cars and drive away in the night. Something connected to a dead sixteen-year-old girl on a cold stone, and a ghostly rider galloping through the forest.

Little Stefan let go of the door handle and took the stairs in three strides. Hurtled out through the porch, down the steps and into his truck.

He started the engine and set off with a screech of tyres. He didn't even glance in the rear-view mirror until he was absolutely certain that Svartgården had disappeared, deep among the trees.

1

'Hi, Margaux, it's Thea. Sorry I haven't called you for a while – there's been a lot to do with the move, but now David and I have arrived in Skåne. Our new life can begin. A new, happier story than the old one. At least that's what both of us are hoping for.'

The drone begins by taking a close-up of the main entrance and the impressive stone steps, then it slowly pulls out until the whole castle can be seen: a large central section with two wings, which from above makes the building look like an elongated H.

The white, freshly cleaned façade, the green copper roof, the coach house and the stables a short distance away to the right, beyond the east wing. The moat beyond the west wing. Then the voiceover.

'Bokelund Castle is situated approximately four kilometres from the small community of Tornaby in the district of Ljung-slöv in north-western Skåne, not far from the southern point of Söderåsen National Park. The castle is one of the oldest in Skåne, dating all the way back to the fourteenth century. The current main building, in the style of the French Renaissance, was constructed around 1880, but remains of the original castle can still be found down in the cellar, where one of the dungeons still exists.'

A slight exaggeration. No one actually knows what the little vaulted room down in the cellar was used for, but Thea has to admit that David was right when he said that a dungeon sounded better than a larder.

The camera zooms a little further out, revealing the mossy green moat. The avenue linking the castle to the main road in the south. The narrow stone bridge leading across to the forest in the north. The marsh, just visible to the east.

'Bokelund Castle lies on an island surrounded by a moat, created in the seventeenth century by diverting water from the nearby Tornaby marsh, which is one of Skåne's largest wetlands. It is also a Natura-2000 area, supporting a wide range of flora and fauna.'

Switch to a shot of deer with the light behind them, ferns, moss, a dragonfly dancing over a tranquil pool, a skein of geese crossing a blue sky.

Back to the drone. A new angle, this time a variation on the opening image, finishing at the top of the stone steps where she and David are now standing.

'Since 1996 the castle has been owned and run by the Bokelund Foundation, which was started by Count Rudolf Gordon, the last private owner. The foundation is unique; its aim is to benefit the Tornaby area and its residents. Among other things, it funds a bus service and a local medical practice, and also awards grants. The castle has recently been restored to its former glory.'

End.

'What do you think?' David looks both eager and nervous at the same time. 'They'll add the interview we're about to do.'

'Great,' Thea says, and immediately regrets her choice of word when she sees his expression. 'Professional,' she adds. 'Extremely professional.'

David looks happier. He closes his laptop and places it on the stone balustrade.

'The producer just sent it to me.' He points to the short man in the baseball cap who's standing a short distance away, talking to the cameraman and the sound guy. 'There's a bit of tweaking to do, plus the music track, but they'll put that on after the interview. I think it's going to be fantastic – as long as the weather holds out.'

He glances anxiously at the sky. It's warm for the second half of April, and the spring sun is shining, but a band of grey has begun to grow on the horizon.

'This has to be perfect,' he mutters, probably as much to himself as to Thea.

She places a hand on his arm. 'It will be. Don't worry.'

David nods, forces a wry smile. He's wearing spotless chef's whites. His beard, peppered with grey, has been neatly trimmed along his jaw line, and his blond hair is neatly slicked back.

A woman with a make-up kit attached to her belt comes up to them.

'Hi – can I just powder your forehead?'

'Sure, no problem.'

The make-up artist is around thirty, a good fifteen years younger than both Thea and David. She's also very attractive. Not so long ago David would already have switched on the charm, given her the confident, wolfish grin that's so difficult to resist. But David is not his usual self. From time to time he nibbles, apparently unconsciously, at one thumbnail; the flesh around it is red, and the make-up artist has to work hard to disguise the sheen of sweat on his forehead.

She turns to Thea.

'Are you appearing on screen?'

'No,' David answers for her. 'My wife is a little shy.' He winks at Thea as if to reassure her that everything is OK, that there will be no more arguments; he respects the fact that she doesn't want to appear on TV. Thea knows it isn't true.

'David, can I have a word?' the producer calls out.

Thea moves over to the wall. She would really like to slink down the stairs, sneak off home to the coach house, stay as far away from the camera as possible, but the TV feature is a big deal for the castle. At the very least she has to stay around and look interested.

'How's it going?' says a voice behind her.

'Fine.' Thea tries to hide her surprise. In spite of her height, David's mother has an unfailing ability to materialise unexpectedly. Ingrid is tall – taller than Thea. Straight back, broad shoulders, no hint of the stooping posture that often creeps in after retirement. Her steel-grey hair is cut short, her eyes sharp behind her glasses.

'The weather looks promising – that's good.'

Thea nods in agreement.

'What time is Dr Andersson arriving tomorrow?' A quick change of subject. That's how Ingrid operates.

'Nine o'clock,' Thea replies, even though she's absolutely certain that Ingrid knows exactly what her timetable is.

'And she's going to take you around the area. Show you the surgery, explain how everything works.'

Statements, not question.

'Mm.'

'Sigbritt Andersson is an excellent GP,' her mother-in-law continues. 'She's meant a lot to Tornaby.'

Thea waits for the reservation that is hanging in the air. And here it is, right on cue.

'But Sigbritt has always been nosy, ever since she was a child. You have to think about what you say in her company, if you know what I mean. Particularly when it comes to personal matters.'

Ingrid pauses for a couple of seconds – just long enough for another abrupt change of subject.

'I hear you're off the medication. Glad you're getting better.'

Thea says nothing. Silently thanks David for overstepping the mark.

'You and David need each other.' Ingrid nods in the direction of her son, who is talking to the producer and the interviewer. 'You need a chance to recover. Get away from everything that's happened.' She continues to nod, emphasising her words. 'By the way, I'm working on the guest list for the preview dinner. So sad that your parents are no longer with us.'

The new topic of conversation seems innocent enough, but it's always hard to tell with Ingrid.

'Yes,' Thea replies. The lie is so well-practised that it doesn't even feel untrue.

Ingrid touches her arm. 'You should know that Bertil and I regard you as our own daughter.'

The gesture surprises Thea, and she doesn't really know what she's expected to say. She and David have been together for a number of years, on and off, but they've only been married since last November. She can probably count the number of times she's met her in-laws on the fingers of one hand, and Ingrid Nordin is not the kind of person who's in the habit of showing her emotions or her appreciation.

'How is Bertil today?' Thea manages to ask.

'Good. He wanted to come, but he was a little tired.' Ingrid points to the TV team. 'I think they're starting.'

David has taken up his position on the steps, exactly where the drone footage ended. The interviewer is a young man with dazzling white teeth and a close-fitting suit. He looks a little too ambitious to be doing this kind of lightweight reporting. Judging by his body language and the irritated glances he keeps giving the producer, he is of the same opinion.

The first question sounds as if it belongs in a sports programme.

'David Nordin – how does it feel to return home after more than twenty successful years as a chef and restaurant owner in Stockholm?'

Thea already knows the answer. She and David have been rehearsing this interview for almost a week, but she is still a little nervous, for some reason.

'Fantastic, of course. Bokelund Castle is a wonderful environment for a restaurant. I'm so happy to be able to promote my local area and the traditional cuisine of Skåne. It's a natural step for me, and one I've longed to take for many years.'

David ends with a smile that radiates self-confidence. Apparently. This part of the narrative is vitally important. He is the local boy made good, triumphantly returning home to attract tourists and summer visitors. Not a disgraced restaurateur who has been forced to quietly close his businesses and scuttle south with his tail between his legs.

'So you and two of your childhood friends are behind this project?'

Thea breathes out. The interviewer is sticking to the agreed questions. David also seems relieved.

'That's correct – Jeanette Hellman and Sebastian Malinowski. Sebastian is one of the founders of the IT company Conexus, and Jeanette has had a long and successful career in finance. We all grew up in Tornaby, and we see the restaurant as an opportunity to give something back to our beloved local area.'

Goodness me. Who wrote that reply for him? It wasn't you, was it, ma chère?

Margaux's voice comes from nowhere. Thea gives a start, quells the impulse to look around. She knows that Margaux can't possibly be here. Although she's right, of course. 'Beloved local area' is way too much.

'An amazing opportunity,' David continues, answering a question that Thea has missed. 'We're so grateful to the Bokelund Foundation for modernising the castle and investing in the restaurant. Paving the way, so to speak . . .' He laughs.

Thea glances at her mother-in-law, who is entirely focused on the interview. No mention of the fact that she is the chair of the foundation, or that Ingrid is behind most things that happen around here, including this interview.

David is comfortable now. His voice is less tense, his smiles more spontaneous. Thea relaxes a fraction.

Next question.

'Is the castle haunted?'

Margaux comes into her head again – her image this time. That chopped-off fringe, those brown eyes, that slightly crooked front tooth she always presses her tongue against just before she smiles.

'Absolutely. We have two ghosts, in fact. In the middle of the eighteenth century a young woman drowned when she fell through the ice into the moat. According to the legend, she was on her way from the castle to a secret tryst with the huntsman's son. In the late nineteenth century another young woman came off her horse during a fox hunt in the forest and broke her neck. It's said that sometimes you can hear the two of them galloping through the trees at night. If you believe in ghost stories, that is.'

The interviewer nods with interest.

'But there's a real-life story too, isn't there? A third girl who died. I'm thinking of the spring sacrifice.'

David's smile stiffens. Thea sees Ingrid straighten her shoulders.

'Yes, it was a tragedy. Maybe we shouldn't . . .' David looks at Thea, then at the producer.

'Cut!' The producer takes the interviewer to one side, and a fractious discussion ensues.

David chews on his thumbnail, his brow once again shining with perspiration. Thea goes over to him, takes his other hand. It is hot and sweaty.

'What was that all about?'

He shakes his head. 'Nothing. I just lost the thread.'

The make-up artist reappears and powders his forehead. The producer and the interviewer are still arguing.

'But why? The true-crime angle is much more interesting. The viewers love that kind of thing, I don't get why we . . .'

The producer interrupts, says something that makes the interviewer turn on his heel and stomp down the steps.

David squeezes Thea's hand. Ingrid goes over to have a quiet word with the producer, who beckons the cameraman and says: 'We'll take it from the top. I'll ask the questions this time, stick to what we agreed. OK?'

David nods stiffly. Thea lets go of his hand and quickly moves out of shot.

'Let's go.'

The producer asks the same introductory question as before, and David immediately trips over his words. They try again and again, but his concentration is gone. His responses sound mechanical and automatic, and there is no trace of his warmth and charm.

Thea sees the producer glance at his watch, then at the sky, where the band of grey is getting closer and closer.

'We'll take a short break. Have a drink of water, David.'

The producer and Ingrid confer once more. David sips at a bottle of water. The make-up artist continues to fight a losing battle with his shiny forehead.

'It's all going wrong,' he mutters. 'Before we've even started.'

Thea takes his hand again. 'You can do this. Just try to relax.'

'It's no good, we'll have to rethink. Come up with something else.' He squeezes her hand, looks pleadingly at her, raising his eyebrows to make sure she understands what he means. 'I can't do this without you, Thea. Please . . .'

She swallows, tries to assess the risks.

Ingrid interrupts her train of thought.

'So, Thea – Peter, the producer, and I have decided it would be good if you were involved in the interview. The supportive wife, the area's new GP and so on.'

Thea can feel everyone's eyes on her. There is a lump of ice in her stomach, her mouth feels as dry as dust. David squeezes her hand again, harder and harder until she almost can't bear it.

She takes a deep breath.

'OK,' she says, and regrets it almost immediately. But it's too late now.

She hears Margaux's throaty voice inside her head.

We all have our ghosts, Thea. Some more than others.

Far away, beyond the darkening grey band on the horizon, the thunder rumbles threateningly.

2

'I'm sure you're wondering how Emee is. She runs away as soon as I let her off the lead. Disappears into the forest, won't come back when I call her. I think she's searching for you, Margaux. She misses you. We both do. Are you missing us? Sorry – stupid question.'

Thea cuts through the box garden and continues across the lawn behind the castle. Emee already knows the way; she is pulling at the lead, eager to get on.

The moat forms a pond here, or even a small lake, divided by the stone bridge leading over to the forest. The bridge is only a couple of metres wide. It was built in the early nineteenth century, presumably so that the fine folk could ride directly from the castle into the forest.

Beneath the bridge the water is bottle-green and slow-moving; the surface is largely covered with aquatic plants and a slimy layer of algae. The water comes from the marsh, bringing with it a smell that Thea recognises from other places: the jungles of Nigeria, the desert landscape of Ethiopia, the forensic pathology lab in Solna and among the ruins of Syria. It is a mixture of earth and yeast, iron and ammonia, insects with vibrating wings, and grubs that live on decay.

Thea shudders. Emee snorts, as if she too wants to escape the musty smell. As soon as they reach the other side Thea lets her off the lead, and she races away among the tall trees like a streak of grey.

Thea follows the path, waiting until she is out of sight of the castle before lighting up. Gauloises with no filter, which Margaux taught her to enjoy. She has promised David that she will stop.

She takes a deep drag, holds the smoke for a few seconds until she feels the pain in her lungs.

What's worse than a doctor who smokes? Margaux used to say. *Two doctors who smoke, of course!*

A silly joke, but Margaux always got away with it. She only had to dip her head, hiding her eyes beneath her dead-straight, cartoon-character fringe to make everyone burst out laughing.

Today's TV interview worries Thea. She tries to tell herself that she only appears on screen for a minute or two, that over twenty-five years have passed, and that no one is going to recognise her. Plus she had no choice; David couldn't have carried on alone. The opening is getting closer and closer, he's working long hours, and the phone is always ringing. He is under enormous pressure.

And yet she is convinced that it was the unexpected question that really threw him. A third dead girl, a much more recent event, something the interviewer definitely wanted to talk about rather than continuing with the sunny positivity. David has never mentioned the story to her. She will have to find the right opportunity to ask him about it.

The castle forest rises above the surrounding marsh on a slight hill, an area of solid ground where the trees have been able to grow bigger than in other places. The Bokelund Foundation has put all its funds into the castle itself, leaving the forest to its own devices. The section closest to the bridge and the castle was once more like a park, but weeds have invaded the gravel paths, the old lampposts are no longer connected to the electricity supply, and only a couple of the benches are sturdy enough to sit on. Not that anyone ever does. During the week or so she has been here, Thea hasn't seen a single person in the forest, but maybe that's not so strange. Tornaby is five kilometres away, and the castle has few neighbours. There are hardly any roads leading here; it's as if the world has forgotten this place, left all its decaying beauty to her. The newly opened leaves have not yet formed a solid canopy, and the sunlight filters down onto the carpet of wood anemones. The birds are singing, the wind is soughing through the treetops. Everything is so lovely, and yet a little sad. Maybe that's why she feels at home here?

A crooked signpost informs her that it is five hundred metres to the castle (heading south, back the way she came), five kilometres to Tornaby (west along the overgrown track to her left), six hundred metres to the stone circle that she hasn't yet explored (straight ahead to the north), and finally five hundred metres to the canal (east along the track on the right).

David has told her that the canal is actually a wide ditch about a kilometre in length. It slices through the forest, diverting the water from the wetland to the moat. He has plans to create a floating restaurant, travelling via the moat and along the canal all the way to the hunting lodge at the far end. Personally, Thea wonders whether the almost stagnant water and the smell of the marsh might make the diners lose their appetite, but of course she hasn't said anything to David.

She chooses the track leading east, taking slow drags to make her cigarette last as long as possible. After a couple of minutes she reaches a glade. On one side there is an ancient tree with a gnarled trunk and heavy, twisted branches. The bark is grey, but the light in the glade makes it look almost white.

Instead of continuing along the track she goes over to the tree. Its girth must be four metres, maybe more. Beside it there is a grubby information board that she hasn't noticed before. She rubs away some of the green algae so that she can read the text.

OAK – *QUERCUS ROBUR*

The oak is one of Scandinavia's largest trees, and can be found from Skåne all the way up to Gästrikland. This particular tree is known as the Gallows Oak, although it is unclear whether it was actually used for executions. According to an investigation carried out in 1998, its age is estimated at over nine hundred years old, which makes it the oldest tree in the castle forest, along with the hawthorn grove by the stone circle. The nodular growths on the trunk are known as burls, and are probably caused by a genetic defect that makes the wood fibres grow in the wrong direction in relation to the trunk itself.

Approximately three metres from the ground there are two large burls and a hole, which together give the impression of a man's face, familiarly known as the Green Man. According to a local legend, the Green Man is a creature who takes on human form on certain nights during the spring, and rides through the forest to chase away the winter and the darkness. This same legend says that spring gifts should be inserted in the Green Man's mouth in order to hasten the return of life.

Thea gazes up at the trunk; the formation is easy to find. Two protruding oval shapes side by side, with swollen edges and a smooth centre, and below them a black, circular hole. It definitely resembles a warped male face with empty eyes and a gaping mouth.

A patch of wood anemones is growing right beside her. Without really knowing why, she picks a few and tucks them into her pocket. She stubs out her cigarette, places her foot on the lowest burl, pushes off and grabs the next one with her hand. She hasn't climbed a tree since she was a little girl, but she remembers the technique her big brother taught her. Use your hands to hold on, your legs to push. She doesn't weigh much, and her back, arms and shoulders are strong.

The pale bark is coarse and rough, full of nooks and crannies that she can use. It doesn't take her long to reach the creepy face. She stares into its dead eyes and suddenly feels ridiculous. This is something Margaux would do. Thea's forte is being sensible and logical, focusing on things that can be measured and organised. She loves jigsaws, always knows where the emergency exits are, keeps a rucksack packed with the essentials just in case the worst happens. *Used to keep*, she corrects herself. Until the worst actually happened.

Thea takes the wood anemones out of her pocket and pushes them into the Green Man's mouth. The hole is bigger than it looked from the ground, and her fist easily fits inside. She feels an edge, as if the thick trunk is partly hollow. She extends her arm as far as she can, closes her eyes and thinks of Margaux. Tries to summon up every detail of her face. Her dark fringe, her eyes, the tiny freckles on her nose. Her smile.

Then she drops the flowers.

To the return of life.

A gust of wind passes by, bending the treetops and sending up swirls of dry leaves from the ground. It carries with it the smell of electricity, of a storm. Thea shivers.

Somewhere deep in the forest, Emee begins to bark.

3

Walpurgis Night 1986

Dear readers!

Every narrative must have a beginning, a middle and an end. This is my beginning.

My name is Elita Svart. I am sixteen years old. I live deep in the forest outside Tornaby.

By the time you read this, I will already be dead. But let's take it from the start, shall we?

Arne Backe realised almost straightaway that the garage foreman was messing with him. The fat bastard leaned across the counter speaking loudly enough for his two colleagues, who were doing an oil change on a Volvo 245, to hear every world.

'What did you say your name was?'

'Police Constable 2971 Backe, Ljungslöv police. I've come to pick up a radio car.'

Arne stroked his moustache in a way that he imagined made him look older and more experienced.

'Have you indeed.' The foreman ran a fleshy finger down the page of his ledger. 'A radio car for the Ljungslöv police. Do you really need one? I thought you mostly drove tractors out there in the sticks.'

Arne could hear the two grease monkeys laughing behind him, but he didn't bother turning around. Instead he rapped on the counter with his knuckles.

'Keys. I'm in a hurry.'

'In a hurry! Why would you be in a hurry? Do you have to get home to do the milking? Or are you helping Hans Holmér to solve the murder of Olof Palme?'

More laughter, louder this time. The foreman straightened up and produced a bunch of keys, which he dramatically placed on the counter in front of him. He obviously intended to draw this out for as long as possible.

Arne was used to people trying to wind him up. He was twenty-two years old, the youngest officer at the station in Ljungslöv. A newly qualified kid, wet behind the ears, who was only allowed to make the coffee, man the reception desk and run errands. Lennartson, the chief of police, had very reluctantly organised a lift to Helsingborg in the mail van so that Arne could pick up the new radio car. Lennartson always adopted a particular expression when their eyes met, a mixture of irritation and distaste that Arne had seen way too often. It seemed to be something he evoked in others, something he couldn't do anything about.

He gritted his teeth. In the summer a fresh batch of newly qualified officers would arrive at the station, and he would move up a notch. Get out on the streets like a real cop. Until then he just had to put up with Lennartson's grimaces and his colleagues' teasing. However, this guy and his two stooges were fucking civilians, and had no right to speak to a representative of the law like this.

The foreman scrawled something down in his stained ledger.

'Backe, you said.' He was grinning now.

'Mm . . .' Arne knew what was coming.

'Backe, that means hill. Uphill or downhill?'

The mechanics guffawed, and Arne dug his front teeth into his lower lip. Arne Nedförsbacke – Downhill Arne – that had been his nickname at school. He'd been a figure of fun because of his grades, because he was useless at football, because his parents had had him when they were older. Sometimes there had been a suggestion that his sister was actually his mother, even though Ingrid was only twelve when he was born.

Regardless of how many times he fought, how many times he got beaten up or went on the offensive himself, the laughter had continued. It hadn't stopped when he'd grown up either. He was a target because he hadn't been accepted for military service, because he couldn't hold down a job, because he would never have got into the police if his brother-in-law Bertil hadn't played bridge with Lennartson.

Downhill Arne.

'Sign here.'

The foreman turned the ledger around and winked at him as if Arne were an errand boy rather than a policeman in full uniform.

'It's the Saab over there in the corner. And don't go trying to plough any fields on your way back.'

Arne scribbled his name and grabbed the keys.

The mechanics were pouring fresh oil into the Volvo. The tray containing the old oil was still on a small trolley on the floor. One of the mechanics had blond streaks in his mullet, the other wore an earring. Arne had no doubt they were both closet gays. They weren't much older than him, but they still thought they had the right to laugh at him.

They straightened up and grinned at him as he passed by; no doubt they were trying to think of a suitable parting shot.

'You need to clean the floor,' Arne said before they had time to open their mouths. He kicked the trolley as hard as he could, sending a wave of black, sticky oil all over their feet. Then he walked over to the police car, jumped in and drove away.

The radio car was a Saab 900 Turbo. The mileage was low, and it still smelled new. He could feel its power.

On the E21 heading east, Arne switched on the sirens and blue lights and managed to push the speedometer over one hundred and eighty. He loved seeing the other drivers move aside to let him pass. He could still see the mechanics, slithering around with their shoes full of oil while the foreman roared like a constipated walrus.

For the first time in ages, Arne was in a good mood. He felt as if something within him had eased. He could drive this car wherever and however he wanted. Lennartson moonlighted as a farmer, and had spent all week worrying about a sow that was due to farrow. He'd probably already left for the day, and wouldn't have a clue where Arne was. As long as he stayed away from Ljungslöv, nobody would know what he was up to. He just had to make sure the car was at the station before eight o'clock tomorrow morning.

He passed the sign for Tornaby, and slowed down. It was high time people saw the new Arne Backe.

4

'You're wondering if I still have the same nightmare. I'd really like to say no, because I don't want you to worry about me. I'm fine, Margaux. We won't talk about it anymore, OK?'

The deafening noise reverberates inside Thea's head. She throws herself out of bed, drops to the floor and covers her head with her arms.

The field hospital in Idlib. The explosions from the barrel bombs that tear apart the buildings and the people inside them, burying everything and everyone beneath the rubble. The concrete dust is choking her. She has to get up, put on her helmet. She has to find Margaux, get out of here . . .

David is standing in the doorway. His lips are moving, but she can't hear what he's saying. Her brain is still in the flattened hospital. She staggers through the devastation, tripping over the dead bodies . . .

Then she feels his hands on her shoulders, shaking her gently. The nightmare recedes and she regains her hearing.

'Thea,' he says softly. 'Are you awake?'

She manages a nod, and suddenly notices how dark it is. The nightlight by the door has gone out, and the external lights are not on. Only a faint glow of moonlight spills into the room, making David's face appear chalk-white.

He pulls her close. Only then does she realise her body has started shaking. Just a little at first, then more violently until her teeth are chattering and she can barely stay upright. Her chest contracts, her breathing becomes shallow.

'It's all right,' he murmurs in her ear. 'It was just the thunderstorm. You're safe here. Deep breaths now.'

She tries to follow his advice, takes deep breaths and presses herself as close to him as she can. The pressure in her lungs eases, the shaking stops as the nightmare gradually goes away.

'OK?'

She nods, pulls back and wipes away the last of the tears with her wrist.

'I have to go up to the castle – the lightning has knocked out the electricity. Do you want to come with me?'

Thea nods again. She definitely doesn't want to stay here alone in the dark.

'Do you know where our raincoats are? It's pouring down.'

She follows him into the kitchen, drinks a glass of water. Something is missing.

'Have you seen Emee?'

'She slipped past me when I opened the front door.'

'How long ago?'

'Just after the clap of thunder. I stuck my head out to check on the lights up at the castle, and she ran out. It's pitch black everywhere.'

David sounds considerably more worried about the castle than the dog. His phone starts ringing.

'Securitas,' he says, turning away to take the call.

Thea opens the front door. The rain is hammering on the gravel and the decking outside.

'Emee!' she shouts, but her voice doesn't even carry across the courtyard.

'Both the fire alarm and the intruder alarm have gone off,' David informs her. 'Probably a short circuit. We need to get up there right away.' He rummages in a drawer, digs out a torch.

'But what about Emee?'

'I'm sure we'll find her on the way. Let's go!'

He runs across to the car, shoulders hunched against the storm. After a few seconds' hesitation, Thea pulls on her shoes and jacket and follows him.

It's only two hundred metres from the coach house to the castle. David puts his foot down, steering with one hand and chewing at the thumbnail on the other. Thea keeps a lookout for Emee, afraid that David will run over her. But Emee is a street dog, she reminds herself. She knows all about the dangers of cars.

Somehow the castle looks even blacker than their little house, as if the high walls, turrets and steeply sloping roof make the darkness even deeper.

David slams the brakes on by the kitchen door in the east wing. Holds the torch in his mouth as he struggles with the key. The sound of the alarms bounces off the stone walls inside.

'There's a portable emergency light in the kitchen – just follow the glow,' he calls over his shoulder as he hurries down the cellar steps.

Thea does as she's told. She finds the light, switches it on and runs with it through the service corridor leading to the main dining room. Could Emee have crossed the bridge and run off into the forest? If so, Thea ought to be able to spot her from the terrace at the back.

The alarm stops abruptly. The dining room is deserted, of course. The new tables and chairs are still stacked in a corner. The walls are covered with gilded panels which have recently been cleaned. She directs the beam of the powerful light up towards the ceiling. Greek motifs, young women in long robes in a forest, surrounded by creatures such as satyrs, centaurs, and others she can't name. Some of the trees look like living beings. She remembers the face on the Gallows Oak, the Green Man to whom she made her offering of wood anemones. A ridiculous idea, with hindsight.

She opens the glass doors. The cloudburst has abated slightly, and is now an ordinary spring downpour. She pulls up her hood and goes out onto the terrace. Sweeps the beam across the low hedges in the box garden, across the grass.

'Emee! Emee!'

A flash of lightning illuminates the whole garden, a blue-white core with red edges that slices through the night and comes down in the forest on the far side of the moat. The thunderclap is almost simultaneous, and so loud that it takes her breath away.

The nightmare returns. The blast wave, the panic, the feeling of not being able to get up, of suffocating. Her body begins to shake again. She crouches down, lowers her head, tries to slow her breathing.

In, out. In . . . out.

Something nudges Thea's back. It's Emee. The dog pushes her nose into Thea's hand and whimpers. Thea pulls her close, and to her surprise Emee doesn't object, but simply allows herself to be embraced.

The rain seeps inside Thea's jacket. She continues to take deep, slow breaths, and after a couple of minutes the panic attack is over. She wipes away the tears and the raindrops with her sleeve.

'Good girl,' she murmurs in the dog's ear. 'It'll be all right in a little while. Nothing to worry about.'

A light flickers in her peripheral vision. It's coming from the west wing, and for a moment she assumes it's David. But he doesn't have access to the west wing, and even if he did, he couldn't have got there in such a short time. Plus the glow is too faint and unstable to come from a torch.

Someone is standing at one of the windows up there – a little man holding a candle. He is half-hidden behind a curtain. Their eyes meet through the rain.

Thea recognises the look in those eyes – she sees it in the bathroom mirror every morning and night.

Sorrow.

The man nods to her, then blows out the candle and is swallowed up by the darkness.

5

Walpurgis Night 1986

In Tornaby no one can escape the past. Everything repeats itself, over and over again, but with different faces. Like one long ritual.

But tonight that will all change. Things have been set in motion, and the Green Man is riding through the forests.

Can you hear him coming? Can you hear him whispering my name?

Elita Svart, Elita Svart . . .

Arne turned off for Tornaby, wound down the side window and rested his arm on the sill. He deliberately drove slowly, nodding casually to everyone he met and receiving surprised nods in return. The ironmonger, the painter, the bad-tempered woman from the post office. People who would never usually dream of acknowledging him. He turned the car around and drove up and down the street a couple more times, then parked outside the bank and got out.

Two other cars were already there: the count's green Land Rover, and the white pick-up belonging to Erik Nyberg, the castle administrator. Under normal circumstances, Arne wouldn't have gone in. He'd been afraid of Rudolf Gordon ever since he was little. The older kids had scared one another with stories of how the count had chased them when they were playing in the forest near the castle, how he'd set the dogs on them and come after them on horseback. Some even claimed they'd seen him riding through the trees dressed as the Green Man on Walpurgis Night.

However, neither ghost stories nor dried-up old men frightened the new Arne Backe. He put on his peaked cap, adjusted his white belt and shoulder strap and entered the bank.

The three tellers who worked for Bertil looked up from behind the glassed-in counter. Gave a start that improved Arne's already excellent mood.

'So how are things today?' he said in his most authoritative voice. He tucked his thumbs in his belt and bounced on his heels, as he'd seen older colleagues do.

'Fine,' the drones chorused.

'Excellent. Is the manager in?'

'He's in a meeting,' the nearest drone informed Arne, who gave him the stern officer-of-the-law expression he'd practised in front of the mirror.

'But I think they've just finished,' the drone added hastily, pressing a button to unlock the door and let Arne through.

He knew exactly where he was going; he'd visited his brother-in-law many times. Bertil's office was on the first floor, with three large windows overlooking the main street. Should he sprint up the stairs, showing off his lithe agility, or should he plod up with a heavy, important tread? He opted for the latter; he could feel the drones' eyes on him all the way to the top.

The office door was open. Bertil, the count and Erik Nyberg were in the corridor, clearly in the process of finishing off. Arne slowed down even more.

'That's all agreed then,' he heard Bertil say. 'It's 30 April, so you'll have to give notice today if you don't want to wait another month.'

'Erik, can you sort that out?' The count's voice was a nasal drawl, typical upper-class Skåne.

'I'll go over there this afternoon.'

'It might be best if you take someone with you,' Bertil suggested. 'I don't think Lasse Svart is going to react very well.'

The name made Arne prick up his ears.

'I know how to deal with Lasse,' Erik said tersely, 'but I'll take Per. The boy needs to learn how to handle things.'

'I hear he's not going to the school of music,' Bertil said.

'No.' Erik exchanged a glance with the count. 'We didn't think it was a good idea. It's best if he stays at home and learns a proper trade.'

'Time we made a move,' the count said. 'Thank you for your help, Bertil.'

The three men shook hands and turned towards the staircase; only now did they become aware of Arne's presence. The count looked at him. Rudolf Gordon was almost seventy, tall and thin with sharp features and sunken eyes. Erik Nyberg was a head shorter and Arne envied him his hard, weather-beaten appearance, which was somehow emphasised by the fact that Erik always wore a scruffy moleskin jacket.

'Gentlemen,' he said as they passed by, doing his best to maintain his stern expression. Much to his satisfaction, he got a couple of nods in response.

'Arne.' Bertil sounded surprised rather than concerned. Arne straightened his shoulders, bounced on his heels again. Bertil was fifteen years older, and had been like a big brother ever since Arne turned ten. They were actually the same height, but for the first time in his life Arne didn't feel as if he had to look up to meet Bertil's gaze.

'How nice to get a visit from the police. Come on in.' Bertil stepped aside, making a sweeping gesture with his hand. 'Take a seat.'

Arne sank down in one of the leather armchairs in the corner. His gun holster caught on his hip, and he adjusted it. There was a large cigar box in the middle of the table, and three stubs in the ashtray. Bertil opened a cupboard and took out a crystal decanter and two brandy balloon glasses.

'I'm sure you've got time for a little drink and a smoke? Not a word to Ingrid!'

Arne opened his mouth to reply, but the words stuck in his throat and he had to make do with a brief nod.

'What was all that about?' he asked when his cigar was lit and he'd taken a sip of Cognac. 'The count and Erik Nyberg. Did I hear Lasse Svart's name?'

Bertil blew a plume of smoke at the ceiling as he considered his reply.

'To be honest, it's confidential . . .' He broke off, removed a flake of tobacco from his tongue, then leaned forward. 'The count's had an offer for the land around Svartgården. The army want to extend their firing range. They're prepared to pay a tidy sum for a run-down farm and several acres of waterlogged marshland.'

Arne felt his chest expand. He and Bertil were equals now, confidants in a way they'd never been before.

'Bloody hell! Lasse Svart, out on his arse!' Arne grinned, then immediately realised what the long-term implications were. 'But where will the family go?' he added so quickly that the cigar smoke went down the wrong way, resulting in a coughing fit.

Bertil shrugged. 'I've no idea. That's Lasse's problem, but I'd be surprised if anyone around here was prepared to take him on as a tenant, given his reputation. It would be best for everyone if Lasse took his women and all the rest of his crap and disappeared.'

Arne tried to look unconcerned. The role of confidant was no longer quite so appealing.

He knew why. Who was responsible.

Elita Svart.

6

'I've found something in the forest, Margaux. A piece of a puzzle from a different story. Someone's else's story.'

Thea takes Emee down into the staff dining room in the castle. Lights some candles, then dries herself and the dog with an old blanket. It's just after five. The residue of the panic attacks still lingers in her body, making its presence felt from time to time like tiny, almost imperceptible vibrations in her hands.

David is wandering back and forth between the rooms. She can hear him on the phone, but he ends the call as he walks in.

'Oh, you found the dog – good! I'm sorry I didn't help you look – it's chaos here. The freezers and fridges are off; I must try and get hold of a generator later today if the power's going to be out for a while.'

He pulls out a chair and sits down opposite her. His expression changes. He looks concerned.

'Are you OK? Have you recovered?'

Thea nods.

'Can I do anything for you?'

'I'm fine, David. I'm more worried about you. We haven't discussed the interview. What the hell happened?'

He waves a dismissive hand.

'Oh, I just lost the thread. I'd eaten badly, had too little sleep, and I just ran out of energy. But you saved me.' He reaches out and takes her hand. 'Without you I'd have fucked up completely. I really am grateful, Thea.'

She smiles at him, pleased that he appreciates her sacrifice. Tries not to think about the risk she has taken.

'What was that interviewer asking about?'

'I don't . . .'

'He mentioned a third girl who died.'

David slowly shakes his head. 'It's a tragic story. A young girl was murdered in the forest back in the Eighties. Absolutely not something we want associated with the restaurant – that's why I didn't quite know what to say, but you rescued the whole situation.'

He releases her hand and stands up. Takes out his phone.

'Sorry, I have to take this.'

Only when he's left the room does Thea realise that she didn't actually hear his phone ring.

She waits until dawn, then goes back to the coach house and changes into dry clothes. It's stopped raining, and the sky is pale blue, streaked with pink. Dr Andersson won't be here for several hours, and Thea is too anxious to sit around and wait for her. She decides to take Emee for a walk in the forest.

The ground is sodden after the storm. The track is full of puddles, and raindrops sparkle on the spiders' webs that have survived the downpour. Thea lights up a secret cigarette, takes several deep drags and blows out the last traces of the panic attacks. However, it isn't the residue of the PTSD that worries her the most.

David tried to trivialise the whole thing, but it's obvious that he didn't want to talk about the dead girl. Why not? If she died in the Eighties, he must have been a child when it happened.

ANDERS DE LA MOTTE

She's finished the cigarette by the time she reaches the glade and the Gallows Oak. Emee has beaten her to it, and is sniffing around the base of the tree with great concentration.

Something has happened to the ancient oak. There is a black mark on the trunk that wasn't there yesterday. Thea moves closer. Emee has started scratching among the leaves at its roots.

The black patch begins right at the top and runs down the trunk like a jagged scar, splitting the Green Man's face in two before it reaches the ground. This must have been where the lightning struck last night. The force and violence of the strike are both horrible and fascinating. She touches the scar. The edges are blackened, the rough bark has been burned away and in the centre she can see the paler wood inside the tree. The smell of charring lingers in the air.

Emee is still scratching, becoming more and more agitated.

'What have you got there, sweetheart?'

Thea crouches down. The scar is broadest at the bottom, as if the power culminated when the electricity reached the ground. It has burned a hole in the trunk, and Emee is kicking up earth and fragments of wood, half-barking and half-whimpering with excitement.

'What is it, Emee?'

Thea can see something shining. She gently moves Emee to one side and reaches within. Her fingers touch a smooth, cold object. She tries to pick it up, but the hole is too small. She breaks off some of the wood to make it bigger. Emee wants to help, but Thea moves so that her own body is in the way. The dog isn't happy, but co-operates.

The object is partially buried in a brownish mixture of rotten wood and dried flowers. With a little persuasion, she manages to get it out and discovers that it's an old paint tin with a lid, about twenty centimetres high and half as wide. The label is gone, the surface pitted with rust. Thea has also brought out an almost fresh wood anemone. It must have been one of the bunch she pushed into the Green Man's mouth yesterday, which suggests that the tin once went in the same way. A very long time ago, judging by the state it's in.

She shakes it gently; it rattles. Emee has sat down beside her with her tongue out and her head on one side. She seems to be as curious as Thea is.

The lid is stuck fast, as if it is determined to preserve its secret at all costs. Thea manages to insert one of her keys beneath the lip. The metal bends and creaks, then suddenly the lid flies off.

Thea tips the contents into her hand. A small figure comes out first, then a few dry leaves. The figure is no more than ten centimetres in height, and is made up of two twigs woven together. The longer twig has been bent in the middle to form a loop, giving the figure a head and a body. The ends provide the legs, and the shorter twig, twisted just below the loop, creates a waist and arms.

For a second she thinks of her father. The wooden doll he carved for her when she was little. She quickly pushes away the thought.

There's something else inside the tin, a rolled-up piece of paper. Thea puts down the figure and fishes it out, only to discover that it is in fact an old, faded Polaroid photograph. She smoothes it out as best she can.

The photo shows a dark-haired young woman in a white dress. She is standing on a flat stone with her arms folded across her chest, her head inclined slightly. Her eyes are closed, and in her hands she is holding two antlers.

Strangely distorted trees can be seen behind her, and on either side of the young woman stand two figures – children, judging by their height. Their faces are concealed by animal masks that remind Thea of the artwork on the dining-room ceiling in the castle. Hare, fox, owl and deer.

Each child is holding the end of a length of ribbon tied around the woman's wrists. It almost looks as if they are keeping her there on the stone. She is very beautiful, a kind of delicate, naïve beauty that exists only in the narrow gap between childhood and adulthood.

The photograph is taken in daylight, and yet there is something unpleasant about the whole thing: the children, the masks, the lovely young woman, the stone and the warped trees. It is somehow reminiscent of a horror film, an impression that is reinforced by the flat perspective and the faded colours.

Someone has written on the white border beneath the image:

Walpurgis Night 1986. Come to the stone circle at midnight.

Then three more words. Thea reads them aloud.

'The spring sacrifice.'

7

Walpurgis Night 1986

I notice them staring at me. Not just the boys in school, but the teachers too, the fathers, the old men in the town square. All of them.

Most of them do it secretly when they believe no one is watching, but I can feel their eyes on me. I know what they think of Elita Svart. What they want to do to me.

School was over for the day, the bus shelter was empty. Arne checked behind the seating at the football pitch, drove past the kiosk. Then he headed down to the common, where the villagers had built a huge bonfire ready for the Walpurgis Night celebrations. Right on the top, leaning against a T-shaped structure, was a figure approximately the height of a man. It was made of interwoven twigs and branches, the head formed by a loop. Arne had seen it many times, in countless variations: a representation of the Green Man.

His big sister Ingrid used to tell terrifying stories of the Green Man and his ghostly horse, just as the residents of Tornaby had done for generations. Arne hated to admit it, but there was something about that faceless object that still made him shudder.

He spotted a few kids on the far side of the bonfire, and wound down the window. They looked at one another when they saw the police car, then picked up their backpacks and turned their bicycles around, ready to disappear.

'David!'

'Hi, Uncle Arne.' The boy let go of the handlebars, looking relieved. 'Cool car!'

Arne nodded with satisfaction. 'What are you up to?'

'Nothing.' The answer came much too quickly.

'So what are you doing tonight?'

David shuffled uncomfortably and looked at his friends. Arne was trying to remember their names; he knew they often hung around at Ingrid and Bertil's place, but he'd never taken much notice of them. The girl was adopted, Chinese or Korean or whatever, and the boy with the cropped hair was a Pole whose parents were something important at the plastics factory. Behind them was another terrified face that presumably belonged to that crazy seamstress's boy.

'Nothing special. We'll probably check out the bonfire,' David replied.

'You're not going to do anything stupid?'

'Of course not!'

David shook his head, and the other three joined in.

'Good. By the way, I don't suppose you've seen Elita Svart?'

For a second it was as if the little group froze in the middle of shaking their heads. Only their eyes moved, darting from side to side like frightened little sparrows. Arne fixed his eyes on his nephew. David opened his mouth a couple of times, but nothing came out.

'No, we haven't, have we, David?'

The little adopted princess had spoken. She gave David an encouraging nod.

'No,' he mumbled.

'She's older than us. We don't hang out together,' the girl added.

'I see. Remind me of your name?'

'Jeanette, but everybody calls me Nettan.'

'Your father's the headmaster at Tornaby school, isn't he?'

'Yes. And Mum's on the council.'

The kid was glaring at him in a way that both irritated and amused Arne.

'You don't say.'

He sucked in air between his teeth. It was obvious that these kids were up to something; could he be bothered to find out what it was? He ran his thumb and forefinger over his moustache. What could a gang of spoilt twelve-year-olds come up with in Tornaby? The answer was simple: nothing that was of any interest to him.

'Just behave yourselves,' he said sternly. 'Otherwise the Green Man might come after you.'

He pointed to the figure on top of the bonfire, and much to his satisfaction he saw four young faces turn a little paler.

8

'Hi, Margaux, it's me again. I promised to tell you about Tornaby. The people here are perfectly ordinary, the kind who mind their own business and do the right thing. They have neatly mown lawns, and the local paper comes out on Sundays. A safe place – on the surface at least. I can't stop thinking about that photograph.'

Dr Andersson is nearing retirement age, a well-built woman with several double chins and small, square glasses. She's wearing an oilskin coat and cargo pants, and groans loudly with the effort of clambering out of her little white Toyota to shake hands.

'Thea – lovely to meet you in person.' Her handshake is firm, her palm slightly sticky. 'That was a hell of a storm we had last night. Thunder and lightning – in April! Did you survive?'

'More or less – we still don't have any power. David's trying to get hold of a generator for the fridges and freezers.'

'Oh dear – let's hope it's back on soon, Thea.'

The doctor clearly likes to repeat names – not an unusual trait among those who work with people. The Toyota is new, and the name of the local car dealer is displayed on the doors in big letters. This seems strange for a local GP, but Thea already knows that this whole set-up is kind of strange.

'Have you settled into the coach house?' Dr Andersson cranes her neck as if she's trying to see in through the windows.

'Absolutely – we're getting there!' A white lie. The boxes of their possessions remain largely untouched.

'Excellent! The sooner the better, that's what I always say.' The doctor remains where she is for a few seconds, as if she's hoping to be invited in, then she gives up and gestures towards the car. 'OK – jump in!'

Thea locks the door of the coach house. She's put the old paint tin in her room, and tucked the Polaroid photograph in her inside pocket. Has the tin really been inside the Gallows Oak since the spring of 1986? It's like a mysterious greeting from the past. Who was the beautiful young woman? Who were her four masked attendants? Why were they dressed like that?

Come to the stone circle at midnight. The spring sacrifice.

She thinks back to the question the TV interviewer asked, the topic David was so keen to avoid. The girl who died in the forest in the Eighties. Hadn't the interviewer referred to her as the spring sacrifice?

Dr Andersson drives past the old stables and heads for the castle. David's car is still parked by the east wing, along with several other vehicles belonging to various trades.

'How's it going? Will the restaurant be ready in time?' the doctor asks as they pass by.

'I think so. David's working around the clock.'

'Ingrid's told me a little bit about what's going on. The foundation has put a lot of money into the renovation.'

Thea suspects this statement is in fact a question, but she refrains from commenting. Dr Andersson continues along the avenue, then turns right onto the main road. The name is misleading; it's actually a strip of bumpy tarmac with no line down the centre, meandering between oilseed rape fields and clumps of trees.

'So, Thea, as you already know this job is something of a special arrangement. It's funded by the Bokelund Foundation and a number of private sponsors, such as our local car dealer.' The doctor pats the steering wheel with something that could be affection. 'It's just a part-time post, and we'll make home visits as well as holding a surgery in the community centre. It's all pretty straightforward – cleaning wounds, giving flu jabs, peering into people's ears and throats, pulling splinters out of fingers and so on.'

She slows down to let an approaching tractor pass by. Sounds her horn and waves cheerily at the driver. 'Little Stefan. He's worked at the castle for many years. Needless to say, the life of a GP is nowhere near as eventful as life with Doctors Without Borders. The idea behind this arrangement is for the residents of Tornaby to have access to their own doctor, someone who's part of the community. A bit like the way things used to be, if you know what I mean. The surgery must be open on Monday and Tuesday mornings. People are used to that. Otherwise you can plan your schedule to suit you, and make sure you post it on the homepage on the Friday of the previous week at the latest. Freedom with responsibility, so to speak.'

Thea nods. Her mother-in-law has already explained all this, but as long as the doctor is talking, she's not asking intrusive questions.

'As I'm sure Ingrid's told you, the Bokelund Foundation exists to promote the good of the community. And this is a wonderful job – the best I've ever had, in fact.'

There is a faint hint of sorrow in Dr Andersson's words, a suggestion that there may be more to this story. But not right now.

The road straightens out, a central line appears along with speed bumps and road signs, plus an electronic board wishing drivers a pleasant day as long as they stay below forty kilometres an hour.

'I'm sure you know the village well by now – you must have been here lots of times.'

Thea nods, even though it isn't true. Prior to the past week, she had only visited Tornaby once before, and now they usually drive straight through the village. David has never wanted to come here. Thea hasn't asked why, because she didn't want any reciprocal questions about the area where she grew up. However, following the interview and his weird behaviour this morning, she can't help wondering if there's a particular reason why they've stayed away. Something to do with a dead girl.

She thinks about the Polaroid in her pocket. Maybe the talkative doctor can tell her what it's about? But first they have to get to know each other better.

In the eastern part of the village the houses date from the 1950s. Gradually the landscape changes – leafy gardens, tall flagpoles, white picket fences. The year of construction is painted on several façades, always from the early twentieth century. One of the largest houses belongs to Thea's in-laws.

Tornaby boasts the almost obligatory pizzeria, a combined ice-cream and fast-food kiosk, plus an ironmonger's that is fighting for survival against the big DIY chains. The fire station resembles a Lego model with its red door and little turrets. The post office is long gone, but there is still a small Konsum super-market, plus a branch of Sparbanken, where her father-in-law was once the manager.

The church is located on a patch of higher ground, surrounded by tall poplars. It is built of depressing grey sandstone blocks, and has several side naves plus an enormous tower, which makes it look far too large in comparison to the rest of the village.

'The oldest stone church in Skåne,' Dr Andersson informs Thea as they pass by. 'The crypt and one wall were built back in the 1000s, but this area was an important religious hub long before Christianity made its mark. Tornaby is named after the hawthorn – *hagtorn* – which was a sacred tree in pre-Christian religions.'

Thea murmurs something in an effort to sound interested.

The red-brick community centre is diagonally opposite the church. David was educated here until the age of twelve, when the school moved to the uninspiring concrete box down by the sports ground. That's more or less all Thea knows about his childhood, apart from the fact that he used to hang out with Nettan and Sebastian, who are now his business partners.

She thinks of the photograph again, the children in the masks, the young woman. Walpurgis Night 1986, that's thirty-three years ago. David was twelve, Thea was fifteen. A completely different person from the one she is now.

TORNABY COMMUNITY CENTRE, announces an unnecess-arily large sign at the end of the drive. And in smaller letters: DOCTOR'S SURGERY, FOLK MUSEUM, MEETING ROOM, CAFÉ, CHARITY SHOP. Two women, each with a pushchair, are chatting beneath a cherry tree. They wave as the doctor pulls into the car park.

'A lot of families with young children move here,' she says. 'The new road has helped, and in two years we'll be linked to the local train service.' She parks the car, still talking as she extricates herself from the driving seat with some difficulty. 'This place is perfect for families. There's a strong community spirit – everyone knows everyone else. This centre is key – a meeting point, thanks to the Bokelund Foundation and the parish council. They've also put pressure on the politicians to make sure we keep the school – much better than bussing all the children to Ljungslöv, as so many of the other small villages have to do. We also have a Facebook group you ought to join, Thea. That's where you'll find out most of what goes on in the village.'

'I'm not on Facebook.'

'Oh?' Dr Andersson raises her eyebrows, but doesn't push it. She leads Thea to a side door. 'You and David don't have children?'

Thea shakes her head. 'No. We're childless.'

Dr Andersson looks embarrassed, as if the word makes her uncomfortable. A simple, if not very nice, trick that Thea learned from Margaux. The truth is that she and David have always avoided the subject, maybe because neither wants to hear the other's excuses. And now they're too old anyway.

The surgery is bigger than Thea had expected – twenty-five square metres, with space for an examination couch, several lockable cupboards and a washbasin. The walls are adorned with old school posters showing various parts of the human anatomy. The room smells of soap, the curtains look new and there is a large bouquet of flowers in a vase on the desk.

Dr Lind – a warm welcome from Tornaby parish council, says the card, in David's mother's slightly old-fashioned handwriting.

'As you can see, they're very pleased to have you here. I expect they're fed up of me after all these years.'

The comment is meant as a joke, but once again there is that hint of sorrow in the doctor's voice, suggesting that she doesn't find it funny at all. The big woman looks at her tiny watch, then rubs her hands together.

'Twenty minutes before we open. How about a cup of coffee and a slice of homemade cake, Thea? The girls in the café look after us very well. It's sponge cake on Tuesdays.'

When they return to the surgery, Dr Andersson shows Thea how to log into the database on her laptop, how to upload her timetable, and how to update medical notes. The patients, who are obediently waiting on the chairs in the corridor outside, present the expected challenges.

Thea vaccinates two small children, dresses a wound and diagnoses one case of inflammation of the ear. Dr Andersson lets her do her job, looking perfectly relaxed as she sits in the corner with her coffee.

Most of the patients are young mothers or pensioners. They all welcome her in a way that suggests she's already been a topic of conversation in the village for some time. The mothers want to know more about David, the restaurant and the opening night. The pensioners prefer to discuss their aches and pains, but almost all of them ask how her father-in-law is, and send their best wishes to both Bertil and Ingrid.

They all open up to her, which seems to impress Dr Andersson. Thea herself isn't at all surprised. People have always confided in her, ever since she was a child. Her older brother, her father, eventually her fellow students, her colleagues, her patients. All she needs to do is start things off with a little small talk, then sit quietly and listen.

'Everyone is searching for someone who will listen to them,' Margaux used to say. 'Someone who understands and doesn't judge. And you're good at it, *ma chère*. So good that even mussels open up to you. That's why you need to devote yourself to the living, not the dead. But be careful. With great talent comes great responsibility.'

Thea thinks about the mysterious photograph yet again. What is the story hiding behind it? And who can tell her that story?

9

Walpurgis Night 1986

'Your mother is so beautiful, Elita.' I've heard that ever since I was a child. Lola is beautiful, but also delicate. She believes in fairies and the creatures of the forest. Spends most of her time talking to her little porcelain figurines.

Father broke one of them once, a white baby rabbit she'd bought at a flea market. Eva-Britt spent hours at the kitchen table with toothpicks and glue until every single fragment was in the right place, and my mother stopped crying. Lola is just like that rabbit — whole on the outside, but still broken. Eva-Britt is the glue. It's thanks to her that everything sticks together.

A rne arrived at Svartgården just before five. He'd driven carefully, trying to avoid the biggest muddy puddles. He should have carried on to Ljungslöv. Put the vehicle away, hung the keys on the hook behind the desk. But he wanted Elita to see him in the police car. Plus he had important news.

He parked in the middle of the yard, got out and adjusted his belt, handcuffs, radio, and white gun holster. Pulled his peaked cap well down over his forehead.

A shower of dogs came rushing at him, bad-tempered little terriers that always barked at him and nipped at his heels. Arne kicked out at the first one, then stared out the others until they slunk away, tails between their legs. He hadn't been here for a couple of years at least, and the place looked worse than he remembered. Slates were missing from several roofs, and the top of the barn was covered with a tarpaulin. There was a general smell of dampness and decay that Arne had barely registered before, but today it made him wrinkle his nose.

A homemade sign stood beside the steps leading up to the house; it wasn't even straight.

LASSE SVART FARRIER

Underneath, in different handwriting:

EVA-BRITT RASMUSSEN AND LOLA SVART HOMEOPATHIC MEDICINES, EQUINE MASSAGE

The front door opened and Eva-Britt appeared, wiping her hands on a dirty rag. She stared at the police car, then at Arne.

Eva-Britt and Ingrid were about the same age, with the same hard expression, the same sharp tongue. But Eva-Britt looked at least ten years older than Ingrid. Her hair was already turning grey, her mouth permanently locked in a bitter grimace.

'Oh, it's you,' she muttered.

Arne glared at her as he mounted the steps. 'Aren't you going to offer me a coffee?'

Normally Eva-Britt would have stood her ground in the doorway, blocked his path and told him to go to hell, but today she stepped aside. She seemed to realise that he was no longer Downhill Arne, Lasse's little errand boy, but a person to be respected.

The kitchen was a mess, as usual. Bottles, cups, containers, little bowls everywhere, and there was an unpleasant, acrid smell.

Elita's mother Lola was heating some concoction on the stove. She didn't respond to Arne's greeting. Lola had always been beautiful: almond-shaped eyes, long dark hair, white alabaster skin. Once upon a time Arne had only dared to gaze at her in secret, but on closer inspection he could see that she was no longer quite as lovely as he recalled. Or maybe the past few years had taken their toll. Her hands were calloused, her back was bent, and her expression was guarded. For a moment Arne was filled with an unexpected feeling of tenderness.

'So what are you two girls up to?' he asked in his smoothest voice.

Lola quickly looked away, which bothered him. He hadn't meant to scare her.

'Nothing,' Eva-Britt snapped, planting herself in front of him with her arms folded, as if she regained something of her old, vicious self. 'And you've got no right to come marching in here, Arne.'

The way she said his name had always annoyed him. She kind of spat it out, as if the letters had a nasty taste.

'No right?' He walked around Eva-Britt to the kitchen table, picked up one of the plastic containers and sniffed the contents. Acted as if he hadn't seen similar containers hundreds of times before. 'This smells like moonshine. As you know, it's illegal to produce or sell alcohol at home. You could end up in jail . . .'

Eva-Britt shrank a little. 'Lasse's down in the paddock,' she said, slightly too loudly.

'And?'

'Elita's there too.'

Arne slowly replaced the stopper and put down the container. Nodded as reassuringly as he could to Lola, then turned and left the kitchen.

10

'Everyone here is really friendly. Almost unpleasantly friendly, if you know what I mean – a bit like the neighbours at the beginning of Rosemary's Baby. You're laughing now, aren't you? Remembering how I hated all those old horror films you made me watch. We used to sit on your bed with the laptop between us, with me trying to hide how scared I was. I miss those times, Margaux. I miss them so much.'

Thea and Dr Andersson get into the Toyota. They're going to visit a patient on the way home. Apparently Kerstin Miller used to be David's teacher. She lives in the hunting lodge, deep in the forest. Thea tries to remember if David has ever mentioned her, but the name doesn't ring any bells.

'When you're doing home visits, it's important to press the business journey button on the sat-nav so that it matches your travel log. The foundation likes to keep an eye on its outgoings.' She groans at the effort involved in turning her upper body as she reverses away from the centre. 'I thought this morning went very well. I was afraid that people might be a little shy, especially with someone from Uppland, but they talked to you as if they'd known you for years. I think you're going to fit in very well, Thea.' She nods with satisfaction at her verdict. 'You haven't worked as a GP before, have you?'

'No. I was a pathologist for a few years.'

'What made you want to change?'

Thea shrugs. 'I became good friends with a woman I met at a conference, and she got me into Doctors Without Borders. She convinced me I could do more good among the living.'

She stops; she has no desire to say any more about Margaux.

Dr Andersson seems satisfied with her answer. She remains silent for all of five seconds before changing the subject.

'Ingrid and I went to school together – maybe she already told you that?'

Thea shakes her head.

'I've known her and Bertil ever since we were little. Ingrid was the class organiser even back then. Bertil was a couple of years above us. He was a good footballer. And he was very handsome.' She laughs. 'Well, handsome for Tornaby! He looked a bit like Elvis, with eyes like velvet and wavy hair. A lot of the girls were after Bertil – much prettier girls than Ingrid, but she decided she wanted him, and all the rest just had to step aside. Even Bertil didn't have much say in the matter.' The doctor laughs again. 'They were made for each other, those two. They were both strong-willed and ambitious, both with a fierce sense of responsibility. Ingrid's father owned the general store and chaired the sports association, while Bertil's father ran the bank and was a local councillor. The cream of the village, if you know what I mean. Ingrid was twenty-one when they got married, and David came along the following year.'

The doctor lowers her voice.

'It could have gone very badly. Ingrid haemorrhaged – she almost died.'

'Oh goodness – I didn't know that.'

'Yes, it was a close thing. Bertil sat by her side at the hospital, refused to move until she was out of danger.'

'Is that why David's an only child?'

The doctor nods sadly. 'They had to perform a hysterectomy, which was very sad, because I know she'd always wanted a big family. Life hasn't been easy for Ingrid.'

She turns to Thea with a wry smile, pauses briefly as if to let her into the conversation.

'Anyway,' she continues when the silence has gone on for a little too long, 'Ingrid's parents died when her brother Arne was in his early teens, so she and Bertil more or less brought him up. Have you met Arne?'

'Only in passing.'

The doctor tilts her head to one side as if she's waiting for a continuation. She looks disappointed when Thea fails to oblige.

'Arne's a bit . . . different. He was married for a while, to a girl from Thailand that he brought over here with her little boy. It didn't work out, and they went back home. He took it pretty hard.'

Dr Andersson seems to have exhausted the topic, or maybe she's finally realised that Thea isn't going to supply her with any tasty details about David's family.

They take a different road out of the village, past the sports ground and the school. On the common people have started building a bonfire for Walpurgis Night, but there is something unusual about this one; it has been constructed around a pole with a crossbar at the top.

'What's that?' Thea asks, pointing at the structure.

'Sorry? Oh, that's for the Green Man. It's a local custom – some say it came over from England with the Gordon family, but others believe it's much older. Maybe you've already heard of the Green Man?' The doctor doesn't wait for an answer. 'Every year the residents of Tornaby burn an effigy of the Green Man on top of the bonfire. They make it together – a bit like the midsummer maypole. You'll see for yourself; it's put in place on the day before Walpurgis Night. It's really an old fertility rite, just like the fire – burning the old and the dead to make room for the new and the living.'

'There's an oak tree in the forest with a Green Man's face on it,' Thea interjects. 'People seem to have put small gifts into its mouth.'

The doctor nods. 'There must be half a dozen similar trees in the area. The business of the gifts or offerings is left over from pagan times, as I'm sure you know. Quite a lot of people around here make their own small Green Man figure and hang it on the door just before Walpurgis Night, so that the Green Man and his huntsmen won't frighten their pets.'

Thea is reminded of the figure made of twigs that she found in the tin.

'Once upon a time,' Dr Andersson continues, 'long before my day, they used to hold a ceremony when the Green Man was burned. A beautiful young girl was selected, and they pretended to sacrifice her to the Green Man before the bonfire was lit. I think the tradition died out at the beginning of the last century, but there are some old photographs in the Folk Museum, if you're interested?'

The doctor is interrupted by her mobile phone. She rummages around in her pockets and manages to find the hands-free headset.

'Hi – no, you're not disturbing me. We're on our way to see Kerstin Miller.'

Thea thinks about the ancient custom, small figures made of twigs, and a young woman pretending to be a sacrifice to the Green Man. This all fits with the items she found inside the Gallows Oak – but who are the children and the girl in the photograph?

They follow the same winding road they took this morning, past the drive leading up to the castle, and after a kilometre or so they reach a deciduous wood.

Dr Andersson is still on the phone to someone who is presumably her husband. She turns left onto a dirt track. The wood closes in around them. Only a narrow strip of sky is visible through the leaf canopy. Thea can see from the sat-nav that they're crossing the marsh on the eastern side of the moat.

Dr Andersson ends the call at last. 'By the way, Thea, I almost forgot. The district medical board rang; apparently there's a problem with your ID number.'

Thea inhales sharply, gives her standard response.

'My personal details are protected,' she says as casually as she can manage. Just like the word 'childless', it usually puts a stop to any further questions. Not this time.

'Oh – why's that?'

'My previous post with Doctors Without Borders was sensitive. We travelled to war zones, worked with people who were being persecuted for various reasons.'

Her second line of defence; few people get past this. However, Dr Andersson isn't giving up.

'But I thought you left several years ago?'

'One year ago.'

'And your details still have to be protected? You must have experienced something really terrible.'

'Mm.' Thea looks away, tries to show with her entire body that she doesn't wish to discuss the matter. Fortunately the doctor takes the hint.

'Anyway, they couldn't carry out a search using your ID number, so you'll have to contact them. Technically you shouldn't take up your post until they've done the relevant checks, so it's probably best if you go down to the regional office in Lund and sort it out this week.'

'No problem.'

Thea allows herself a smile, tries to look as if it's the simplest thing in the world. Which it is – Dr Thea Lind's record is as pure as the driven snow.

The road twists and turns even more, with the number of puddles increasing as the marshy forest takes over. The GPS shows that they have gone around the moat and begun to follow the canal to the hunting lodge. They drive over several culverts where the ditch or narrow, slow-flowing streams take the water from the marsh to the canal at the bottom of the dip to their left.

It's hard to work out how wide the canal is. The banks are steep and the dip itself is full of undergrowth, reeds and fallen trees; it's difficult to see the surface of the water, let alone the far side by the forest. Thea doesn't believe that David's proposed floating restaurant would be able to get through.

Almost without warning the forest opens up in front of an attractive Skåne longhouse, with a thatched roof, leaded windows and red-painted shutters. A short jetty extends into the green pool that forms the end of the canal, and behind the house, among the trees, Thea can see a stable and a barn.

A small van is parked in front of the house, and a stocky man in overalls and a cap is up a ladder painting the gable end of the stable. Just above him there is an enormous set of antlers. The sun breaks through the thin leaf canopy, the shadows play across the façade and for a brief moment Thea imagines she sees a huge, terrifying creature with long legs and horns. The vision is so real that her heart skips a beat, but then the man turns around and the spell is broken.

'Hi Jan-Olof!' Dr Andersson calls as she gets out of the car.

The man on the ladder merely raises his brush in greeting; Thea catches a glimpse of an unshaven, fleshy face.

'Jan-Olof Leander,' the doctor whispers. 'Something of a handyman around here. His mother is one of our regular patients. She's a little . . .'

Before she can finish the sentence, the door of the house opens and Kerstin Miller emerges. She's the same height as Thea, and her grey hair is cut in a neat bob. Her nose is red, she is wearing a bobbly old cardigan and a scarf carelessly knotted around her neck, but somehow she manages to look elegant.

'Thea! Welcome – lovely to meet you at last,' she says. 'Come on in, I've made the tea.'

'Thank you.'

Thea steps forward and sees that there is something hanging on the wall to the right of the door: a figure about half a metre long, made of interwoven twigs. It looks familiar.

'Is that a Green Man?'

The question is directed at the doctor, but it is Kerstin who answers.

'Yes – you know the legend, then. Exciting, isn't it? I live all by myself out here in the forest, so of course I have to keep in with the Green Man. You can never be too careful,' she says with a laugh.

Kerstin and the doctor go inside, but Thea remains on the top step. She reaches out and touches the Green Man. It's bigger and the twigs are still green, but there is no doubt that it's made in exactly the same way as the figure she found in the tin.

Come to the stone circle at midnight. The spring sacrifice.

She gives a start. A thorn that was hidden under the leaves has pierced her index finger so deeply that she is bleeding. She licks the little wound, then follows Kerstin and the doctor indoors.

11

Walpurgis Night 1986

Father is lethal, everyone knows that. Especially when he's been drinking. I've seen him hit both Eva-Britt and Lola. Leo too. Poor Leo . . .

Once Father knocked down a horse dealer who was trying to cheat him. He kicked him until he was barely moving. Eva-Britt managed to distract Father so that Leo and I could get the poor man into his car. Father chased after him and threw a rock straight through the rear windscreen.

One day Lasse is going to kill someone, Eva-Britt whispered to me. Maybe she's right.

A rne followed the muddy little track from the house down to the paddock and parked the police car as close to the fence as possible.

Lasse was standing in the middle of the paddock with a long whip in one hand, while Elita was riding bareback. The horse was called Bill, a muscular stallion that belonged to some rich guy in Kristianstad. He was as black as coal, apart from a white sock on one hind leg, and he was almost broken in.

Arne placed his foot on the lowest bar and leaned nonchalantly on the fence. Elita had inherited her mother's eyes, but instead of Lola's fragility there was a feistiness about her. There wasn't a man around who didn't know who Elita Svart was, who didn't drool over her. Anyone who thought differently had to be gay, a eunuch, or a fucking liar.

Lasse cracked the whip and Elita urged the horse on, digging the heels of her boots into his sides. Her long dark hair streamed out behind her, and her breasts bounced gently beneath the tight sweater.

'Well done, Elita! Now gallop!'

Elita continued to drive the stallion. His hooves thundered on the ground, echoing Arne's heartbeat. Bill snorted, foaming at the mouth.

Just as horse and rider passed by, Elita turned her head and winked at Arne, who almost forgot to breathe.

When they'd finished, Lasse sent Elita back to the stable with Bill, then came over to the car.

'Well, if it isn't Constable Arne Backe. Nice car – is it yours?'

'Yes!' Arne didn't know why he'd lied. His self-confidence suddenly dissipated.

He always used to admire Lasse Svart. Lasse did exactly what he wanted; he never let anyone mess him around. Plus he had the kind of good looks that women like – dark hair, brown eyes, and a white scar running down his cheek.

'You've managed to grow a moustache as well,' Lasse went on. 'And you've got yourself a gun. Just like Magnum PI. Things seem to be going well for my old sidekick.'

Arne nodded in a way that he hoped was cool. Lasse took out a tin of tobacco, tucked a substantial plug beneath his top lip, then wiped his hand on his trousers.

'You've come at a really good time,' he went on. 'My usual driver was arrested for drink driving last week. I've got a new moonshine distiller and thirsty customers all the way up to

Nedanås. No one will suspect a police car. You'll be well paid, of course – much better than when you used to drive for me in the past.'

He patted Arne on the shoulder. Arne made an effort not to flinch; Lasse had big, powerful hands that bore the marks of many years working with a hammer and tongs.

'I need to send several containers to Ljungslöv today. I was going to take them myself, but a farmer in Reftinge called a while ago. He wants to sink a new well, and he's offering double pay.' Lasse leaned closer, lowered his voice and gripped the shoulder he'd just patted. 'Walpurgis Night is a perfect opportunity to go water divining. There are many forces on the move tonight, let me tell you. Nature is hungry and the Green Man will ride through the forests, so you be careful, little Arne.'

As usual Arne couldn't tell whether Lasse was teasing him. All that nature hocus-pocus sounded like a joke, as if Lasse were trying to scare him, just like he'd done with those kids earlier on. At the same time, Lasse's expression was deadly serious. He kept his hand on Arne's shoulder, eyes boring into his.

A screech from the marsh made Arne jump – presumably some kind of bird. What else would it have been? He managed to stop himself from shuddering.

'Anyway. The containers are in there. You can take them right away.' Lasse released his grip on Arne's shoulder and pointed to a small shed, half-hidden among the undergrowth beyond the paddock.

Arne took a deep breath, tucked his thumbs in his belt and rocked on his heels.

'I don't do that kind of thing anymore, Lasse.'

Lasse drew back. Frowned and looked Arne up and down.

'No? So you've turned over a new leaf?'

Arne shrugged apologetically. 'I'm a police officer now, I have to consider my actions.'

'I see . . .'

Lasse was still staring at him. There was something hypnotic about his gaze, something that threatened to melt the last remnants of Arne's self-confidence. Arne cleared his throat, tried not to look away.

'The thing is, Lasse, I really can't . . .' His voice wobbled. *Shit!* He cleared his throat again. He was Arne Backe, Officer Arne Backe.

'I can't,' he said, his voice steadier now. He pushed his hips forward, tucked his thumbs further under his belt.

'I understand,' Lasse said, spreading his hands in a gesture of resignation. 'You've got a new job now. You don't have time to help your old friends.'

Arne nodded, hugely relieved.

'Not even old friends who were there for you in the past.'

The relief was replaced by a lump of ice in Arne's belly.

'Old friends who actually helped you to get this fancy job, with a car and a uniform. Who swore to the police that there was no way Arne Backe had been looking through little girls' windows, because he'd been helping out here when that perverted little Peeping Tom was creeping around Tornaby. It would be a shame if the truth came out now. All it needs is a phone call to the chief of police in Ljungslöv – Lennartson, isn't it? I believe he's a close friend of your brother-in-law?'

Arne felt the air go out of him, felt his shirt gape at the collar and his belt slip down over his hips.

'OK, so this is what we're going to do,' Lasse continued, grasping Arne by the shoulder again – harder this time. 'You back that smart police car up to the shed and you load twenty five-litre containers into the boot. Actually . . .' Lasse squeezed until Arne grimaced with the pain. 'Take twenty-one. You can keep the last one. After all, we're old friends.'

12

'You'd have liked Kerstin Miller, I'm sure of it. She's the kind of person who has a glow about her. A good soul.

'I can hear you snorting, saying that surely I've experienced enough misery to realise that anyone is capable of doing bad things. That genuine goodness doesn't exist. I'd like to believe that you're wrong.'

The kitchen in the hunting lodge is warm and cosy. There are bunches of dried herbs hanging on the walls, a wood-burning stove crackles in one corner, and a big fluffy cat is stretched out on the stone floor in front of the fire.

Kerstin Miller has a subtle sense of humour that immediately appeals to Thea. She offers rhubarb tea, chatting away as if they already know each other.

'You really didn't need to drive all the way out here for my sake. I'm already better. I'm intending to be back at school in a couple of days; the supply teacher is having a few problems.'

'You need to stay home for the rest of the week,' Dr Andersson insists.

'It's nothing, just a bit of a temperature. Alvedon will sort it out. We've got so much to do before the summer. I don't want the children to suffer because I've got a cold.' Kerstin turns to Thea. 'So tell me – how are you settling in at the coach house? Are you coping with the lingo? You can always ask me if there's something you don't understand – we northerners must stick together!'

Kerstin comes from somewhere in the north, and speaks a charming mixture of 'standard' Swedish and the Skåne dialect.

'I've picked up a few words,' Thea assures her.

'There you go – you'll be speaking fluent Skåne in no time.' Kerstin's smile is inviting. 'Will you get everything done in time for Walpurgis Night?'

'Absolutely. David's working flat out, but I'm sure it'll be fine. There will be a lot of people at the dinner.'

'Yes – both Jeanette and Sebastian have been in touch and said they're coming. I think it's wonderful that they're going into business with David after all these years. They were such good friends when they were children. Hard-working. Conscientious. Let me show you something.'

Kerstin gets up and goes into the room next door. Thea hears the sound of drawers opening.

'Here they are in their first year.'

Kerstin places a scrapbook on the table and turns to a faded colour photograph. *Tornaby School 1981, Year 1* is written neatly beside it.

There are only fifteen children in the class. Some of them are shyly looking down or away, others are more interested in the camera or the photographer. Kerstin is at the far side. She's about twenty-five years old with long, dark blonde hair. Her face is young, full of energy.

'There he is.'

David is in the back row; he's easily recognisable. His mother Ingrid probably knitted the sweater he's wearing.

'And there's Jeanette.'

Kerstin points to a girl with an Asian appearance in the front row. She's wearing dungarees and a blue hair band, and she's beaming at the camera. Thea can see the gap between her slightly too large front teeth.

Jeanette's ethnicity comes as a surprise. Thea has never met her, and somehow she's always imagined her with blonde hair and freckles, as if all children who grew up in the country automatically looked like Pippi Longstocking. Ridiculous, of course.

'Jeanette was usually top of the class, except in Maths.' Kerstin moves her finger to a third child, a shy-looking boy with cropped hair and glasses that are much too big for his face. 'Sebastian was the mathematician. His parents moved here from Poland when he was a baby. He was a wonderful boy, quiet but kind. And as I said, very gifted when it came to Maths.'

'And David?'

'He was good too, especially when it came to his verbal skills. He knew how to capture an audience.'

Kerstin turns the pages, stops at a newspaper cutting from *Helsingborgs Dagblad*.

'Look at this.'

David, Nettan and Sebastian again, a few years older now. Nettan has grown into her front teeth, Sebastian into his glasses. David is displaying an early version of that charming smile.

TORNABY TRIO'S SUCCESS IN RADIO QUIZ

Thea skims the text. David is quoted the most; he says he wants to be a fighter pilot and fly a Saab 37 Viggen when he grows up. Nettan wants to be an actress or a company director, or a musician because she plays the piano. Sebastian has the least to say. He wants to be an engineer like his father, or maybe a chess player.

'They went all the way to the semi-final – lost by one point to the team that won the whole thing.' Kerstin's voice is filled with pride. 'I know teachers shouldn't have favourites, every class and every pupil is special in their own way – but there's something about your first class. I can still remember all their names, and their parents were so supportive. I'd only just qualified, and I'd never set foot in Skåne, but the village welcomed me with open arms and made me feel at home right away.'

'So how come you ended up in Tornaby of all places?' Thea asks.

'Oh, the usual reason when someone moves halfway across the country – love. It didn't work out, but I fell in love with the area instead. I rented the lodge, got myself a horse, and that was that.'

'And you're not afraid of the dark?' Dr Andersson interjects, as if she's feeling left out of the conversation. 'I'd be too scared to live out here in the marsh on my own, with no neighbours for several kilometres.'

Kerstin shakes her head. 'After a tiring day in school I appreciate the peace and quiet. And of course I have the horses and Vanderbilt here to keep me company.' She points to the cat, who has moved from the floor to the sofa. 'I love this house, and the forest, and I intend to stay here as long as I have my health, and the foundation allows.'

She pauses, catches a sneeze in a handkerchief that she produces from her sleeve. Then she turns her attention to the scrapbook once more. Another newspaper article, a much later date.

BELOVED TORNABY TEACHER CELEBRATES
TWENTY-FIFTH ANNIVERSARY

'That was 2006. The house was full of flowers, and Jeanette came all the way from Switzerland to see me!'

She shows Thea a large colour photograph with smiling people arranged in two rows. There is a banner above them:

CONGRATULATIONS, MISS MILLER! WE LOVE YOU!

It takes a few seconds for Thea to realise that this is the same group who were in the first picture, in the same room and standing in exactly the same places twenty-five years later. The rounded, childish faces have acquired beards and double chins, the serviceable school clothes have been replaced by smart shirts, jackets and pretty dresses.

David is handsome now, his teeth are sparkling white and his gaze is full of confidence. Nettan has shaken off her provincial roots and is wearing a trouser suit. Her hair and make-up are perfect – she is a businesswoman to her fingertips.

'Isn't it wonderful?' Kerstin sounds even prouder, if that were possible. 'They did it for me – as a surprise!'

The new version of Sebastian has swapped his glasses for contact lenses, and his hair is clearly thinning, even though he can't be much more than thirty in the photograph.

'Sebastian did his doctorate in Lund, then started a business with some friends. Microprocessors – very technical. The company was bought up by Sony, and he made a fortune. He bought a big house in Poland for his parents when they retired.'

'How lovely.' Thea can't think of anything else to say.

She thinks she recognises someone else – a square-built man with a fleshy face. He's wearing an ill-fitting blazer, and he looks extremely uncomfortable.

'Isn't he the guy who was up the ladder outside?'

'Jan-Olof? Yes, that's right. He was the fourth member of their little gang. A quartet, you could call them.'

The final sentence hangs awkwardly in the air, and suddenly Thea thinks back to the Polaroid photo. Four children in the spring of 1986.

'Could I just check something?' She points to the scrapbook.

'Of course.'

Thea leafs through the pages until she finds what she's looking for.

TORNABY SCHOOL 1986, YEAR 6

She runs her finger over the faces, spots David and his three friends. Dr Andersson clears her throat and looks meaningfully at her watch.

'Time we made a move, Thea.'

Thea ignores her. She takes the Polaroid out of her pocket, smoothes it down and places it next to the scrapbook. One of the masked children is wearing a striped jumper that is a lot like the one Sebastian has on in the school photo. It can't be a coincidence.

'Where did you get that from?' Dr Andersson asks sharply. Both she and Kerstin have moved to stand behind Thea.

'I found it in an old tin in the forest yesterday. Could this be David and his friends? Nettan, Jan-Olof and Sebastian?'

Kerstin and the doctor exchange a long look, which answers the question as far as Thea is concerned. 'What's this about?'

'Hasn't David told you anything?' Kerstin asks quietly.

'About what?'

Another look, followed by an almost imperceptible shake of the head from the doctor, who is no longer so talkative.

Kerstin takes a deep breath. 'About poor Elita Svart. The spring sacrifice.'

13

Walpurgis Night 1986

Men are so easy to manipulate. They lie at home in their beds, fantasising about me. What they want to do to me. Elita Svart is the kind of girl you screw, not the kind you marry. A gypsy, a slut, a little whore.

Which is why I behave exactly as everyone expects. I tease and tempt them. I'm good at it, I've had plenty of practice, but deep down I'm tired of this role.

One final performance remains. And then, dear reader, it will all be over.

You haven't forgotten that I'm going to die, have you?

'Fucking hell!' Arne swore out loud as he loaded the white plastic containers of moonshine into the boot of the police car. Lasse's 'distillery' was a shed mounted on blocks of concrete out in the marsh, hidden by brambles and undergrowth. Only the muddy tyre tracks on the ground outside revealed the presence of the low wooden building.

Inside it stank of damp and mould. Arne's uniform shirt had sweat patches under the arms, and his shoes were covered in mud. He should never have come here, he should have stayed far away from this fucking swamp, far away from Svartgården. Instead he'd allowed himself to be dragged back, down into the morass.

He'd been seventeen when the incident happened. It had all started on the school bus, coming home from Ljungslöv. He'd been secretly in love with Ida Axelsson for years, and she was sitting just a few rows in front of him. She'd always been pretty, but that particular evening there was a kind of glow about her. All their contemporaries on the bus had flocked around her, and when they reached their destination, Arne wanted to see more. He wasn't ready to say goodbye just yet. And so he'd followed Ida at a distance. He hadn't meant any harm.

Without knowing exactly how it had happened, he found himself standing in the darkness outside her window. He didn't remember how long he was there. Five minutes maybe, or ten. He watched Ida as she moved from room to room. She played a record, sang along, danced.

For a few short, wonderful moments it was as if he was sharing it all with her. As if he was inside in the warmth. Until her mother arrived home, and he was caught in the car headlights. He'd fled, ran home, jumped on his moped and got as far away as he could. He went to Svartgården. Lasse was one of the few in the area who didn't look down on him or call him Downhill Arne. Lasse had even given him work, made him feel important.

When the police started asking questions, Lasse had provided him with an alibi, and since neither Ida nor her mother could be absolutely certain that it was Arne they'd seen in the garden, the matter was soon forgotten.

Stupidly, Arne had assumed that all the favours he'd done for Lasse over the years would have evened things out, but he should have realised that a debt to Lasse Svart could never be paid off. Then again, maybe there was hope? He hadn't said anything to Lasse about what he'd heard at the bank, but it sounded as if the count and Erik Nyberg were going to solve the problem for him. Make sure Lasse disappeared for good.

'Hi, Arne.'

He gave a start; Elita was standing right behind him, carrying a little case with a strap.

'Nice car.'

She took a step closer and slowly adjusted his tie.

'You look good in uniform.'

'Thanks!' Arne didn't know what to do with himself. She was standing so close that he was all too aware of her smell: sweat, horse and something else, something incredibly appealing. In some ways Elita reminded him of Ida Axelsson; she was a dark-haired, much prettier version of Ida. She was still fiddling with his tie, her hip brushing against his. Arne swallowed hard.

'There you go.' Elita stepped back, dangling the case in front of him. 'Thanks for the loan.'

Only now did Arne recognise the case; it contained the Polaroid camera Ingrid and Bertil had given him when he graduated from high school.

'No problem. Can I see the pictures?'

'Maybe. If you're nice to me.' Elita winked at him, just as she'd done in the paddock.

Arne chewed his moustache. 'And the ghetto blaster?'

'I need that a while longer, if that's OK.'

'No problem,' he said again. He turned and closed the boot of the car so that she wouldn't see the containers.

'Are you going into the village?'

'Yes!' His hands were wet with perspiration; he wiped them on his trousers.

'Can you give me a lift to the castle forest?'

'And why do you want to go there?'

She shrugged. 'I've got to get something ready for tonight.'

'Tonight? Don't do anything silly now, will you?' Arne swore silently to himself. Why did he suddenly sound like such an old killjoy?

'We'll see,' she said with a smile. 'We're meeting up at the stone circle. Why don't you come? I think you'll enjoy it.'

Her voice was inviting. Arne realised he was staring at her lips. They were so perfect, so soft, so . . .

'Who knows – maybe the Green Man will turn up,' she added.

Arne tried to speak, but his mouth refused to co-operate. The sound of a car engine made Elita spin around.

'Leo!' she shouted, and began to run. Something in her voice made Arne feel as if a rusty knife had just been plunged into his heart.

14

'The story behind the photograph is horrible. It's about a dead girl, and it touched me deeply, in a way I daren't explain to you – not yet. There's so much you don't know about me, Margaux. So much I haven't told you. About the person I used to be. About the people I've left behind.'

They say goodbye to Kerstin Miller and drive back the way they came. Dr Andersson remains silent, as if she doesn't know what to say – for once.

'So the girl in the photograph is Elita Svart,' Thea says. 'And she was murdered in the forest.'

That's all Kerstin was prepared to tell her. Maybe she thinks it's up to David to fill in the rest, but Thea can't wait that long.

The doctor drums her fingers on the wheel, as if she is engaged in some kind of internal battle.

'What happened to Elita was very sad,' she says eventually. 'A family tragedy. They lived at Svartgården, deep in the marsh. There used to be a track, but it's gone now. Elita's father, Lasse Svart, was a farrier, but he did all kinds of other things as well. Water divining, curing sick animals, breaking in horses. There were rumours that he had other irons in the fire too . . . He went to prison more than once, and a lot of people were afraid of him.'

The doctor pauses while she negotiates a water-filled pothole in the road.

'Lasse lived with two women, Eva-Britt and Lola. Eva-Britt was about the same age as Lasse. She took care of his business affairs, and she made and sold homeopathic medicines. Her son Leo lived at Svartgården too.'

Another pothole, another pause.

'Lola, Elita's mother, was a little . . . strange. She never really went anywhere, couldn't look you in the eye. The whole family was . . .' Dr Andersson hesitates. 'I don't really know what the right word is these days, but back then people like that were described as gypsies.'

Thea's skin crawls, her upper lip twitches.

'Right,' she hears herself say in a surprisingly neutral tone.

'As you can see from the photograph, Elita was a very pretty girl with a special aura. And she knew how to exploit all of that.'

'In what way?' Thea asks, mainly to stop her brain repeating that word.

'Elita loved to be the centre of attention, and she could wrap boys and men around her little finger. Including her stepbrother – Leo did everything she asked him to do. Everything.'

The doctor takes a deep breath.

'On Walpurgis Night 1986, Elita had set up a little performance. It turned out later that she'd seen the photographs in the Folk Museum and wanted to recreate the old rite of spring. And that she'd persuaded four younger children to help her.'

'David, Nettan, Sebastian and Jan-Olof.'

'Exactly,' the doctor says with a sigh. 'They gathered at the stone circle in the forest, lit a fire, then Elita and the children danced, just like in the old ritual. Then her stepbrother turned up on horseback.'

She breaks off again, searching for the right words.

'Leo killed Elita. Laid her down on the sacrificial stone with her hands folded across her chest. The newspapers called her the Spring Sacrifice.'

Thea inhales sharply. 'And David and his friends saw all this?'

'More or less. It was a terrible business, as you can imagine – both for the children and their families. They were questioned by the police, then there was the trial . . . Has David really never said anything about this? Or Ingrid?'

'Not a word.'

There is a silence as Thea tries to process what she's just heard. With hindsight, it's hardly surprising that David lost the thread during the TV interview, but why wouldn't he tell her what was going on?

'Why did the stepbrother do it? What was his motive?'

Dr Andersson shakes her head.

'Elita had left a letter in her bedroom. She wrote that she didn't want to grow up, along with a lot of other teenage nonsense. She'd planned the whole thing. Planned to die.'

'And Leo agreed to kill his stepsister?'

The doctor nods slowly. 'He confessed, and was convicted of murder – but with a reduced sentence, because the court believed that Elita had manipulated him. A terrible business, as I said.'

It's clear that the doctor is trying to bring the conversation to an end, but Thea isn't done yet.

'Were you their GP?'

'No, I was working at the hospital in Helsingborg back then, so I wasn't involved – except that we lived in Tornaby and knew the family.'

'So what happened to Lasse and the others?'

'They're long gone, all of them. The thing is, Thea . . . What happened to Elita Svart was dreadful, and we've put it behind us. Tornaby is so much more than . . .' Dr Andersson fumbles for the right phrase.

'A dead gyppo kid,' Thea supplies before she can stop herself. The words taste of poisonous mushrooms, perhaps bitter almonds.

'Well, yes, no, I don't . . .' Dr Andersson shifts uncomfortably in her seat. 'What I mean is, people don't want to be reminded of all that. Dragging it up isn't going to help you fit into the village community. Do you understand?'

Thea nods, but that word is still reverberating in her head. She hasn't heard it since she was a teenager, when other people used to spit it at her the way the residents of Tornaby no doubt did at Elita.

In another life, another time.

Gyppo, gyppo, gyppo . . .

15

Walpurgis Night 1986

Leo is my big brother, even though we're not actually related.

Eva-Britt has an old photograph of us on her bedside table. Leo's ten, I'm six. We're sitting on a bench together. He's looking at something behind the camera, his expression serious. I am gazing admiringly at him, as if he's the most fantastic person I've ever seen.

Now he's the one who looks at me almost the same way. He wants us to run away together. He's put it in his letters. Leo would do anything for me. Whatever I ask of him.

Leo lifted his duffel bag out of the baggage compartment of the minibus. He slung it over his shoulder, adjusted his moss-green beret and straightened his shoulders. Waved to his comrades as the minibus drove off.

He'd been looking forward to this moment for a long time, fantasising about every detail. How he would stand there in the middle of the yard in his uniform, what the place would smell like, sound like.

The dogs rushed towards him, wagging their tails and whimpering with excitement. His mother came down the rickety steps, with Lola following cautiously.

'Leo! Leo!'

The voice made him turn around. Elita was running along the track from the paddock, mud splashing up over her riding boots, eyes sparkling. Leo's heart began to pound. This was exactly how he'd imagined it, even down to the sun peeping through the clouds.

Elita threw her arms around his neck and he drew her close. Her hair smelled of horses and the herbal shampoo that Eva-Britt and Lola made themselves. Leo closed his eyes, determined to hold this moment in his memory forever.

'My turn,' Eva-Britt said, and Elita stepped aside. 'Let me look at you! You've certainly grown – the food must be good up there in Norrland.'

Leo nodded; he still couldn't take his eyes off Elita.

'And you've got medals!' His mother touched the row of small gold-coloured merit awards on his breast. 'But your hair . . .'

She reached up as if she were about to remove his beret; he turned his head away and laughed.

'Everyone has a buzz cut, Mum. It's the most practical solution – we're on our bellies in the mud nearly every week.'

'I think it looks good,' Elita said.

Her words made Leo's heart beat even faster. He looked her up and down.

'Have you been riding Bill? You wrote that he was almost broken in.'

Elita nodded. 'They're coming to pick him up after the weekend, but there'll be time for you to try him out. Dad's not around this evening.'

'What does ND stand for?' Lola pointed to the badge on his beret. Her expression was distant, and Leo guessed that she was having one of her 'absent days' as his mother called them – days when a part of her was somewhere else.

'Norrland Dragoons,' he said proudly. 'You're given the beret when you've completed the winter training and the commando assessment.'

Lola didn't appear to have heard him; she just carried on staring at his beret.

Elita took his hand, wove her fingers through his. Her skin was warm, almost burning him.

'Let's go in. Eva-Britt and I have baked you a cake.'

They set off up the steps, but paused by the door. Lola was still in the yard, staring up at Leo. She raised her chin as if she could hear sounds that were inaudible to everyone else.

'Many things are on the move tonight,' she said loudly. 'Nature is hungry, the Green Man is riding through the forests, and the old must be replaced by the new.'

'What did you say, sweetheart?' Eva-Britt went back down the steps and gently took Lola by the arm. 'Come along – let's go inside and celebrate Leo's homecoming.'

16

'I've told you about David's father, haven't I? Bertil has dementia, but both David and Ingrid are determined to pretend that everything is OK. They cling to Bertil's lucid moments, blame tiredness, a cold, the wrong medication for any aberrations. Support each other in their denial while Bertil slowly disappears into his own mind. Sorry, I didn't mean to upset you. Some things are just so sad. Losing the person you love is bad enough, but to do it slowly, until all that remains is an empty shell, is almost unbearable.'

They have dinner with David's parents. The house, which is Ingrid's childhood home, is in the middle of Tornaby, and is one of the oldest and largest in the village. Enormous garage, guest accommodation at one end of the perfectly manicured garden.

To the right of the front door hangs something that Thea recognises: a Green Man figure. This one is made of pale green hawthorn twigs instead of brambles.

'Welcome! I was just telling Bertil how well the TV recording went.' Ingrid hugs her with unexpected warmth. 'You saved the day,' she whispers in Thea's ear. 'But don't tell David I said so!'

After pre-dinner drinks David and his mother disappear into the kitchen, leaving Thea in the library with Bertil. She doesn't really mind. They've met on only a handful of occasions, but she's fond of him.

David bears a close resemblance to his father. The same square face and well-defined nose, the same neatly trimmed beard, although Bertil's is white and rather more sparse.

The library is spacious, with fitted shelves. One wall is covered with framed photographs, awards, pennants – so many that the wallpaper is barely visible. Most of the photographs feature Bertil with politicians, businessmen and women, and sports stars. Her father-in-law is always equally smart; he appears only occasionally without a jacket or blazer. In fact, Thea has never seen Bertil in anything other than a shirt and tie. Tonight is no exception, although he has replaced his blazer with a cardigan.

In one of the photographs ten-year-old David is standing with Ingrid outside a wintry Stockholm City Hall along with a young man in a peaked cap and an old-fashioned police uniform. This must be Ingrid's younger brother Arne, probably on the day he qualified as a police officer. The uniform and the cap are a little too big, and his moustache seems out of place on his childish face.

Christmas 1985, it says at the bottom. Only four months before Elita Svart's death.

Thea had intended to ask David about the spring sacrifice in the car on the way over, but he was on the phone all the time, so she didn't get the chance.

In another photograph David must be about thirty. He's wearing his chef's whites, standing in the doorway of his first restaurant with his arm around his mother. He looks happy – so does Ingrid. She is looking at her son with such pride.

The best picture is right in the centre of the display: Bertil and Ingrid's wedding. They're so young – not much more than twenty. Their faces are smooth, unmarked, but it's the expression on their faces that moves Thea. They are gazing at each other with so much love that it still, almost forty-five years later, radiates from the frame.

A low, subtly lit display cabinet completes the collection. Cups, plates, vases, bowls, most with the date, the name of the award and some special citation engraved.

'Look at this, Thea.'

Bertil opens the cabinet and takes out a pewter goblet. It's not the biggest in the collection, but Thea already knows it's the most important piece.

'The national bridge championship in 1980,' he says proudly. 'We won the whole thing!'

Thea nods, giving no indication that he showed her the goblet the last time she was here.

'Fantastic, Bertil.'

He beams, for a moment looking much younger than his sixty-nine years. Then the expression vanishes, replaced by confusion as soon as he puts the goblet back in the cabinet.

'So how's it going with . . .' Bertil frowns, waves his hand.

'The castle. Very well, I think. David's working extremely hard.'

Bertil nods, then looks irritated, as if he didn't mean the castle at all. He shakes his head.

'You'll have to forgive me. I'm on new medication, and it makes me a little . . .' He taps his temple. 'Shall we sit down?'

He takes one of the leather armchairs, signals to her to take the other.

'And your job?' he asks. 'How are you getting on as . . . ?'

'Good, thanks – I started today. I'm taking over as the local GP from Sigbritt Andersson.'

Bertil takes a sip of the whisky and soda Ingrid put out for him a little while ago, next to his pipe and ashtray.

'And you're happy at Bokelund?'

'Yes.'

'Have you met the count? Rudolf?' Bertil shakes his head crossly. 'No, I mean his boy. Hubert.'

'No, we've only seen each other from a distance.' Thea thinks of the face she saw at the window during the thunderstorm. The sorrowful man in the west wing.

Bertil nods slowly. 'Just be careful. A lot of bad things have happened at Bokelund.'

'Like what?'

Bertil frowns. He suddenly looks irritated again, as if he'd intended to say something completely different.

'How . . .' he says after some thought. 'How's it going with . . .' He waves his hand again, as if he's trying to catch the right words. Thea realises that the conversation has reached its conclusion. Regardless of who David's father once was, the people he's met and the things he's achieved, he is now on his way into the great oblivion. The thought makes her feel very sad.

'Dinner's ready!' Ingrid calls from the hallway with exaggerated cheerfulness. The sound of her voice makes Bertil's eyes light up.

'Wonderful! Let me escort you to the table, my dear.'

He gets to his feet and gallantly proffers his arm.

They chat their way through the starter. The castle, the preview dinner, the weather, the TV report. Ingrid and David do most of the talking. Bertil sits in silence at the head of the table, concentrating on his food, and Thea doesn't have much to contribute.

'So how was your first day at work, Thea?' David's mother asks when the main course has been served.

'Good, thanks. Dr Andersson showed me the surgery, then we made a home visit to Kerstin Miller.'

'She's not ill, is she?' David asks.

'Just a touch of the flu. I think it will be difficult to stop her from going back to work too soon.'

Thea thinks she sees Ingrid cast an anxious glance at her husband, but Bertil is fully occupied with his meal, and doesn't appear to be paying any attention to the conversation.

'I heard an old story while I was out there,' Thea adds.

'Oh? What story was that?' Ingrid asks.

Thea hesitates, then realises she's said too much to stop now.

'It was about Elita Svart.'

Bertil drops his fork onto his plate with a crash. His face is ashen.

'The spring sacrifice,' he says in an unexpectedly clear voice. 'Poor child. You must never tell anyone. Never, never, never . . .'

He stops, then bursts into tears.

17

Walpurgis Night 1986

Hoof and horn, hoof and horn. All that dies shall be reborn.

Eva-Britt taught me that rhyme when I was a child. She and Lola always recite it when they're mixing herbs.

What does it mean? I wanted to know.

It means that death is necessary for new life to flourish, little Elita, Eva-Britt replied.

Many people are frightened by the thought of death, the idea that everything comes to an end. Not me. Nothing ever comes to an end. Now let's say it together:

Hoof and horn, hoof and horn. All that dies shall be reborn.

Don't you feel better already?

Per Nyberg and his father found the one-year-old fawn in the enclosure nearest to the castle forest. The carrion crows led them to the right place, a huge flock circling above the cadaver.

The belly was open. The crows and other carrion-eaters had made in-roads, but the wound in the throat was still clearly visible.

'How many is that?'

Erik Nyberg took off his cap and wiped his forehead with the sleeve of his jacket. 'Three. The count won't be pleased.' He stomped around on the grass, looking for tracks.

'Do you still think it's a wolf or a lynx?' Per wondered.

'Have you got a better explanation?' The response was rapid and a little too sharp. Erik paused, crouched down.

'What have you found?'

No reply. Per went and looked over his father's shoulder; there were a number of U-shaped indentations in the ground.

'Hoof prints?'

Erik quickly straightened up, brushed the dirt off his knees.

'They're old,' he muttered. 'Nothing to do with this.'

He nodded toward the dead animal.

'We need to go over the enclosure again. There must be a gap in the fence somewhere that we've missed – but first we have a job to do at Svartgården.'

The name made Per's heart beat faster, and he had to make a real effort to maintain his composure.

'What kind of job?' he asked, keeping his tone as neutral as possible.

'We're terminating the lease.'

'Shit – why?'

'Because the count is selling the land to the army.'

'So what happens to Lasse and his family?'

Erik shrugged. 'Not our problem. The count can do what he likes with his land. Grab hold of the front legs.'

He seized the deer's hind legs, while Per fumbled in his pockets for his gloves, only to realise he'd left them in the car. He could feel his father's eyes on him, staring at Per's smooth hands.

'For fuck's sake, Per – just do it. Getting dirt under your fingernails occasionally is part of what we do. You have to get used to it.'

Reluctantly Per seized the front legs. The fur was rough and cold. He suppressed a shudder.

Between them they carried the body to the car, with Per doing his best not to stare at the wound in the animal's throat. The patches of dark red blood on the white belly. The big, empty eyes, reflecting the sky above.

The whole thing was so harsh, so brutal. So far from what he really wanted to do. The person he wanted to be.

He thought about Elita, about his dreams.

His heart beat even faster, bringing a flush to his cheeks. He glanced anxiously at his father, hoping he hadn't noticed anything, but fortunately Erik seemed to be completely focused on the task in hand. His lips were moving, murmuring words that were barely audible:

'Nature is hungry and the Green Man is riding through the forests.'

18

The atmosphere is subdued during the drive home.

'I'm sorry,' Thea says in an attempt to fix things. 'I had no idea . . .'

'It's fine,' David murmurs. 'Dad's not himself. Mum had high hopes for the new medication, but it doesn't seem to be helping. Not yet, anyway.'

'What do you think he meant?'

'Nothing – he mixes things up. Names, people, events. Everything somehow blends into one.'

'But he remembered Elita Svart. Dr Andersson told me the whole story. All four of you were there – you, Nettan, Sebastian and Jan-Olof. You saw Elita's brother . . .' She breaks off. 'Why have you never mentioned any of this?'

David sighs. 'It happened such a long time ago. I don't want to rake up the past.'

'It must have been terrible – to see your friend . . .'

'Elita Svart wasn't our friend.' His tone has hardened.

'Oh – I thought . . .'

'You thought wrong.' He doesn't say anything for a little while. 'Elita was sixteen, and very . . . mature for her age. We were only twelve, nerdy kids who played board games. As far as we were concerned, Elita was in a different league. When she suddenly started taking an interest in us, it was amazing. She made us feel special. She was good at that – she knew exactly what to do.'

He slows down, turns left out of the village and follows the narrow lane leading to the castle. There are no street lamps here, and the darkness closes around the car.

'So what did Elita get out of it?' Thea wonders.

'I don't know, to be honest. Maybe she enjoyed being in the centre of attention. Whatever it was, she started sending us on little errands – to buy sweets, collect her clothes or school books, take messages. We became her secret little servants, but the sick part is that we were more than happy to go along with it. We were completely bewitched by her.'

He shakes his head as if he finds it hard to believe what he's saying.

'Even though she was a gyppo?'

That word again, bitter as bile.

'That was the kind of thing other people said behind her back. Adults, mostly.'

'Your parents?'

David pulls a face, confirming Thea's suspicions.

'Elita made us promise not to tell anyone what we were doing. It wasn't difficult; none of our parents would have approved of us spending time with her, which of course made the whole thing even more exciting.' He falls silent.

'So what happened on Walpurgis Night?' Thea ventures after a moment.

No answer. David is clutching the wheel, eyes fixed on the road ahead. He looks as if he might be working up to telling her.

They come from nowhere, suddenly appearing in the beam of the headlights. Black creatures with humped backs, pouring across the lane.

David slams his foot on the brake and wrenches the wheel to the side. The tyres screech on the tarmac and Thea just manages to grab the handle on the roof before the car lurches across the ditch and ends up in a field of rape. The front wheels sink into the soft ground, bringing the vehicle to an abrupt stop. The engine dies, and there is total silence for a few seconds.

'Are you OK?' David asks eventually.

Thea nods. Her heart is racing, the air inside feels thick, it smells of petrol and exhaust fumes.

'W-what the hell was that?'

'Wild boar. A whole fucking herd of them.'

He gets out and walks around the car to inspect the damage. She hears him swear, and decides to join him. The cold air makes her shiver. It's dark, but she can clearly see the front wheels buried in the ground. One of the headlights has stopped working.

David jumps back in the car, starts the engine and tries to reverse. Earth and greenery spurt up around the tyres, but the only result is that the car sinks even lower.

'Fuck!' He slams his fists against the wheel. Gets out again and kicks one of the tyres.

'Shall we call the roadside recovery firm?' Thea suggests.

'We can't do that, for fuck's sake! We've both been drinking. If the recovery guy calls the police and I go down for drunk driving, the restaurant is fucked!'

He takes several deep breaths then spreads his hands in an apologetic gesture.

'What I mean is, we can't risk any negative publicity. Not now, with the preview night coming up.'

Maybe you should have thought of that before you decided to drive home, Thea thinks, but decides to keep her opinion to herself. To be fair, she could have stopped him, suggested they ring a taxi.

'So what do we do now?'

David is chewing his thumbnail. 'I'll call someone who can help us. Get back in the car and keep warm.'

She does as he says, leaves the door open for a minute or so to get rid of the fumes. She can hear him on the phone, but she can't work out who he's talking to.

She finds it difficult to understand why he's never mentioned Elita Svart. On the other hand, there are plenty of things she hasn't told him, things she hasn't even told Margaux. The reason why Elita Svart's story feels so personal. So close.

She leans her head back and closes her eyes. David's conversation fades to a faint murmur, before being replaced by her big brother Ronny's voice.

Jenny, Jeeenny!

She opens her eyes, sees lights approaching, dazzling headlights accompanied by the sound of a powerful engine. A tractor with double front and rear tyres rolls easily off the road and stops a few metres behind their car.

The driver clambers down from the cab and shakes hands with David. Thea gets out of the car. She shades her eyes against the bright lights and waits for David to introduce her, but the tractor driver gets there first. He's in his early fifties, dressed in a fleece jacket, overalls and heavy boots. His hair and the stubble on his chin are peppered with grey, his eyes so intensely blue that Thea can see them in the darkness. He pulls off one glove.

'Hi – Per Nyberg. We're neighbours.'

His hand is surprisingly soft.

'Thea Lind.'

'I live over at Ängsgården – my father Erik and I lease most of the castle's land.' He smiles broadly. 'He's one of your patients – I think you're due to see him tomorrow. He can be pretty bad-tempered, just so you know, but he doesn't mean any harm.' Per winks at her in a way that could almost be flirtatious, then turns back to David.

'Wild boar, you say – it doesn't surprise me. The population has exploded since we were young. They do a tremendous amount of damage to the crops.' He inspects the car. 'Good job you managed to swerve – you don't want to crash into a herd of wild boar. It's like hitting a concrete block.'

Per releases a chain wound around the weights at the front of the tractor and attaches it to the back of their car.

'If you get behind the wheel, David, I'll pull you out. Thea, move back so that you're not too close to the chain, in case it breaks.'

He climbs into the cab, puts the tractor in gear then begins to reverse slowly so that the chain gradually tightens.

Within a couple of minutes they're back on the road. The car looks somewhat the worse for wear, with only one functioning headlight and the sides covered in mud.

'Thank you so much for your help,' David says. 'And Per . . . It would be good if we could keep this little incident between us.'

'You're welcome. And don't worry, this isn't the first car I've hauled out of a ditch. Out here in the country we help each other. We keep each other's secrets, don't we?'

He turns to Thea, winks again in that way that's so hard to interpret.

'Good to meet you, Thea. I hope to see you again soon.'

19

Walpurgis Night 1986

Leo has always been afraid of Father. Crept along close to the walls, keeping his gaze lowered. Jumped every time Lasse raised his voice.

'Leo is a cuckoo in the nest, Elita,' Father says. 'An unwelcome little interloper who must be kept in line to stop him taking over completely.'

But Leo is no longer little, neither on the outside nor the inside. Something has been growing within him ever since we were children. Something dangerous that can escape at any moment. It frightens me, yet at the same time I find it attractive. Isn't that strange?

A rne lingered by the car for quite some time, hoping that Elita would return. He took the opportunity to go around the back of the shed and pee in one of the muddy puddles. Stood among the bracken thinking about her sitting astride the powerful horse, controlling its movements. His shirt was sticking to his back. He loosened his tie, looked over at the house for what must have been the fiftieth time.

Elita had rushed off as soon as she heard the car, called out Leo's name in a way that still caused Arne physical pain in his chest.

Shit!

He got in the car. The rubber mat was covered in mud, and the smell of the marsh seemed to have seeped into the upholstery. He started the engine and drove slowly up to the house.

The yard was quiet; there wasn't even any sign of the dogs. Arne waited for a few more minutes before going up the steps. He could hear loud voices from inside; one of them was Lasse's.

He reached for the door handle, hesitated. He wasn't sure why. He was a police officer, he could walk straight in, exactly as he'd done only an hour or so ago.

The voices grew louder. Arne briefly considered leaving, but he'd promised Elita a lift, and the thought of having her in the police car with him was still far too tempting. He knocked, opened the door and went in.

Lasse was sitting at one side of the kitchen table in the middle of an arm-wrestling match with a young man in military uniform. There was an open moonshine container on the table, several coffee cups and a half-eaten cake.

Eva-Britt, Lola and Elita were so focused on the contest that they didn't even notice Arne.

'Come on, Leo!' Elita shouted.

Eva-Britt's son had always been a scaredy-cat, but he was all grown up now. He was taller and more broad-shouldered than Arne. There were medals on his tunic, and Arne noticed the green beret tucked under one epaulette. However, what bothered him was the way Elita was looking at Leo, as if the little soldier boy was the most fantastic thing she'd ever set eyes on.

The stupid idiot had obviously been persuaded to take on Lasse, and that could only end one way. Lasse's arms were as thick as pythons, and as far as Arne knew, he'd never lost a match. So now it was the soldier boy's turn to be humiliated.

They'd only just started; their arms were still vertical, and the veins on the back of their hands were bulging with the effort.

Lasse had adopted his usual tactic. First of all he tired his opponent by simply keeping his hand still, then when he thought he'd played out the drama for long enough, he would slowly force down the other man's hand one centimetre at a time, occasionally pausing just to show how superior he was.

Lasse grinned, but Leo didn't seem worried. He was leaning across the table with his chest much closer to his hand than Lasse's was. Nor did he appear to be trying as hard as he should be at this stage. Instead he slowly moved his upper body and his hand a fraction to the side.

The technique looked professional, as if Leo knew exactly what he was doing, which worried Arne. Fortunately Lasse stopped the movement, but his grin wasn't quite so confident now.

'Come on, Leo!' Elita called out again, and her voice sent a shard of ice into Arne's heart.

Leo repeated the manoeuvre. Lasse stopped grinning and frowned as doubts began to creep in. He couldn't believe what was happening. Leo continued to move his body to the side, and Lasse did his utmost to stop their hands from doing the same. Sweat was pouring down his face, and a prominent vein was throbbing at his temple. Leo did it again.

One of Lasse's nostrils twitched, his hand began to tremble and then slowly, slowly sank towards the table. Arne held his breath. There wasn't a sound in the little kitchen, as if everyone there had realised that something incomprehensible was happening.

The colour drained from Lasse's face and his eyes were transformed into two pieces of coal. He drew back his lips, exposing all his teeth, and the vein at his temple looked as if it was about to burst. However, his resistance was futile. Leo's technique forced Lasse closer and closer to inevitable defeat.

Lasse leaped to his feet and overturned the table, sending the moonshine, cups and cake flying. The three terrified women pressed themselves against the worktop. Leo got to his feet, showing no sign of fear. He was a head taller than Lasse, and at least as muscular, but in spite of this Arne thought Lasse was about to attack the younger man. He probably ought to do something to calm the situation; after all, he was a police officer. Then again, that cocky little soldier boy deserved a beating.

Lasse stepped forward, fist raised. Leo still didn't have the wit to be scared. Instead he clenched his fists, lowered his chin and bent his knees; he knew exactly what he was doing.

At the last second Lasse realised the same thing. He dropped his arm and produced a large flick knife from somewhere. Released the blade with one thumb.

Someone gasped, and out of the corner of his eye Arne saw that Lola and Eva-Britt's faces were rigid with fear. Elita, however, was looking from Lasse to Leo and back again, seemingly unaware of Arne's presence. The kitchen stank of spilt booze.

Lasse tightened his grip on the knife. 'You little fucker! You come back here thinking you're something – this is my fucking house!'

Arne had to do something.

'OK,' he began in his most authoritative tone of voice. He stepped forward, positioning himself between the two men. 'Let's all calm down, shall—'

'Shut the fuck up!' Lasse yelled.

Arne recoiled as if he'd been punched, but stood his ground. One foot had landed in the remains of the cake, and the alcohol fumes were making the membranes in his nose smart. What the fuck was he supposed to do now? His baton was still in the car, and it would take too long to draw his gun.

He heard the dogs barking outside, followed by the sound of an engine.

This seemed to bring Lasse to his senses. In a second he flicked the blade shut and slipped the knife into his pocket.

'Get this mess cleaned up!' he shouted at the women, who didn't move a muscle.

He gave Leo one last filthy look, pushed past Arne without so much as a glance, and slammed the door behind him.

20

'I'm sure you're wondering what it is about this story that fascinates me, Margaux. Why I'm so interested in something that happened over thirty years ago.

'I'd like to say it's for David's sake, because whatever went on back then, it still torments him. I want to help him, just as he helped me.

'But that's not the whole truth. There's another reason, but you'll have to be patient for a while longer. Wait until I've gathered the courage to tell you.'

Thea wakes early, as always. It's just before four; Emee is asleep on the floor next to her bed. The nightlight is on. The moonlight seeps through the blind, drawing a pattern of stripes on the ceiling. Thea gazes up at it, following the lines. She notices a small patch of damp where the wall meets the ceiling. Best not to mention it to David, at least not at the moment. He's got enough to think about. Things she could never have imagined.

Poor child. You must never tell anyone. Never, never, never . . .

What did Bertil mean by that? What was it that must never be told, and why had he reacted so strongly to Elita's name?

She takes out her phone, opens a search window and enters 'Tornaby 1986 murder'. She finds articles from various Skåne newspapers that have been scanned in; they don't tell her much more than she already knows.

The reporting seems to have died down pretty quickly after the lurid headlines of the first week. Words such as 'ritual murder', 'sacrificial rites' and 'child killer' are replaced by the significantly less charged 'family tragedy' and 'sibling drama'. The size of the typeface clearly shows how interest has waned. Olof Palme had been assassinated only two months earlier, and the twists and turns into the investigation still preoccupied almost every media outlet.

However, one of the tabloids does try to squeeze the last little bit out of the story by running a summary piece with the headline:

SPRING SACRIFICE VICTIM MADE BROTHER KILL HER!

The article is illustrated with photographs of both Elita and her stepbrother. Leo seems to be in uniform; his hair is cropped, and his eyes are covered with a black rectangle that is theoretically supposed to protect his identity. The image is grainy, but Thea can make out a straight nose and a square chin.

Elita is smiling confidently in what is presumably a school photo. She looks very different from the girl in the Polaroid. Bolder, angrier in a way that Thea recognises all too well.

Elita is referred to throughout as the sacrificial victim, while Leo is either the stepbrother or the elite soldier. The writer revels in the details surrounding Elita's death, and much is made of the fact that she left behind a letter in which she said she was planning her own death.

The last article Thea can find is from August 1986, a brief report stating that the court in Helsingborg had convicted Leo of murder and sentenced him to six years in jail, but that the sentence had been reduced because he was only twenty years old and was heavily influenced by his stepsister. Then nothing. The press pack has moved on, and no one cares about a dead gypsy girl anymore.

She switches off her phone, lies back on her pillow and closes her eyes.

Fucking gyppo . . .

She was twelve years old when the word was spat in her face for the first time. A boy yelled it at her in the school playground after he'd asked her to be his girlfriend and she said no.

Admittedly she'd heard whispers about her family before, but there was something about that particular word that made her flinch. It hit her hard, even though she wasn't really sure what it meant.

Ronny had beaten the shit out of the kid the next day. Her big brother dealt with everyone who used that word. Not that it helped.

Ronny never understood that the more violently he tried to fix things, the worse they would get. The word became branded into his skin until it was impossible to remove, like an invisible tattoo that marked him for life.

It would be many years before she did anything about the situation, but she'd already realised what she had to do.

Before you can become the person you want to be, you have to get rid of the person you are.

21

Walpurgis Night 1986

I know that Eva-Britt is worried about Leo too. She's done her best to keep us together, while keeping Lasse and Leo apart, but it's getting more and more difficult. The walls and the ceiling in the house are closing in. We are heading for a catastrophe, if no one does anything to stop it. If no one sacrifices himself or herself.

Walpurgis Night is fast approaching. You haven't forgotten what's going to happen, have you? How this story ends for Elita Svart?

Everything had gone exactly as Leo had hoped. The bitter coffee burned in his belly as he stood there in the middle of the kitchen, his head buzzing with intoxication and pride. He'd broken the spell, shown them all that it was possible to defeat Lasse Svart.

Now he wanted to speak to Elita alone, tell her about the cottage, show her the key. Tell her that it was all for real, that they could leave, just as he'd promised her before he went off to join the army.

Unfortunately, after Lasse had walked out and slammed the door, Lola had run upstairs and Elita had followed her, leaving only Leo and his mother in the kitchen.

'You shouldn't have done that,' Eva-Britt whispered as she fastened the top button of his shirt and straightened his tie.

'Why not? I've been practising all winter. One of the guys in my platoon is a Swedish champion in arm wrestling.'

Eva-Britt shook her head. 'Lasse's dangerous. You need to be careful – you saw the knife!'

Leo snorted. 'He was only trying to scare me. Have you ever seen him stab someone?'

Eva-Britt didn't reply.

'I'm not scared of Lasse,' Leo went on. 'Not anymore.' He placed his hands on his mother's shoulders. 'And you and Lola and Elita don't need to be afraid either. We can take the car and leave right now, all four of us. One of my comrades has a cottage outside Ystad that we can borrow. Elita and I have already talked about it. I've got the key in my duffel bag. It's all set up.'

Eva-Britt removed his hands, glanced around with a worried look on her face.

'Don't say that. Lasse will never let us go. You and me maybe, but not Lola, and definitely not Elita. He would never allow it – never! He'd rather kill both of you.'

22

'By the way, do you remember the man in the window that I mentioned earlier? Hubert Gordon – he lives in the west wing. A strange man with a strange story. Or rather a sad story, maybe. You can make up your own mind, Margaux. There are many stories here, if you just scrape beneath the surface.'

D r Andersson picks her up just before eight. Thea couldn't get back to sleep; she cannot shake off the tale of Elita Svart and her fate.

Did Elita persuade her stepbrother to kill her? Did she really have that kind of power over him? And why would a pretty sixteen-year-old with her whole life in front of her want to die on a cold stone?

The whole thing reminds her of a jigsaw puzzle. She already has a picture of what it will look like in the end; the challenge is to put together the pieces. Although of course this story is something very different from a five-thousand-piece Ravensburger.

'I thought we'd call on Erik Nyberg,' the doctor says when they've turned onto the main road. 'He's diabetic and is having problems with the sight in one eye. He still refuses to slow down, so I drop by occasionally, check his levels and make sure he's taking his medication properly. Erik is the biggest farmer in the area, but these days it's his son Per who runs Ängsgården.'

Per Nyberg, the smiling man with the tractor. Thea thinks back to last night's incident, which she has absolutely no intention of sharing with Dr Andersson.

Out here in the country we help each other. We keep each other's secrets.

'Oh yes, I think David's mentioned him,' she lies. 'Something to do with the castle, maybe?'

The question is innocent and so vague that it could be referring to almost anything. Dr Andersson doesn't need any more encouragement.

'That's right, the Nybergs take care of the estate – they mow the grass, cut the hedges, clear the snow when necessary. They've done it ever since the foundation took over Bokelund. Per's a good boy. Well, I say boy – Erik's seventy-five, so Per must be in his fifties. He's a bit of a local celebrity.'

'Oh?'

The little nudge is unnecessary. Dr Andersson is in full flow; all Thea needs to do is sit quietly and listen.

'Yes indeed! Per plays the guitar and sings in his spare time – he travels all over the area. He's good – I've heard some of his songs on the local radio. Per and the little count are childhood friends too, of course.'

Thea has heard the nickname before, but the doctor misinterprets her silence.

'The little count – Hubert Gordon. I thought you knew each other. You're neighbours up at Bokelund, after all.'

'I have seen him, but only from a distance. He tends to stay in the west wing.' Thea thinks back to the night of the storm.

'Yes, Hubert is something of a loner. Most people feel sorry for him – a lodger in his own castle. I assume you know the story?'

Thea doesn't even need to answer. The doctor turns onto a dirt track between green fields; several large buildings are visible over by the edge of the forest.

'The old count, Rudolf Gordon, married late; he was almost fifty when Hubert arrived. Unfortunately the boy bore no resemblance to his father, either in his appearance or character. Rudolf sent him to the best boarding schools in England, determined that Hubert should carry on the family traditions, but poor Hubert was a dreamer, and had issues with his nerves, like his mother. Rudolf gradually came to realise that his son wasn't cut out to run a large estate, with all that entails.' The doctor shook her head. 'In the early Nineties, when Rudolf's health began to fail, he set up the Bokelund Foundation and transferred the castle and most of the grounds. He also gave several hundred acres of land to the Åkerlunda monastery. Rudolf was a Catholic – I believe there's a small chapel in the castle?'

The doctor raises her eyebrows, making it clear that this is a question.

'Maybe. In which case it must be in the west wing; I've never been in there.'

They arrive at Ängsgården, passing a row of well-kept stables and storage sheds.

'Anyway,' Dr Andersson says. 'When Rudolf died in 1994, Hubert received only a small amount of money plus the right to use a number of rooms in one wing of the castle for the rest of his life. Oh, there's Erik.'

She nods in the direction of the farmhouse where an elderly man is leaning on a stick at the top of the steps. He is wearing dark glasses, a scruffy moleskin jacket and trousers that don't match.

'He was the old count's administrator for many years – one of the few people Rudolf trusted. He's been the treasurer of the foundation ever since the start.'

Erik raises a hand in greeting as they get out of the car. 'Welcome.' His voice is rough. 'Erik Nyberg.' The dark glasses hide his eyes, yet Thea immediately has the feeling that he's examining her very closely.

Erik is small and sinewy, and there is an innate dignity about him. He's polite, but doesn't say any more than he has to.

The house smells of cleaning fluid. The wellington boots and clogs by the kitchen door are in a dead straight line. Erik Nyberg seems to be the kind of man who gets things done – and done in the right way.

He sets out coffee and cake while the doctor chats to him. The kitchen is warm. On one wall there is a tapestry of a Bible quotation, while on the others small oil paintings depict English fox-hunting scenes with horses and dogs.

When they are seated at the table a red-and-white spaniel appears and shows a great interest in both Thea and Dr Andersson's shoes and trouser legs. The dog is well-trained and obeys its master's slightest gesture. Thea sees an opportunity to get Erik to open up.

'I've got a dog too – a street dog I brought back from Syria.'

'Oh?' Erik sounds interested.

'Her name is Emee. She looks a bit like a cross between a greyhound and a dingo.' Margaux's description; not very flattering, but fair. 'My colleague and I found her in a ditch outside Idlib. She was badly emaciated, so we took turns to feed her with milk substitute whenever we were off duty. We hadn't intended to keep her, but as soon as she'd recovered, she started to follow us wherever we went.'

Or Margaux, at any rate, she adds to herself.

'What colour is she?' Erik asks.

'Grey – both her coat and her eyes. Like a ghost. Emee means ghost in the Yoruba language, which is spoken in Nigeria.'

She stops herself, leaves out the fact that she and Margaux first met in Nigeria. Sixteen years ago now . . . She pushes aside the thought.

'A street dog, you say? And she looks like a ghost.' Erik leans forward, full of curiosity. 'How did you get her into Sweden?'

Thea describes the import procedure, doesn't say that it was David who flew down and took care of all the practicalities while she lay in a hospital in Cyprus. Or that she remembers very little of the time immediately after the bombing.

The story clearly interests Erik. His initial reserve has gone, and he chats away as if they've known each other for a long time.

'How did you get on the other night?' he asks. 'Any damage from the storm?'

Thea tells him about the lightning strike and the power outage.

'We once talked about getting both lightning rods and a reserve generator,' Erik says. 'But the count decided it was too expensive. Rudolf didn't like spending money. We have both here on the farm; it would be too risky to do without. Most of our operations are mechanised nowadays – feeding, mucking out, the machinery. You can never be too careful.'

'So shall we start the examination, Thea?' Dr Andersson opens her bag and hands Thea the blood pressure cuff.

Thea wraps it around Erik's arm; he needs no encouragement to keep the conversation going.

'Have you and David settled into the coach house?'

'Absolutely.'

'That's good. I'm looking forward to seeing what David does with the castle. How's his father, by the way? I haven't bumped into Bertil for a long time.'

'He has good days and bad days,' Thea answers truthfully. She thinks about how upset he'd become during dinner, and feels a pang of guilt at having caused it by bringing up Elita Svart.

'Growing old is no picnic,' Erik mutters. 'Alzheimer's, isn't it?'

Thea doesn't reply. David's father isn't her patient, but she still prefers not to discuss other people's medical conditions.

'God knows we've had our differences over the years, Bertil and I,' Erik continues. 'But I've always respected him. Everyone around here respects Bertil Nordin. He was on the executive committee of the Centre Party, and chaired both the sports club and the local community council for many years. He was re-elected over and over again. People trusted him. They knew he'd keep his word, and always had the village's best interests at heart. And he was discreet – that was why the count asked him to help set up the Bokelund Foundation.'

Erik suddenly stops talking. Thea has experienced this before: all at once a patient is overwhelmed by their own unexpected chattiness, and falls silent. She leaves him in peace while she completes her examination. He doesn't flinch when she pricks his finger to measure his blood sugar.

'Does he talk a lot of rubbish?' Erik asks when she's finished. She can't read his eyes behind those dark glasses, but once again she feels sure that he is watching her closely. 'Bertil,' he adds when she doesn't respond. 'Does he say stupid things? I've heard that people with Alzheimer's often do that.'

Before Thea can say anything, the kitchen door opens and Per walks in, followed by an older man with a bushy red beard, wearing a baseball cap.

'I saw the car and realised we had visitors. You must be our new doctor.'

Per smiles and holds out his hand, as though this is their first meeting. 'Per Nyberg. This old fox is my father,' he adds, patting Erik on the shoulder.

'Thea Lind.'

The whole thing makes her feel kind of ridiculous, but as Per has started it, she has to play along.

'David Nordin's wife,' Erik informs his son.

'I knew that. I read about you on Facebook.'

Per holds onto her hand for a second too long, squeezes it gently before letting go. As before, she is struck by how soft his skin is. She glances at his left hand; no wedding ring, no telltale trace of one. Around his wrist he wears several braided leather bracelets, which briefly remind her of her father.

'This is Little Stefan,' Per says, gesturing towards his companion. He works for us. He's in the middle of cutting the hedges up at the castle, so you're bound to come across him again before long.'

Thea nods to the other man, who gives her a little wave.

'So how's it going with the restaurant?' Per asks. 'Dad and I are looking forward to the dinner.'

'They've had a power outage,' Erik says. 'After the storm the other night.'

'Oh dear. If you need help with anything, you only have to ask. David has my number.' Per winks conspiratorially at Thea.

'And Dad knows everything there is to know about the castle and its secrets. Where all the bodies are buried, so to speak.'

He fires off another smile which is definitely flirtatious.

'Thanks – good to know,' Thea says.

In spite of Erik's dark glasses, she thinks the old man is glaring angrily at his son.

23

Walpurgis Night 1986

The dragonfly is my favourite insect. It starts life as an egg, then lives as a nymph at the bottom of the muddy pools deep in the bog. The nymph catches tadpoles and lives on them so that it can grow bigger and stronger. When it is strong enough, it crawls up out of the mud to begin its final metamorphosis. To become something better, more beautiful.

As soon as the legs and abdomen harden, it spreads its fine wings and drifts with the wind like a new, perfect creation, far away from the dampness and mud where it was born. Far away from everything that has held it down.

Do you understand where I'm going with this? Or are you still interested only in my death?

Arne walked out of the front door of Svartgården. He'd paused for a minute just inside the porch, wiped the sweat from his forehead, adjusted his uniform and attempted to regain at least some of his dignity.

The truck he'd heard was now parked between his own and Lasse's. The same white pick-up he'd seen outside the bank. Erik Nyberg, this time accompanied by his pretty-boy son.

Erik and Lasse seemed to be involved in an angry discussion. Erik held out a piece of paper, but Lasse knocked his hand aside. Arne realised what was going on: Erik was serving notice.

'Go to hell, Nyberg!' Lasse roared. 'Both you and the count can kiss my fucking arse!' With that he jumped into his own pick-up, started the engine and shot away, gravel spraying up around his wheels.

Slowly Arne went over to the Nybergs. Noticed in passing that there was a dead fawn in the back of their truck.

'Hello,' he said.

Erik looked him up and down. Raised an eyebrow, presumably at his muddy shoes and trousers and his grubby shirt.

'Are you here in an official capacity, Arne?'

Arne didn't bother answering. He couldn't stand Nyberg or his son. Per was only a couple of years younger than him. Sang and played the guitar, had an earring in one ear.

'It's good that you're here,' Erik went on. 'You can be a witness to the fact that we've given Lasse notice to quit, even if he refuses to sign.' He folded up the paper he'd tried to give Lasse and tucked it away in his inside pocket, then turned his back on Arne to show that their conversation was over.

Arne ambled over to his car. Opened the door, got in and pretended to busy himself with the police radio. After a minute or so he realised that no one was looking at him. He'd just decided to leave when the front door opened and Elita emerged.

His heart began to beat faster. Maybe the day could be saved after all. But Elita ignored him, walked straight past his car.

Eva-Britt had come out too, and Erik Nyberg went over to her. He dug out the notice to quit again, and Eva-Britt reluctantly took it.

Arne turned his attention to Elita. She and Per Nyberg had moved a short distance away and were talking to each other. A little too close together, a little too intimate. Elita reached out, touched Per's arm, and Arne saw her slip something into his hand, a little white square that he recognised only too well.

A Polaroid photograph. A photo of her, taken with his camera. A private photo, and she'd given it to Per fucking Nyberg.

Another person came out onto the steps: Leo in his uniform. He put on his beret and pulled it down over his forehead. Then he caught sight of Elita and Per. His confident, relaxed expression gave way to something else.

Arne knew exactly what it was. The same thing he was feeling.

Disappointment, jealousy.

Rage.

24

'You could never understand why I liked doing jigsaw puzzles, Margaux. The satisfaction of creating order. The faint click when a piece fits, forming a clear pattern where before there was chaos.

'Yes, I admit it – I'm fully committed to the puzzle that is Elita Svart, and I won't give up until I have the whole picture.

'Why? you wonder yet again. What is it that draws me to this story?

'I'll tell you: Elita Svart reminds me of someone I know. Or rather – someone I used to know.'

There are already patients waiting in the corridor outside the surgery. Dr Andersson and Thea work their way through them, and once again Thea is struck by the fact that almost all of them already seem to know about her. They ask questions about David and the castle, and several have already booked tables in the restaurant even though the official opening is still a month away. Many also know that she and David are living in the old coach house, they know where she used to work – they even know the name of her dog. When Thea discreetly questions one of her most talkative patients, it turns out that the information comes from the Facebook group both Per and Dr Andersson have mentioned.

Just before midday, the doctor takes a phone call.

'I have to pop out,' she says. 'I won't be gone for more than an hour. Is it OK if I leave you here on your own, then we can have lunch when I get back? You could log into the records system, see if there's anything you're still unsure about.'

'No problem.' Thea has nothing against being alone for a while with her thoughts.

'Great – see you later.'

The doctor's rapid footsteps fade away along the corridor, then the outside door slams shut.

Thea realises that she still has the packet of cigarettes in her pocket, and decides to nip outside for a sneaky smoke.

There is a large garden behind the community centre. A set of goalposts, some broken swings and a strip of asphalt with the remains of hopscotch grids suggest that it was once a playground. This must have been where David and his friends hung out. She narrows her eyes, tries to visualise the faces from Kirsten's scrapbook: David, Nettan, Sebastian and Jan-Olof. Four nerdy twelve-year-olds who suddenly attracted the attention of Elita Svart – someone who was older, cooler, and beautiful. Thea can easily understand why their heads were turned.

She takes a deep drag, thinks of her own school playground.

Fucking gyppo!

She shakes off the memory, finishes her cigarette as quickly as she can.

On the way back inside she peers through one of the windows overlooking the garden. She sees display stands and glass cabinets, walls filled with photographs. This must be the Folk Museum. Didn't Dr Andersson say something about

Elita being inspired by photographs of the rite of spring she'd seen there?

Once inside, Thea follows the signs until she is standing in front of the right door. It's locked. She tries the surgery key; it must be some kind of master, because the lock clicks open.

The room is approximately twice the size of the surgery. It smells of dust and old artefacts. The stands and cabinets she saw through the window contain everything from embroidered cloths and traditional hand tools to Stone Age axes and fossils. Hand-written signs indicate the theme of each area: HANDICRAFTS, HARVEST, THE HISTORY OF TORNABY.

On one of the walls she finds what she's looking for: LOCAL CUSTOMS. A dozen black-and-white photos, taken around the beginning of the twentieth century, grouped in threes. One group is labelled THE CEREMONY OF THE SPRING SACRIFICE.

The pictures take Thea's breath away. The similarity with the Polaroid photo is striking. The same arrangement: a young woman in the centre with antlers in her hands, long silk ribbons attached to her wrists. Four children beside her, wearing grotesque animal masks. Hare, fox, owl, deer.

The next group is BURNING THE GREEN MAN, and shows a Walpurgis Night bonfire. In the first one the fire must just have been lit; the figure at the top is clearly visible, tied to the same kind of T-shaped frame that she saw down on the common. The head and arms are easily distinguished, while the rest of the body is a shapeless mass of leaves and branches. In the last picture the flames have begun to lick at the Green Man; the heat has caused the leaves to shrivel, and you can almost see right through him. In front of the blazing fire stands the young woman and her masked helpers.

ANDERS DE LA MOTTE

Thea shudders. Just as with the Polaroid, there is something deeply unpleasant about this image. Beneath the photograph there is a typewritten caption:

> During Walpurgis Night the veil between life and death is at its thinnest. Things are on the move, nature is hungry and the Green Man is riding through the forest.

She photographs the pictures and the caption on her phone and returns to the surgery.

Back at her desk she repeats the Google search she carried out earlier. She doesn't really know why, or what she's hoping to find. Once again the old newspaper articles are listed, but this time she scrolls down the page. As expected the hits become less and less relevant, but a couple of times she sees references to a book with the title *False Confessions*.

She checks it out with an online bookseller. It's written by a journalist called Kurt Bexell, published in 2004, and as the title suggests it looks at why certain people confess to crimes they haven't committed. According to the blurb, the book contains both notorious international cases and several Swedish examples, including the murder of Elita Svart in 1986.

So Bexell doubted Leo's guilt – but why? And who did he think murdered Elita? With each new piece of the puzzle Thea's fascination grows; the idea that there are other theories beside the official line is riveting.

She is still wondering about David's role in all of this. Was he questioned? What did he and his friends actually see?

You must never tell anyone. Never, never, never ...

She clicks on the link and orders the book.

When she's finished she remains where she is, staring into space. As far as she is aware, she has exhausted the internet when it comes to facts about the murder of Elita Svart, but of course there are other possibilities. One of them is right in front of her on the desk.

She opens up the practice laptop and logs into the patient database. Types Elita's name in the box, then hesitates. Technically it's illegal for her to run a search on someone who isn't her patient; on the other hand, the risk of being caught is negligible. Who would check out her search history?

After a few seconds she clicks on enter. All that comes up is a single line: Elita's name and ID number, followed by *deceased 30-04-1986*.

She looks for a link that will take her further, but all that appears is a fact box informing her that patient records before a certain date have not been digitalised, but that hard copies can still be found in the regional archive in Lund. She jots Elita's ID number down on a Post-it note. She's so absorbed in what she's doing that she doesn't hear the footsteps in the corridor.

Someone clears their throat in the doorway, and Thea looks up in surprise. A man is standing there with a blood-soaked cloth wrapped around one hand.

'Excuse me,' he says in English. 'Are you a doctor?'

Thea quickly closes the laptop and gets to her feet.

'I am – come on in!'

The man looks relieved. He is a few years older than her, tall and muscular with an angular face and short hair, thinning on top. He's wearing an army jacket, jeans and sturdy boots.

She sits him down and begins to unwind the cloth. Blood is flowing freely from a large gash in the lower half of his palm.

'I cut myself. Stupid.' He attempts a smile.

'Lie down,' she says, raising his hand as high as possible in an attempt to reduce the bleeding. She washes the wound; it's deep, almost to the bone, but fortunately it doesn't look as if any tendons have been damaged.

'It happened not long ago. I was going to drive to A & E in Helsingborg, but then I remembered there was a surgery in the village.' His English is good, but Thea thinks there's a faint accent. His face is ashen now, his lips white. She has to stop the bleeding so that she can suture the wound, but can't find anything to use as a tourniquet. She resorts to an old trick.

'Lift your arm a little higher.'

The man does as she asks. She wraps the blood pressure cuff around his wrist and pumps it up until the blood stops.

'Keep still – I'll give you some local anaesthetic before I start stitching.'

He nods, then obediently lies there motionless while she numbs the area, inserts six stitches, then dresses the wound.

'There you go. Stay where you are for a while until you feel better. Would you like a drink?'

'Yes, please.'

She pours him a plastic cup of water.

'Thanks.' His eyes are brown and friendly. 'My name is Philippe Benoit, by the way.' He holds out his uninjured hand.

'Thea Lind. Are you French?'

'Almost,' he replies with a smile. 'Québécois. Do you speak French?'

'Of course.' Thea switches languages and realises that she too is smiling. It's a long time since she spoke French to anyone except Margaux. 'What happened to your hand?'

'A stupid accident. I was cutting a piece of rope and the knife slipped. In my defence, I was on the phone at the time. Then again, maybe that's not a point in my favour.'

'So what's someone from Quebec doing in Skåne?'

'I work in mineral prospecting.'

'Gold?'

He laughs. 'Nothing quite as exciting. Vanadium – at least that's what we hope to find when we do the test drilling. If I can manage not to slice through an artery before then.'

Maybe it's the fact that they're speaking French, but something about this whole situation has put Thea in a good mood.

'Nice trick.' He points to the blood pressure cuff. 'Very smart. I'm guessing you didn't learn that at medical school?'

'No. I used to work for Doctors Without Borders. Africa, the Middle East. You learn to improvise.'

'Aha – that explains why your French is so good. I imagine you've seen worse things than a little cut.'

'I have.'

'I'm pleased to be in experienced hands if anything else happens.'

Philippe is just about to get up when Dr Andersson comes bustling in. She stops dead, stares at the blood-soaked cloth and the stranger half-lying on the couch.

'Goodness me – what's going on here?'

'A gash to the hand. Six stitches.'

Philippe holds up his hand, displaying the dressing. *So he understands Swedish,* Thea thinks.

'Very dramatic! Have you updated the daily log?'

'Not yet – I've only just finished.'

'No problem – I'll do it.'

The doctor sits down at the desk and opens the laptop. Thea thinks she looks a little taken aback, but it passes so quickly that she can't be sure. Then she realises that she might not have deleted the illicit search for Elita's notes. She studies the other woman's face carefully, but Dr Andersson gives nothing away.

25

At the end of the working day, Dr Andersson drops her off at the coach house. It might be Thea's imagination, but she thinks her companion has been a little less talkative than usual. She can't shake off the feeling of having been caught out.

There's a pick-up and trailer outside the house. A man in overalls and goggles is cutting the hedges with some kind of power tool. He waves as she approaches the front door, and she recognises him. He's the man with the bushy red beard who was in Erik Nyberg's kitchen.

Emee is pleased to see her. Thea is about to fetch the lead to take her out when there's a knock on the door. The man with the beard is standing there.

'Sorry to bother you, but could I possibly use your bathroom?'

'Of course.' She steps aside. 'It's on the left in the hallway.'

'I know – Per and I worked on the renovations.'

He disappears, and returns after a couple of minutes.

'We're still in a bit of a mess – we haven't settled in properly yet,' Thea says, waving a hand in the direction of the piles of boxes and removal crates.

'This is nothing. I helped my eldest daughter to move before Christmas, and she's still got stuff in boxes.' His smile is wide and infectious. 'Stefan Holmkvist, usually known as Little Stefan.'

'Why?'

He laughs. 'You're the first person who's asked that question for many years. There were two Stefans in my class when I started school. I was small and skinny back then, so . . .' He spreads his arms wide. 'I overtook the other Stefan within a few years, but by then the name had stuck.' He laughs again. Little Stefan seems to be a very likeable person. He's also worked for both the castle and for Erik Nyberg, so he probably knows a great deal about the area. Thea decides to postpone the dog walk.

'Would you like a coffee?'

'Yes, please.'

They go into the kitchen and she makes them both an Americano in David's ridiculously expensive coffee machine. She even manages to find a packet of biscuits.

'How many children do you have, Stefan?' she asks, softening him up.

'Three, plus two grandchildren and another one on the way.'

He takes out his phone and shows her pictures of his grandchildren while telling her an anecdote about their nursery school. Thea lets him talk for a while before gently nudging the conversation in the direction she wants it to go.

'Dr Andersson and I were out at the hunting lodge the other day.'

'Kerstin Miller's place? She's a fantastic teacher – she taught all my children.'

'She and Dr Andersson told me about Elita Svart. What an awful business!'

Little Stefan nods.

'Did you know Elita?'

'No, although I bumped into her occasionally on the estate. She lived at Svartgården, deep in the marsh. A terrible place.'

'In what way?' Thea does her best to sound vaguely interested.

'Lasse Svart ran it down to the ground. He wanted the castle to pay for every little repair, even though the tenancy agreement stated that he was responsible for the upkeep of the property. And he didn't pay the rent on time. We often went out there to . . .'

He breaks off, helps himself to a biscuit and takes a bite.

'We?' Thea says encouragingly.

'Me and Erik Nyberg. Per too, sometimes. It was best if there were two of us when it came to dealing with Lasse Svart. He was a dangerous man.'

'How do you mean?'

'Violent – at least according to the rumours. There was a lot of gossip; plenty of people were afraid of him. I know he had a hell of a temper. It can't have been easy for those he lived with – Eva-Britt and Lola.'

'What about Elita's stepbrother?'

'Leo?' Little Stefan pulls a face. 'Things weren't easy for him either. Lasse gave him a hard time, but I always thought Leo was a nice kid. Certainly not someone who was capable of killing his own sister. On the other hand, I've lived long enough to learn that you never know what goes on in other people's heads. And like I said, Svartgården was a dreadful place.'

He shakes his head slowly, as if an unpleasant memory has just surfaced.

'So what happened to the family?'

Little Stefan takes a deep breath.

'They all took off, the day after the funeral. Disappeared without a trace as soon as the girl was in the ground.'

'Disappeared?'

'Yes. I was the one who found out. I went over there to read the water meter; both cars were gone and the house was empty. It was kind of creepy, to be honest.' He hunches his shoulders a little. 'Although with hindsight, I suppose it wasn't that strange. Lasse had already been given notice to quit, and then Elita died, so . . .'

He looks at his watch, straightens up.

'Thanks for the coffee – I must get on. Per wants the hedges finished today. The clippings need a few days to dry out so that they'll burn better on the bonfire.'

Thea can see that he's just realised how much he's said. He's regretting it now, as Erik Nyberg did the other day. However, she's not ready to let him go yet.

'What happened to Svartgården after the family vanished?' she asks as he gets to his feet.

Little Stefan hesitates, checks his watch again. Then he glances over his shoulder as if he's worried that someone is eavesdropping. He leans forward and lowers his voice.

'Erik Nyberg told me to board up the whole place that same day – windows, doors, the whole lot. Old Gren and I did it in a few hours, worked as if the devil himself was at our heels. As if there was something inside that house that absolutely mustn't be allowed to escape.' He shakes his head again. 'The following day the track was ploughed up. The count sold the whole lot to the military and they extended the fence around the firing range.'

He breathes out through his nose as if he's accomplished a difficult task, then he nods to Thea and heads for the door.

'Thanks again. I'm sure I'll see you around.'

'Is it still there?' she asks his back.

'What?'

'Svartgården. Is it still standing?'

He shrugs. Or maybe he's trying to suppress a shudder.

'I've no idea. I haven't been anywhere near since the spring of 1986. Ask Erik Nyberg – he's bound to know.'

When Little Stefan has returned to his hedges, Thea puts Emee on the lead and goes over to the castle to say hello to David. From a distance she can hear him arguing with one of the builders. Money, of course, and the schedule. She's heard several similar conversations over the phone during the past few weeks, but this one is more agitated, more aggressive. She hears a shout, gravel spurting up around feet.

'Fucking idiot!'

Thea rounds the corner of the east wing to see the builder lying on the ground. David is bending over him; he's grabbed the man's jacket with one hand, while the other is raised in a fist.

'David!' she shouts.

He turns, his eyes black, his lips a thin line.

Emee starts barking, hurls herself in David's direction, baring her teeth and snapping at thin air. Thea has to grasp the lead in both hands and dig her heels into the ground to hold her back.

David blinks a couple of times, becomes his normal self again. He lets go of the builder's collar and straightens up. Emee stops barking but continues to growl, hackles raised. She doesn't take her eyes off David.

'Sorry,' David mutters. Thea's not sure who he's apologising to. He turns on his heel, disappears through the kitchen entrance and slams the door behind him.

The builder scrambles to his feet.

'I do apologise,' Thea says. 'David's under a lot of stress. There's so much . . .'

The man nods, brushing the dirt off his jacket.

'He's bloody lucky he's Bertil Nordin's boy,' he mutters as he lumbers towards his van.

26

Walpurgis Night 1986

'Love is hard, Elita.' That's what my grandmother used to say. The hardest thing in life.

I only met her a few times. Lola didn't like going there. Grandma was always nice to me, but I understood that she hadn't been that way with Lola. The few times they were together, there was something strange about Lola's expression, as if she both adored and hated her mother.

Sometimes Lola gets the same look on her face when Lasse is around, but only when he has his back to her. The other day I saw her tuck a knife into her pocket.

Love and hatred are very close to each other, Grandma said.

I understand exactly what she meant.

Arne drove fast through the forest, ploughing through muddy puddles, ignoring the branches and undergrowth scraping against the wing mirrors and paintwork.

Elita had used him, just as her father had done. Treated him as a lackey, pretended to be his friend, toyed with his emotions. She'd borrowed his camera so that she could take a picture for her fucking boyfriend. She hadn't even had the wit to hand it over secretly; instead she'd done it right in the middle of the yard where everyone could see them. Elita and that fucking mother-in-law's dream Per Nyberg. The very thought made him feel sick.

Arne slammed on the brakes, leaped out of the car and grabbed the camera in its case. He didn't want it anymore, didn't want to be reminded of what it had been used for. He swung it back and forth by the strap a couple of times, intending to throw it as far as possible into the bog, deep into the mud where no one would ever find it, but the catch came undone and the camera fell to the ground.

'Shitshitshit!' He kicked at the camera, then saw that something else had fallen out. Another white rectangle, another photograph.

He picked it up, brushed off the dirt.

Elita, in a white dress with her hair loose. She was standing on a stone with her eyes closed, hands folded across her chest, holding two antlers. Long silk ribbons were attached to her wrists, and two small figures in animal masks stood on either side of the stone – four in total, clutching the ends of the ribbons. Arne was sure he'd seen a similar picture somewhere else, but where?

He stared at the photograph, held it close to his eyes so that he could pick out every tiny detail. Something about the image made him feel weird. Dizzy, feverish, sick, all at the same time.

Elita had written beneath the picture:

To Arne. Walpurgis Night 1986. Come to the stone circle at midnight.

Then three more words.

His heartbeat pulsated through his whole body. Reached his throat, his temples, his stomach, his crotch, repeating the words she'd written.

The spring sacrifice
The spring sacrifice
The spring sacrifice

27

'They boarded up her house – can you imagine that, Margaux? Blocked up every opening and took away the access road. Why would anyone do that? What secrets were they trying to seal up inside?'

David is himself again by the evening. He cooks dinner, lights candles, opens a bottle of decent red wine. He doesn't mention the altercation with the builder, and nor does Thea. The TV piece on the restaurant is due to be broadcast tonight. Thea is nervous, but tries not to show it.

'How was work today? Are you starting to get to grips with everything?' David asks.

'Oh yes – I now know the history of Tornaby all the way back to pre-Christian times! Today Dr Andersson told me about the old count and the Bokelund Foundation. And about poor Hubert over in the west wing, who was robbed of his inheritance. By the way, I saw him the other night – I forgot to mention it.'

'Hubert?'

She nods. 'He was peeping out from behind a curtain when I was looking for Emee. Isn't it a bit odd that he hasn't called round to say hello? Shouldn't we go and introduce ourselves?'

David pulls a face.

'Hubert's . . . different. I've only met him once since it was agreed that we were going to rent the castle. He's something of a recluse, plus I think he's away quite often.'

'Can he afford that? According to the doctor the count only left him a pittance.'

'I've no idea – you'd have to ask my mother. Madam Chairman can account for every krona that passes through the foundation. Nothing escapes her eagle eye, I can promise you that.' He smiles, pours himself another glass of wine.

Thea leans back in her chair. She's missed this David. He's attractive too, especially when he relaxes. She tries to remember the last time they made love, and concludes that it was much too long ago.

Outside the window the moat is in darkness. Some of the lamps on the bridge have been fixed, but on the other side the night is impenetrable. She wants to bring the conversation back to Elita Svart. She wonders how to do it, then decides to come straight to the point.

'I found something in the forest the other day.'

'Oh?'

'A photograph. I'll show you.'

She fetches the Polaroid from her jacket pocket and places it on the table in front of him. 'That's you, isn't it? You, Nettan, Sebastian and Jan-Olof.'

David stiffens. 'Where did you find this?'

'In an old paint tin inside the Gallows Oak,' Thea says eagerly. 'Someone must have pushed it through the hole in the face.'

David is ashen.

'It's exactly like the old pictures of the spring sacrifice in the Folk Museum,' Thea goes on. 'Was it Elita who persuaded you to dress up? Where did you get the masks from?'

She pushes the photograph closer to his plate. Only when she meets his eyes does she realise she's gone too far.

'Take it away,' he hisses. 'I don't want to talk about Elita fucking Svart – haven't you got that yet? I've got other things to think about, like how we're going to bring this massive project in on budget and on time. Don't you realise how much is down to me? How many people are monitoring every little thing I do?'

He shoves the picture away.

'I'm sorry, I didn't mean . . .'

'You saw what happened yesterday. How upset Dad got when you mentioned Elita. Mum too, although she didn't show it.'

'I'm sorry, David. You're right.'

She removes the photograph and tops up their glasses, but the pleasant atmosphere is gone. They both make an effort, but they can't get it back.

They sit down on the sofa and watch the TV report, everything from the drone shots to the interview. It's a warm, positive piece, just as David had hoped, yet he seems dissatisfied. Meanwhile Thea tries to suppress her anxiety at having appeared on TV, tells herself that she was on screen for no more than a minute or so, almost thirty years have passed, no one will recognise her.

Later they have sex anyway, but the feeling from earlier just isn't there, and it becomes a series of dutiful, mechanical movements.

David stays in her bed for exactly as long as politeness demands, then retires to his own room, blaming an early meeting.

Thea lies there staring at the ceiling. The damp patch seems to have grown since this morning. The edges have become more irregular, as if it's slowly expanding into the room.

Maybe it's a sign? However much you renovate and clean, all it takes is a tiny little crack in the façade for the dampness to seep in and begin the destruction.

28

'Dreams are strange, aren't they? They transport us through time, open doors to things we thought we'd forgotten. Things we've put behind us.

'Do you dream, Margaux? I so want to believe that you do. Happy dreams.'

She is in a forest. Conifers, anthills, self-seeded birch. Their house is in a dip right at the bottom of the slope. She, her big brother and his friends are playing up among the trees.

They've built two dens near the top, one for Ronny and one for her. It's Ronny who's made all the decisions, helped her to put up the frame and fix the poles. Inside she's made a little pen out of four branches, filled it with pine-cone animals that she and Ronny have made together. The wooden doll her daddy whittled for her is sitting beside the pen. He carved eyes, a nose and a mouth into a sturdy branch, with four protruding twigs forming arms and legs. She's called it Stubby. She has prettier dolls at home – two Sindys with lots of different outfits, but still she likes Stubby best. Likes sitting in her den with him in her arms, listening to the older boys outside. She feels safe, secure.

Then suddenly it's evening. Blue lights flashing down by their house, doors slamming, agitated voices.

Ronny and his friends have disappeared, but someone else is running up the slope towards her. Daddy. His face is white, he's carrying something. An object wrapped in a Konsum carrier bag. He takes Stubby off her, pushes the bag into her hands.

'Jenny – take this and run and hide it. Quickly! Good girl!'

She gets to her feet and runs as fast as she can. Behind her she can hear more shouting, dogs barking.

In the forest she falls over. Hurts her knee, but doesn't cry. She has to help Daddy. Has to be a good girl.

She scrabbles with her fingers, digs a hole in the ground, pushes the plastic bag into the hole. Presses a piece of turf down on top and covers the whole thing with dry branches. Then she goes back to her den and hides right at the back with her eyes tightly closed.

Afterwards, when Daddy comes back, he praises her. Says she's his best girl. Promises to buy her something nice. But when he asks her to show him where she buried the bag, she can't remember. Everything looks so different in the dark, and she can't find the right spot.

Daddy goes crazy, he smashes up both dens, stamps all over the pine-cone animals. He shouts horrible words at her, at Mummy, at Ronny. Grabs her by the arm, it hurts, puts his face close to hers and hisses that the bag doesn't belong to him, that this is a fucking disaster. Says he's going to lock her in the cellar and throw away the key if the bag doesn't come to light.

She is crying now. So is Ronny.

Daddy isn't listening. He makes them spend the whole of the next day searching in the forest.

In the afternoon Ronny finds the bag at long last, which makes Daddy calm down. She is spared the cellar this time, but Daddy barely looks at her for weeks. She never sees Stubby again. Maybe Daddy threw him on the fire, like he said?

Ronny and his friends rebuild the dens, bigger and better. They help her to make new pine-cone animals and carve a new wooden doll for her. But it's never the same again.

Thea wakes in the early hours again. The nightlight glows faintly, keeping the darkness at bay, slowing her pulse.

The dream echoes inside her. How many years since she last had it? She can't remember.

Emee is awake, gazing at her with those pale eyes as if she understands exactly what thoughts are going around in Thea's head.

Thea gets up, gets dressed. Checks that she has her cigarettes and lighter, fetches the dog lead from the hallway.

David's bedroom door is closed. Her first instinct is to creep out as quietly as possible so as not to wake him, then she changes her mind, opens the door a fraction.

The bed is unmade, the clothes valet where David usually hangs his shirt and trousers is empty.

Thea closes the door. Has a cup of coffee before pulling on her jacket and boots. She tucks the Polaroid in her pocket and steps outside. The sun is rising, so she doesn't need a torch.

She cuts across to the path leading to the back of the castle. David's car isn't in its usual place. When he mentioned an early meeting last night, she'd assumed it was an excuse to avoid staying in her room, but maybe she was wrong. Then again, who has a meeting at this hour?

It's just before six. The morning mist covers the moat like a woollen blanket. She crosses the bridge, lets Emee go in the forest as usual. Lights a cigarette. It's her last.

She stops at the signpost. The stone circle lies straight ahead in the forest; she can just make out the contours of an almost overgrown path. She follows it through the trees. To begin with, it's easy. The deciduous trees are tall, the ground is covered only in wood anemones and moss. But as the terrain starts to slope downwards, the vegetation becomes wilder. The moss is wet, the wood anemones give way to bracken, and time and time again she is forced to take a detour around thick, impenetrable brambles.

She thinks about what Little Stefan told her: that Svartgården was boarded up and the track destroyed. An attempt to obliterate all memories of Elita Svart and her family. To wash away the stain on the village's reputation.

The morning sun is low in the sky, penetrating the leafy canopy only occasionally. It is no longer possible to make out the path, and Thea is worried that she's lost her way in the gloom. Has she gone too far to the west and missed her target? She stops, checks her watch and tries to work out which direction she's going in. It's ten minutes since she left the signpost.

She hears rustling behind her, then the sharp crack of a branch breaking. Emee, probably. She calls her name, but there's no sign of the dog.

Thea turns slightly to the east and sets off again. She thinks she can smell the marsh, which ought to mean that she's going the right way.

She circumvents another patch of brambles and finds herself in a glade. Six standing stones, each approximately one metre in diameter, are arranged in a circle, with a seventh flat stone in the centre.

The glade is surrounded by gnarled old trees of a completely different type from the rest of the forest. Each one consists of several slender trunks leaning outwards in different directions until they form the crown. In the dim morning light it looks as if these trunks are actually tall human beings whose feet have become part of the trees' roots, their hands part of the crown. The veils of mist slowly swirling over the wet grass add to the sense of unreality.

There is a pole beside Thea which reminds her of the one next to the Gallows Oak. The information board is lying on the ground, overgrown with grass. With a little effort she manages to lift it. The first part of the text is barely legible, but she manages to work out that the strange, humanoid trees are hawthorn. She remembers what Dr Andersson told her the other day – that Tornaby got its name from the hawthorn, once regarded as a sacred tree.

The rest of the text is easier to read.

The stone circle probably dates from the sixth century, marking a grave or possibly a meeting place of some kind. At this time the castle forest was an island, surrounded by extensive marshlands, which made it suitable for religious ceremonies.

The central stone is older than the rest. On the top there is a small bowl-shaped hollow, common during the Bronze Age. It was probably used during fertility rites, when grains of corn or small figures made of twigs were 'sacrificed' in the hollow to ensure a good harvest. The custom lived on in the area until the mid-nineteenth century. The stone is still referred to locally as the sacrificial stone.

The smooth surface of the stone is dark with dampness. The hollow is about ten centimetres wide and maybe half as deep. The dew has formed a small puddle in the bottom.

Thea takes out the Polaroid. Steps back. The background in the photograph looks slightly different. The trees aren't so tall or overgrown. The stone, however, is exactly the same. She moves around until she finds the precise angle from which the photograph was taken. She half-closes her eyes, pictures Elita standing on the stone, David and his three friends on either side of her. The spring sacrifice and her four attendants. Five people in total.

But there must have been a sixth person present – the photographer. Unless the camera had some kind of automatic timer, of course.

She looks closely at the picture, trying to see if there's a shadow from the person behind the camera, but the image is too pale, the colours faded.

A sound interrupts her train of thought, another branch snapping, but this time she can tell where it's come from. Among the trees, more or less opposite the point where she emerged into the glade. She is just about to call Emee when she hears more noises, branches scraping against clothing, a faint metallic click.

She sees a movement among the hawthorns and realises she's holding her breath. A dark silhouette appears through the mist. A man pushing a bicycle. He is on his way into the glade, eyes fixed on the sacrificial stone. He doesn't seem to have noticed her, not until he's almost there. He stops dead, drops the bicycle. The colour drains from his face, his eyelids flicker, and for a second she thinks he's going to faint.

'Hi, Bertil,' she says. 'What are you doing here?'

29

Walpurgis Night 1986

I'm sure you've heard about the other girls who died in the forest. Isabelle who drowned in the moat, and Eleonor who fell off her horse and broke her neck.

Soon it will be Elita's turn.

Beautiful women dead that by my side. Once lay.

Isn't that lovely?

There's something appealing about dying when you're at your most beautiful, don't you think?

The young man loved to ride. Loved the feeling of controlling something so big and strong, yet as sensitive as a horse. He himself was short and had been born with a cleft palate, which still gave him problems with his speech. He had to make an effort to master certain letters, just as he had to make an effort to control his involuntary twitching. But on horseback none of that could be seen. Up here he raced along. Agile, complete.

He loved to ride, and he loved the land: the meadows, the pastures, the forest, the marsh. It all belonged to him, as far as the eye could see. Or it would belong to him. Soon.

His father was getting old now. He was a hard man, a man who never talked about his love for the land, but about crops, yield and tenancies. Practical matters. Things that could be counted and measured.

His father feared no one, apart from God. The only time his expression softened somewhat was when they prayed together in the chapel. Prayed for the young man's mother. For her immortal soul. Asked God to forgive her weakness.

Sometimes the young man could feel his father's eyes on him. Studying him closely, as if he were searching for something in his face or movements. A feature, a gesture of some kind. But every time his father seemed disappointed.

Over the years the young man had realised why. It was because he was his mother's son. Because he was different.

Elita was waiting by the Gallows Oak, just as she'd promised. He galloped up to her, made the muscular stallion stop right by her feet, thanks to a combination of perfectly executed movements with the reins and his legs. Elita's expression didn't change. She was just as good a rider as he was – maybe even better, which was one of the reasons why he loved her.

As always he was struck by how lovely she was – the coal-black hair, those eyes, the olive skin.

'I've got something for you.'

She held out an envelope. He took it, felt the square card inside.

'Are you ready for tonight?'

He nodded. Nelson did a little pirouette, his hooves digging into the soft ground. He was a thoroughbred, the most difficult horse to ride, but also the most beautiful, the fastest, the strongest.

'What's that?'

The young man pointed with his crop to the paint tin by the oak tree. As usual he kept his sentences short so that his speech impediment would be less noticeable.

'A little offering.'

She smiled in a way that irritated him. He'd opened up to her, confided his deepest secrets to her, and yet she insisted on teasing him.

'To whom?' His voice sounded more brusque than he'd intended. Nelson snorted. Performed another little pirouette.

Elita's smile broadened. She pointed up at the nodular growths on the tree trunk that resembled a face.

'To him. The Green Man.'

She tipped her head back and laughed. Her teeth were so white, so perfect. Like his mother's pearl necklace.

For a brief moment the young man wished he could own her. Lock her up in a box, as his father had done with the necklace. Preserve the memory of her, equally untainted and precious.

'Are you worried?'

The young man shook his head, but as usual she saw straight through him. She grabbed the reins, stroked Nelson's forehead, which instantly calmed the stallion. Then she looked up at him with those eyes that reminded him so much of his mother's.

'Don't worry, Hubert,' she said softly. 'Everything will be fine.'

30

Thea gets Bertil to sit down on one of the stones. Her father-in-law is still as white as a sheet. His lips are constantly moving, whispering the same two words over and over again. She leans closer to hear what he's saying.

'Poor girl, poor girl, poor girl . . .'

'What girl? Do you mean Elita Svart?'

The name makes him fall silent. He lowers his eyes.

'What are you doing here, Bertil?'

No response.

'Does Ingrid know you're out on your own?'

Nothing.

He's wearing a shirt, jacket and checked pyjama bottoms. Wellingtons on his feet. No coat, in spite of the cold morning air. His legs are shaking, his lips turning blue.

Thea takes off her own coat and wraps it around his shoulders, then gets out her phone and calls David. It rings six times, then goes to voicemail. She tries again, with the same result. His phone is clearly switched on, so either he can't hear it or he's ignoring her.

She finds Ingrid's number; her mother-in-law answers almost right away.

'Hi, it's Thea. I've got Bertil here; he seems to have gone off by himself.'

Ingrid doesn't waste any time on her own reaction. 'Where are you?'

'In the forest, at the stone circle.'

A brief pause. 'Where's David?'

The question takes Thea by surprise; surely Ingrid should be asking how Bertil is?

'He said he had an early meeting. He's not answering his phone.'

Another pause. 'Where can I meet you?'

Thea looks around the glade. Trying to drag Bertil back the way she came doesn't seem like a good idea; the terrain is too difficult. Obviously he cycled here by a different route, but she doesn't know the back roads to the village.

'I can take him to the hunting lodge – it can't be far, I'm sure I can find it.'

A third pause, a fraction longer this time.

'Do that,' Ingrid says, and ends the call.

The sun disperses both the darkness and the mist, helping Thea to locate the muddy canal quite quickly. They follow it to the left. Bertil is exhausted, and has to stop to catch his breath every couple of minutes. He says next to nothing during the walk, he merely continues to move his lips silently as if he's fully engaged in some internal dialogue. However, he follows her instructions, and seems to have an idea of where he is.

The roof of the hunting lodge appears through the trees. There is smoke coming out of the chimney, which suggests that Kerstin is up and about.

A freshly cut strip of weeds that must be Jan-Olof's work marks the boundary between the forest and the property. They pass the paddock; as they approach the house Thea can't help glancing at the figure of the Green Man on the wall. She thinks about the dream she had last night. About Ronny and her father.

The door is flung open before they reach it and Kerstin comes out onto the steps.

'What's happened?'

Her voice makes Bertil look up, and his face breaks into a smile.

'Kerstin,' he murmurs. 'Dear Kerstin. There was something I had to do. Something important. But I must have got a little bit lost.'

The two of them shepherd Bertil into the kitchen, wrap him in a blanket and settle him on the sofa next to the wood-burning stove. Kerstin pours tea; the hot drink make Thea realise how cold she's got without her coat. She examines Bertil as best she can. The colour has returned to his cheeks, his pulse is steady and she can't find any sign of injury.

'Dear Kerstin, I really am sorry to be such a nuisance,' Bertil says.

'No problem. It's a good job Thea found you.'

'It is. She found me in the forest. By the stone circle.' He looks anxious again, and shakes his head. 'Poor child . . .'

'Drink your tea, you'll soon feel better,' Kerstin says, gently rubbing his back.

He nods and does as he's told. The anxious expression disappears. After just a few sips his eyelids grow heavy. Thea helps Kerstin to pile cushions behind him so that he can have a nap.

'He's worn out. I added a little camomile to his tea; it's very calming.'

Kerstin signals to Thea to sit down at the table. The kitchen has a different smell this time, probably thanks to the bunches of fresh nettles hanging above the stove. Kerstin follows her gaze.

'Nettles are good for the immune system, and they're at their most nutritious now, in the spring. Another of my tea blends.' She frowns. 'It really was a stroke of luck that you found Bertil. Things could have gone very badly. What if he'd fallen into the canal?'

She waves towards the kitchen window and the green water outside. Thea nods; the same thought occurred to her. 'Why do you think he came out here, of all places? He must have cycled five kilometres from the village.'

Kerstin is considering her answer when they hear the sound of a car engine.

'That must be Ingrid,' Thea says, getting to her feet.

But the car is not her mother-in-law's dark grey Mercedes, but a black three-door BMW. The driver's door opens and a man with a moustache climbs out; he is wearing jeans and a leather jacket. He takes the steps in one bound and opens the door so fast that the cat who has fallen asleep on the kitchen floor shoots away, terrified.

It's Arne. Ingrid's younger brother, David's uncle. He nods a greeting. 'Ingrid said you needed help.'

They wake Bertil and lead him out to the car. Bertil thanks Kerstin over and over again, keeps calling her 'dear Kerstin'.

Arne, on the other hand, says very little. He supports his brother-in-law, eases him into the passenger seat carefully, almost tenderly.

'Thanks for your help, Kerstin,' Arne mumbles when Bertil is settled.

'You're welcome. I hope he soon feels better.'

Arne flips down the driver's seat so that Thea can get in the back. The car smells of a Little Tree air freshener, coffee and leather clothing.

Within minutes Bertil has gone back to sleep.

'Where did you say you found him?' Arne asks.

'By the stone circle.'

'Mhm.' Arne meets her gaze in the rear-view mirror. 'And what were you doing in the middle of the forest so early in the morning, if I may ask?'

'I woke up early and took the dog out.'

She knows what the next question will be a millisecond before he asks.

'So where's the dog now?'

Emee. Shit! She's been so focused on helping Bertil that she's forgotten all about Emee.

'I expect she ran off home. I had my hands full with Bertil.'

Arne nods, still watching her in the mirror. 'Did he say anything about why he was there? Was he rambling?'

Thea takes a deep breath, playing for time to give herself a chance to think.

'He just said "poor girl".'

'Poor girl? Is that all?' Arne sounds as though he doesn't really believe her.

'Yes.' She pauses, considers whether to continue. 'He meant Elita Svart. The spring sacrifice.'

No answer, just a long stare. They reach the turning for the castle and lose eye contact.

He drops her at the coach house. There is still no sign of David's car.

Arne holds out his hand. 'Thank you so much, Thea.'

'No problem.'

He squeezes her hand a little harder.

'The thing is, Thea . . .' He leans forward in a way that she doesn't really like. 'It would be best if we kept this . . . incident to ourselves. Within the family, so to speak. There's already enough gossip in the village.'

'Absolutely.'

'Good.'

Another squeeze; he stops just before it begins to hurt. He lets go, jumps in the car and drives off. Bertil is still sleeping peacefully in the passenger seat.

31

Thea shouts for Emee as soon as Arne's car is out of sight. She walks around the little garden surrounding the coach house, but there is no sign of the dog. It's almost eight o'clock, and Dr Andersson will be here to pick Thea up at any minute.

What if something has happened to Emee? What if she's found her way out of the forest, run out onto a road, been hit by a car? The thought makes it difficult to breathe.

'Emee! Emee!' She blows the dog whistle, but to no avail.

She hears a car approaching and hopes it's David rather than the doctor, but in fact it's neither of them. A green Land Rover, one of the older models, pulls up outside the coach house. The sunlight is reflected on the windscreen, and she can't see the driver until he gets out: a short man aged about fifty, in a scruffy oilskin coat, a flat cap and leather gloves. She recognises him from the night of the storm.

'Hubert Gordon,' he says without offering his hand. 'We're neighbours.'

Thea notes that he has a slight speech impediment, and seems keen to avoid eye contact.

'Thea Lind.'

Hubert has already turned his back on her. He goes around the car, opens the boot. Emee jumps out, skips happily around Hubert's legs then runs to Thea. She is soaking wet, her coat is dirty and full of mud. Thea lets out a long breath.

'I found her over by the western meadow.' Hubert points diagonally across the moat. 'Between the forest and the main road, just by the deer enclosure.'

'Goodness, she'd gone a long way – I let her off the lead by the bridge.'

'It might be best if you don't allow your dog to run loose in the future.' His tone is brusque, verging on unfriendly. He turns away to get into the car.

'Thanks for your help,' Thea says. 'I really appreciate it. Emee isn't actually my dog. She belongs to a friend of mine who's ill . . .'

The words unexpectedly stick in her throat. She coughs, but it comes out like a sob, which is annoying.

Hubert stops, turns back to face her again. His expression softens a little. His eyes are brown, sorrowful. For a few seconds Thea experiences that same mutual understanding she felt on the night of the storm. Hubert seems to feel the same, because although neither of them says anything, the silence between them is not uncomfortable.

The mood is broken by the sound of Dr Andersson's car approaching.

'I hope your friend gets better soon,' Hubert says. He gives her a wry smile of farewell that could be interpreted as friendly.

Thea takes Emee indoors, fills up her food and water bowls, then changes out of her muddy boots and trousers. When she gets into the car Dr Andersson glances at the clock, but doesn't comment on Thea's lateness.

'So you've met Hubert?'

'Yes, my dog had run away. He found her over by the deer enclosure.'

'Oh. As I said, Hubert is a little . . . different. He can seem . . . unfriendly.'

Dr Andersson tries to winkle out more details about their conversation, but Thea has nothing to tell. She sinks down in her seat and tries to gather her thoughts. What the hell has happened over the past few hours? What was Bertil doing out there in the forest all on his own? And why did Ingrid send Arne instead of jumping in the car herself?

Arne had asked her if Bertil had been rambling, and the other day Erik Nyberg had wondered the same thing, but why? It must have something to do with Elita Svart, but what?

You must never tell anyone. Never, never, never . . .

What was it that mustn't be told?

They have a gap in consultations after lunch, and Thea nips over to the Konsum mini-market to buy cigarettes, although obviously she doesn't share this with Dr Andersson. The morning's sunshine has given way to a fine drizzle.

When she's made her purchase she pauses outside the shop, looking towards the church. She suddenly remembers what Little Stefan said: that the Svart family disappeared the day after Elita's funeral. Is Elita buried here, opposite Thea's workplace? She crosses the street. The churchyard gate squeaks as she opens it. The air smells of box and wet shingle. She passes a number of tall monuments from the late nineteenth century. Dark metal, chains, gold lettering. Combined with the large building itself and the tall poplars, they create an impression of gloom.

She can hear organ music coming from inside the church. She tries the door; it's unlocked. After a brief hesitation, she goes inside. The space overwhelms her: the Gothic arches, the tall stained-glass windows, the organ music winding its way around the pillars. Frescoes and statues everywhere: faces, figures, some Biblical, some not. The ceiling is so high that she has to tip back her head to see all the way up.

One of the figures right at the top is a man's face, covered in leaves and with a gaping mouth. She is so preoccupied with staring at it that she bumps into a table and knocks a pile of hymn books onto the floor.

The music stops immediately and footsteps descend the steps from the lectern.

'I'm sorry, I didn't know there was anyone here.'

The voice belongs to a woman in her late twenties. She has fair hair tied back in a ponytail, a stud in one nostril, round Harry Potter glasses, dungarees and a fleece top with the emblem of the Swedish Church.

'I'm the one who should be apologising,' Thea says, picking up the books. 'Do you work here?'

The woman nods. 'I'm a member of the churchyard administrative committee. My husband Simon is the cantor; we moved here two years ago. I sneak in occasionally to play the organ – it's hard to resist for someone who enjoys music as a hobby. My name is Tanya, by the way.'

'Thea Lind – I moved here quite recently.'

The woman doesn't seem to know who she is, which is a welcome change. Her accent suggests that she's from western Sweden.

Thea's eyes are drawn to the ceiling once more, to the face up there. Tanya follows her gaze.

'I see you've discovered our Green Man. There are examples in various churches, including Lund Cathedral. I'm sure you're aware of the local Walpurgis Night tradition? The figure by the front door of the house, and the effigy placed on top of the bonfire?'

'Yes, I've heard about that.'

'Wait until you see it for real. Where I come from, we make little straw men for 13 January – *tjugonde Knut* – and put them outside one another's houses, but the Green Man is more exciting.' She stops, as if realising that she's taken over the conversation. 'Sorry – is there something I can help you with?'

'Yes, I'm looking for a grave.'

'Have you checked our homepage? Almost all the graves are listed.'

Thea shakes her head. She feels stupid, walking into the church and expecting someone to know exactly where one grave is among the hundreds out there.

'I have a pretty good memory, so maybe I can help you anyway. Is it a new or an old grave?'

'Somewhere in between – 1986.'

'OK – most graves from the Eighties are over on the eastern side. What's the name?'

'Elita Svart.'

Tanya smiles. 'Aha – number 407. The mystery grave.'

'Sorry?'

'That's what Simon and I call it, but maybe you can solve the mystery. The grave is tended by the church council. A couple of years ago they considered reclaiming it, because there were no relatives, but then an envelope arrived in the post. It contained a bundle of cash and an anonymous typewritten letter saying that the money was for the care of grave 407.'

'What happened next?'

Tanya shrugs. 'The members of the church council didn't quite know what to do, but in the end they decided to go along with the wishes of the letter writer and retain the grave. Simon and I were curious; we did a little research and heard the story of the poor girl who was murdered by her stepbrother. We thought the idea of a secret benefactor was quite exciting, so we decided to keep an eye on the grave. We've never seen anyone there, but on more than one occasion I've found a memorial candle burning by the headstone, so someone must visit.'

The headstone is simple, a small black rectangle sunk into the grass.

> *ELITA SVART 12.02.1970–30.04.1986*
> *LOVED. MISSED.*

In front of the stone lies a white rose.

Thea carefully picks up the flower, turning it this way and that as if she were a detective examining a piece of evidence. It is almost fresh, the petals are damp from the drizzle.

Someone must have been here very recently. Someone who still remembers Elita Svart, in spite of the fact that most people seem to want to forget her.

But who?

32

Thea and Dr Andersson go through a few more things on the computer together, but as the time approaches two o'clock, the doctor begins to finish off.

'I think that's all you need to know. Good luck, Thea. I'm sure you'll be fine,' she says, with a hint of sorrow in her voice.

'So you're done with your working life?' Thea says.

The other woman sighs. 'To be perfectly honest, I'd have liked to carry on for another year or so. I'm in good health, I love my job, and I like the idea of doing something important for the village.' She straightens her spine. 'But as Ingrid pointed out, it's time to pass the baton to someone younger. Time for new blood.'

Thea doesn't know what to say. She's suspected this ever since the idea of the move was first broached. It seemed like too much of a coincidence that there just happened to be a vacant post as GP in the village; she wondered whether her mother-in-law had used her influence.

Dr Andersson gives a wry smile.

'So – you've got the keys, the telephone and the computer. One last thing – we need to call at Ängsgården on the way home. Erik Nyberg's blood sugar monitor is playing up. If necessary we'll have to swap it for ours. And don't forget you have to go to Lund; your security clearance has to be handed into the regional office this week. You could do that tomorrow, while the surgery's closed. The practice car is yours now.'

'OK.' Thea realises she's looking forward to being her own boss. And the doctor is right – best to get her clearance out of the way.

The drive to Ängsgården takes ten minutes. Once again Dr Andersson makes a big show of pressing the GPS button to register that the car is being used for work, then fills the time with a lengthy anecdote about her holiday plans. Thea is lost in thought, listening with half an ear.

Her mother-in-law clearly has a hand in most aspects of village life. The coach house, the TV interview and the renovation of the castle is one thing, but Thea is far from comfortable with the idea that poor Dr Andersson has been kicked out in order to provide a job for her. She thinks about this morning's phone call; Ingrid didn't even sound surprised. Didn't ask how Bertil was. And why didn't she come to the lodge to pick him up herself? Why send Arne?

It would be good if we could keep this little incident between us.

When they arrive at Ängsgården, Erik, Per and Little Stefan are standing next to an open shed. A dead deer is hanging from a butcher's hook just inside. The men are absorbed in their conversation, and don't look up until Thea and Dr Andersson have got out of the car.

'Bit early for hunting deer,' the doctor says.

None of the men laugh at her joke.

'Killed by a predator,' Per says. 'We found it this morning in one of the enclosures with its throat ripped out.'

'Oh dear!' Dr Andersson immediately becomes serious. 'What predator is big enough to take a fallow deer?'

Per shrugs. 'A wolf, or maybe a lynx.'

'A wolf?' Thea exclaims. 'This far south?'

'It does happen, although it's rare. A couple of years ago a lone wolf was hit by a car just outside Malmö, and a guy I hunt with who lives up by Vedarp found wolf tracks as recently as last winter.'

'This is no wolf,' Erik mutters. 'More like a big dog.'

Thea freezes. Emee was missing all morning. Where did Hubert say he'd found her? *Over by the western meadow, just by the deer enclosure.*

'Which enclosure was it?' she asks, afraid that she already knows the answer.

Per points in the direction of the castle.

'The one over by the western meadow. Why do you ask?'

'No reason – I was just curious.'

Her eyes are drawn to the body. The bloodstains on the cement floor. The gaping hole in its throat.

They leave Per with the deer and follow Erik's car to the house.

'Does Per live here too?' Thea asks, mainly in an attempt to shake off thoughts of the dead animal.

'He does – he and Erik share the house. Per has been in relationships with various ladies, but they never last very long.'

The doctor looks as if she has a lot more to say on that subject, but they've already arrived.

'One of my dogs has had puppies – would you like to see them, Thea?' Erik asks as Dr Andersson sits down at the table and starts to check his blood sugar monitor.

'Yes, please!'

Erik opens a door and she follows him along a short corridor to a laundry room. In a basket in one corner there is a spaniel, feeding a heap of puppies.

'They're six weeks old,' he says. 'All reserved except for one.'

He raises one eyebrow above the rim of his dark glasses. Thea laughs.

'Thanks, but I've got my hands full with the dog I already have.'

The image of the dead deer comes into her mind again; her smile stiffens.

'I thought I'd ask. By the way, I heard that Bertil was wandering around in the forest this morning. Is he OK?'

'He's as well as can be expected.'

'Good to know. What was he doing out there?'

Thea doesn't answer right away. Her first instinct is to brush him off, but this is the second time he's asked about Bertil. Maybe this is her chance to find out what lies behind his interest.

'I'm not sure. He was rambling about the girl who died in the stone circle – Elita Svart.'

One of Erik's nostril's twitches.

'Oh? What did he say?'

Thea decides to go for a counter-question.

'Did you know her?'

Erik purses his lips. 'No, but her father leased the farm from the count, so it was my job to make sure that Lasse behaved himself and . . .' Erik breaks off. 'So what did Bertil say about Elita?'

Thea comes back at him with another question.

'What happened to the Svart family?'

Erik shrugs. 'God knows. When Little Stefan got there the morning after Elita's funeral, they were gone – all three of them. No one ever heard from them again.' He pauses, raises both eyebrows this time. 'What did Bertil say?'

Thea wonders whether she ought to keep Bertil's words to herself; on the other hand, she has to give Erik something if she wants more answers.

'He said "poor girl".'

'Poor girl. Was that all?'

'Mm.'

Erik holds her gaze for a few seconds.

'Why did you board up Svartgården and destroy the track?' she asks.

He scratches the tip of his nose. Seems to be giving his response careful consideration.

'The count told me to do it.'

'And you didn't think it was strange? What if the family came back? What if they'd just gone off to do something?'

She's been thinking about this ever since she spoke to Little Stefan.

Erik spreads his arms wide.

'I worked for Rudolf Gordon for over thirty years. We respected each other, respected the importance of discretion. It was the count's farm, his land, and what he wanted done with the place was his business. Plus Lasse had already been given notice to quit.' Erik moves a step closer. 'Is that really all Bertil said?'

'He just kept repeating "poor girl, poor girl". Nothing else.'

Erik is about to say something when the doctor calls them. They head back to the kitchen.

'I believe the land was sold to the army?' Thea says.

Erik nods.

'Did they demolish the farm?'

Erik stops with his hand on the doorknob. 'Why do you want to know that?'

'Why do you want to know what Bertil said?'

She can feel his eyes through the dark glasses; she is determined not to look away. 'Did they demolish the farm?'

'I've no idea.'

He opens the kitchen door.

'There you are!' Dr Andersson says cheerfully. 'I've fixed the monitor; it just needed new batteries. Didn't you try that yourself, Erik?'

He shrugs apologetically. 'I did, but I must have had some spent batteries in the drawer. It's not easy, getting old and absent-minded.'

Thea is watching him closely. There are two things she's absolutely certain of when it comes to Erik Nyberg.

One: he's anything but absent-minded.

Two: there's something he's not telling her about Svartgården.

She drops Sigbritt Andersson at her 1970s house. Once again the doctor wishes her well, draws out the leave-taking for as long as possible, but at last Thea manages to escape. The practice car is hers now, and she loves the freedom of being able to go wherever she wants, whenever she wants.

David's car is outside the east wing when she drives past, and back at the coach house Emee is delighted to see her, behaving just as she normally does. Thea checks her grey coat carefully, searching for any trace of blood around her mouth. Nothing, which makes her feel a little less worried. She puts Emee on the lead and walks over to the castle.

David is on the phone outside the kitchen door, but ends the call as soon as he sees her.

'Hi, darling, everything OK?' He kisses her cheek. 'I've just been talking to my new sous chef – he starts on Monday. And everything's ready for the welcome dinner on Saturday for Nettan and Sebastian.'

'Great!'

He takes her hand, squeezes it.

'Thank you for rescuing Dad this morning. Mum called and told me what had happened.'

'I tried to contact you, but you didn't answer. Where were you?'

'At Kastrup. There were problems with the coverage in Denmark. I must have had ten missed calls when I got back.'

'Kastrup?'

'I told you yesterday – I was picking Nettan up from her flight.'

She shakes her head. 'No, you didn't. You said you had an early meeting.'

'. . . with Nettan at Kastrup. That's what I said.'

His expression is perfectly innocent, as it always is when he's lying.

33

Walpurgis Night 1986

I hate Tornaby. Hate the people who live there. The people who stare at me and call me horrible names. Who tell their kids to keep away from the likes of Elita Svart.

Gyppo, tart, trash.

To them I'm just a nymph in a muddy pool. A tempting morsel that will drag them down into the shit. They haven't realised who I can become when my wings have dried and I am ready to fly.

Arne dreamed that he was running through the forest. He was twelve or thirteen, seven or eight, yet at the same time he was grown up in that weird way things are in dreams.

The darkness was pressing against him from all directions, twigs and branches tearing at his face, lashing him with a whining sound that reminded him of a riding crop. He didn't know why he was running, at least not at first. He just knew he was terrified.

Behind him he could hear the dull thud of horse's hooves drumming against the soft ground. The air was thick and hard to breathe, his heart was pounding in his chest.

The hoof beats came closer and closer, the horse snorting with every step as if it were eager to catch him up.

He was running blind, the darkness was impenetrable now. He tripped over a branch and fell so slowly that he had time to think that his landing would be painful.

He crashed down heavily, yet at the same time the ground was soft, sinking beneath him. There were creatures all around him, creeping and crawling, animals with slimy bodies and shiny backs, with scales and blue transparent wings. They were trying to get into his mouth, his nose, his ears.

His arms flailing wildly, he tried to find something to hold onto so that he could pull himself up, but his legs were heavy, dragging his body down until only his head was protruding above the mud.

Horse and rider broke through the greenery, and the horse was Bill yet at the same time something else, something ancient that might not even be a horse.

And the rider ... The body was covered in leaves, tendrils writhing like snakes. The arms were branches, the fingers plaited bramble, the face hard circles of bark beneath a crown of antlers.

Arne closed his eyes, felt the rush of wind as the Green Man and his steed leaped over him. The smell of stagnant water, rotting wood and dead leaves, of things that crept and crawled and transformed what had recently been alive into earth and mould.

He screamed, but no sound came out of his mouth, just a stream of white grubs that stripped the flesh from his legs. Emptied him completely and let the night into his head.

He woke as usual right in the middle of that silent scream. Automatically checked whether he'd wet himself, which was ridiculous because he was a grown man, not a teenager who was easily scared.

His clothes were sticking to the car seat, his mouth felt like grade three sandpaper. The full moon shone high above the treetops.

Arne belched loudly and shook off the unpleasant dream. Once when he was a little boy he'd got lost during a mushroom foraging expedition, and had fallen into a sump of mud. His boots had stuck fast, and he hadn't been able to get out. His father had found him after fifteen minutes – filthy, scared and covered in mosquito bites, but otherwise unharmed.

His father had told him off, firstly for straying from the path, and then because Arne couldn't stop crying. It was nothing, really, and yet for some reason the incident had stuck in his mind, got mixed up with Ingrid's ghost stories about the Green Man, tormenting him with nightmares that meant he'd had to sleep with a rubber undersheet until well into his teens.

It must have been ten years since he'd last had that fucking dream. All Lasse Svart's fault, of course. His eyes, that burning stare.

There are many forces on the move tonight, let me tell you. Nature is hungry and the Green Man will ride through the forests, so you be careful, little Arne.

Arne shuddered. He'd parked the police car on a narrow track. The smell of newness had gone, replaced by a miasma of perspiration, the marsh itself, and fried food. He glanced at the Coke can and the screwed-up foil tray on the passenger seat. Checked his tie and discovered greasy stains left by his supper, just as he'd suspected.

He could have stayed in Ljungslöv after delivering Lasse's moonshine, but instead he'd returned to Tornaby. Now he was sitting here in the middle of nowhere, half-dozing while he waited for . . . what? He had no idea. He just knew that he had to be here, that she'd invited him. He took out the Polaroid again.

Come to the stone circle at midnight.

Bewitched. That was how he felt. And maybe that was the truth?

It was because of Elita that he'd driven out to Svartgården this afternoon, because of her that he'd been dragged back down into the mud. He'd been well aware of the risks, and yet he couldn't stay away. And now he was sitting here.

There are many forces on the move tonight.

He picked up the container on the passenger seat, unscrewed the lid and took a deep slug of neat alcohol. It seared his throat, offering a brief respite.

He sat there with the container on his knee, fingering his tie. Found a new patch of grease, on his shirt this time. Then several more on his trousers. He spat on his thumb and rubbed it over the coarse fabric, to no avail.

Suddenly he felt sick. Everything was going downhill. He was going downhill. And it was all because of her. Elita Svart. He ought to get out of here. Right now, before it was too late.

He looked at his watch. The luminous hands showed eleven thirty. Time to make a decision.

He took one last swig, then put the container back on the seat beside him. Took his binoculars out of the glove compartment, then opened the car door and stepped out into the night.

34

'OK, I admit it. I've become completely obsessed with the mystery of Elita Svart. A dead girl whose spirit seems to hover over the area, even though her house was boarded up the day after her funeral. A dead girl whom nobody wants to talk about, yet someone still lays flowers on her grave.'

The drive to Lund takes just under an hour in the morning traffic, which gives Thea the opportunity to consider the events of the previous day.

Why are Erik Nyberg and Arne so interested in what Bertil might have said? The broken blood sugar monitor was clearly an excuse; Erik wanted to question Thea about her father-in-law. How did he even know that Bertil had been in the forest that morning? Was it Kerstin who'd told him, or Arne? Or someone else?

One thing she is sure of: there is something going on around her that everyone is trying to hide. Something to do with Elita's death, but she still can't see the pattern.

A friendly clerk in the regional office deals with her declaration. Fortunately he doesn't ask any questions about her protected ID; he simply taps away on his keyboard.

'There you go, all done. I'm sorry you had to come down, but now everything's updated on our system. Sometimes there's a bit of a mismatch between hard copies and digital documents.'

'No problem – it's nice to get it sorted.'

Thea is struck by a thought as she reaches the door.

'By the way, I was looking for some patient notes the other day, but they haven't been digitised. Do you happen to know where I can access a copy?'

'Absolutely. All documentation is stored in the regional archive, which is only ten minutes from here. I can tell you how to get there if you like.'

The regional archive in Lund turns out to be housed in an enormous complex called the Archive Centre, which occupies an entire block on an industrial estate on the edge of the city.

On the way, Thea has had time to think about what she's doing. Requesting the notes of a person who is not her patient isn't allowed, strictly speaking, and there is a risk that she will get a flat refusal. However, the archivist on reception is unexpectedly helpful, possibly because Thea is a doctor and the notes are so old. Whatever the reason, he raises no objections.

'Take a seat on the sofa – this could take a while,' he says before disappearing through a door.

Thea fetches a cup of coffee from the machine, then settles down with a magazine. The archivist returns after about fifteen minutes.

'I'm so sorry – I can't find the notes you wanted.'

'Why not?'

'I'm afraid I don't know. We have very strict rules on how items are archived. Of course things end up in the wrong place occasionally, but my guess is that these notes were never sent over from the clinic in Ljungslöv.'

'But isn't that compulsory?'

'Well yes, but we handle millions of documents every year. No one would notice if one set of notes goes missing – unless someone asks for them.'

'You mean like now?'

He nods. 'Once again, I'm sorry. Anything else I can help you with?'

Thea is about to say no when she notices an information board on the wall, listing all the types of documentation held in the archive.

'What about court cases?'

'Yes – anything that took place within the district of Skåne before 1990. For anything after that date you'd have to contact the relevant court directly. Or the police.'

'I'm interested in a police investigation and the subsequent court case from 1986.'

'That shouldn't be a problem.'

It's almost midday when the archivist returns with a thick blue file under his arm.

'There you go. We have private areas if you'd like to read it in peace?'

Thea checks her work phone and her own. No calls from patients or from David. The surgery is closed today, so she has plenty of time.

'Please – that would be good.'

He shows her to one of several glass cubicles. Lingers for a little too long until she almost exaggeratedly thanks him for his help.

'No problem – just let me know if you want anything copied.'

There must be a hundred documents in the file. The verdict is at the front, so she begins with that.

It states in formal language that the court sentences Leo Rasmussen to six years' imprisonment for the murder of Elita Svart, and that this term is significantly reduced because of the fact that he was only twenty years old at the time of the offence, and that he was also 'heavily influenced by his stepsister'.

This is followed by a summary of the reasons for Leo's conviction, namely his own confession and forensic evidence linking him to the scene. He was also identified by four witnesses. As Thea had already guessed, these witnesses are David, Nettan, Sebastian and Jan-Olof.

She turns to the police investigation – pages and pages of typewritten records of interviews and handwritten notes that will take her many hours to go through. The initial report was made by the first officer on the scene. It describes how Elita's body was found on the sacrificial stone in the middle of the circle on the morning of 1 May. The body was lifeless, the face covered by a white handkerchief. It was immediately clear that she had been killed, and the area was cordoned off to allow for a crime scene investigation to take place. Erik Nyberg and Bertil Nordin were present; they were the ones who contacted the police.

Thea looks up from her reading. So Erik and her father-in-law were at the scene together, before the police arrived. She raises an eyebrow and continues.

As she was hoping, there is a short interview with both men. Bertil says that he was on his way home from a Walpurgis Night party at the community centre and met David and his three friends, shocked and terrified. They told him that something terrible had happened to Elita at the stone circle.

Bertil initially thought it was a joke, but his wife persuaded him to check out the situation. He called Erik Nyberg, who was responsible for the castle estate; there had been problems in the past with teenagers and unplanned Walpurgis celebrations. Erik set off to investigate.

Erik states that he arrived at the stone circle just after six o'clock in the morning and found what he thought was a pile of clothes on the sacrificial stone. Only when he came closer did he realise that it was a body. He hurried to the nearest telephone, which was in the hunting lodge.

Thea thinks about that; he must have told Kerstin Miller about his horrific discovery, which explains why she seems so invested in the tragedy.

After contacting the police, Erik called Bertil Nordin, who arrived shortly before the police. Neither of the men saw anyone else near the scene of the crime.

Thea turns to the post-mortem report from the duty doctor called to the scene to pronounce Elita dead. Severe damage to the os frontale, ossa nasalie, maxilla and os zygomaticum, which in plain language means that someone has violently smashed the poor girl's face. She wonders if David and his friends saw it happen. Saw the terrible injuries.

She is just about to move on to the interviews with the children when her phone rings. David.

'Where are you?'

'Still in Lund.'

'Shit.' He sighs. 'Emee's taken off again.'

'Taken off? How?'

'I was going to take her out for a walk at lunchtime. As soon as I opened the door she pushed past me and ran off.'

'When was this?'

'About half an hour ago, maybe a little more. I've searched and shouted, but there's no sign of her. I've got two meetings this afternoon so I can't do any more.'

'OK, on my way.'

She closes the file and takes it back to the archivist.

'I'd like a copy, please.'

'Of course – which documents?'

'All of them.'

As soon as the copying is done, Thea drives home as fast as she dares. She gets there in less than fifty minutes. David's car and two others are parked outside the castle; she decides not to disturb their meeting. If Emee had turned up he would have called, or at least shut her in the house.

She goes inside; no Emee. She puts the file in her chest of drawers, pulls on her wellingtons, grabs the dog whistle and lead and sets off.

She crosses the stone bridge, calling Emee's name and blowing the whistle. Nothing. Maybe Emee has headed for the deer enclosure again? Thea turns left at the signpost and follows the track that will take her out of the forest.

Panic is bubbling up inside her; she tries not to think about the dead deer that she saw yesterday. *Emee isn't aggressive,* she tells herself.

That's not true though, is it? Margaux's voice comes from nowhere. *Don't you remember how she used to catch rats in the yard outside the hospital? And that time there was a dead cockerel on the steps? We laughed, said she was a predator deep down.*

Thea increases her speed, blows the whistle, shouts as loud as she can.

'Emee! Emee!'

Something is crashing through the undergrowth up ahead. She sees a movement, a grey, muscular body hurtling towards her. The relief makes her want to cry.

Emee dances around her and Thea sits down, pulls her close and strokes her nose.

'Good girl! Where've you been?'

Emee can't keep still. She's excited, pulls away, jumping up and down. Her eyes are shining, ears pricked, tongue hanging out.

Thea realises that her hand is wet. She looks down. There is a red, sticky mark on her palm.

35

Walpurgis Night 1986

Everyone has their secrets, that's what they say. Tornaby is full of them. A morass of dishonesty and lies.

Soon I will leave it all behind me, spread my wings and fly away from here. Because no secret is greater than mine.

Arne had completely miscalculated the route. He'd thought that all he needed to do was cross the canal that separated the forest from the marsh. Five minutes and he'd be at the stone circle.

However, the canal turned out to be much wider than he expected. It was more like a stagnant river than the ditch he'd imagined: almost ten metres of mud, reeds and murky water that absorbed both the moonlight and the beam of his torch. He knew there was a ford somewhere, but it was impossible to find in the darkness.

He followed the water for some distance, treading in barely visible pools of mud and almost losing a shoe. The warmth of the spring day had disappeared, and the temperature had dropped below ten degrees. The damp air and his wet feet made it feel even colder.

He looked at his watch: ten to twelve. If he didn't find a way to get across the canal very soon, he would miss the whole thing.

He was in luck. Just as he glimpsed the lights of the hunting lodge, he came across a large tree that had fallen across the water, creating a bridge to the other side.

He scrambled up onto the trunk. It was wet and slippery with algae, and had presumably been there for several years. He adjusted the binoculars around his neck, then took a moment to get his balance before he began to cross. Within a few metres he realised he wasn't entirely sober.

The further he went, the worse the smell became. Stagnant water, rotting wood and dead leaves. The same as in his nightmare.

When he reached the middle, the water was greenish black, with insects dancing on the surface. Something made a loud splash. Arne stiffened, feeling the fear creeping up his spine. What if he slipped and fell? The canal looked deep, two or three metres, maybe more. It must be full of larvae and tadpoles and other creatures that he didn't know the names of. Creatures with slimy bodies, shiny backs covered in scales, blue transparent wings, creatures that crept and crawled and . . .

Arne squeezed his eyes tight shut, swallowed hard several times. He'd come five metres, and he still had five metres to go. Trying to turn around and go back would be even more hazardous than carrying on.

All he had to do was take one step at a time. Calmly and cautiously.

He took a deep breath. One small step. Then another.

When he finally reached the other side he was so relieved that he had to go behind a tree and empty his bladder.

The noise frightened Arne at first, even though he didn't want to admit it. A dull, rhythmic drumming that got louder and louder as he approached the stone circle. Between the tree trunks up ahead he could see a flickering glow, and he quickly switched off his torch. He plodded on through the darkness, but immediately lost the winding track and ended up among the brambles. The vicious thorns pierced his flesh through his shirt and trousers. He slowed down and eventually came to a stop; the brambles were too thick to allow him to proceed.

The drumming continued, accompanied now by chanting voices. The luminous hands on his watch showed five to twelve.

He had to see what the hell was going on, right now before it was all over. He fought his way onwards with blood trickling between his fingers until he reached a tree with low-growing branches that enabled him to pull himself free of the brambles. He kept on climbing until he could see the glade.

See what she had wanted him to see.

The spring sacrifice.

36

When Thea reaches the stone bridge she see that some-one is leaning over the balustrade – a short man in dark clothing, puffing away at a cigarette.

It's Hubert Gordon. He straightens up, touches the peak of his cap.

'Good afternoon,' he says.

Emee, who is normally so reserved, wags her tail and rubs up against his legs like a cat. Thea has wiped her nose and mouth with some leaves. There wasn't much blood, but enough for the feeling of disquiet to linger. Has Emee been up to no good in the deer enclosure?

Hubert tosses his cigarette into the moat, crouches down and scratches behind Emee's ear.

'Good girl,' he murmurs. 'Good girl.'

Thea doesn't really know what to say. The behaviour of both man and dog has taken her by surprise.

'Thanks for your help the other day,' she manages eventually.

Hubert merely nods. He stands up, strokes Emee's head.

'She likes you,' Thea says unnecessarily.

The comment evokes a wry smile. 'Animals usually do.'

'Don't you have a dog of your own? Most people around here seem to.'

Hubert shakes his head. 'We used to have them when I was little. Hunting dogs, outdoors in the kennels over by the stables. That was how my father wanted it. His dogs, not mine.'

Thea notices that he speaks in short sentences.

He produces a packet of cigarettes and offers it to her. She takes one, waits while he lights it and another for himself. She ought to go home really. Carry on reading the documents, find out what David and his friends saw that night. But this strange little man interests her.

The cigarettes he smokes are slender, with no filter. They remind her of the ones Margaux used to smoke. He turns towards the water. The smell of the marsh is unmistakable. Emee sits down between them, and they smoke in silence for a while.

'What did you do before you came here?' he asks.

'I worked for Doctors Without Borders. At a field hospital in Idlib in Syria. We were bombed . . .'

She takes a deep drag, holds the smoke in her lungs. Why is she telling him this? She doesn't even know him. And yet . . . The feeling is there again, the sense that she and this little man share something. The same kind of pain. The same kind of sorrow.

'It was utter chaos,' she goes on. 'I lost colleagues, friends. I spent several weeks in hospital. I'm not fully recovered yet, to be honest.' She falls silent. Her eyes are smarting. Maybe it's the smoke, maybe not.

'Your friend who's sick – was she there?' Hubert asks without turning his head.

'Yes.'

He doesn't ask any more questions; she is grateful for that. Instead he finishes his cigarette and tosses it into the moat, just as he did with the first one.

'May I offer you a cup of coffee?' he says.

The front door is small in comparison to the wing itself. Hubert's old Land Rover is parked outside.

They go up the stone staircase and find themselves at the end of a long corridor on the first floor. To the right are two tall double doors equipped with a heavy steel bolt. There is a cross on one of the doors; this must be the chapel, which Dr Andersson mentioned. Straight ahead another door leads to the rest of the castle; it too is bolted.

Hubert guides her to the left. The ceilings are high, the floor made of huge, smooth slabs of stone. On the walls are gloomy paintings of stern men in wigs and uniforms, with the odd woman in a shiny dress, her face whitened with powder.

'My ancestors,' Hubert says, anticipating her question. 'Eight generations of Gordons in chronological order.'

They pass several more closed doors until they reach one that is open. Thea is surprised to see a modern little kitchen.

'Take a seat in the library.' Hubert points towards the end of the corridor. 'I'll bring the coffee. You can let the dog off the lead if you like.'

Thea does as he suggests, and Emee runs off ahead of her, as if she already knows the way.

The room is large, it must be over a hundred square metres, with triple aspect windows. There are thick, valuable rugs on the floor, and the walls are lined with dark bookcases; you would need a ladder to reach the top shelves. The smell of cigars and old books makes Emee snuffle and sneeze before she gets down to the serious business of investigating the corners.

Thea goes over to the window facing onto the garden. She pushes the heavy velvet curtain aside and looks out. This must have been where Hubert was standing when she caught sight of him on the night of the storm.

She moves to another window on the short wall of the wing, with a view of the moat, the bridge and the forest. A skein of geese is flying high in the sky, and over to the right she can see the roof of the coach house.

Emee is still checking out the room, and has stopped by the drinks trolley. Up above her on the wall hangs a more modern portrait than the ones in the hallway. A hook-nosed, grim-faced elderly man in a suit is standing beside a beautiful, considerably younger woman with skin like alabaster. Between them is a boy in a sailor suit. He must be seven or eight years old, and the artist has done his best to tone down the scar on his upper lip. There is no mistaking the fact that the boy is Hubert Gordon, which means the adults must be his parents.

'Mother and Father,' Hubert confirms as he enters the room with a tray. 'The last Count Gordon. The family dies out with me.'

He places the tray on a table between two wing-backed armchairs and gestures to her to take a seat as he pours the coffee.

'No more Gordons at Bokelund,' he continues. 'Probably just as well . . .'

'Why do you say that?'

He leans back in his chair. 'Because the Gordons are terrible people.'

Thea raises her eyebrows.

'Have you heard about the girls who haunt this place, Isabelle and Eleonor? How they died?' Hubert's tone is lighter, less tense.

'One fell through the ice on her way to a secret tryst with her lover, and the other came off her horse,' Thea says, remembering what David said during the TV interview.

Hubert shakes his head.

'Isabelle drowned at the end of April 1753. At least that's what it says in the parish records. The ice on the moat has never lasted beyond the end of March, not even in the worst of winters.' He takes a sip of coffee. 'And Eleonor was expecting a baby when she broke her neck in 1891. A pregnant woman riding out on a fox hunt sounds a little strange. According to the rumours, her own father was the father of the child.'

'You mean . . .'

'I mean that both girls were actually murdered, probably by their fathers or someone doing their fathers' bidding. One drowned, one beaten to death. As I said, the Gordons are terrible people. Generations of incest and marriage between cousins gives rise to certain defects, both on the inside and the outside.'

Thea doesn't quite know how she's expected to respond.

'What a wonderful library,' she says when the silence has gone on long enough.

'That's mostly thanks to my mother. She organised the collections when I was small. She loved books.' He stares down into his cup.

'Have you always lived at Bokelund?'

'Mostly. I went to boarding school in England for a while – a family tradition. The Gordons are originally British.'

'And the rest of the time you went to school in Tornaby?'

The question isn't as innocent as she is trying to make it sound. Hubert is only a few years older than Elita Svart. His father owned Svartgården. Maybe he knew her?

To her disappointment, Hubert shakes his head.

'I was educated here in the castle. The schoolroom is over in the east wing, and the governess lived in the room next door. That was Father's decision. He didn't want me mixing with the villagers.'

Thea tries to work out whether the last comment is a joke; she's not sure.

'You mentioned your sick friend . . .' Hubert points to Emee, who has settled down on the floor beside them. 'The one with the dog. What's her name?'

'Margaux. She's French.'

'From Paris?' His face lights up.

'Yes, actually. Have you been there?'

'Once, when I was very young. My aunt lived there, and my mother and I went to visit her. I remember it as a fantastic place. I dreamed of going back there when I was older, but Father and my aunt hated each other, and after Mother died he wouldn't let me go anywhere. And since I grew up, it just hasn't happened. Maybe I'm afraid the city won't live up to my expectations, that it won't be as perfect as it is in my dreams. Things rarely are.'

He takes another sip of coffee, seems surprised by how talkative he is, like so many people who meet Thea.

'Have you known each other long, you and Margaux?' he asks, turning the focus of the conversation back to her.

'Yes.' Thoughts she usually manages to suppress are threatening to come pouring out. She wants to tell him that Margaux was her best friend. Her only friend. That she meant much more than that. Instead she is a coward, hiding behind her coffee cup.

Hubert gazes at her. His eyes are soft, full of sorrow.

'I've also lost someone who was close to me,' he says. 'It's a long time ago now, but the pain never really goes away. It leaves an empty space inside you.' He glances up at the portrait.

Neither of them says anything for a long time, but as before, the silence isn't in the least uncomfortable.

'What about you and David? How long have you been together?'

'About five years, on and off.'

'On and off?'

'We dated whenever I was home from my travels – nothing too serious. But after the bombing he was there for me. He flew down to the hospital in Cyprus, took care of everything. It was the same when I came back here. I've been suffering from the after-effects for almost a year, but David's supported me, helped me to get back on my feet.'

'Was that why you married him?'

The question surprises her. So does the answer.

'Yes.'

She hasn't shared that thought with anyone except Margaux, but when you get behind his slightly morose façade, Hubert is very easy to talk to. It's as if he has the same effect on her as she has on other people. The admission makes her feel strangely relieved. Hubert doesn't say a word; he merely nods.

They sit in silence again. The feeling of affinity between them has grown even stronger.

Thea looks at her watch. David must be wondering where she is. Whether she's found Emee. Maybe he's worried? She stands up, even though she would rather stay.

'I'm afraid I have to go. Thanks for the coffee.'

Hubert accompanies her into the corridor.

'Wait a minute,' he says when they reach the top of the stairs. He disappears through one of the closed doors and returns after a few seconds. Thea catches a glimpse of a narrow bed and a TV, and guesses that it's his bedroom.

'I think you might enjoy this.'

He hands her a well-thumbed book: *Selected Poems* by Stanley Kunitz.

'It's helped me sometimes, when things have been difficult. Maybe it will help you.'

'Thank you.' The gesture is so kind that a warm glow spreads through her body.

'You're welcome. I hope you'll come and see me again.'

'I'd love to.'

They go downstairs and she hears him close the front door behind her. And double lock it.

37

Walpurgis Night 1986

I have chosen them with care, my little tadpoles. Chosen the children whose parents snigger at me behind my back and pull faces when they talk about me, as if my name has a nasty taste.
Those children will witness the death of Elita Svart.

A rne pressed the binoculars to his eyes so hard that he couldn't see properly. A big fire is burning over in the glade, casting long, flickering shadows over the stones. Elita and the children were standing in the centre of the circle, right next to the flat sacrificial stone. The whole thing looked exactly like the Polaroid: Elita's white dress, the antlers, the silk ribbons, the masked children. The full moon riding high above them intensified the sense of unreality.

His ghetto blaster was on one of the other stones. The recorded sound of drumming reverberated around the glade, along with voices chanting something in English that Arne didn't understand at first.

Elita gestured to the children, said something. They formed a circle around her, fully extending the ribbons attached to her wrists. Arne adjusted the focus, managed to sharpen the image.

Elita began to move, taking slow steps in time with the drums. She was barefoot on the wet grass; Arne thought he could see the moisture gleaming on her shins.

The chanting continued, and by now he had heard it often enough to be able to make out the words.

'*Hoof and horn, hoof and horn. All that dies shall be reborn.*

'*Corn and grain, corn and grain. All that falls shall rise again.*'

The rhyme was repeated over and over again, each time a little faster than the one before. Elita's feet were moving faster too. She swung her arms, spun around on the spot, taking the children with her.

'*Hoof and horn, hoof and horn. All that dies shall be reborn.*'

Elita's movements became more frantic. She threw her head back and raised the antlers high in the air, drawing the children closer.

The circle spun faster and faster, closer and closer. Arne swallowed, felt himself grow hard.

'*Corn and grain, corn and grain. All that falls shall rise again.*'

The children pulled on the ribbons, locked Elita in the centre of the circle with her arms outstretched.

The tempo of the drums continued to increase. The circle was spinning so fast now that Arne could barely make out the children. But he didn't care about them; Elita was all that mattered. Her eyes were closed, her chest shining with sweat above the neckline of her dress. She looked as if she was in a trance.

Arne's mouth was as dry as dust, his face was burning, his trousers straining at the crotch. He reached for the zip with his free hand, but something made him pause. At first it was only a barely perceptible vibration in the darkness, then a pulsating beat that clashed with the rhythm of the drums.

He lowered the binoculars and twisted around, almost losing his balance in the process.

The beat grew louder, turning the hairs on the back of his neck into tiny, needle-sharp ice crystals. He'd heard it before, many times. The sound of hooves, of branches and twigs breaking. The sound from his nightmare, a rider approaching.

The hoof beats came closer and closer, thundering inside Arne's chest, his head, his crotch. His cock shrank to the size of a pathetic little worm.

Horse and rider burst through the greenery directly below him. He caught a glimpse of a huge black horse that was something else at the same time, something ancient that might not even be a horse. And the rider . . .

Arne screamed, but exactly as in his dream, not a sound came out.

He closed his eyes, heard the Green Man and his steed crash through the undergrowth beneath him.

The smell of stagnant water overwhelmed him. Rotting wood and dead leaves, the stench of things that crept and crawled and transformed what had recently been alive into earth and mould. Transformed a grown man into a little child.

He lost his balance and fell backwards out of the tree. Hung in the air just long enough to think that the landing would be painful.

He could hear terrified screams from the glade, almost drowned out by the bellowing of an animal.

The sound was cut off abruptly as Arne hit the ground, letting the night into his head.

38

'I've had a look at Hubert's book. The poems are beautiful, melancholy in a way that I really like. They express a kind of longing, both for what has been and what never was.

'Hubert has written inside the cover that the strongest love is unrequited love. I've searched for the quotation in the book, but I can't find it. Anyway, I understand exactly what he means.'

David is playing the good husband. Preparing meals, asking about her work. In spite of his efforts, Thea can tell that his thoughts are elsewhere. He's irritable, flares up at the least thing. She can't help recalling his outburst the other day when he attacked the builder; he still hasn't said anything about the incident. He gets phone calls until late into the evening, and he doesn't protest when she says she's tired and closes the bedroom door so that she can concentrate on the file the archivist gave her.

David, Nettan, Sebastian and Jan-Olof were interviewed at the police station in Ljungslöv. Together, apparently, which Thea finds a little strange. On the other hand, the police had also questioned Bertil and Erik together earlier that same day, so maybe it wasn't against the rules.

The interviews seem to have been taped and then transcribed. In a couple of places whoever did the transcription has added brief notes in brackets.

Present in the room were the children and their fathers. All the men are listed in an old-fashioned way, with their professions: *bank manager Bertil Nordin, headmaster Staffan Hellman, engineer Pawel Malinowski, machinist Eskil Leander.*

David answered most of the questions. Sometimes he was prompted by Nettan, less often by Sebastian. Jan-Olof, on the other hand, says nothing unless he is asked directly, and then he answers in monosyllables.

```
INTERVIEWER: What were you doing in the
   stone circle?
DAVID NORDIN: We . . . We were pretending
   to act out a ceremony.
JEANETTE HELLMAN: Carry out a ceremony.
INTERVIEWER: What kind of ceremony?
DAVID NORDIN: A spring sacrifice. Like they
   used to do in the old days.
JEANETTE HELLMAN: They pretended to sacri-
   fice a virgin so that spring would come.
INTERVIEWER: I see. And whose idea was that?
DAVID NORDIN: Elita's. She'd read about it.
   Seen old photographs. She'd sorted out
   animal masks for us so that it would look
   exactly the same.
INTERVIEWER: And what did this ceremony
   consist of?
JEANETTE HELLMAN: We were going to sacrifice
   Elita to him. Pretend to, I mean.
INTERVIEWER: To him?
(SILENCE)
```

INTERVIEWER: Who were you going to sacrifice Elita to?

SEBASTIAN MALINOWSKI: (clears his throat) To the Green Man.

INTERVIEWER: The Green Man? The figure that people burn on the Walpurgis Night bonfires?

DAVID NORDIN: Yes . . .

INTERVIEWER: OK . . . So you were at the circle because you were going to play at sacrificing Elita to the Green Man.

JEANETTE HELLMAN: It wasn't a game.

INTERVIEWER: No? What was it, then?

DAVID NORDIN: Well, maybe it was a kind of game. But it didn't feel that way. It felt kind of . . .

JEANETTE HELLMAN: Real.

DAVID NORDIN: Yes. Real.

INTERVIEWER: What do the rest of you have to say?

(INAUDIBLE MURMURING)

INTERVIEWER: Can you repeat that, Leander?

JAN-OLOF LEANDER: Too fucking real . . .

39

Walpurgis Night 1986

Walpurgis Night is here at last. Nature is hungry, and the Green Man is riding through the forests. He is coming to fetch Elita Svart. His spring sacrifice. And nothing will ever be the same again.

The boy was frightened. The eye-holes in his mask were tiny, and he had difficulty seeing what was going on around him.

Elita had just switched on the ghetto blaster. The sound of drums reverberated around the glade, bouncing off the stones and tree trunks. His breath inside the mask smelled sweet and cloying. For a moment the boy thought he was going to throw up.

The girl in the owl mask turned towards him. He could only just glimpse her eyes, but he could tell that she was just as scared as him. So were the other two boys. It had all sounded so exciting when Elita first talked to them. The full moon, the ritual, the spring sacrifice. The Green Man coming to fetch her. Although of course none of them believed that bit.

They'd recorded the drums the other night, all four of them sitting around and banging on plastic buckets while Elita directed them. They had to repeat the rhyme she'd taught them over and over again; she'd said that druids and priests used it thousands of years ago.

'Hoof and horn, hoof and horn. All that dies shall be reborn.

194

'Corn and grain, corn and grain. All that falls shall rise again.'

They'd carried on for so long that they'd almost lost track of time, and now their words were pouring out of the ghetto blaster's loudspeaker. Strangely enough, the voices didn't sound like theirs; they were much deeper. More unpleasant.

The boy swallowed. His mouth felt dry, the ground was moving beneath his feet. He mustn't be sick, not now, not here.

Elita had brought a bottle with her. Said it contained a magic potion made according to an ancient recipe, which of course was more of her nonsense, just like the rhyme. They'd all drunk it though. Swallowed the sweet, slippery contents because none of them dared to say no.

He felt the others' eyes on him as they stood in silence around Elita in their horrible masks. She was wearing a white dress, and holding two sets of antlers in her hands.

She looked in his direction, and as always there was something about her that made him want to do whatever she asked. She nodded to him, indicating that he should pick up the end of one of the silk ribbons attached to her wrists. The others did the same.

'What do we do now?' said the girl in the owl mask. Her voice mingled with the drums and the chanting, but there was no mistaking the fear.

Elita closed her eyes and crossed the antlers over her chest.

'Now we dance.'

The drumming began to speed up. Elita started to move, slowly at first, then faster and faster. She pulled on the ribbons, whirling around and forcing all four of them to follow her.

'Sing!' she yelled. 'Sing, my little tadpoles!'

The rhyme echoed out across the glade, accompanied by their trembling voices.

'Louder! Faster! Extend the ribbons!'

They obeyed, moving further away so that the ribbons drew Elita's arms outwards. She spun faster and faster; they had to run to keep up. The moonlight turned the grass to silver, the shadows cast by the fire flickered over the hawthorn trees.

'Faster! Faster, louder! The Green Man is riding through the forests. Soon he will be here!'

The boy tripped over a branch and almost fell. His heart was pounding, sweat was pouring down his back.

The drumming and the chanting continued, but suddenly the boy became aware of another sound, increasing in volume and making his stomach contract. The sound of approaching hooves.

The others seemed to have heard it too. Their movements slowed as they glanced anxiously towards the forest.

Elita was beside herself. 'The Green Man is coming! The Green Man is coming! He's coming!'

The trees in front of them parted, revealing a sight that could have come straight out of their nightmares.

A huge black horse, foaming at the mouth. On its back a tall, faceless rider with a shapeless body made up of leaves and branches. On top of his head was an enormous crown made of antlers.

The boy stood there as if he had been turned to stone. Every muscle was tensed, and the silk ribbon was cutting into his palms.

The horse stopped no more than a metre away, then it reared up and made a noise that sounded like a scream. Or was someone else screaming? Was it his own scream he could hear?

Or Elita's?

40

Thea continues to read the transcript with rising excitement. There is something strange yet deeply fascinating about reading twelve-year-old David's words, while the forty-five-year-old version lies sleeping on the other side of the bedroom wall. She feels as if she is getting much closer to him with every sentence.

INTERVIEWER: So you played music on a tape recorder and danced. Then a man arrived on a horse. What happened next?

DAVID NORDIN: Someone screamed. We ran away as fast as we could. Tore off our masks and dropped them in the forest. We were terrified.

INTERVIEWER: All of you?

ALL FOUR CHILDREN: Yes.

INTERVIEWER: Did you see who was riding the horse?

DAVID NORDIN: It was Leo. Elita's stepbrother.

INTERVIEWER: Leo Rasmussen?

DAVID NORDIN: Yes.

INTERVIEWER: And you're sure of this, even though the rider was dressed up as the

Green Man? Even though you were wearing
masks, and Elita had given you alcohol?

JEANETTE HELLMAN: Yes, we are.

INTERVIEWER: But how can you be? You said
he was disguised as the Green Man.

JEANETTE HELLMAN: We recognised the horse –
Bill. We've seen him at Elita's place several
times.

INTERVIEWER: Did you see what happened
next? What Leo did to Elita?

(SILENCE)

INTERVIEWER: Did any of you see what happened
next?

(SILENCE)

INTERVIEWER: Nordin, did you see anything?

DAVID NORDIN: Mm.

INTERVIEWER: What did you see?

DAVID NORDIN: I . . . I stopped in the forest
and went back.

INTERVIEWER: Back to the stone circle?

DAVID NORDIN: Yes.

INTERVIEWER: And what did you see there?

Thea realises that she is holding her breath. Her fingers are
shaking, it's hard to turn the pages.

41

Walpurgis Night 1986

T he boy ran. He'd already pulled off the mask and dropped it when he left the glade. Sharp branches whipped his face, brambles tore at his legs, but he hardly noticed.

The scream echoed inside his head, lingered on his lips, in his throat. His three friends were running too – terrified, panic-stricken. They were running away from the stone circle, away from the Green Man and his phantom steed.

The nausea he'd been fighting for so long suddenly gained the upper hand, forcing him to stop. He doubled over, hands resting on his knees, and vomited into the darkness.

He could hear the other three up ahead of him, running towards the place where they'd hidden their bikes. He was desperate to follow them, but his body refused to co-operate.

He threw up over and over again until his stomach stopped contracting. The fear loosened its grip a fraction, enabling him to think a little more clearly.

What had just happened? What had they actually seen?

The boy straightened up and took a couple of deep breaths. His friends were gone, cycling towards safety. But what safety? If the ghosts really existed, they would never be safe again. Not anywhere.

He turned and began to creep back to the stone circle. He had to know. However scared he was, he had to find out if the ghosts really existed.

And what had happened to Elita.

42

Thea turns the page. She can picture David out there in the dark forest, a solitary, frightened little boy who somehow manages to pluck up his courage and go back to see what has become of his friend.

INTERVIEWER: So what did you see when you reached the stone circle, David?

DAVID NORDIN: She . . . Elita was lying on the sacrificial stone. Leo was bending over her. Her face was covered in blood.

INTERVIEWER: Go on.

DAVID NORDIN: Then he covered her face with his handkerchief.

INTERVIEWER: Did you see anything else?

DAVID NORDIN: No. I ran back to the others. To the bikes. Then we cycled to my house. Told my dad as soon as he got home.

INTERVIEWER: And you're absolutely certain that it was Leo Rasmussen you saw?

DAVID NORDIN: Yes.

INTERVIEWER: Was he dressed up?

DAVID NORDIN: What?

INTERVIEWER: You said the rider was dressed up as the Green Man. Did Leo still have the costume on?

DAVID NORDIN: Oh, yes. I think so. Although I did see his face. It was Leo.

INTERVIEWER: I ask you once again: are you absolutely certain? Even though it was dark, you saw him from a distance, and he might still have been wearing the costume?

UNKNOWN VOICE: David has answered the question. He's already told you he's sure.

INTERVIEWER: The last comment was made by David's father, Bertil Nordin. I must ask you not to interrupt, Bertil. David, let me ask you one more time. Are you sure it was Leo Rasmussen you saw bending over Elita?

DAVID NORDIN: Y-yes I am.

The interview comes to an end. Thea slowly closes the file. Her heart is beating fast, and she is suddenly overwhelmed with a feeling of tenderness towards David.

So he saw Elita. Saw her battered face, saw the man who murdered her. He was also forced to relive the experience when questioned by the police, and when he testified in court. It's hardly surprising that he moved away from the area as soon as he could, that he stayed in Stockholm and came home to visit only when he couldn't avoid it. But he's here now, living only a kilometre or so from his childhood trauma. Partly for his own sake, partly for hers, so that they can both make a fresh start. Have a second chance.

She gets out of bed and goes into the hallway. David's bedroom door is ajar.

'Are you asleep?' she whispers.

He doesn't answer, but he moves slightly in bed. She lifts the covers and slides in beside him. Puts her arm around him and presses her body to his back.

43

Walpurgis Night 1986

Every story needs a beginning, a middle and an end. And now my end is near.

Who was it? you ask. Who killed Elita Svart?

Why should I tell you? By the time you read this, I will no longer exist. I will be floating high above your heads like a dragonfly.

Can you see me, dear readers?

I can see you.

Arne stumbled through the forest. The moon had slipped behind the clouds, everything was pitch dark. The ghetto blaster in his left hand was heavy, and one corner kept banging against the back of his knee. The binoculars were bouncing around on the strap around his neck, and the brambles ripped holes in his clothes and his skin.

He switched on his torch, tried to direct the beam in front of him. Searched for a path, a gap in the undergrowth, the quickest way out of here. Out of this fucking nightmare.

His head was pounding, his back was aching, his right hand could hardly hold the torch, but the adrenaline would keep him on his feet for a few more minutes.

He saw the gleam of water and stopped. Swept the torch back and forth, looking for the fallen tree he'd used as a bridge. Suddenly he became aware of car headlights on the other side of the canal, and switched off the torch. The track was at least twenty metres away from him, and the headlights weren't pointing in his direction, but still he threw himself on the ground.

The movement made the fall from the tree replay in his head. How long had he been unconscious? He looked at his watch. Quarter to one, so he must have been out for half an hour, maybe longer.

He pulled the ghetto blaster towards him. Ran his fingers over the letters etched into the plastic on the back.

Property of Arne Backe, Tornaby.

The car had extra lamps on the front. It passed by slowly, as if the driver was looking for something. A short distance away the headlights were reflected in a parked car, which must be his. The driver braked, and now Arne recognised the vehicle; it was Lasse Svart's old red pick-up.

What if Lasse stopped, got out of the car and started wandering around? What the fuck would Arne do then? He was soaking wet, shivering like a dog, and couldn't lie here in the mud for much longer.

For a moment he was on the verge of bursting into tears. This was all Elita's fault. She was the one who'd lured him here, toyed with his emotions and made him dance to her tune like a lovesick fool. Well, now she'd got what she deserved. His sorrow was mixed with anger now; he rubbed his eyes with his uninjured hand.

The brake lights went out. Lasse drove past the police car and continued along the track.

Arne used his anger to get to his feet. He had no intention of allowing himself to be dragged down into the mud. He wasn't going to let the Svart family destroy his life.

He found the fallen tree. It was even harder to scramble onto it this time. His legs felt wobbly, and the ghetto blaster almost made him lose his balance right away.

He was about halfway across when he slipped, pitched forward, hit his head on the tree and dropped both the torch and the ghetto blaster. He heard the splash as the black water swallowed them up; he scrabbled wildly at the slippery surface to stop himself from following them. If he fell he would sink deep into the stinking mud, just like in his nightmare. The thought made his body begin to shake uncontrollably. His mouth was filled with the taste of iron.

Pull yourself together, for fuck's sake.

He heard the sharp crack of a branch breaking in the forest behind him. Was someone there? Someone who'd seen him, seen what he'd done? Someone who was following him . . .

Arne managed to get up on all fours. Crawled along the fallen tree with trembling arms and legs until he reached the other side. He staggered up the slope to the car, fumbling for his key. His hand was shaking so much he had difficulty unlocking the door.

He slumped down on the driver's seat, pressed the button to lock the car and managed to pull off the heavy binoculars; the strap was cutting into his neck. The relief at having reached safety was so great that he was close to tears again.

After a while he looked up and saw his reflection in the rear-view mirror. *Jesus.* His face was streaked with dirt, his lips were swollen, a huge graze covered one cheek. When he raised his left hand to rub away the worst of the mud, he saw several rusty-red stains on the cuff of his shirt.

Blood.

Elita Svart's blood.

The nausea overcame him again. He covered his mouth with his hand and just managed to get the door open before the contents of his stomach spurted out between his fingers. Now his mouth was filled with the taste of shame.

He really ought to switch on the police radio, call it in, get his colleagues over here and tell them what had happened. But if he did that, his life would be smashed to pieces. All those who'd fucked him around, called him Downhill Arne, would be proved right. Bertil and Ingrid wouldn't be able to hold their heads up for the rest of their lives.

He had to get out of here, right now. Get as far away as possible from this terrible place. Cover his tracks.

The fact that the ghetto blaster had his name on it was unfortunate, but he didn't think it would ever be found. The canal was several metres deep, and by now it must be buried in the mud, along with his police-issue torch.

The car started immediately. His right hand had turned into a swollen blob, but he managed to push the gear stick with his knuckles. He put his foot down.

But where the hell could he go? In six hours this car had to be at the station in Ljungslöv, spotlessly clean. It was also his job to make the coffee ready for morning briefing at eight o'clock, then sit at the back of the room, smartly dressed and with some kind of reasonable explanation for his injuries.

Elita's body would be found, there would be a murder inquiry. A team from Helsingborg would move in. He had to think, had to work out what the fuck . . .

The animal appeared in the headlights right in front of the car; Arne's heart almost stopped. For a second it felt as if time had done the same. He could see the animal hanging in the air.

Slender legs, a powerful, dark body, like something from his nightmares.

Somehow he managed to swerve to the side. The right-hand wheels chewed up a considerable part of the ditch before he was able to get the Saab back on the track. He stared in the mirror, but the animal had disappeared into the forest.

It must have been ten seconds before Arne realised what he'd almost hit. Not an imaginary creature, but a black horse with no saddle, reins dangling. A black horse with a white sock on one hind leg. The same horse he'd seen just a few hours earlier in the paddock at Svartgården.

Suddenly a thought began to take shape in his head. It grew bigger and stronger the further he got from the marsh. Things he'd seen and heard during the day came together, and a crystal clear picture emerged of what he'd actually seen at the stone circle.

And he knew what had to be done. What he had to do.

44

Thea can't find the phone at first, she fumbles around on the bedside table for a while before she manages to silence the alarm. She's had a dream she only partly recalls: a rider in a dark forest, and stagnant, muddy water. Hardly surprising, but she's also dreamed about her father, which as always makes her uneasy.

Suddenly she realises she's in David's bed, not her own. He must have brought her phone in before he left. She stiffens, jumps out of bed and runs into her room. The file with the transcripts is under the bed. Is that where she left it last night before she went to join David? She's not sure, but eventually manages to convince herself that she must have done.

She pushes the file into her work bag so that David won't find it. After reading the transcript she understands why he doesn't want to talk about Elita Svart, yet at the same time she's keen to know more. Get even closer. She takes Emee to work with her; she daren't leave her at home and risk her running away again. The wind seems to be blowing from several directions at the same time, lashing the side windows with rain as she drives along the narrow track between the fields.

When they arrive Emee wanders around the surgery looking miserable, but after a while she flops down on the blanket by the radiator with a loud sigh.

There are no patients waiting, which means that Thea can go back to the file. After the interviews with the four children,

Elita's mother Lola was questioned. Her responses are disjointed; presumably she was still in shock. As before the interview was recorded, then transcribed.

> INTERVIEWER: What was Elita doing in the stone circle in the middle of the night?
> LOLA SVART: She was the spring sacrifice.
> INTERVIEWER: What does that involve?
> LOLA SVART: Something old must die so that something new can rise again.
> INTERVIEWER: I don't really understand.
> LOLA SVART: (INAUDIBLE MUTTERING)
> INTERVIEWER: Who do you think killed her?
> LOLA SVART: Him.
> INTERVIEWER: Who?
> LOLA SVART: The Green Man. He was the one who took her.
> INTERVIEWER: Who is the Green Man?
> LOLA SVART: (CRIES)
> INTERVIEWER: Who is the Green Man, Lola?
> LOLA SVART: (CRIES)
> INTERVIEWER: Interview suspended 14.08.

The Green Man took her. What does Lola mean by that? It could, of course, be a way of dealing with the incomprehensible, because she can't bring herself to utter Leo's name. Or perhaps Lola has simply lost her grip on reality.

The next interview is with Eva-Britt Rasmussen, Leo's mother.

She is more matter-of-fact, but doesn't say much either. She and Lola both went to bed at about eleven o'clock. Lasse was out working, and Eva-Britt assumed that Elita was in her room. She didn't see Leo, because he lived in a small cabin behind the main house.

Lasse Svart is even more taciturn in his interview, and yet Thea thinks she can read both suppressed grief and anger in the short lines. Lasse is quite hostile towards the police, but when pressed he confirms that he was in the Reftinge area, dowsing for water. He reluctantly gives the name of the farmer who asked for his help, then adds that he got home around midnight, went straight to bed and didn't see either Elita or Leo. That's all he has to say.

Thea recognises his attitude. The distrust of the police and the authorities – everyone outside the family, in fact. Her father was exactly the same.

There is a short interview with Kerstin Miller, who says that she went to bed just after ten on Walpurgis Night, as always. Erik Nyberg turned up at six thirty in the morning, told her the terrible news and asked to use the telephone.

Then comes the first interview with Leo. It was conducted at the police station on the evening of 1 May. Leo claims that he spent the evening alone in his little cabin, drinking. He got drunk and fell asleep, and has no memories of that night. When the interviewer asks about the scratches and bruises on his face and hands, he replies that he doesn't remember how he got them. He insists that the last time he saw Elita was just before ten o'clock. The interviewer then states that Leo is suspected of murdering Elita Svart, which Leo denies. The interview ends.

Thea finds a total of nine interviews with Leo, but she decides not to read the rest of them until she is more familiar with the details surrounding the murder. She finds a report from the scene of the crime, and several pages of photographs. These are copies of copies, but the quality is surprisingly good.

Elita is lying on her back on the sacrificial stone. Her hands are folded across her chest. In the first picture her face is covered by a handkerchief that is sodden with dark blood. In the subsequent pictures the handkerchief has been removed, and just as Thea has already read in the doctor's report, the upper part of Elita's face is a bloody pulp.

She takes out the Polaroid and places it on the desk.

Elita is dressed in exactly the same way in both images. The dress, the ribbons around her wrists, the antlers, all identical. Which means that the Polaroid must have been taken on Walpurgis Night.

Thea flicks through the remaining interviews. The same names recur: Lasse, Eva-Britt, Lola and Leo. No one else. No outsiders.

A family tragedy.

She goes back to the crime scene report and reads through the summary of the forensic evidence.

The ground inside the stone circle consisted mainly of flattened grass with clearly visible hoof prints. Dogs were brought in, and a search of the terrain revealed a track with freshly broken branches and trodden-down undergrowth, heading directly east towards a ford where the canal was shallower. Again, hoof prints were found. The track continued on the other side of the canal, coming to an end when it reached the road. The technicians stated that as far as it was possible to tell, this coincided with the time of the murder, and that it involved a large horse. The animal must have been both wet and muddy after crossing the canal. As if to back up their conclusions, the technicians attached close-ups of the hoof prints in the mud.

Thea leafs through the pages, finds pictures of Svartgården – a collection of gloomy, low buildings surrounded by dense greenery. Then Leo's little cottage, and the stable. Even Bill in his stall.

Elita's room seems familiar in many ways. Sloping ceiling, a single bed, an IKEA desk, an armchair and a lamp. If you swap the wooden floor for a fitted carpet and the Duran Duran poster for Wham!, this could have been Thea's room when she was a teenager.

The letter Elita left behind is on her desk. It has been photographed from several angles, and there is a copy on the next page. Her heart begins to beat a little faster.

Dear readers!

Every narrative must have a beginning, a middle and an end. This is my beginning.

My name is Elita Svart. I am sixteen years old. I live deep in the forest outside Tornaby.

By the time you read this, I will already be dead.

Thea reads on. Elita's handwriting is rounded, still a little childish. She sometimes uses words and phrases that are too overblown for a sixteen-year-old girl, and her tone becomes rather melodramatic, not least when she writes about herself in the third person.

Sometimes she can seem ironic and manipulative, sometimes more vulnerable, which suggests that she didn't write the letter all in one go. In certain sentences she is cocky and confident, in others so cryptic that she doesn't make sense. At times she sounds afraid, especially when she writes about her family and the relationship between her father and Leo.

Leo, who is prepared to do anything for her.

As Thea reads on, she can almost hear Elita's voice. The voice of a sixteen-year-old girl who lives in the middle of a marsh, trapped in a keg of gunpowder, near a village where the inhabitants simultaneously desire and despise her.

Or is it her own voice Thea can hear? Her own sixteen-year-old self who wants to tell the whole world to go to hell?

She carries on reading, gobbling up the words. Elita's tone becomes darker, her voice clearer and clearer.

Soon I will leave it all behind me, spread my wings and fly away from here. Because no secret is greater than mine.

Thea stops, looks up. What secret? Is Elita referring to the death pact between her and Leo? That seems likely.

Another section captures her interest.

I have chosen them with care, my little tadpoles. Chosen the children whose parents snigger at me behind my back and pull faces when they talk about me, as if my name has a nasty taste.

She leans back on her chair. Repeats the words out loud.

'The children whose parents snigger at me behind my back.'

She can imagine Ingrid turning up her nose at Elita Svart. A dirty little gyppo, not good enough to associate with her darling David and his friends.

That explains why Elita chose to surround herself with four twelve-year-olds. These weren't just any children. David's father was a bank manager, Nettan's a headmaster, Sebastian's an engineer. The children, with the possible exception of Jan-Olof, represented the society that rejected her.

Thea reads the rest of the letter, all the way to the highly charged ending.

Who was it, you ask? Who killed Elita Svart?
Why should I tell you?

A tap on the door makes her look up. She quickly closes the file and slips it into a drawer.

'Come in!'

The door opens to reveal Hubert Gordon. He is wearing his oilskin coat as usual, shaking the rain off his flat cap.

'Sorry to disturb you.'

'You're not disturbing me at all – come on in and sit down.'

Emee leaps to her feet, walks around Hubert a couple of times, then settles with her head on his knee.

'Thanks for yesterday, by the way,' Thea says.

'No, thank you. I'm sorry I didn't have anything to offer you; I rarely have visitors,' he says with a small smile.

'Is there something I can help you with?'

'Yes; I wonder if you can renew my prescription?'

'Of course.'

She opens the laptop and asks him for his ID number. His list of medications comes up.

'Stesolid, is that right?'

'Yes.' He clears his throat. 'I've had problems with muscle spasms ever since I was a child. Father had them too, so it's probably hereditary.'

'Mm,' she says, for want of a better response. Stesolid is actually Valium in new, more modern packaging. Good for spasms, but also anxiety, panic attacks, insomnia and so on.

'The Gordon gene pool really is a mess,' he says, smiling again in a way that immediately makes her do the same. Hubert has a dark, subtle sense of humour that appeals to her.

'I've had a look at the book you gave me,' she says, tapping away at the keys.

'I'm pleased to hear it. Did you approve of Stanley Kunitz?'

'Absolutely. I liked the one about the summer.'

'"End of Summer"? Good choice. But I have a different favourite.'

'Which one?'

'You have to guess.'

'But I haven't read all the poems yet.'

'Well, you do that then maybe we can have another coffee.'

'Is that a challenge?'

'Perhaps.' Another smile.

She closes the laptop. 'I've put your prescription through. You can collect it from the nearest chemist.'

'Thank you, Thea. Goodbye – I hope to see you again soon.'

He gets to his feet, pats Emee for one last time, then tips his cap in farewell before he leaves.

Thea locks the door behind him and takes the file out again. She decides to go back to Leo. The children have blamed him, but in the first two interviews he flatly denies everything and insists that he never left his cabin. The change comes in the third interview.

```
INTERVIEWER: Have you anything to add since
    the last time we spoke?
LEO RASMUSSEN: No.
INTERVIEWER: So you still claim that you
    fell asleep in your cabin, and spent the
    whole night there?
```

LEO RASMUSSEN: Yes.

INTERVIEWER: At this point I must inform you that your father has changed his statement.

LEO RASMUSSEN: Lasse is not my father.

INTERVIEWER: OK, your stepfather. He now says he arrived home at about midnight and found the stable door open and Bill gone. Bill is a horse that was stabled at the farm because Lasse was breaking him in.

Thea assumes that this remark is aimed at Leo's defence lawyer. She reads on.

INTERVIEWER: Lasse thought that Bill must have somehow broken out of his stall and escaped. He went to wake you so that you could help him search, but you weren't there.

LEO RASMUSSEN: Lasse's talking crap, as usual.

INTERVIEWER: Lasse says that he began to suspect that something was wrong. He returned to the stable and realised that Bill's bridle wasn't on its hook. He took his truck out to search. At about one o'clock he found Bill on one of the dirt tracks in the marsh, less than two kilometres from the stone circle. The horse was muddy, wet, and dripping with sweat. He was wearing his bridle, but the reins had been torn off. Lasse led him back to his stall and washed him down. It was gone two o'clock by the time he finished. He checked your cabin again, but you still weren't there. He went up to bed and says that he saw you from his bedroom window, limping across the yard.

LEO RASMUSSEN: That's crap.

INTERVIEWER: In what way?

LEO RASMUSSEN: He's lying. Lasse can't have seen me from his bedroom window; – it doesn't even face that way.

INTERVIEWER: But you did come home and cross the yard?

(SILENCE)

INTERVIEWER: Do you want to change your statement, Leo?

LEO RASMUSSEN: Er . . . C-can we take a break? Is that possible?

INTERVIEWER: No problem. Interview suspended 14.16.

Thea eagerly turns to the next page. The interview resumes less than twenty minutes later.

INTERVIEWER: OK, Leo, so you've had the opportunity to speak to your lawyer. Do you want to change your statement?

LEO RASMUSSEN: Mm . . . I did go out for a while on Walpurgis Night. I'd had an argument with Elita. I needed to speak to her.

INTERVIEWER: What was the argument about?

LEO RASMUSSEN: I . . . I wanted her to . . . to run away with me. Get away from Svartgården and Lasse. I'd arranged for us to borrow a cottage near Ystad – it was all sorted. But she didn't want to come.

INTERVIEWER: Why not?

LEO RASMUSSEN: She said she had other plans.

INTERVIEWER: What other plans?

LEO RASMUSSEN: She wouldn't tell me. Elita could be very secretive.

INTERVIEWER: Did that bother you? The fact that she was keeping secrets from you?

LEO RASMUSSEN: A bit, maybe.

INTERVIEWER: Were you in love with her?

LEO RASMUSSEN: (INAUDIBLE)

INTERVIEWER: Could you please repeat that, Leo? Were you in love with her?

LEO RASMUSSEN: Yes. Yes, I was.

INTERVIEWER: So you got angry when she refused to run away with you?

LEO RASMUSSEN: Mm. I said a whole lot of stuff. Stupid stuff. Then I locked myself away in the cabin and drank. I was hurt. Then I started to regret what I'd said. I wanted to talk to her, maybe apologise. I don't really remember what I was thinking.

INTERVIEWER: So what did you do?

LEO RASMUSSEN: I knew she was going to be at the stone circle, that she'd planned to act out the spring sacrifice ritual. But it was too far to walk, so I took Bill.

INTERVIEWER: What time was that?

LEO RASMUSSEN: I'm not sure – eleven thirty? I'd drunk quite a lot. I rode off towards the castle forest. There was a full moon, so it was easy to see the way, but Bill was skittish.

INTERVIEWER: Skittish?

LEO RASMUSSEN: Agitated. The least sound spooked him. He's not fully broken in yet. Something in the forest scared him, an animal maybe. He went crashing straight through a thicket and a branch hit me on the head and knocked me off.

INTERVIEWER: Go on.

LEO RASMUSSEN: I lay there for a while, I think. I don't know if I passed out, or if it was just the effects of the booze. When I came round Bill was gone. I knew Lasse would be furious, so I spent ages looking for him before I went back to Svartgården. When I got there Bill was back in his stall, so I went to my cabin and got into bed. I was bruised and drunk – I fell asleep right away.

INTERVIEWER: Why didn't you tell us this from the start?

LEO RASMUSSEN: Because Lasse hates me. Because I knew he'd try and blame all this on me. I thought the less I said, the better.

INTERVIEWER: So if I've understood you correctly, you never made it to the stone circle.

LEO RASMUSSEN: No, I didn't. I never even reached the ford over the canal.

INTERVIEWER: You didn't see Elita?

LEO RASMUSSEN: No.

INTERVIEWER: And your injuries? How do you explain the scratches on your face and hands?

LEO RASMUSSEN: I got them when Bill was galloping through the trees. It was pitch dark, I couldn't protect myself.

INTERVIEWER: And you still deny that you murdered Elita?

LEO RASMUSSEN: (INAUDIBLE MUMBLE)

INTERVIEWER: Could you please repeat your answer. Did you murder Elita Svart?

LEO RASMUSSEN: (CLEARS HIS THROAT) No, I didn't.

Thea takes a break, stretches as she tries to digest what she's just read. To begin with, Leo had lied about where he'd been on Walpurgis Night. Then, when Lasse suddenly and unexpectedly made a statement dropping him in it, he'd changed his story so that it explained Lasse's story and his own injuries. It sounded a lot like something he'd come up with after the event. Not a word about a death pact – not yet, anyway.

Emee has started wandering around the room. Thea grabs her jacket and puts the dog on the lead. The corridor outside the surgery is still empty. Maybe the weather is keeping people at home? At least it's almost stopped raining.

She puts a BACK SOON sign on the door and takes Emee for a walk around the former schoolyard, then crosses the road and enters the churchyard.

The church itself is in darkness, and the wind is whistling through the tall poplars. The rose is still on Elita's grave, but a few of the petals have fallen off.

There is something about what Thea has just read that is bothering her. Perhaps it's connected to the fact that she dreamed of her father last night.

Lasse Svart was openly hostile to the police at first, saying virtually nothing, which fits perfectly with his character. Men like Lasse and Thea's father never talk to the police; it's part of their DNA. In spite of this, Lasse suddenly changed his mind and became much more talkative. Not only that, he dumped a family member in the shit. Something that should have been unthinkable.

Why did he do that? Why did he break the unwritten rule?

Thea lights a cigarette, remains standing by Elita's grave as she smokes it.

> ELITA SVART 12.02.1970 – 30.04.1986
> LOVED. MISSED.

By whom?

Emee moves restlessly, whimpers. Maybe it's the dog's reaction that triggers something in Thea, because all at once she feels as if she's being watched. As if someone is standing behind her, hidden in the gloom between the poplars and the wall, observing her.

She turns her head a fraction, thinks she sees a faint movement out of the corner of her eye, but when she spins around there's no one there. The only thing that's moving is the churchyard gate, slowly closing.

45

There are still no patients waiting when Thea returns. She unlocks the door, takes down the BACK SOON sign.

Emee pushes past her, stops dead in the middle of the room, ears pricked, sniffing the air.

Thea stops too. The dog is right; there's something different about the surgery, a faint smell of wet clothes that isn't coming from Thea.

Her heart rate increases. She checks the drugs cabinet, but it's locked, and there's nothing to suggest that anyone has tried to break in. Plus her laptop is still on the desk.

Next to the laptop is the bouquet of flowers with the welcome card from Monday. It was waiting for her when Dr Andersson unlocked the surgery, which means that other people have keys. Maybe all the keys are skeleton keys, like hers?

She sniffs, but any sense of an intruder has been replaced by the smell of wet dog.

Of course it could be Dr Andersson who'd forgotten something, or one of the ladies from the café who came looking for her. However, she can't quite shake off the feeling of unease from the churchyard, the feeling of being watched.

She sits down at her desk. Elita Svart's case file is in front of her, closed. Did she leave it like that?

Get a grip, Thea!

She opens the file, turns to the second interview with Elita's father. She is disappointed to find a summary read out by the interviewer and formally accepted by Lasse Svart, rather than a transcript of the tape recording.

Lasse gave the same information that Thea has already read in Leo's interview. He got home just after midnight, discovered the Bill and Leo were gone, found the horse in the forest, agitated and covered in mud. He washed the animal down, then went up to the house. Saw Leo limping across the yard at about two.

Lasse's unexpected talkativeness clearly surprised the interviewer too.

```
When asked why he had chosen to alter his
previous statement, Lasse Svart states
that he does not want to see a murderer
get away with his crime, and that the man
who has killed his little girl must be
brought to justice.
```

The answer sounds entirely logical, yet Thea finds it hard to believe. She tries to imagine her own father in the same situation. What would he have done if she'd been murdered? Certainly not this. He would probably have taken matters into his own hands.

The interview is dated 5 May, which means it took Lasse five days to decide to co-operate with the police. Five days – does that have any significance?

She turns back to the interviews with Leo. The one she read before taking Emee out was held the day after Lasse altered his statement. It is followed by five more in which Leo sticks rigidly to his second version, which is that he fell off the horse and never went to the stone circle.

The next change comes in the ninth and final interview, dated 27 May. By then Leo has been in custody for almost four weeks. Four weeks in a cell. What might that do to a twenty-year-old?

46

27 May 1986

L eo was woken by the racket from the cell next door, loud yelling followed by a rhythmic banging that passed through metal and concrete, causing a faint vibration in his bunk.

He shook his head, trying to clear his mind. Had he slept, and if so, for how long? Was it night or day? Day, presumably, because his neighbour usually kicked off just before lunch.

He'd requested a move several times, but had been told that the custody suite was full. A lie, along with the lie that the flickering fluorescent tube on the ceiling couldn't be switched off.

Leo rolled over onto his side, covered his eyes with his forearm.

The sagging waterproof mattress stank of sweat and fear; it was almost impossible to find a comfortable sleeping position. Although sleeping was the wrong word. He hadn't slept properly for several weeks. The closest he came was a grey fog in which his thoughts metamorphosed into images, faces, voices.

Did you kill her, Leo? Did you kill Elita?

'No,' he mumbled, and was shocked by the rasping sound of his own voice.

Elita was dead. It still felt so unreal – like a nasty joke, an absurd nightmare from which he would wake at any moment.

He could see her face in his mind's eye, the way she'd looked the second after he'd beaten Lasse at arm wrestling. Her smile, the promises he thought he'd seen in her sparkling eyes. But he'd been mistaken.

You wanted her to run away with you, but she rejected you.

Elita toyed with your emotions. You were angry with her, weren't you, Leo?

'No,' he mumbled again.

He tried to gather his thoughts, repeat the story he'd practised so many times, but it was becoming more and more difficult. The words slithered around, slid away in the fog that filled his head.

Yes, he'd been disappointed.

Yes, he'd drunk more than he usually did because he was upset. Yes, he'd made a stupid decision.

You dressed up as the Green Man, took Bill out, rode into the stone circle. We know that. We've matched the hoof prints. You scared the children who were there half to death.

And then, when they'd run away, you were alone with Elita.

He shook his head, tried to silence the voices.

Bill threw him off in the forest. He definitely remembered lying on the ground on his back, looking up at the treetops, a patch of sky, the moon and the stars. He could see them now, as clearly as the flickering fluorescent light.

Bill had thrown him.

But maybe he did that on the way back?

Maybe you were so shocked, so shaken by what you'd done that you lost control of the horse?

Maybe you fell so hard that you don't remember what happened?

Maybe . . .

'No!' He shook his head, tried to blink away the scalding tears. He hadn't done it. Hadn't done it, hadn't . . .

. . . killed Elita. Are you absolutely certain of that, Leo? Are you sure it wasn't you?

The images tormented him, disturbed his sleep even more than his crazy neighbour and the flickering light.

Elita on her back on the sacrificial stone. Her hands crossed over her chest, holding the antlers, her face covered with a white handkerchief.

A perpetrator covers his victim's face because he's ashamed, Leo. Because he can't stand to see the victim's eyes.

The next image was worse.

Elita's face . . .

Beaten to a pulp. A single, powerful blow with a stone, according to the forensic pathologist. It takes real strength to cause injuries like that. You're strong, aren't you, Leo?

He turned over again, covered his eyes with his hands, desperate to escape the blinding light. He needed to talk to someone. His mother. When had he last heard from her? It must be at least a week ago.

No visits, no phone calls, no letters. Not since Elita's funeral. Why not?

Because she's started to have doubts, Leo. Just like you. Not even your mother believes you're innocent now. We have a witness who saw you bending over Elita on the sacrificial stone.

'No!'

He buried his face in the paper pillowcase.

The voice grew softer, working its way into his brain.

You loved her, didn't you, Leo? You'd have done anything for her. She says so herself, in her letter.

Is that what happened? You didn't do it out of anger, but out of . . .

Love.

Do you love me, Leo?

He sat bolt upright, rubbed his eyes with his fists. His neighbour had fallen silent. When? Impossible to tell. He'd completely lost track of time.

'Leo would do anything for me. Whatever I ask of him.' That's what she wrote in her letter. She wrote that she was going to die, that she'd chosen someone to help her. Is that what happened, Leo?

'No . . .'

He wrapped his arms around his knees, shook his head.

The image appeared once again, the same image that broke through the grey fog inside his head with increasing frequency. It could be a dream – at least that was what he kept telling himself, but it felt so real.

Elita lying on her back on the sacrificial stone. Eyes open. Looking straight through him.

Do you love me, Leo?

'Yes,' he sobbed. 'Yes, I love you.' He hid his face between his knees.

I am the spring sacrifice, Elita whispered. *All that dies shall be reborn.*

She gasped. Her eyes widened. He could see his own reflection in them. One hand was raised above his head. It felt as heavy as a stone.

Do you love me?

Did you kill her, Leo?

Do you love me?

Did you kill her . . .

The bang made him jump. The sound of one of the guards hammering on his door.

'Up you get, Rasmussen. The police want to question you again.'

47

INTERVIEWER: You said you were never at the stone circle.

LEO RASMUSSEN: That's correct.

INTERVIEWER: And you're absolutely sure of that?

LEO RASMUSSEN: Yes.

INTERVIEWER: Just like you're absolutely sure that you didn't see Elita.

LEO RASMUSSEN: Yes. Can I ask a question?

INTERVIEWER: What?

LEO RASMUSSEN: My mother hasn't been to see me for over a week. Not since Elita's . . . (INAUDIBLE)

INTERVIEWER: Not since Elita's funeral?

LEO RASMUSSEN: Yes. She used to come every day.

INTERVIEWER: I know.

LEO RASMUSSEN: I'm worried that something might have happened to her.

INTERVIEWER: So she didn't say anything to you?

LEO RASMUSSEN: About what?

INTERVIEWER: Your family have gone, Leo. Left you in the lurch.

LEO RASMUSSEN: When?

INTERVIEWER: The day after the funeral. One of the guys from the castle called round and the place was empty, the cars gone. No one has seen Lasse, Lola or your mother since then.

LEO RASMUSSEN: That can't be right. Are you looking for them?

INTERVIEWER: Why would we do that? None of them is suspected of a crime. And you're an adult – twenty years old, with your own lawyer. You don't need any help from your mummy, do you?

LEO RASMUSSEN: (INAUDIBLE)

INTERVIEWER: Let's go back to Walpurgis Night. So you're absolutely certain that you weren't at the stone circle, and you didn't see Elita?

LEO RASMUSSEN: Yes.

INTERVIEWER: The thing is, we've found something very close to the spot where the body was discovered. Can you tell me what this is?

LEO RASMUSSEN: It's . . . It's my cap badge. From my beret.

INTERVIEWER: ND. Norrland Dragoons. A cavalry regiment originally, I believe. I myself was a coastal ranger. I know how hard you have to work to be awarded your beret and badge. It's something precious, isn't it?

LEO RASMUSSEN: Well, yes . . .

INTERVIEWER: So how do you explain the fact that your badge ended up in the forest only twenty-five metres from Elita's dead body?

LEO RASMUSSEN: I . . . (INAUDIBLE)

INTERVIEWER: Could you repeat that, please?

LEO RASMUSSEN: I can't explain . . .

INTERVIEWER: 'Leo would do anything for me. Whatever I ask of him.' That's what she wrote in her letter. Is that what happened, Leo? Did Elita want you to kill her? Was that why she was waiting for you in the forest? Was the whole thing actually her idea?

LEO RASMUSSEN: No, no, no!

INTERVIEWER: Elita was manipulative – plenty of people have said so. She was fascinated by death, and wanted to be the spring sacrifice. Did you agree to help her, Leo? Did you pick up a stone and hold it above your head as she lay there on her back in her white dress? Maybe you didn't intend it to go any further?

LEO RASMUSSEN: No, no . . .

INTERVIEWER: You were angry with her – perhaps that made it easier. She'd rejected you. If you couldn't have her, then nor could anyone else. Or was it all just a game? Elita liked games, dressing up, acting out little stories. She liked to be the centre of attention. She didn't want you, didn't want to run away with you, and yet she'd had the nerve to ask you to help her with this stupid charade. You were angry, hurt and drunk. And now she was lying there in front of you, kitted out as the spring sacrifice, asking you to kill her. The woman who'd just turned you down, laughed at your pain. All you had to do was bring the stone down on her face – that would stop her laughing. Maybe you didn't even do it deliberately. Maybe you just dropped the stone. Maybe the whole thing was just a tragic accident?

LEO RASMUSSEN: (SOBS)

INTERVIEWER: Perhaps your mother can't stand any more of your lies, Leo. She's realised what actually happened, and she's not coming back until you tell the truth.

LEO RASMUSSEN: (CRIES)

INTERVIEWER: I can see you're suffering, Leo. You'll feel better as soon as you get it off your chest. Was it an accident, Leo?

LEO RASMUSSEN: I . . . I don't remember. I fell off the horse. (CRIES) My mother . . .

INTERVIEWER: But you do remember being there? In the stone circle?

LEO RASMUSSEN: M-maybe.

INTERVIEWER: And that you were angry with Elita?

LEO RASMUSSEN: Yes. (CRIES) But I loved her.

INTERVIEWER: So you did it out of love? Could it have been an act of love? Because she asked you to do it?

LEO RASMUSSEN: Maybe. (CRIES)

INTERVIEWER: It's OK, Leo. You're doing really well.

LEO RASMUSSEN: (SOBS HELPLESSLY)

INTERVIEWER: So shall we say that you did it out of love?

INTERVIEWER: You're nodding, Leo, but you have to say it out loud for the tape. Did you kill Elita out of love?

LEO RASMUSSEN: Mm . . .

Thea lets out a long, slow breath. In spite of the dry, typewritten transcript, she can feel the charged atmosphere in the room. The interviewer was manipulative, exploiting Leo's isolation, his love for Elita, the sense of abandonment he must have felt, knowing that his mother had gone.

She doesn't know if the police are allowed to do that. Her only experience is what she's seen on TV crime shows, and it's nothing like what she's just read.

She rubs her forehead, feeling overwhelmed by the whole thing. Exhausted. But there is one document she hasn't yet read, and which interests her. Something she knows a lot more about than police interrogation and crime scene reports.

The form is old and typewritten, but she is familiar with the language of the autopsy report from her time as a forensic pathologist.

The summary on the first page is aimed at non-medical personnel, such as police officers, prosecutors, defence lawyers and judges. It states baldly that Elita Svart died as a result of blunt force trauma to the head. Her injuries indicated that she was subjected to one or possibly two violent blows to the upper part of the face, which led to instantaneous death. The murder weapon is described as a large blunt object, probably a stone.

There were no traces on the body that could be linked to a possible perpetrator. No fragments of skin under Elita's nails to suggest a struggle, although there was a certain amount of soil. Several strands of hair were found on her clothing; the reader is referred to a different technical report. Thea checks and learns that these hairs come from horses and dogs – the animals that lived at Svartgården.

A more detailed account of the autopsy itself follows the summary. Thea soon realises that something isn't right. The beginning and end are there, but a chunk is missing in the middle. She assumes that the original document pages stuck together, so the archivist failed to copy this section. However, when she checks the pagination, she sees that there are no pages missing – and yet the report is definitely incomplete.

She takes a closer look at the numbers from the middle onwards. The typeface looks slightly different, and the numbers are about a centimetre further to the right than in the rest of the document. She photographs some of them with her phone, then enlarges the image on the screen and plays around with the brightness. In a couple of places she thinks she can see a faint, uneven shadow right next to the numbers – as if someone has Tippexed over the original then typed a different one.

Maybe it doesn't mean anything. If the pathologist had found something significant, it would have been included in the summary on the first page. She photographs that too, adjusts the brightness once more. No Tippex shadows this time, but there is something almost at the bottom. A thin line across the page could indicate that someone placed a piece of white paper over the original so that the last sentence didn't appear on the copy. A kind of Eighties version of Photoshop.

Thea goes through the autopsy report once more just to make sure, and reaches the same conclusion.

One page is missing – the examination of Elita's stomach. Someone has removed that page, and tried to hide the information.

What could they have found in her stomach that was so controversial that someone went to so much effort to keep it quiet?

A sentence from Elita's letter pops into Thea's head.

Because no secret is greater than mine.

She rubs her forehead again. Tries to tell herself that she's wrong, that there must be a perfectly simple explanation for the missing page. But the suspicion has already taken root in her mind. It grows and grows until it becomes a conviction.

Elita Svart must have been pregnant when she was murdered.

48

The hea spends the drive home trying to get her head straight. Elita's pregnancy is not mentioned in any of the interviews, which means that the interviewer probably didn't know about it. Therefore, the person who removed the page from the autopsy report must have come across the information at an early stage and taken steps to ensure that no one else found out.

The autopsy was just a formality, really. The cause of death had already been established, and there was no evidence pointing to Leo. Therefore, it's likely that the investigating officers would have read the summary and nothing else, and the pathologist wasn't called to give evidence at Leo's trial.

But if Thea is right, if Elita really was pregnant, then who concealed that information – and why? The report should have been sent to the senior investigating officer.

She slows down at a junction and is so lost in thought that she barely notices that the car on the opposite side of the road is flashing its lights at her. The driver is waving as if he wants something.

She stays put as he drives towards her and stops with his side window next to hers. It's Per Nygren.

'Good afternoon, Doctor,' he says with his usual smile. 'Everything OK?'

'Yes, thanks – I'm just trying to get into the daily routine.'

'Excellent. It'll be great to see Bokelund all fixed up soon. I haven't been inside the castle for years – not since the old count's time.'

Another smile, just on the borderline between charming and flirtatious.

'What was he like?' She thinks of the painting in Hubert's library.

'Rudolf? A hard master. I don't think I ever saw him smile, but he and my father got along well. He was actually my godfather.'

'Oh – so you must know Hubert?'

Per nods. 'We used to play together when we were children. Have you met him?'

'Yes, a couple of times.'

'Good. Hubert needs to get out and meet people.' Per leans out of the window a fraction. 'As you might know, he didn't go to the village school with the rest of us; he had a private tutor. Unfortunately, that made him a little reclusive. A bit different. But he's well worth getting to know.'

The tenderness in Per's voice surprises her a little.

'Anyway, I must go – I don't want to be late for rehearsal.'

'Rehearsal?'

'I'm in a band – we get together a couple of times a week. It's mostly for fun, but we play the odd gig – weddings, fiftieth birthdays, that kind of thing. Plus I run an open mic night at Gästis in Ljungslöv. You ought to come along some time.'

Only now does Thea notice the guitar case on the passenger seat. 'I might just do that.'

'I'll look forward to it. Have a nice evening, Doctor!'

He is about to close the window when she stops him. The question has been burning in her brain ever since she found the blood on Emee's coat.

'Any news on the deer? Was it a wolf?'

The smile fades. 'We still don't know. Whatever it is, it took a pregnant hind yesterday.'

'Where?' She wishes she hadn't asked. Holds her breath, waiting for the answer.

'Same place as before – over by the western meadow.'

'That's so sad.' She glances in the rear-view mirror at Emee, whose head is sticking up above the back seat.

'Yes. We're going to have to come up with a new strategy soon; this can't go on. But don't worry; it's not the first time we've had problems with predators in the enclosures. Hunting is all about patience. And cunning. A bit like love.' He winks at her, closes the window and drives off.

David's car is in its usual place. Just like yesterday evening, Thea is struck by a sudden desire to be close to him. It's as if every little piece of Elita's story makes her understand him better, helps her to know who the real David is.

She parks her car and goes into the castle, calling his name. She thinks she can hear noises from upstairs; she searches around for a while before she spots the ladder and the open loft hatch in the bridal suite. That's where the voices are coming from.

'Hello?' she shouts.

David's face appears in the gap. 'Hi, Thea!' He looks pleased to see her.

'What are you doing?'

'We're getting ready to install a lightning rod. We can't afford to have a power cut in the middle of the high season. Come up and see!'

Thea clambers up the steep ladder. She says hello to the workman in dungarees and small round glasses who is inspecting the inside of the roof by the light of a builder's lamp. The loft is huge, the floor covered with sturdy planks. Removal crates and old pieces of furniture are dotted here and there. Beyond the glow of the lamp, the darkness is dense.

'Cool, isn't it? We could have ghost walks up here. Get a couple of the summer staff to dress up as the dead girls.'

Thea is taken aback, then realises he's talking about the two girls Hubert mentioned, not Elita Svart.

'The loft runs all the way through the castle, so we could finish above the old chapel,' he goes on, pointing into the gloom. 'There are some crosses and a pretty horrible statue of a saint over there that nearly frightened us to death. Take a look for yourself.'

'No thanks!' Thea says. There's plenty of headroom up here, but the smell and the darkness somehow remind her of a cellar.

'I'll be another hour or so,' David informs her. 'Mum and Dad have invited us to dinner. Nettan will be there too, so you'll be able to meet her at last. See you later.'

Thea hesitates. To be honest she has no desire to have dinner with David's parents yet again, particularly with Nettan as an unexpected guest. However, David is in a good mood. Presumably he didn't see the file this morning, which is a relief, so she decides not to raise any objections.

Her in-laws' Mercedes is parked outside the coach house. In the kitchen Ingrid has made coffee and set out fresh rolls with a selection of toppings.

'Hi, Thea, come on in. I thought you'd be hungry after work. I've got a bone for the dog too – there you go, sweetheart.'

Ingrid holds out a big meaty bone. Emee immediately grabs it and settles down under the kitchen table.

'Coffee?'

'Please.'

Thea takes off her jacket and shoes and sits down. The place looks different from when she left this morning. The removal boxes that were stacked by the walls have been unpacked and cleared away. The furniture is where it's meant to be, the books are in alphabetical order, and even her jigsaws have been allocated their own space on a shelf. The whole house smells of detergent.

Ingrid pours the coffee while Thea tries not to show how much it bothers her that her mother-in-law has been poking around among her things.

'How's it going at work? Has Dr Andersson handed over the reins?'

'She has.'

'Excellent.' Ingrid pauses, just long enough to enable her to change the subject. 'Listen, there was something I wanted to talk to you about. People have started talking about you.' She breaks off, takes a sip of coffee.

'Talking?'

'In the village. On Facebook. The word is that our new much longed-for doctor is taking a slightly unhealthy interest in an old murder case.'

'That's not true.'

'No? Well, that's what people are saying. You have to under-stand . . .' Ingrid leans across the table. 'If you and David are going to build a future here in Tornaby, it's important for you to become a part of the community. Learn the village's unwritten rules. One of them is not to bring up that terrible business of Elita Svart and her brother.'

Thea nods, mainly because she doesn't have a choice.

'The police investigation and the trial were terribly traumatic for David and his friends.'

'And for Elita's family,' Thea blurts out.

Ingrid recoils slightly, narrows her eyes.

'Elita's family disappeared as soon as the girl was in the ground,' she says dryly. 'They left the farm without so much as a word, with the rent unpaid. But that was probably the wisest decision Lasse Svart ever made.'

'Why do you say that?'

Ingrid pursed her lips. 'In the past he'd always been able to lie low, keep himself to himself out there with his women and his dodgy dealings. But because of what happened to Elita, all that changed. He was in the spotlight. All eyes were on him, and he was smart enough to realise that.'

She tilts her head to one side.

'I know the story might seem fascinating to an outsider. Ritual murder, a death pact – that's what the newspapers wrote at the time. In fact, Elita Svart's death was nothing but a . . .'

'Family tragedy,' Thea supplies.

'Exactly.' Ingrid has either missed the ironic tone or, more likely, has chosen to ignore it. 'A terrible story that no one in the area wants to be reminded of. Especially David.'

'Or Bertil.'

Ingrid's face stiffens.

'Bertil isn't the man he used to be – I think you already know that.' She gives a strained smile. 'But there are few people who have been as important for Tornaby as Bertil has. He's helped so many families with their problems. The village and its residents have a great deal to thank him for, let me tell you. Without Bertil . . .'

Ingrid purses her lips again, this time as if to stop herself from saying any more. She gets to her feet, brushing a few imaginary crumbs from her dress.

'Well, I'd better make a move. I have to go shopping before dinner. If you have any further questions about Elita Svart, I suggest you speak to Arne. He was involved in the investigation, and he knows all the details. And he's not interested in gossip. OK?'

Ingrid doesn't wait for an answer, but picks up her handbag and heads for the door. Then she stops.

'I'm so glad we've sorted this out, Thea. I'll see you this evening. Oh, by the way – I brought in the post.' She points to the hallstand. 'I think there's a letter for you.'

The front door closes behind her. Thea remains seated at the kitchen table. Has her mother-in-law just warned her off digging into the case of Elita Svart? Not in so many words, but this unexpected visit must surely be seen as a warning. What is it about Elita that still bothers people so much?

She collects the post and settles down on the sofa. There's a parcel on top; it must be the book she ordered. Then bills, but right at the bottom she finds an envelope with her name and address written by hand. She opens it slowly, filled with trepidation even before she unfolds the letter. As she begins to read, she feels as if all the air has been knocked out of her lungs.

Hi, Jenny!

It's been a while. You seem to be doing well.

Dad saw you on TV. He'd like to talk to you. No need to worry, he's not angry with you, but he wants you to come home. Right now.

Best wishes,

Ronny

49

The rest of the afternoon passes in a fog. David comes home, they change their clothes, get in the car, drive to David's parents. It's as if Thea is observing the whole thing from the outside.

All her defences have been torn down – because of a stupid TV feature. The latest in a series of very bad decisions she's made over the past year.

She shouldn't have married David, shouldn't have moved down here, shouldn't have stood there on the castle steps, shouldn't have let herself be persuaded to appear on camera.

'Are you OK?' David asks as they arrive. 'You're very quiet.'

'I'm just tired.'

'We don't have to go in if it's too much for you. Do you want me to take you home?'

He sounds as if he means it, and she fights the urge to say yes.

'No, it's fine. I'll feel better when I've had something to eat.'

They greet David's parents. Thea has to force herself to hug her mother-in-law. This is all Ingrid's fault: the move, the restaurant, the TV feature. It was all her idea.

But you went along with it. For David's sake . . .

She would like to tell Margaux to shut up. In fact, she would like to tell them all to shut up so that she can sort out the mess inside her head.

Just as David had said, Nettan is there. She's a smart woman, she's worked all over the world, and she's both friendly and polite. Thea does her best to be present and friendly in return, and yet there is immediately a tension between them. Perhaps it's because Nettan calls David's parents Aunt Ingrid and Uncle Bertil. Or because she touches David's arm in a special way from time to time.

David notices the strained atmosphere, flaps around them in a way that Thea doesn't like.

'I'm sorry if I stole David away from you the other day,' Nettan says. 'I could have taken a taxi, but he insisted on picking me up from Kastrup.'

'No problem,' Thea mutters. She is trying to be pleasant, but it's difficult. Her head is spinning, not only because of the letter, but everything she's read over the past few days. Every time she looks at Nettan, she can hear the twelve-year-old girl's voice in the interviews.

'Do you often visit Tornaby?' she manages to ask.

Nettan shakes her head. 'No. My father died a while ago, and by then he and my mother had already moved to Malmö. This is the first time I've been back for years. I couldn't wait to get away, for various reasons.' She pulls a face which is hard to interpret. 'Mum lives with me in Switzerland now; she helps out with the children when I'm away.' Nettan takes a sip of her drink. 'How about you? How are you finding life out here?'

'Good,' Thea replies.

Nettan leans a little closer. 'You don't have to be polite. David's told me about your travels. You're restless, just like me. It's difficult to stay in one place for very long. So why would you want to settle here, in the middle of nowhere?'

The comment surprises Thea. It seems honest rather than snide.

'I . . . I've grown tired of going from one place to another.'

'Grown tired?' Nettan raises an eyebrow. 'Is that possible?' She leans even closer, lowers her voice. 'I mean, don't misunderstand me. David's a good guy, but neither of you should be here. There's still a lot of old crap bubbling away beneath the surface. More than you can imagine. You need to be careful.'

'Careful about what?' David appears from nowhere.

'Oh, nothing. Thea and I were just chatting,' Nettan says. 'If you'll excuse me I'm going to top up my drink.'

David's Uncle Arne has also been invited, presumably to even up the numbers. He's dressed for the occasion; he's wearing a scarf with his shirt and jacket, his moustache is neatly trimmed, and he smells of aftershave. He glides over to Thea and David in a way that is presumably meant to convey self-confidence.

'So have you settled in, Dr Lind? Worked out who has piles and who suffers from erectile dysfunction?'

'Absolutely. Don't worry, your secrets are safe with me.'

She doesn't know why she says that. Maybe because the part of her brain that normally filters her behaviour is otherwise occupied.

Arne stiffens, then bursts out laughing.

'Your wife is very funny, little David,' he says, thumping his nephew on the back. 'You hang onto her!'

David smiles, but Thea can see that the comment irritates him. He doesn't like being called little David, doesn't want to be reminded of the person he was. Nor does she.

She can't stop thinking about the letter. Her father wants her to come home. What happens if she doesn't go? Dare she even contemplate that idea?

Bertil is having a pretty good day – possibly because of his new medication.

He joins in the conversation over pre-dinner drinks, remembering names and places. Thea hasn't seen him since the incident in the forest, but neither Bertil nor anyone else mentions it. At one point he gently pats her on the back and gives her a little smile, which is presumably a silent thank you.

After their drinks they sit down at the table. The food is delicious as always, and David has brought several bottles of wine from the castle. Ingrid gives Arne a meaningful look every time he refills his glass; Thea is keeping an eye on him too. He's trying to charm Nettan, telling her stories about his police work that become more and more detailed as his wine consumption increases. He ignores his big sister completely. The interaction – or lack of it – between the two of them is actually quite entertaining, and makes Thea forget the letter for a little while.

'So when's the big day?' Arne asks when he finally reaches the end of a lengthy tale about a huntsman, a dog with diarrhoea and a bullet that accidentally hits a windscreen.

'You mean the launch?' David says. 'End of May, but we're having a dinner on Walpurgis Night. The first test, so to speak.'

'When's Sebastian arriving?' Nettan wants to know.

'He had a meeting in London, but his flight lands first thing tomorrow morning. He'll be here in time for lunch.'

'Sebastian has done very well,' Ingrid says, half-turning towards Bertil. 'He started a technology company when he left university, remember? He has over a thousand employees right across the world.'

'Of course I remember.' Bertil sounds slightly offended. 'How are his parents?'

'They moved to Helsingborg, then home to Poland when Pawel retired,' Ingrid says. 'Sebastian bought them a big house by the sea. I'm friends with them on Facebook. Theresa's still hoping for grandchildren, but Sebastian isn't ready to settle down.'

'Am I invited?' Arne fills his glass over-enthusiastically, splashing red wine onto the cloth. 'To the Walpurgis Night dinner?'

David shuffles uncomfortably, exchanges a glance with his mother, who comes to his rescue.

'David didn't think it would be your kind of thing, Arne.'

'Not my kind of thing? A dinner with good food and expensive wines?' He points unsteadily at David. 'Tell the truth – you're afraid I'll show you up in front of all your fine friends.'

David shuffles again. Ingrid opens her mouth, but Arne silences her with a gesture. His eyelids are heavy, his face red and puffy.

'No, let the boy answer for himself. Why am I not invited? After everything I've done for you? It's thanks to me that the two of you and that poverty-stricken little Pole ended up with such successful lives.'

He wags his index finger at David, then at Nettan.

'If Uncle Arne hadn't stepped in and sorted things out that night . . .'

'Shut the fuck up, Arne!'

'What?' Arne jerks back as if he's been punched in the face.

'Shut the fuck up, you stupid bastard!' Bertil's voice is rough, the look in his eyes ice-cold.

249

Arne blinks a couple of times, stares blankly at Bertil, then his sister.

'I was just having a little joke with the boy, Bertil. You know I'd never . . .'

He clears his throat, looks away. Bertil is still staring at him. Ingrid places a hand on her husband's arm.

'Of course you're welcome at the dinner, Arne,' she says. 'Our family sticks together, isn't that right?'

She smiles at Bertil, squeezes his arm. After a couple of seconds his expression softens.

'Of course, of course,' he murmurs.

They have coffee and cognac in the library. Bertil shows Nettan his bridge trophy; she pretends to admire it, just as Thea did. Thea is trying to stop studying the other woman, but Nettan touched on a sore point earlier.

Is she really intending to stay here with David forever, give up travelling for good?

And what did Nettan mean when she told her to be careful?

Arne still looks cowed. He glances at Bertil from time to time, clearly embarrassed. Thea is about to go over and talk to him when David slips an arm around her waist.

'Feeling better?'

'Definitely.'

'Good . . .' David sounds as if he doesn't believe her. 'Sorry about that business with Arne. You have to take whatever he says with a pinch of salt. He's a bit too fond of . . .' David pretends to drink from an invisible glass.

'Well, your dad certainly put him in his place,' she says.

David laughs. 'Yes, Dad's always kept an eye on Arne. He was the one who got him into the police back in the day, otherwise God knows what would have happened to him.'

'What do you mean?'

David shrugs. 'He used to get into trouble when he was a teenager, but Dad sorted him out. He's always been something of a father figure to Arne.'

Thea glances at Arne. He'd come rushing over to the lodge the other morning, treated Bertil with a kind of respectful reverence that can be seen in his anxious glances this evening. He'd probably do anything for Bertil, just as Ronny would for their own father.

Dad wants you to come home. Right now.

50

'You're right, Margaux. It's time for me to talk about my own ghosts. About the ones I've left behind. About the person I once was.

'Jenny Boman. That was my name.

'At a different time. In a different life.'

Mum is so thin lying there in the bed, her cheekbones look as if they could pierce holes in her skin, which is almost transparent. The little hair she has left almost disappears into the pillow.

They've been sitting with her for half an hour, maybe more, and Dad is getting restless. Even though he is in cancer's innermost room, he is desperate for a cigarette. One heel waggles up and down, his fingers drum on his thigh. Mum is sleeping. Her eyelids flicker like a butterfly's wings. Her breathing is shallow.

Dad looks at his watch for at least the third time. Gets to his feet.

'We need to go. There's something I have to do on the way home.'

There's always something he has to do, but no one is allowed to ask what it is. He tosses the car key to Ronny.

'Fetch the car and I'll see you out the front. I'm just going for a smoke.'

Ronny nods, kisses Mum gently on the cheek before he leaves the room.

Dad's hand on her shoulder. 'It'll be OK, Jenny. You can always try again.'

She knows he's trying to console her, and yet she can't take in what he's saying. Her head is empty. Her belly hurts.

Miscarriage. A bloody fragment in her knickers a few mornings ago. A child she didn't even realise she was expecting.

'I'm sure it'll work out next time,' Dad whispers, his breath smelling of cigarette smoke. 'You and Jocke have your whole lives in front of you. He's a good lad. Reliable.'

She knows what he means by that. What Jocke must have done to deserve that accolade. Dad heads for the door.

'Are you coming, Jenny?'

'In a minute.'

He nods, disappears into the corridor.

She goes over to her mother. Bends down and kisses her cheek. The tears are not far away. She really wants to push aside all the tubes and crawl into the bed. Be six or seven years old again, be comforted. For a moment she is on the way to becoming a child again, and Mummy is no longer dying, but young and healthy.

Then Mum opens her eyes and Jenny is back in the moment. Mum's expression is clear, full of sorrow. She takes Jenny's hand, squeezes it, pulls her close. Her fingers are cold and warm at the same time.

'The life insurance,' Mum whispers. 'Take the money, Jenny. Get away from here. Forget about us!'

It is still dark in the bedroom when Thea opens her eyes. The only point of light is the faint glow of the nightlight by the door. It is just after five, and as usual she is wide awake.

She switches on the bedside lamp. The damp patch on the ceiling has grown, it reminds her of a handprint, its long yellow fingers reaching further and further into the room.

Mum's words echo in her mind.

Forget about us!

Thea has tried, done her absolute best, but clearly her family haven't forgotten her. So what should she do? Ignore them?

What if Ronny sends his next letter to David? What if David finds out that she's lied about her background? That she isn't an orphan after all, that she's just a fucking . . . *gyppo*, like Elita Svart.

The idea that her father's world might somehow be linked to David, the castle or Tornaby is so unpleasant that her stomach turns over. A part of her brain, a terrified part, just wants to pack a bag, leave everything behind once more. Another part is resisting. For a while longer, at least.

She picks up her phone and opens a search engine. As usual she can't find any trace of her father. Leif stays away from the internet, he doesn't even have a registered address. Ronny is still at the same address as usual, which doesn't necessarily mean that he lives there. However, she's pretty sure he does. *Dad wants you to come home!*

She gets out of bed and goes over to the window. Emee looks up, watching her with those grey, ghostly eyes. The forest is dark and forbidding beyond the moat.

Thea fell pregnant at nineteen. Elita Svart was only sixteen. She must have been so frightened, but would she really have planned her death if she was carrying a child?

And an equally interesting question: who was the father? Could it have been Leo? For some reason Thea doesn't think so.

Because no secret is greater than mine . . .

What did Leo actually know? Maybe the book she ordered can throw some light on the matter, or at least help her to focus, shut down the part of her brain that is screaming at her to pack a bag.

False Confessions is a slim, stylishly written volume. The author, Kurt Bexell, lists a number of psychological mechanisms that can lead to false confessions; he also provides lots of statistics. The phenomenon of false confessions, he states, is more common among younger suspects, particularly if the crime may have been committed under the influence of drugs, and the suspect is subjected to aggressive interrogation methods combined with isolation.

Bexell goes through various cases that strengthen his hypothesis, all overseas. Thea recently saw a documentary about one of them: the police in New York got five young men to confess to a rape they hadn't committed.

She turns to chapter twelve.

In 1986, Leo Rasmussen confessed to the brutal murder of his stepsister Elita, who was four years his junior. At the time he was only twenty. Rasmussen stated that he was drunk when the crime took place, and couldn't remember his actions in detail. However, he flatly denied any involvement during eight interviews, and confessed only in the ninth. By then he'd been held in isolation for almost four weeks.

Rasmussen admitted killing his stepsister, and explained that he had acted in accordance with her wishes. He was convicted of manslaughter, and because of his age and the circumstances surrounding the crime he was sentenced to six years in prison. On the advice of his lawyer he decided not to appeal, since there was a significant risk that he would be handed a much longer sentence.

Rasmussen served his time, but later expressed doubt about his guilt. He claims he was subjected to enormous psychological pressure while in custody, that he was deliberately deprived of sleep, and was isolated from his family.

The witnesses who claimed to have seen Rasmussen at the scene of the crime were all children, and were initially interviewed together. This type of interrogation is against police regulations, and means that the children could have influenced one another's testimony.

The forensic evidence in the case was largely circumstantial, and certainly not definitive. There were no blood traces or fingerprints linking Rasmussen to the crime, and no murder weapon was found.

However, no alternative perpetrator for the murder of Elita Svart was ever sought. All resources in the police investigation were immediately concentrated on Leo Rasmussen.

Thea puts down the book. The sun is beginning to rise. She dresses quietly so as not to wake David. Emee comes out with her, reluctantly allowing herself to be put on the lead outside the front door. The birds in the forest are slowly waking.

Emee pulls on the lead, turns her head and glares at Thea to show that she wants to run free, but the incidents with the deer mean that Thea daren't let her go.

Her mind is darting between what she's just read, and Ronny's letter.

Was Leo the victim of a miscarriage of justice? And if so, is the doctored autopsy report a part of something much bigger?

Her father and her older brother want her to come home. It must have something to do with money. The money she took, the money she can't repay. So what is she going to do?

A branch snaps somewhere behind her. The sharp sound makes her stop dead. Emee flattens her ears and growls.

Suddenly the feeling Thea had in the churchyard is back. The feeling of being watched.

'Hello!' she calls out. 'Is anyone there?'

The only answer is the wind, soughing in the treetops.

51

'It feels as if everything is falling apart. The dampness has destroyed my walls, and is slowly seeping into what remains of my world. Maybe it would be best to leave, float away like a dragonfly. After all, I've done it before.

'Would anyone even miss me here? Would you miss me, Margaux?'

Sebastian Malinowski arrives just after ten. He is driving an expensive sports car and is accompanied by a young woman who can't be more than twenty-five, and is much too attractive for him.

He hasn't changed a great deal since the school photograph. He's about the same height as David and also has fair hair, but Sebastian is considerably slimmer and has a bald patch stretching a long way back from his forehead. He comes across as a mixture of a professor and a dynamic entrepreneur – but once he was just a frightened twelve-year-old, Thea thinks.

Nettan turns up a few minutes later in a dark blue rental car, followed by David's parents in their Mercedes. Ingrid is driving as usual.

David shows them up the castle steps. 'This way, ladies and gentlemen.' He's in a good mood.

In the entrance hall they are met by two waitresses who serve champagne. David then guides the group through the great hall, telling them about the history of the castle. Thea listens with half an ear; she's heard it before. Instead she discreetly studies Sebastian and Nettan. They are trying to act like old friends, yet they both seem a little stressed.

David stops by one of the portraits.

'This is Isabelle Gordon, who drowned in the moat during the tragic winter of 1753, on her way to a secret tryst with her lover. The first of our two beautiful ghosts.'

Thea suddenly remembers a phrase from Elita's letter.

Beautiful women dead that by my side. Once lay.

An odd construction, especially for a sixteen-year-old. Had Elita read it somewhere?

She recalls what Hubert told her about the two deaths, and wonders what David would say if he found out the truth. She suspects it wouldn't matter. He has chosen a narrative that suits him, so the truth is less relevant. Just as she did when she became Thea Lind.

David continues his guided tour, taking them through the drawing room and into the newly renovated kitchen, where he spends almost fifteen minutes talking about the ultra-modern equipment. They then move on to the dining room.

The curtains are open and the spring sunshine floods in through the tall windows. The chairs and tables have been set out, white cloths and napkins are in place. The gold panelling on the walls shimmers, the crystal chandeliers sparkle, with the lovely ceiling paintings high above.

'Space for ninety covers,' David says proudly. 'We've already got bookings well into the autumn.'

The doors to the terrace open, the waitresses return and top up their glasses. David pauses to chat to a member of staff and everyone starts mingling. Sebastian and his companion, whose name Thea didn't catch, go over to talk to David's parents. She decides to slip outside. This morning's breeze has died down, and it's warm enough to enjoy the fresh air without a jacket. She glances up at Hubert's window, hoping to catch a glimpse of him, but there's no sign. She thinks about the book, those beautiful, melancholy poems. About what he'd written on the flyleaf.

The strongest love is unrequited love.

For some reason the words make her feel better. They open a door inside her head to which her father has no access. To which no one has access.

She hears a movement behind her. Nettan has come out and is taking an e-cigarette out of her handbag when she sees Thea.

'I'm trying to give up smoking,' she says apologetically. 'It's not going too well, to be honest. These things aren't the same at all.'

Thea pulls a face which she hopes is sympathetic.

Nettan clicks the cigarette, takes a drag and exhales a puff of vapour.

'So what do you think about this circus? Can you cope?'

'Of course. This is what David has wanted for a long time.'

Nettan shakes her head slowly.

'David had no choice – we both know that. All this is down to Aunt Ingrid. She organised the whole thing – the castle, David, me and Sebastian. Brought the three of us together again after almost thirty years.'

Something in Nettan's tone irritates Thea. Gives her a reason to express her frustration.

'So why did you say yes, if you didn't want to be involved?'

Nettan takes another drag. Exhales and gazes at Thea with a wry smile.

'Because no one says no to Aunt Ingrid. I thought you'd have realised that by now.'

They end the tour upstairs as David shows off the recent renovations.

'This used to be the old schoolroom,' he says as they reach the bridal suite. It smells of paint and new furniture. The loft hatch is closed, barely visible against the freshly painted panel. Thea tries to picture Hubert in here, with only his governess for company.

A lonely little boy with no friends.

The thought makes her feel sad.

They have a light lunch in the breakfast room in the east wing. Their glasses are refilled, first with white wine, then red. Sebastian chats to David's parents, but Nettan is preoccupied with her phone and seems bored. David notices.

'We're going to have coffee somewhere else,' he announces. 'I've organised a little surprise.'

He points to the courtyard where the local taxi firm's minibus has just pulled up. Everyone gets to their feet, except for Ingrid and Bertil.

'Aren't you coming?' Thea asks.

'No, Bertil's tired,' her mother-in-law replies. 'You young people go and enjoy yourselves without us.'

Thea is the last to board the minibus. The atmosphere is lighter now. Sebastian and David are telling Sebastian's girl-friend a story; apparently her name is Bianca. Nettan is still busy with her phone.

As soon as they turn off the road into the forest, Thea realises where they're going: to the hunting lodge and Kerstin Miller.

Maybe it's her imagination, but the atmosphere seems to change again as they travel across the marsh; it's more relaxed, yet at the same time highly charged. They follow the winding track. The greenery has grown thicker in just a few days, and the canal is barely visible in the dip below them.

None of the others seem bothered by their surroundings. David and Sebastian talk louder and louder, and now Nettan is involved in the story too. They talk over one another, until the volume is so overwhelming that Bianca starts to glance enquiringly at Thea.

Kerstin Miller is waiting for them outside the lodge, with Jan-Olof by her side. He's smartened himself up; he's wearing a shirt and jacket, although the sleeves are too long.

David, Sebastian and Nettan jump out. They greet Kerstin warmly, Jan-Olof slightly less warmly. Thea sees David shake his head discreetly at Sebastian and Nettan, as if to indicate that he didn't know Jan-Olof was going to be there. They're all trying to hide it, but there's definitely a problem between the three of them and Jan-Olof. Could it be connected to Elita Svart? Thea would like to think so, but maybe there's another explanation.

Kerstin offers freshly baked buns, coffee and her homemade tea. She takes out the scrapbook and goes through old memories, just like the last time Thea was here.

David has brought dessert wine and cognac; he tops up everyone's glasses as soon as they're empty. He's so taken up with playing the role of the host that he barely exchanges more than a few words with Thea. She, however, feels as if she's observing things from a distance. Neither David nor any of the others has provided a clue as to what the problem is with Jan-Olof; in fact, they are almost exaggeratedly polite to him.

Thea slips away to the bathroom. The medicine cabinet door has been left ajar, and she glimpses a bottle of pills. She opens the door a little wider, sees that they are strong sleeping tablets prescribed by Dr Andersson. She feels guilty for prying into Kerstin's private life, but can't help wondering why the teacher has difficulty sleeping. She closes the cabinet and sits down on the toilet seat, resting her chin in her hands.

There is definitely something strange about the way David and his friends are behaving, as if it's all play-acting, where those involved pretend to be delighted to see one another even though they're not. She can't help thinking back to the Polaroid. David, Nettan, Sebastian and Jan-Olof standing around Elita Svart. Those four were the last to see Elita alive, apart from her killer.

What does that do to a twelve-year-old? What effect does it have on the rest of their lives?

David, Nettan and Sebastian were all keen to get away from here as soon as possible, returning only when they were forced to do so. Jan-Olof stayed. But now they're here, all together. Under duress.

She has no problem putting herself in that situation. She still hasn't abandoned the idea of packing a bag and simply leaving.

When she returns to the kitchen the others have moved into the living room, but the yearbooks are still on the table. She picks out the one from '85/'86 and finds the right year group. Elita Svart is in class 9B, sitting right in the middle and gazing confidently into the camera, as if she already knows that she will be the obvious focus for the photographer. The picture must have been taken during the autumn of '85 – just six months before Walpurgis Night.

'Thea – we haven't had time to chat.'

Kerstin glances at the photo and her smile falters. Thea feels caught out, but decides to ask the question that's been on her mind.

'Did you know the Svart family? You were practically neighbours, after all.'

'I knew Eva-Britt and Lola. Good people, but a little . . . different. They came here occasionally. I tutored Lola in English one summer, and Eva-Britt used to drive her over. Lola said she wanted to travel, see the world, but I think that was just a pipe dream.'

'And Lasse?'

Kerstin's upper lip curls involuntarily. 'Lass and I had no direct contact.'

Thea looks at the photo again. 'Did Elita have a boyfriend?'

Kerstin looks surprised. 'Why do you ask?'

'She's a pretty girl, with real magnetism. The boys must have been crazy about her.'

Kerstin stares at Thea for a few seconds.

'Well, yes, I suppose most of the boys in school were after her, but I don't think she was interested. That's usually the case.'

'What do you mean?'

'Girls of that age tend to prefer older boys. Or men, in fact.' Kerstin closes the yearbook firmly and places it at the bottom of a pile. 'Wasn't it like that for you, Thea?'

'David's three years younger than me . . .'

'I know that, but what about your first love? I'm sure he was older.'

Thea doesn't reply. Jocke's face flickers through her mind. Then her own. She is nineteen years old, standing in the toilet on a train. In her hand is a battered suitcase, in her pocket a bank book that still smells new.

She has to make a decision. And soon.

52

After coffee at the hunting lodge, David, Nettan and Sebastian return to the castle, while Thea hurries home to the coach house. She takes her suitcase out of the wardrobe and places it on the bed, then sits down and stares at it.

She promised herself that she would support David, help him in the same way as he'd helped her. But maybe it would be better if she left, before something comes out that could damage the restaurant project? Or is she trying to justify leaving him in the lurch? Avoiding a confrontation with her father?

Her thoughts are interrupted by a knock on the front door.

It's Hubert Gordon. The little man is in a tweed suit beneath his oilskin coat; he is also wearing his usual flat cap, and wellingtons.

'I wondered if you and Emee would like to come for a walk?'

She's about to say no, but Emee has already pushed past her and is winding herself around Hubert's legs, delighted at the prospect of an outing.

Thea reluctantly pulls on her jacket. They walk for a while in silence.

'Have you read any more of the poetry book?' Hubert asks.

'A little – but there's been a lot going on.'

'Have you worked out which is my favourite poem?'

'No!' She can hear how snappy she sounds. Hubert hears it too.

'Is everything all right, Thea?'

'Have you . . .' She stops dead. 'Have you ever felt as if you might be exposed at any moment? As if the people around you are about to find out that you're actually a sham? That you're a completely different person from the one you're pretending to be?'

He laughs, much to her surprise.

'Of course. I think that's one of my most common nightmares. That and standing naked in the middle of the village square.'

In spite of the situation, Thea can't help smiling.

His tone grows more serious. 'We all have our secrets, things we absolutely don't want to come out. Although sometimes you have to wonder . . .'

He pauses.

'Wonder what?'

'Whether it would really be so terrible if those secrets were revealed. Then at least we would have to carry them alone. Loneliness is fucking worse than almost anything.'

He falls silent, and they continue their walk.

The f-word surprises her. Hubert doesn't usually swear. Although he has a point. She's kept her family a secret for almost three decades – or rather kept herself a secret, constantly worried that they might catch up with her, expose her, turn her back into what she once was.

But she's no longer a frightened nineteen-year-old, Daddy's little girl who suddenly realises that the world he's dragged her into contains nothing but crap and stagnant water. Who flees in the middle of the night with nothing but a battered suitcase, a bank book and a train ticket.

She's a grown woman who has worked in war zones, been bombed and shot at. Lost everything she cared about.

Hubert is right. What is she so afraid of?

'Thank you, Hubert,' she says.

'For what?' He gives that wry smile she likes so much.

'For listening.'

53

'I've made up my mind, Margaux. I'm tired of running away, tired of hiding. It's high time I did what you would have done. High time to take the bull by the horns.

'I'd be lying if I said the prospect doesn't scare me. Think of me – promise!'

It's just after five in the morning when she coaxes Emee into the car. She's left a note for David, telling him she's meeting an old friend from Doctors Without Borders who's unexpectedly turned up. He probably won't be too bothered; he's completely obsessed with the restaurant, Sebastian, Nettan, and planning for the preview dinner.

It's still dark, and she drives carefully. A couple of times her headlights are reflected in eyes among the trees – deer, or maybe wild boar. She follows the narrow, winding tracks until she reaches the main road and heads north.

Just after eight o'clock she stops, lets Emee out to stretch her legs, and has breakfast at a café. She smokes a cigarette and texts David to check that everything is OK. Judging by his response, he hasn't seen through her lie.

She tries to clear her head during the rest of the journey, but it's impossible. All the different strands come together to form a narrative that plays over and over again as the road signs flash by.

Dad and Ronny, Elita, Lasse and Leo.

David, Nettan, Sebastian and Jan-Olof.

Lola Svart and Leo's mother, Eva-Britt.

Her own mother. Jocke.

The child she lost.

The child Elita was carrying.

And finally, the person who never really leaves her thoughts.

Margaux. Always Margaux.

The drive takes just over five hours, as the GPS promised, and it is almost half past ten when she reaches her home village.

The contrast with Tornaby's neat and tidy appearance is striking. The houses are dotted around in a random fashion; some are so close to the road that the car's wing mirrors almost scrape against them, while others are much further back. There are FOR SALE signs everywhere; some look pretty old. The coniferous forest is encroaching from all directions, swallowing up the light and spreading its shadow.

She passes her old school. It's closed down, and seems to be the venue for a flea market on Saturdays and Sundays. The bus shelter opposite has been vandalised.

The ICA mini-market where Ronny used to pinch beer is also gone. All that remains of the village's shops is a combined petrol station and grocery store. She decides to stop.

PAY FIRST, THEN FILL UP, a cardboard notice above the pump instructs her.

Thea goes inside. A woman in her twenties with long multicoloured nails is standing behind the counter. She's on the phone.

'Tell him to go to hell!' Thea hears her say. 'He can take his fucking PlayStation and go home to his mummy if it doesn't suit him. Why should you pay all the bills while he sits at home smoking and wanking while he watches *Emmerdale*?'

Thea turns away, wanders around the shop until the conversation is over. She picks up an energy drink and a packet of cigarettes.

'Sorry,' the young woman mutters as Thea pays. 'My sister. Her boyfriend is a total fucking loser. Did you want petrol as well?'

Thea nods. The woman is looking closely at her.

'You're not from round here, are you?'

'No.'

'Lucky you.'

'What do you mean?'

'It's just ...' The question seems to have embarrassed the assistant. 'This is such a fucking hole. I can't wait to get out of here.'

'I understand.' Thea takes her purchases. 'By the way, do you know who Ronny Boman is?'

'Who the fuck doesn't?'

'Does he still live by the old mine?'

She hopes the answer will be no. The woman is looking at her differently now, as if she's wondering how someone like Thea knows Ronny Boman.

'He does.'

'OK, thanks.'

Thea fills up the car, then goes back inside to collect her card. The woman is on the phone again. She barely looks at Thea as she hands over the card, and doesn't return her goodbye.

It starts to rain just before she turns onto the dirt road. She doesn't really recognise the place, which is hardly surprising.

It's many years since she walked along here for the last time, heading for the bus stop. Heading out of here.

The fir trees have taken over; everything is much gloomier than she remembers. The persistent drizzle doesn't help.

The road slopes gradually downhill and stops after a kilometre or so at a large gravelled area. To the left, surrounded by a rusty wire fence, are a couple of abandoned industrial units that once belonged to the old mine. To the right several brick buildings that once housed offices and accommodation for the workers. Her father owns the lot. He bought them when the mine went bust years and years ago. He probably paid cash.

The collection of buildings is in a dip, with forest all around. The water finds its way down the slope, gathering at the bottom and forming huge brown pools. Sometimes, when it rains a lot, it's like living by a lake. Or a bog.

Ronny lives in the first house. Two old bangers are parked on the drive; Thea sees a collapsible pool on the overgrown lawn, with a trampoline leaning drunkenly to the side a little further away.

Thea parks behind the other cars, rubs her hands on her jeans to wipe away the sweat. She is greeted by the sound of barking as she approaches the front door. She can hear Emee barking back through the cracked window of her car.

The bell isn't working, so she knocks instead. Her heart is pounding so hard she can almost feel it through her shirt.

The door is opened by a plump woman of her own age, in a vest top and tracksuit bottoms. Her arms and shoulders are covered in tattoos, and she looks vaguely familiar.

'Hi – is Ronny home?'

The woman looks her up and down. 'And who are you?'

Thea takes a deep breath. 'His sister.'

The woman is clearly taken aback. 'Jenny?'

Thea nods reluctantly.

'What the fuck . . . Don't you remember me? Sofie Nilsson. We used to go into town to nick make-up together.'

Thea forces a smile. 'Of course.'

'I didn't recognise you, Jenny. Look how smart you are! Don't just stand there, come on in. Ronny!' Sofie yells over her shoulder.

The house smells of cigarette smoke and fried food. A row of children's shoes are lined up – surprisingly neatly – inside the door.

'Ronny!'

'What?'

Ronny is wearing a lumberjack shirt and scruffy jeans. He hasn't really changed much, apart from being heavier and greyer. The muscular arms, the sharp nose and the dark eyes remind her of Dad. The scar down one cheek is old, but it's new to Thea. Combined with the beard, it makes him look like a hard man.

'Hi!' she says, managing to keep her voice steady.

Her big brother stares at her for a few seconds, then breaks into a wolfish grin.

'Well, if it isn't my missing little sister. How nice to see that you're still alive.'

They sit down on the glassed-in veranda. Sofie sets out a bottle of Coke and two plastic glasses, then sensitively withdraws into the house.

'So you've got kids,' Thea says.

'That's right – two with Sofie, and one with Lollo. You remember her? Jocke's sister?'

'Of course. I read that he'd died.'

She realises that she's giving herself away, letting him know that she's googled them from time to time. However, Ronny doesn't comment. He merely nods, then takes out tobacco and cigarette papers, starts to roll his own.

'Thea Lind. Where did you get that name from?'

She would really prefer to get to the point, find out what she has to do to keep the door leading to this part of her life firmly closed, but she decides to play along for a little while.

'Thea was a girl who helped me revise for my college exams. It was thanks to her I got a place in medical school.'

'And Lind?' He licks the paper and seals the cigarette.

'Another girl who lived on the same corridor as me. Veronica. She also came from the back of beyond and was determined to stay away, like me.'

'Had she stolen money from her family too?' Ronny lights the cigarette.

Thea takes a deep breath. It's just as she suspected.

'Mum gave me that money. It was her life insurance.'

'Mm . . .' He blows out a column of smoke. 'Three hundred thousand. What did you spend it on?'

'My education. I rented a little student room in Umeå. Studied at the adult education institute for a year. Lived on noodles, revised like a demon for my exams. Got into medical school by the narrowest possible margin.'

Ronny doesn't say anything for a moment. He merely carries on smoking, watching her.

'And now you're the lady of the castle, married to a restaurant owner.'

'I work part time as a GP. The castle is David's project. We live in a little house behind it.'

Ronny takes another drag.

'We haven't got any money,' Thea continues. 'David's practically broke. He did some bad deals and had to sell up.'

'But he owns a castle?'

'He's renting it from a foundation. Two of his old school friends are financing the project.'

'So you say . . .' Ronny stubs out the cigarette and immediately starts rolling another. Remains silent, letting her squirm.

Frustratingly, it works.

'Was Dad really angry when I left?' She doesn't want to ask the question, yet at the same time she wants to hear the answer.

'What do you think? You were his favourite. He thought you and Jocke were going to get married and give him grandchildren. Instead you took off with his money.'

'It was your money and mine too . . .'

Ronny ignores the comment.

'He looked for you for a long time. That business of getting a protected identity – very smart. He asked all his contacts to keep an eye out for you; he even persuaded a cop to check their database. But it was as if you'd gone up in a puff of smoke. At least until you popped up on TV.'

He grins, lights the second cigarette.

'What is it you want from me, Ronny?'

He shakes his head. 'Not me. The old man. He wants to see you.'

'Now?' She peers out of the window. The house where she and Ronny grew up is just visible on the edge of the forest.

'As soon as possible.' He follows her gaze. 'He's not there.'

'So where is he?'

'What do you think? In jail. Eight years for serious drugs offences. He's still got four left to serve – that's the issue.'

'What do you mean, that's the issue?'

'I'll let him tell you.'

Ronny looks at his phone. 'It's an hour's drive – you'll be just in time for visiting.'

Thea wants to protest, explain that she has to get back, that she has absolutely no desire to drive to a prison, or to see her father. But she doesn't have a choice, and in a way she's surprised. Why isn't Ronny angry with her? He used to have a terrible temper, almost on a level with Dad's. Has he mellowed over the years, or is there something she's missing?

It's still drizzling. She lets Emee out of the car, takes her for a walk along the dirt road, dodging the huge puddles.

Her childhood home is built of grey brick, and backs onto the forest and the slope. The blinds are down, a couple of them hanging askew. The cellar windows have been boarded up, and an old wreck of a car without wheels sits on the drive. A few pieces of plastic garden furniture are sticking up among the knee-high grass, and several planks are missing from the rotting fence.

She stops by the mail box; she doesn't want to go any closer. The house makes her feel uncomfortable, particularly those boarded-up windows. How many times did Dad lock her in down there in the dark? More than she can count. The smell is still embedded in her brain. Dampness, earth, fear. Sometimes urine. If she stopped crying and kept really quiet, she could hear the faint sound of insects scuttling across the floor. The ones with hard bodies and vibrating wings.

She'd promised herself that she would never come back, and yet she's standing here. Is it just because she's afraid of being exposed, caught out having lied about her past? Or is there another reason? Does some small part of her still long for Daddy's approval, or even his forgiveness?

Ronny is waiting by her car, wearing a filthy hi-vis jacket. Two dogs are sniffing around him. Scruffy, muscular bodies. Square jaws, short snouts. They race towards her barking wildly as soon as they see Emee.

'The boys just want to say hello,' Ronny says.

Emee lies down on the ground and Ronny's dogs stand over her, legs apart, growling and baring their teeth. Emee presses herself even lower, head down.

Thea hates to see her like that. Diminished, cowed. She tries to push away the two male dogs but the paler one snaps at her. Thea dodges to one side and drops the lead.

Emee leaps to her feet, lets out a kind of roar and attacks the paler dog. The onslaught is so fierce that the animal rolls right over on the gravel.

The darker dog goes for Emee, but she is ready for him. The two of them collide in mid-air, but Emee is bigger and stronger, knocking him over too. He quickly gets up and the two male dogs take up their positions a couple of metres away, hackles raised, but neither dares approach.

Emee has been transformed from a submissive bitch into a predator with bared teeth. There is a look in her eyes that Thea has never seen before. She crouches down, preparing to attack, but at the last second Thea manages to grab her lead.

'Calm down, sweetheart,' she says, trying to pull her close.

Emee flatly refuses to move. The muscles in her powerful body are tensed, and a low rumble is coming from deep in her chest.

'Calm down,' Thea says again. Emee stops growling, but continues to glare menacingly at the other two dogs.

Ronny hasn't intervened; he seems faintly amused.

'Tough chick,' he says.

'She doesn't like being walked all over,' Thea replies.

Ronny shouts a command, and after a couple of seconds' hesitation his dogs shamble over to his house and lie down on the steps, keeping an eye on Thea and Emee from a safe distance.

'I wanted to ask you something,' Thea says. 'Did you ever come across a young guy called Leo Rasmussen? He's from Skåne, three years older than you. He was convicted of murdering his stepsister in 1986. He got six years.'

She knows it's a long shot, but somehow Emee's reaction has given her a dose of self-confidence.

Ronny shakes his head. 'Doesn't ring a bell.'

'Do you know anyone who might know something about him?'

One corner of his mouth lifts in a wry smile.

'I've tried to stay on the right side of the law over the past few years; I didn't want to get dragged into all that again. But you could always ask the old man. He's got contacts everywhere.'

Thea puts Emee in the car and gets ready to leave. Ronny's hard expression has softened.

'Dad's ill, Jenny. He's not like he used to be.'

'No?'

Ronny shrugs. 'Not really. I'll call the prison, let him know you're coming.'

She wonders whether to thank him, but decides against it. She's here because he forced her to come; it wasn't her choice.

'One more thing,' he says as she opens the car door. He tugs at his beard, looking indecisive. 'If he ... If he gives you too much grief, ask him how Jocke died.'

'Jocke?'

He nods. For a brief moment she sees the Ronny who built dens and made pine cone animals for her. Then the moment is gone.

'Drive carefully, sis. Good to see you.'

54

The prison looks nothing like the institution Thea had imagined. No walls, no watchtowers, no steel gates. Just a simple fence enclosing a number of red two-storey buildings.

The visitors' room smells of coffee and cinnamon buns. The walls are painted in a familiar shade of hospital orange.

Everything becomes clear when her father shuffles slowly into the room. He is gaunt, his clothes hanging off him, eyes sunken, his skin so thin that she feels as if she can see the blood vessels through it.

Before she went in she hung around in the car park for at least ten minutes. Smoked four cigarettes and tried to gather her courage. Not that she succeeded. She has broken out in a cold sweat, her mouth is as dry as dust and she is sitting on her hands to stop them shaking.

He stops by the table. Thea isn't sure whether to stand up. Chooses to remain seated.

'So here you are. The runaway. The lost child.' His voice is hoarser than she remembers.

'Hi, Leif.' It's the best she can come up with. She is surprised that her own voice holds.

He pulls out a chair and sits down. It is clearly an effort. The weight loss, the skin taut over his scalp, the little tufts of hair – they all tell the same story. Chemotherapy. Cancer. Poor prognosis.

His smile makes him look like a grinning skull.

'I searched for you, little Jenny. Wondered where you'd gone with my money. I left no stone unturned, from Ystad in the south to Haparanda in the north.'

Thea stays silent. Tries to stop her hands from trembling.

'Imagine my surprise when I got a call from an old friend, telling me he thinks he's seen you on TV. Says you're a doctor, married to a man who owns a castle.'

'David doesn't have any money,' Thea says as firmly as she can. 'The castle doesn't belong to him.'

'Oh, you want to get straight to the point. Fine, let's do that.' He leans forward, fixes his gaze on her. Thea swallows hard. 'I trusted you. Let you take care of my affairs. And what thanks did I get? You stole from me.'

'It was our money. Mum . . .'

'Your mother was an idiot,' he snaps. 'A stupid woman. You, on the other hand . . . you were smart. You knew how to get people exactly where you wanted them. Ronny, Jocke, even me.' He shakes his head. 'I had such high expectations of you, Jenny. But you let me down. Let your family down.'

He coughs a couple of times.

'But the past always catches up with us sooner or later, doesn't it?'

She doesn't answer. For some reason she can't take her eyes off his hands. They used to be rough and hard, now they look like thin birds' claws. The backs are covered in brown liver spots, the nails are clean.

She and Ronny used to be so scared of those hands.

'And now you're living in a castle,' he goes on. 'In a lovely little village, with a lovely little husband. But no children? Why not?'

She shrugs. 'Because I didn't want any.'

'Aha. You don't like being tied down. You don't want the responsibility of being a parent. The disappointment you risk when your child lets you down.'

She knows he's trying to provoke her, and yet she can't help taking the bait.

'Or maybe I didn't want to risk the child inheriting your genes.'

His mouth twitches, then the death's head grin returns.

'Sometimes I think about how different things would have been if you hadn't lost Jocke's child.'

Thea doesn't speak. She has no intention of pursuing that particular topic.

'Poor Jocke – he was completely devastated when you left. He'd believed the two of you were going to get married. I was planning on giving you the house next door to Ronny's, so that the whole family could be together. You and me, Jocke, Ronny and all the grandchildren.'

'What do you want from me, Leif?' She is surprised at how calm she sounds.

Scorn is written all over his face.

'Thea Lind. A fine name, much more elegant than Jenny Boman. A perfect name for the lady of the castle.'

He coughs, more violently this time. He takes out a handkerchief, wipes his mouth, leaving a blob of yellow sputum at one corner of his lips.

'Did you know that I worked at a castle when I was a boy? From the age of twelve. In the stables. I had to groom the horses, clean their hooves, muck out – all the jobs the fine folk didn't want to do themselves. I liked horses. The owner used to give me riding lessons sometimes, and he'd slip me a bit of extra cash now and again. One Christmas he and his wife came to our house with two bags of second-hand clothes for me and my brothers and sisters. Playing Lord and Lady Bountiful.'

He clears his throat, spits into the handkerchief. A dark stain appears on the white cotton.

'Do you know what my father did?'

She shakes her head.

'He burned the lot in the back garden. Beat the crap out of me and forbade me from ever setting foot in that fucking stable again. People like that look down on the likes of us, he said. They can smell us, like dog shit on the sole of your shoe.'

He points at her with a skinny finger.

'The same thing will happen to you, Jenny. You can do your best to try and scrape us off the sole of your shoe; you can change your name, lose your accent, pretend to be someone you're not. But sooner or later people will smell you. Expose you.'

He sits up a little straighter. 'Unless someone else gets there first, of course.'

'You, for example.'

'This is an open prison. I can move around freely, call who-ever I want, use the internet. One well-aimed Facebook post is all it would take for your husband to get a whole lot of unwanted publicity around his restaurant project. Married to the daughter of a convicted criminal . . . well, you can imagine.'

She takes a deep breath, holds it for a few seconds. Her head is pounding.

'What do you want? I've already told you we don't have any money.'

He leans back, watches her for a little while.

'As I'm sure you've realised, I'm sick. Lung cancer. The doctors have given me four months, six at the most. I want to die in my own home, in my own bed, not in the cheap fucking sheets of the criminal justice system.'

He pushes the handkerchief into his pocket.

'I want someone to write me a petition for a reprieve. Not some fancy lawyer, but someone who knows me, who can explain why I ought to be allowed to die in freedom. A reliable citizen with a snow-white past.'

Thea places her hands on the table. They've stopped shaking. At last she knows what he wants.

'And you think I'm going to do that?'

He reaches out, rests one hand on hers. His long fingers are ice-cold.

'You're still my little girl, Jenny, in spite of everything. Whether you like it or not.'

She slowly withdraws her hands.

'And if I do it, you'll leave me and David in peace?'

He winks at her. 'Maybe. You'll just have to trust me, Jenny. You don't have a choice.'

She goes through the scenario in her head. A petition for a reprieve is presumably a matter of public interest, a traceable document that will reveal that she's his daughter, even if he keeps his word. She needs to play for time. Time to think things over, work out a plan.

He's leaning back on his chair again, watching her carefully.

'If . . .' She clears her throat. 'If I agree to consider it, I want a favour in return. Proof that I can trust you.'

He raises his eyebrows.

'What makes you think you have the right to ask for anything?'

'Because I'm your only option. Who else is going to give them your sob story? Ronny?'

He stiffens, narrows his eyes.

'Are you trying to blackmail me, little Jenny?'

'No, I just want your help with something.' Now it's her turn to lean forward. 'In 1986 a girl was killed in the forest by the castle where we live. Her stepbrother confessed and was convicted of murder. His name is Leo Rasmussen.'

'And why does this interest you?'

'Because I don't believe the whole truth has come out.'

'What makes you think that?'

'She was pregnant, but someone made sure that information was removed from the case file.'

'Aha – so things ended badly for a pregnant young girl. I can see the appeal. Go on.'

Thea swallows her irritation.

'There is also a suggestion that the stepbrother retracted his confession. He claimed that the police had put him under extreme pressure, brainwashed him.'

Her father continues to gaze at her with that annoying smile, making it clear that he's enjoying himself at her expense.

'So what do you want my help with?'

'I'd like to find out whether any of your friends knows someone who might have been in jail with Leo. Whether he talked about the murder when he was inside. Where he went after he got out.'

Her father chews his lower lip, keeping her in suspense.

'Why should I waste my time on this, little Jenny? I'm the one who's holding the trump card. I can crush you like a louse if you don't do exactly as I ask.'

He taps his index finger on the table, just like he used to do when he wanted to scare her.

'Be a good girl and do what Daddy says, then I might consider forgiving you for what you did. For abandoning your own family.'

She looks down, eyes burning with anger. She has to submit. Let him walk all over her if she's going to have any chance of sorting out this tangled mess. Because nobody fucks with Leif Boman.

She takes a deep breath, suddenly remembers what Ronny said just before she left. It's worth a try.

'By the way, what happened to Jocke?'

Her father becomes very still, apart from his eyes, which are darting from side to side for the first time during this conversation.

'Jocke's dead. He died in '96.'

'How?'

He shuffles in his seat.

'How did Jocke die?' She's determined to push him.

'Car accident. He tried to get away from the cops in a stolen car, high as a kite. They crashed into a truck.'

It takes a few seconds for her to process what he's just said. *They*. Before she realises why Ronny handed her this tiny piece of kryptonite.

'Who else was in the car with Jocke?'

Leif's lips are a thin white line.

'His girlfriend, Jossan. She was pregnant. None of them survived.'

She can see the rest in his eyes. The logical conclusion to this tale.

It could have been me in that car with Jocke. It probably would have been if I hadn't left. Me and our child. Leif's grandchild.

They sit in silence for a few seconds.

'OK,' he says eventually. 'I'll ask around about Leo Rasmussen. Do you have an ID number or anything else I can use?'

'I've got the case file in the car if you want to read it.'

It's a throwaway remark. She isn't expecting him to bite, but he does.

'Good. Ask Sigurdsson in the guards' office to make a copy. Tell him I said so, if he complains. And leave a phone number where I can reach you.'

He gets to his feet laboriously, then stands beside her as he did when he came into the room.

'You're not trying to fool me again, are you, Jenny?'

'Maybe, maybe not. You'll just have to trust me, Leif. You don't have a choice.'

The corner of his mouth twitches. A tic, perhaps, or the hint of a smile.

'You haven't changed, Jenny,' he says as he shuffles towards the door.

55

'What shall I do now, Margaux? I so wish you were here. To help me, give me advice.'

It is gone ten o'clock at night when Thea pulls up outside the castle. Two cars are parked by the stone steps – Nettan's and Sebastian's. Thea's head is empty, she feels completely flat and doesn't want to talk to anyone.

Emee is restless after the long drive, so she takes her for a walk, following the path to the castle garden as usual. There are lights on in the dining room, and one of the doors leading onto the terrace is wide open. She can hear the sound of angry voices, and can't help edging closer. She creeps up the steps, trying to keep both herself and Emee in the shadows.

All three of them are sitting around a table crowded with wine bottles, plates and glasses, but the atmosphere is far from festive. David is red-faced, gesticulating wildly. Sebastian is leaning forward, elbows resting on his knees, hands clasped in front of him. Nettan's expression is determined.

Thea moves a little nearer to the open door.

'You can't go on like this,' Nettan says. 'Sebastian and I are not made of money. We have a budget, and we expect you to stick to it.'

'Fuck the budget! If we want a top-class restaurant, then it's going to cost. We're aiming for a Michelin star within three years.'

'That's what *you're* aiming for, David. Sebastian and I were perfectly happy with the original plan, which had a realistic chance of turning a profit. This . . .' She points to something on the table, presumably a document or drawing. 'This is a daydream. A fucking utopia that we're not prepared to pay for.'

'Take it easy, Nettan . . .' Sebastian ventures.

'I'm trying to do something good for the area. Give back.' David waves his arms, just as he always does when he's on the defensive.

'Bullshit! You're only thinking of yourself.' Nettan is slurring her words.

'That's rich, coming from you! You took off for Switzerland with a week's notice, for fuck's sake! We hardly had time to say goodbye!'

'We were seventeen. We weren't even together anymore.'

'Calm down, both of you!' Sebastian gets to his feet. 'Can we please stick to the matter in hand? We're worried about the budget, David. Costs are spiralling, and you're still making changes without consulting us. You seem to assume that we'll be happy to pay for them.'

'You mean you can't afford it?' David gives a mirthless laugh. 'How many millions is your company worth? A hundred?'

'That's irrelevant. We agreed to finance the restaurant for old times' sake, because we were friends, but we can't carry on pouring money into something that isn't going to make a profit. This isn't a charity project.'

'Charity!' David hisses. 'Thirtieth of April 1986 – do you remember that date? What we went through together on that terrible night?'

'Shut the fuck up!' Nettan leaps up from her chair. 'You promised you'd never bring that up again! You promised . . .' Her voice gives way.

'Sorry, I didn't mean . . .' Now David is on his feet too, suddenly looking regretful. The three friends stand there staring at one another.

'I should never have agreed to any of this,' Nettan says quietly. 'Maybe I thought that the castle and the restaurant would some-how put things right, help us.' She spreads her arms wide. 'But we're fucked, aren't we? Elita's ghost will always haunt us.'

She turns on her heel and weaves her way towards the door.

'Wait, Nettan!' David follows her. Sebastian remains at the table. He picks up his wine glass and unexpectedly glances over at the window.

Thea steps back, but it's too late. Sebastian has already seen her. He stiffens, stares at her for a moment, then raises his glass in a toast. He empties it and follows the others out of the dining room.

Thea leads Emee down the terrace steps. The new moon hangs above the forest, its reflection just visible in the moat. There are no lights on in Hubert's apartment, but she sees a movement behind the curtains at one of the library windows.

She stops. The window is ajar, offering an excellent view of the terrace and dining room. Has Hubert seen her eavesdropping? Probably, but for some reason she thinks he was there because he was every bit as interested in the conversation in the dining room as she was.

56

'Fuck, Margaux. How did I end up in the middle of this mess? That's a good question, isn't it? If you like it, I have plenty more.'

Thea wakes just before sunrise again. Emee is snoring on the floor next to her bed.

Thea has been dreaming, but she can't quite remember the details. Something about her father, and horrible little Green Man figures.

She doesn't switch on the light; she lies in the darkness trying to gather her thoughts. Is she really considering helping her father with his petition? Does she have a choice? And does she seriously think he'll help her get closer to the truth about Elita Svart's death?

This all began with her wanting to find out what David had gone through, hoping she could support him. It's clear that both he and his friends are haunted by the experience. However, that explanation no longer holds water. She has become obsessed by the spring sacrifice, by what happened on Walpurgis Night 1986.

Bill's hoof prints place Leo in the stone circle, as do his cap badge and the testimony of the children, mainly David. Leo confessed to having killed Elita, said she'd asked him to do it. So why isn't Thea convinced of his guilt?

Two reasons, apart from what she read in *False Confessions*.

First of all, there's the missing page from the autopsy report. Someone did their utmost to conceal Elita's pregnancy, but who and why? Who was the father of Elita's child, and how is the pregnancy linked to her death?

Secondly, Thea doesn't believe Lasse Svart's story. Why should he, after a life lived on the fringes of society, suddenly decide it's his duty to speak to the police, make sure justice is done? The question seems even more apposite after yesterday's encounter with her father. Leif would never have gone to the police, she's sure of it. Lasse must have felt the same at the start – so what made him change his mind?

The discovery of the cap badge is also kind of strange. Why didn't it turn up when the crime scene was first searched? According to the interviewer, it was found by a witness.

She switches on the light, takes out the folder and turns to the section marked *Evidence*. It takes her a few minutes to locate the right form.

The witness who found the badge was Erik Nyberg. He says he'd gone to the stone circle to clear up after the police, and that was when one of his dogs came across it.

She checks the date; Nyberg signed the form the day before Lasse Svart walked into the police station and changed his statement. So on a single day, Leo's defence suffers two serious setbacks – setbacks which, possibly combined with Eva-Britt's disappearance, finally make him confess.

Thea realises she hasn't given much thought to where the Svart family actually went. She picks up her phone and googles first Lasse, then Lola, then Eva-Britt. Nothing, not even in the national address database or on Facebook. Have they left the country? Changed their names? Are they somehow living beneath the authorities' radar?

Erik Nyberg said the count had ordered him to board up the windows and destroy the track leading to the farm as soon as it became clear that Lasse and his women were gone. But why? Why was it so urgent?

There are too many questions. The whole thing is a morass of questionable threads. She feels as if she can't even trust the police investigation, but she is becoming increasingly certain that the truth hasn't come out. Someone – more than one person? – has tried to simplify the narrative as much as possible.

Manipulative, extrovert girl murdered by her stepbrother. Case closed.

It would be best to forget all about it, of course. She has plenty of other things to think about, much more important than a long-dead teenager, and yet Elita Svart will not leave her in peace. The sense that their stories are intertwined has grown stronger since she was forced to go back home.

She gets up, opens the window and lights a cigarette. The air is heavy with dampness, carrying the distinct smell of the marsh. She can almost taste it.

The sun is slowly rising. Over to the north east she can just make out the marsh as a dark mass. She wonders if Svartgården is still there – beyond the fence enclosing the military range, in uncharted territory, untouched since the remains of the Svart family closed the door behind them.

She fetches her laptop and gets back into bed. Opens up Google Maps and types in 'Bokelund castle'. The satellite image is crystal clear, showing the H-shaped main building, the coach house, the old stables. The green surface of the moat almost merges with the adjoining forest.

She zooms out, follows the canal down through the dip, all the way to the hunting lodge. The trees are so dense that she can barely make out the water and the track.

She changes to hybrid view so that the track is clearer, moves back and forth at random, looking for buildings. No luck. The marsh is too big, the vegetation too thick.

She tries a different tactic, starting from the hunting lodge and trying to identify the spot where Dr Andersson claimed that the way down to Svartgården lay. After zooming in and out for a while she thinks she's found a route where the greenery is paler. She follows this route to the east, attempts to work out where it passes the fence surrounding the firing range, but it's no good – she can't see the fence, and the route itself becomes more difficult to discern. It changes direction, is interrupted by pools of water and thickets of trees, then disappears completely.

She zooms in as close as she can. It's still difficult, but she thinks she can make out a right angle beneath the trees.

Nature abhors right angles, Margaux used to say. *Abhors everything that is precise and identical. Mankind invented right angles to control that which is wild and incalculable.*

Thea gets out of bed.

'Come on, Emee – we're going on an adventure.'

She drives across the marsh in the direction of the hunting lodge. She has three hours until the surgery opens; that should be enough.

What exactly is she planning to do? What is she hoping to find at Svartgården? She doesn't really know. Maybe she's looking for a fixed point in the story, something concrete that she can get hold of. Or maybe she just needs to do something, anything, to ease her frustration.

She finds the place where the old track probably ran, and manages to park the car on solid ground. She pulls on her wellington boots and lets Emee out of the car. Picks up her rucksack, which contains a torch, a bottle of water and a crowbar that she found in the tool shed behind the coach house.

After checking Google Maps again, she sets off through the marsh. Visibility is limited to ten to fifteen metres thanks to the bracken and undergrowth. The air is cold and damp; it smells of rotting wood and stagnant water.

To begin with she keeps Emee on the lead, but after a few minutes this turns out to be impractical, and she lets her go. Fortunately, Emee stays close, happily exploring her new surroundings.

Thea's conclusion about the old track was well-founded. Along a five-metre strip the trees are younger, not as tall as the rest of the forest. Nor are they covered in lichen and creepers, which explains the colour difference on the satellite image.

She hunts for some kind of path, but to no avail. Instead she has to cut across the terrain, picking her way over moss, leaves and dead wood. Here and there the huge roots of fallen trees are sticking up, and she has to circumvent rotting logs and pools of water. A couple of times her foot sinks deep into the mud, and on one occasion she almost loses a boot.

Emee is still with her, and after ten minutes they reach the fence. It's not particularly off-putting; it's rusty, and the barbed wire at the top is sagging. A yellow notice informs her that this is a military firing range, and that unauthorised access constitutes danger to life. After a short distance Thea finds a spot where an animal has been digging, enabling both her and Emee to crawl under the fence.

The terrain slopes downwards, and the pools of water increase; in some places they are so big that she has to take a detour. Mouldering branches, partly hidden beneath the moss, make the ground treacherous. She slips on one of them and her knee sinks into the porous surface. The cold surprises her, makes her realise that she mustn't fall in under any circumstances.

Emee has begun to roam further afield; sometimes she vanishes for a minute or so before reappearing. The vegetation thickens, the tall trees are joined by bushes that make it even harder to see what is ahead. Her phone is also finding it more difficult to establish her position. She keeps pausing to adjust the direction, but the arrow jumps around the screen and she's afraid that she might have lost her bearings. Every time she updates the map the arrow moves. First of all it's very close to the place she's trying to reach, then suddenly it's some distance away. She searches for an opening among the trees, but the leaf canopy blocks out the light, leaving nothing but a spooky gloom.

Thea decides to keep going for another five minutes, then she will give up. A natural track seems to lead in the right direction, until a huge muddy pool, several metres across, forces her to stop. Insects are dancing across the surface of the water, and she can't help thinking about what Elita wrote in her letter: she saw herself as a nymph, waiting to metamorphose into a dragonfly. Waiting to float away from this damp, stinking place. Just as Thea did from her childhood home.

Suddenly it strikes her. Was that the kind of metamorphosis Elita was talking about? Killing Elita Svart, just as Thea killed Jenny Boman? Creating a new identity, getting away from the people who had already written her off? That could explain why Elita sometimes wrote about herself in the third person, particularly towards the end.

Who killed Elita Svart? Not: *Who killed me?*

The thought excites her. She needs to re-read the letter to see if her theory holds. If so, what does it mean? That there was no death pact, that Elita never asked Leo to kill her, and therefore Leo really was innocent?

She pulls herself together, works her way around the pool. Battles through a hazel thicket and comes to a group of gnarled old trees that seem to be crouching beneath the leaf canopy high above. These trees don't look as if they belong in the forest; could this have been an orchard? Her suspicions are confirmed by several square blocks of stone and a pile of planks, which look like the remains of a shed. She pushes at the planks with her foot and sees some plastic containers, grey with age, and a stainless-steel pipe attached to a gauge and a plastic tube.

Thea has seen something like this before, in her father's garage back home. She's pretty sure it's part of a home distillery.

As she sets off again, a noise makes her jump – a sharp crack, like a branch breaking somewhere behind her. She looks around, trying to work out where it came from, but there is nothing. It was probably Emee – she's been gone for quite a while now.

She calls to the dog, blows the whistle, but there is no sign of her. What could it have been? A deer? A wild boar?

She's read somewhere that wild boar can be a danger to people. At the same time she realises that the birds have stopped singing. All she can hear is a crow, cawing somewhere in the distance, followed by a faint rustling in the undergrowth.

The hairs on the back of her neck stand on end. She takes out the crowbar, but it's only half a metre long. It seems a little inadequate as a defence against a charging wild boar. She stands motionless, staring at the spot where she thinks the rustling came from.

Nothing happens. The birds burst into song once more.

Thea lets out a long breath, feeling silly. She pushes on. The ground on the other side of the pool is less boggy, and here and there she can make out hard-packed gravel and shards of tarmac. The remains of a road. She follows them all the way to an uneven row of fence posts. At the end of the row she sees large, dark silhouettes.

Her heartbeat speeds up.

She is in the right place. She has found Svartgården.

57

Svartgården consists of three buildings, as Thea saw in the photographs in the case file. The forest has almost swallowed them up, taken over the yard, crushed the roof of the stable and the barn, leaving only the gables intact.

The house itself looks more or less undamaged, but the vegetation around the walls, which are thick with lichen, has grown so tall that the place appears to be sinking into the ground. Grass and moss on the roof contribute to the look of dilapidation, weeds are growing through the cracks in the stone steps, and rust has eaten away the handrail.

The boarded-up doors and windows make the house resemble a face with neither eyes nor mouth. The boards are held in place with sturdy bolts, as if someone wanted to make sure that it remained both dumb and blind.

Thea calls to Emee, blows the whistle again, but the dog still doesn't respond. This worries her a little, but she consoles herself with the thought that they're a long way from the deer enclosure.

She tries the bolts on the front door. Almost thirty-five years of dampness have done their work. The wood is rotten, the nails brown with rust. She inserts the crowbar between the bolt and the board; there is a faint creaking sound.

She glances anxiously over her shoulder; of course there's no one there, but she can't help feeling tense. She's about to do something illegal. Literally open a door that she shouldn't be opening.

A pheasant crows somewhere deep in the forest, making Thea's heart beat faster. Is she really going to do this?

What is she hoping to find?

She hasn't come here to ask more questions, but to find answers. She pushes down on the crowbar; the bolt resists for a second, then gives up with a faint crack as the nails part company with the damp wood.

Thea repeats the manoeuvre twice more to remove the other bolts, then she tears off the boarding bit by bit to reveal the front door. She is prepared to break in, but discovers that it isn't locked. However, it has swollen, so opening it is a struggle.

The musty smell of an old house fills her nostrils. It's pitch dark inside; all she can make out is a pile of shoes on the floor, and a few items of outdoor clothing on hooks underneath the hat shelf.

She puts down the crowbar, switches on her torch and cautiously moves forward. The smell gets worse; it reminds her of the cellar back home. Dampness, earth, old wood and something indescribable. She shudders.

The house isn't very big. There's a closed door to her right, the bathroom straight ahead, next to the stairs. She can just see the kitchen on the left.

She opens the closed door. A double bed, neatly made. A bedside table, a chest of drawers, a mirror. Two wardrobes.

On the bedside table there is a book, its covers warped by the damp, plus a faded photograph in a metal frame. Thea picks up the photograph, which shows a girl and a boy on a bench. The boy is looking into the distance, while the girl gazes admiringly at him. Someone has written on the white strip at the bottom:

Leo ten years old, Elita six years old. Thea feels her excitement rising. This is the photo Elita mentioned in her letter, so this must have been Eva-Britt's bedroom.

It's a strange feeling, holding the picture in her hand – as if the years have been erased and she's stepped straight into Elita's world.

She sweeps the beam of the torch across the walls. The paper is yellowed and has fallen off in places, lying in a heap by the skirting board. Above the bed hangs a watercolour in the naïve style: various forest creatures dancing in a glade. It reminds Thea of the ceiling paintings in the main dining room at Bokelund.

She opens one of the wardrobes. It's full of clothes. So is the other – and the chest of drawers.

Why would you leave your home without packing some clothes?

She heads for the bathroom. Washbasin, toilet, bath, mouldy shower curtain. The bathroom cabinet is open, and the contents have been dumped in the washbasin.

Creams, ointments, toothbrushes, plasters, bottles of pills.

She looks at the labels. The first contains tranquillisers for Lola Svart, prescribed only two days after Elita's death. Flunitrazepam. Strong, but not surprising in the case of someone who was already fragile and had lost a child.

The other bottle was prescribed for Eva-Britt Rasmussen in February 1986 and contains Levaxin, a hormone tablet given to patients with thyroid problems. It's more than half-full. It might be possible to explain why Lola left her tranquillisers behind, but medication for thyroid deficiency is usually prescribed for life. And yet Eva-Britt didn't take it with her.

The impression of a hasty departure is reinforced when Thea enters the kitchen. The smell in here is more acrid than in the rest of the house. There are glasses and plates on the table; judging by the mould, they'd been used. One of the chairs has been knocked over.

On the cooker Thea sees a greasy frying pan, and a saucepan with something black and unidentifiable in the bottom. She opens a cupboard; it's full of empty packets, mouse droppings, dead mealworm beetles and various other insects that have eaten themselves to death on a selection of dry goods.

The next cupboard has an array of bottles and jars, with both solid and liquid contents. She reads the labels: castoreum, digitalis, valerian. This must be Lola and Eva-Britt's natural medicine cabinet.

There is a white plastic container on top of the fridge; it's the same as the ones she saw in the ruins of the shed a little while ago. It's half-full of a clear liquid.

Thea shines her torch on the table. Three people sat here eating. Two of them had lost a child, the third person's child was accused of murder. How do you deal with a situation like that? What do you talk about over dinner?

She directs the beam at the overturned chair. Someone seems to have leaped to their feet. She thinks it was Lasse, maybe because the chair was at the head of the table.

She shudders again, not just because of the smell this time. Svartgården is a deeply unpleasant place, but she can't leave. Not yet.

The steep stairs are covered in a thick layer of dust; they creak beneath her feet. There are two bedrooms, one at each end, with a landing and a toilet in between. She begins with the room on the left, which contains a double bed, two wardrobes and a chest of drawers. The furniture and sloping ceiling make it feel cramped. This must have been Lasse and Lola's room. The bed is unmade. A movement among the sheets makes Thea jump, and she almost drops the torch.

Shit!

A mouse, who was obviously just as scared as she was.

She waits until her pulse slows before looking in the first wardrobe. Men's shirts, covered in damp patches. She can't help touching one of them. Lasse Svart's shirts have hung here for over thirty years, and yet it's as if they still hold a small part of him, make him appear more clearly to her. He somehow resembles her own father, even though she actually has no idea what Lasse looked like.

The other wardrobe is full of women's clothes. A blue silk blouse catches her eye. Everything else is cheap and ordinary, but the blouse is different. Thea takes it out, shakes off the dust and hooks the hanger over the door. The fabric has aged well, keeping its sheen. This must have been Lola's best blouse, the one she wore on special occasions, the one that made her feel really good about herself. So why is it still here? Just like her medication, Lola didn't take it with her.

Thea checks under the bed and sees two suitcases.

She straightens up. Something made Lasse and the two women jump up from the table in the middle of dinner. Get into their cars and disappear into the night without suitcases, clothes or medication.

But what?

She goes along the landing to the other bedroom. As she gets closer she realises the door is covered in a beautiful, hand-painted pattern of leaves.

She can just make out ELITA'S ROOM through the dust. And underneath, in smaller letters that almost blend in with the artwork:

Nature is hungry and the Green Man is riding through
the forests.

She's seen those words before, read them in Elita's letter, but this time they feel more creepy, somehow.

She reaches for the door handle, hesitates. The feeling she had earlier is back, the feeling that she's about to cross a line. Do something she shouldn't do.

She pushes down the handle and slowly opens the door.

58

Thea pauses in the doorway, shining her torch around the room. She has a sense of unreality; Elita's room is exactly the same as in the photographs in the case file. A single bed, an IKEA desk, an armchair, a lamp, a wardrobe.

She goes over to the desk, directs the beam at the place where the letter had lain.

My name is Elita Svart. I am sixteen years old. I live deep in the forest outside Tornaby.
By the time you read this, I will already be dead.

Thea opens the desk drawers. Pens, a biology textbook, a pile of cassette tapes. One of them is labelled TOP TRACKS, but she doesn't think it's Elita's handwriting. Another says BRYAN ADAMS. She looks around for a tape player, but can't see one.

In one of the drawers, beneath papers yellow with damp, she finds a Polaroid photograph of Elita sitting on her bed. Judging by the angle, she must have put the camera on the desk and used the automatic timer. Dampness has caused the surface to bubble, and the colours have faded; even though Elita is smiling, the image is unpleasant.

Thea slips it in her pocket and goes over to the wardrobe. Elita Svart has worn these clothes. She pictures the girl standing here trying things on in front of the mirror on the inside of the door. Listening to *Top Tracks*. Miming to Duran Duran, Wham!, Madonna. Dreaming of getting away from this place.

Half of the hangers are empty. Thea thinks back to Lola's wardrobe; her best blouse was still there. The opposite is true of Elita's clothes. The items that are left are old, faded, or too childish for a young woman.

She bends down and peers under the bed. A few pairs of worn-down shoes, a pile of books, an empty space.

She takes out the photograph again. The top of the pile of books is visible, and there is something blue and rectangular where the empty space is now. A suitcase.

A blue suitcase in which Elita packed her nicest clothes, not because she was planning to die, but because she would be flying away from here. Floating high above everyone's heads.

Can you see me, dear readers?

I can see you.

Thea is absolutely certain now. Elita was going to run away, on the very night when she died. She'd packed her suitcase, left a cryptic letter explaining why. So where did the case go? It's definitely not mentioned in the police investigation.

She uses her phone to take some shots of the room, the wardrobe and the space under the bed.

Another thought occurs to her: Was Elita really intending to leave alone? Just her and the child she was carrying? Or was the father involved? Was he waiting somewhere with the case, waiting for a girl who never showed up?

A sound makes her jump; was it the creak of a floorboard?

Her heart misses a beat. She listens hard, but there is only silence. No doubt old houses are always moving, making all kinds of noises.

She edges onto the landing, shines her torch down the stairs. Nothing. She heads down to the ground floor. It's just after eight; she needs to leave if she's going to open the surgery in time.

Maybe she ought to take the medication with her, or at least photograph the bottles?

As she enters the bathroom she notices something on the floor in one corner, something she recognises. Empty green plastic packaging. She picks it up, turns it over.

EMERGENCY DRESSING.

She used dozens of these when she was out in the field. She always carried at least one, usually two, in her trouser pockets.

She takes a closer look at the washbasin and the floor. In spite of the dust, she thinks she can see several dark patches.

They could be anything. But they could also be blood.

Someone could have stood in here dressing an injury. Tried to staunch a bleed that was too serious for a plaster.

She glances around for towels, but the hooks next to the basin are empty. She steels herself and draws back the disgusting shower curtain. She can't suppress a gasp.

Two dark towels lie screwed up in the bottom of the bath. In the middle of the wall, dried onto the white tiles, is a big, rust-coloured handprint.

59

Thea photographs the handprint, the towels and the empty packaging. She compares the print with her own hand; it's much bigger. A man's, presumably Lasse's, unless a fourth person was here.

She returns to the kitchen.

Lasse Svart leaps to his feet, knocking over his chair. But what happens next? She sweeps the beam of the torch all around the room, looking for more bloodstains, but the wooden floor is too worn and dirty. She crouches down; there is a piece of dark material next to one of the table legs. It takes a few seconds before she realises what it is: a green beret. Someone has written *223 Rasmussen* inside with a black felt tip. This must be Leo's beret, the one with the cap badge that definitively tied him to the scene of the murder. So what is it doing here?

Thea tucks the beret into her pocket and continues to examine the floor. She soon makes another discovery; among the rag rugs there is a hatch. She glances at her watch; it really is time she left. It will take her a good half hour to walk back to the car, then it's a fifteen-minute drive to the surgery. Plus she has to find Emee.

She can't help it; she has to at least open the hatch and take a look.

The recessed bolt also acts as a handle. She gets hold of it and pulls as hard as she can, but the hatch refuses to move. She goes back to the porch and fetches the crowbar; she also steps outside for a few gulps of fresh air, and looks around for Emee.

The yard is silent. Maybe too silent. The birds have stopped singing again, just as they did a little while ago. She suddenly feels uneasy. She clutches the crowbar, peers into the gloom beneath the trees.

'Emee! Emee!'

Nothing. She can't wait any longer. Either she leaves now, or she goes back inside and forces the hatch.

She chooses the latter option, and the hatch gives up the fight surprisingly quickly, releasing a gust of that familiar cellar smell. Thea puts down the crowbar, shivers, and directs the beam of the torch down the hole.

A narrow wooden staircase leads to a large cellar directly below the kitchen. A shelf obscures her view; the only way to see what's behind it is to go down there. She hesitates. It's getting late; is she really going to investigate a pitch-dark cellar? If she doesn't, she might miss something important. She hasn't come all the way out here to leave without following every possible lead.

Slowly she begins to make her way down the steps. The smell is nauseating, making her breathe in short gasps.

When she reaches the bottom, she stops and takes in her surroundings. The shelf is packed with old-fashioned glass jars; the contents are cloudy, but the labels are still legible. Apples, pears, plums, even eggs. Bottles of elderflower cordial.

Cautiously she edges around the shelf. Pipes, a rusty boiler, a huge pile of wood. She's about to turn and go back to the stairs when she hears something. A faint scraping, followed by the creak of a floorboard. She looks up, sees a flash of light. There's someone up there.

Rapid footsteps, a different kind of creak, and she realises what's happening. She makes a run for the stairs, but trips and falls head first. Her torch bounces across the floor and goes out. She looks up and glimpses a pair of wellington boots before the hatch is slammed shut, and she is plunged into total darkness.

60

The crash of the hatch bounces off the cellar walls. Thea hears the rattle of the bolt, then footsteps crossing the kitchen floor, followed by the front door closing.

She is alone here. Alone and locked in a pitch-black cellar.

Her heart is racing. In her head she is five years old, or eight, or ten. It's a different cellar, but it smells the same. Dampness, earth, fear.

She can already hear the faint sound of insects scuttling across the floor. The ones with hard bodies and vibrating wings.

She is almost paralysed with terror, but forces herself up onto all fours. Gropes around in the darkness, but fails to find the torch. Her hand brushes against something alive, and she snatches it back. Presses her back against the wall, wraps her arms around her knees.

She is alone. No one knows she is out here in the forest, no one except the person who's locked her in, left her alone in the darkness. She could die here without anyone realising. Sooner or later the old house will collapse, like the stable and the barn. Bury her under a pile of rubble and dust, just as in her nightmare.

Her chest contracts, her breathing becomes shallower. Her vision flickers.

She has to calm down, stop hyperventilating before she faints. She is no longer a terrified little girl, she is a grown woman who has worked in war zones, seen people die, continued operating even though bombs were shaking the building she was in.

She fumbles in her pocket, takes out one of Emee's poo bags. Breathes into it. The trick works. The flickering stops, her pulse slows.

She must try to think. The priority is to find her torch. She pushes the bag back into her pocket; her fingers touch something hard.

Her phone – Jesus, how stupid!

She brings the screen to life, clicks on the torch. There is enough light to find her proper torch and, maybe more importantly, to chase away the worst of the fear.

She checks the phone, but as she suspected there is no coverage down here. She climbs the steps and pushes at the hatch, but it's rock solid. She searches the cellar, but can't find anything that might help her to break out. Presumably the crowbar is still on the kitchen floor. Why the hell didn't she bring it with her?

She sits down on the bottom step and tries to gather her thoughts. How long will it be before someone misses her? Before David starts searching for her? Not until this evening, or tonight. Will the torch batteries last that long?

A sudden noise makes her jump.

Barking. Emee is barking, right outside the cellar. Thea moves towards the sound, shines the torch on the wall behind the pile of wood. She can hear Emee scratching at something; a wooden hatch that must lead out to the front of the house.

She pulls down enough logs to be able to scramble up onto the pile and try the hatch. It refuses to move. Presumably it's bolted on the outside, like the doors and windows, but unlike the hatch in the kitchen, this one must have been exposed to the weather. The wood feels porous, rotten.

Thea rearranges the logs until she has created a flat platform. She lies on her back, draws up her legs and kicks hard. After four kicks she feels something give way. After six she can see the light, finding its way in between the planks. Emee is still scratching and whimpering on the other side.

'Out of the way, sweetheart!'

She keeps on kicking, harder and faster. Five more kicks – the bolt gives way and the hatch flies open. Thea crawls out into the yard and Emee hurls herself at her, clambering all over her, licking her face.

Thea gets to her feet, brushes off the dirt and fills her lungs with air. Relief and Emee's welcome have brought her to the verge of tears, but she mustn't cry. She has to stay alert.

Someone locked her in, someone who presumably followed her to Svartgården. But who, and why?

She looks at her watch, realises that she doesn't have time to go into that now. She also suspects that the answer isn't here. The person responsible has too much of a head start. She must get back to the village.

She sets off as fast as she can, and finds the track almost without needing to ask her phone for help. As she walks she looks in vain for traces of the person who must have followed her, while trying to recall what she saw from the bottom of the steps. The person's torch dazzled her, so she couldn't make out any facial features, or even be sure if it was a man or a woman. The wellington boots aren't much to go on.

It starts raining just as she reaches the car, a cold spring rain that hammers on the roof. She jumps in and starts the engine, but as she's about to switch on the wipers she sees something sitting on the windscreen.

A little Green Man figure.

61

The shock doesn't catch up with her until she's left the marsh. Suddenly she's sweating, feeling totally exhausted. She's already late for work, and considers calling in sick, driving back to the coach house, taking a long shower and thinking through what she's seen and experienced.

However, before she reaches the turning for the castle, her phone rings.

'Where are you?' Dr Andersson says without preamble.

'Er . . . In the car.' Stupid answer – she should have pretended to be ill, but the sound of the engine would probably have given her away.

'Why aren't you at the surgery? It should have opened half an hour ago. I've already had two calls at home from angry patients.'

'I overslept. Sorry.'

'Overslept?'

The doctor doesn't seem to be buying the lie. For a moment Thea gets the idea that the other woman knows where she's been.

'Yes – I really do apologise,' she says hastily. 'It won't happen again.'

'OK.' Dr Andersson still doesn't sound convinced. 'When do you think you'll be at the surgery?'

Thea passes the turning for the castle. 'In ten minutes.'

'Good. It's important to stick to the opening times, Thea. Otherwise people start talking. Rumours spread quickly in the village.'

'I understand. As I said, it won't happen again.'

'Fine.' Her voice softens. 'We'll keep this little blip between us, Thea. Just this once. Drive carefully!'

Four patients are waiting in the corridor. Thea apologises, asks for two minutes to sort herself out. The look on their faces suggests that she might need longer.

She goes into her room and inspects herself in the mirror above the hand basin. Her face is streaked with dirt, her hair is full of dust. Her legs still feel wobbly.

She cleans herself up as best she can, then starts seeing her patients. She apologises once more; they make reassuring noises, but she can't help feeling that she's messed up.

At twelve o'clock she has a gap. She pops out to buy something for lunch, and takes Emee along. Her head is bursting with impressions from the morning. That gloomy boarded-up house, still standing deep in the marsh, filled with silent secrets. The terror of being locked in the cellar hasn't left her.

Someone must have followed her, watched her from a distance, hidden in the shadows. It's a horrible thought, and it gets worse as she goes through the details. She drove straight from the castle to the marsh as soon as it was light. She didn't meet anyone on the main road, and if a car had followed her along the narrow forest track, then surely she would have seen it.

So how had the person in the wellington boots found her? How did he or she know that she was on the way to Svartgården, and why did they lock her in? She can answer the last question at least: for the same reason as they left a nasty little Green Man figure on her windscreen. To scare her, stop her digging into Elita Svart's death.

As she leaves the community centre, a sports car pulls into the car park. It's Sebastian. He stops in front of her and gets out.

'Hi, Thea. I was coming to see you.'

'Right – I'm on my way out, so . . .'

'It'll only take a minute.' He looks around as if he wants to make sure that no one is listening. 'It's about the conversation in the dining room last night.'

'I wasn't eavesdropping.'

The lie is out before she has time to think. It's obvious that she was eavesdropping, and Sebastian knows it, but he plays along.

'Of course not, but as I'm sure you heard, we had a slight difference of opinion. Actually, I'd like to ask you a favour.'

'Oh?'

'When Nettan and I were approached about the castle project we were happy to get involved, both for the village and for David, particularly when we realised that the two of you were in some financial difficulties.'

The choice of words irritates Thea, but she decides not to say anything.

'As you perhaps heard, David has kind of gone off the rails. The project has seriously exceeded the budget, and now he's trying to give us an ultimatum. Either we come up with more money, or we lose the capital we've already invested. Nettan and I were hoping you might be able to persuade David to come to his senses. Stick to the plan.'

Thea shrugs. 'David does what he wants. He doesn't like other people telling him what to do.'

'I know. He's always been like that, ever since we were in school.' Sebastian shakes his head, looking faintly amused. 'The three of us took part in a radio quiz, did you know that? We got as far as the semi-final, and the scores were even. The last question was the decider. Nettan and I knew the answer, David didn't agree – but it was two against one. David was our designated speaker, and when it was our turn he ignored what we'd said and gave his own answer.'

'And you lost.'

'By one point. The team that beat us went on to win the final. If David had stuck to the plan, then . . .' He spreads his hands in a gesture of resignation. 'We're worried that he's well on the way to making the same kind of mistake now – reaching the wrong decision off his own bat, and leaving Nettan and me to suffer the consequences.'

Thea nods. There's a question she simply has to ask.

'You were talking about Elita Svart yesterday, weren't you?'

Sebastian stiffens.

'So you heard that, even though you weren't eavesdropping. How much do you know?'

'That all four of you were there when she died – you, David, Nettan and Jan-Olof.'

'We were.'

'You told the police it was Leo who killed her.'

'We said he was riding the horse,' Sebastian corrects her. 'Leo confessed to killing Elita.'

'There are suggestions that he made his confession under duress.'

Sebastian shakes his head angrily.

'That's crap. It was Leo we saw. Elita had arranged for him to come galloping into the stone circle and frighten us away, and he did. We ran for our lives.'

'Except for David. He went back. He saw Leo bending over Elita.'

'Yes, but you need to talk to him about that, not me.'

Sebastian takes a deep breath, glances demonstratively at his heavy watch.

'One last question,' Thea says. 'A Polaroid was taken at the sacrificial stone at some point before Walpurgis Night. Elita was dressed as the spring sacrifice, and the four of you were wearing animal masks. Who took the picture?'

He stares at her for a few seconds.

'I've no idea. I think maybe Elita took it using the automatic timer, but it's all so long ago. I can't really recall the details, and to be honest, it's not something any of us wants to rake over.' He looks at his watch again; he's had enough of her questions. 'Anyway, I have to go, but as I said, Nettan and I would really appreciate it if you could help us out with David. Stop him from making a mistake that could cost us all dearly.'

He gives her a meaningful look before getting back in the car. As he drives past, Thea glances at the cramped back seat. On the floor is a pair of wellington boots.

62

S he takes Emee for a walk and buys lunch at the local pizzeria.
Tries to force it down at her desk.

She thinks about the wellington boots in Sebastian's car; were
they the same as the ones she saw at Svartgården? A pair of boots
doesn't make him a suspect, and what would Sebastian have to
hide? He was twelve years old when everything happened.

Thea gets out her finds from Svartgården: the bubbly Polaroid
Elita took of herself sitting on the bed, and the beret without its
badge.

She looks at the photograph first, the blue case under the bed.
Elita had packed her best clothes. She was planning to run away,
not to die. But the case is missing.

She fingers the beret. The fabric smells of damp. Leo's handwriting inside is unexpectedly neat. *223 Rasmussen.*

There are several things about the beret that bother her.
David and the others claimed that Leo was dressed as the
Green Man when he came galloping into the glade, that he
had a pair of antlers on his head, not his beret. He could have
had it in his pocket, of course, but in that case how did he
lose the badge? And what was the beret doing on the kitchen
floor?

However, that's far from the greatest mystery at Svartgården.
The remaining three inhabitants clearly left in haste. Judging by
the handprint, one of them was injured. Possibly Lasse.

So what happened? Why did they flee without packing any clothes or even grabbing their medication? And where did they go?

Thea adds those questions to the growing list in her head. What should she do next? She googles the book about false confessions.

The author has a homepage with both an email address and a mobile number. He answers almost right away. Kurt Bexell has a soft, melodic voice, and seems pleased that someone is interested in his work. Thea spins him a line, tells him she's also a writer and is planning to write a true crime book about the case.

'The spring sacrifice? Oh yes, I remember it well. It was an old friend in the probation service who gave me the heads up and put me in touch with Leo Rasmussen. The whole thing seemed very promising at first.'

'Did you meet Leo?'

'No, we spoke on the phone a few times. He was living overseas. I explained the premise of my book and told him about some similar cases. I said I'd read the transcripts of his interviews and thought he'd been affected by memory distrust syndrome. Do you know what that means? I describe it in considerable detail in the book.'

He doesn't wait for her response; he's excited to have the opportunity to hold forth on his area of expertise.

'The suspect is under so much pressure that he no longer trusts his own memories. Eventually reality, fantasy and police claims merge, until he believes in his own guilt, or at least doubts his innocence. Stress, sleep deprivation and isolation combined with lengthy, difficult interviews and leading questions are strong contributory factors, and Leo was subjected to all of those things. He was also mentally fragile after his stepsister's violent death, and the fact that his family had left him in the lurch.'

'What did he say about your theory?'

'Very little; he was pretty vague. He said he didn't remember much, and that he'd served his time. I tried to get him to open up, but his answers became shorter and shorter, then he ended the call. However, I got the feeling that he'd started to think about what had happened. I put together a short chapter and moved on to other cases, hoping he'd come back to me in the future.'

'And did he?'

'Yes, but not exactly in the way I'd hoped.' There was a brief silence on the other end of the line. 'Leo called me a month or so after our original conversation. He was crying, and was obviously drunk. He kept saying that he loved his stepsister, and could never have hurt her.'

Thea can almost hear her heart beating.

'I asked him to call me back when he was sober, but he never did. Instead his phone number stopped working. I finished the book, and after some hesitation I decided to include the case anyway. There weren't many Swedish examples to choose from.'

'Do you have an address for him?'

'I'm afraid not – he never gave it to me. I believe he was living in the USA. That's all I can tell you, I'm afraid.'

Thea thinks for a moment.

'Did you ever hear that Elita Svart was pregnant when she died?'

'No.' Bexell sounds a little taken aback. 'Was she? I have no recollection of that at all.'

'I'm pretty sure she was, but the information seems to have been removed from the autopsy report.'

'Interesting. I always had a vague feeling that not everything had come out. I actually drove down to Ljungslöv to speak to the officers who'd conducted the interviews. I really had to lean on the chief of police just to get a copy of the preliminary inquiry. Things got quite nasty towards the end; one of his heavies threatened to beat me up if I didn't stop poking around in the case.'

Thea presses the phone closer to her ear.

'What did he look like? Do you remember?'

'Oh yes – it's not often you get threatened by a cop in full uniform. He had a moustache; he was a nasty piece of work.'

'Arne Backe?' She can hear the agitation in her voice.

'He never introduced himself – he just made it clear that it would be best if I got in my car and drove away, unless I wanted my balls crushed. I followed his advice,' Bexell said dryly.

Thea tries to gather her thoughts. She has one more question.

'Do you believe . . .' She pauses, decides to carry on. 'Do you believe Leo was telling the truth, that he really was innocent? After all, there were witnesses and forensic evidence.'

There is a brief silence.

'It's true that a lot of things pointed to him. Wasn't some part of his uniform found at the scene?'

'Yes, a cap badge. Plus there were hoof prints from a horse that was stabled at Svartgården, and the witnesses said they'd seen him on the horse.'

'But those witnesses were children, and they ran away immediately, as I understand it. Except for the boy who came back, they can't have seen much.'

'David Nordin.'

'That's right, that was his name. David was the only one who said he'd seen Leo without the Green Man costume. He could easily have influenced his friends. They were interviewed together, which is highly irregular. Children have a tendency to back up one another's stories. If one of them claimed that it was Leo they'd seen, and that person held a strong position within the group, it's not impossible that the rest would just go along with him.'

'So you do think Leo was innocent?'

Another silence.

'Let me put it this way,' Bexell says eventually. 'I think there are certain aspects of Leo's confession, the witness statements and the investigation as a whole that suggest he *might* have been.'

63

*'Do you remember the time we got a puncture out in the
bush, and that bull elephant appeared? He stood and stared
at us, maybe only fifteen metres away, snorting and scraping
at the ground. Do you remember that sense of fascination, of
danger? Then you'll understand what I'm feeling right now.'*

In her dream she is back in the cellar. At first, it's the one
from her childhood. Maybe she's little too, little and terrified.
Sitting with her back pressed up against the wall, listening to
Daddy shouting on the other side of the door. Then everything
changes. The cellar is older, damper. The ceiling is not made of
solid concrete but of planks of wood, a small amount of light
seeping through the gaps.

She can hear voices in the room above, a man and two
women. She moves back and forth across the cellar floor, trying
to peek between the planks, but all she can see are legs. A pair of
wellingtons, two pairs of clogs.

The voices grow louder, angrier. A crash as a chair is knocked
over directly above her head. She instinctively closes her eyes,
protects her head with one arm.

Footsteps, shouting. Then a scream of pain.

Suddenly she is somewhere else. In the stone circle. Veils
of mist hover around the ancient hawthorns. She is wearing a

white dress, clutching two sets of antlers in her hands. Her feet are ice cold against the stone.

Elita Svart is standing opposite her. She looks the same as in the school photo. She has a Polaroid camera on a strap around her neck, and she is carrying a blue suitcase.

'Who killed you?' Thea asks.

The girl doesn't answer; she merely gives a sad smile.

'Who killed Elita Svart?'

Suddenly there is the sound of approaching hoof beats. The girl turns her head, fear in her eyes.

'He's coming,' she whispers. 'Be careful!'

The hoof beats come closer and closer. Become a roar, become the sound of barrel bombs ripping apart a building and the people inside it.

Thea tries to scream but her mouth is full of concrete dust. The darkness envelops her, takes her back to the cellar of her childhood.

Someone is there, right beside her.

Are you trying to blackmail me, little Jenny? her father whispers the second before she wakes up.

She looks at the clock. Four thirty, and the chances of getting back to sleep are non-existent. The nightlight spreads a faint glow through the room. The damp patch has grown darker, as if the plaster, or whatever the bedroom ceiling is made of, is becoming saturated.

She lies there gazing up at the patch for a while. She thinks of her father, and the letter she hasn't written yet. How long will he wait? What will happen when he gets tired of waiting?

She pushes away the thought, replaces it with yesterday's conversation with Kurt Bexell. It is surprisingly easy.

Bexell told her that he'd fallen out with the chief of police in Ljungslöv, who sent Arne Backe to threaten him.

Why was the chief of police so keen to put him off? Who was he?

She turns to Google, enters *chief of police Ljungslöv* in the search box and immediately gets a hit from the local paper.

Crowds turn out to say goodbye to valued chief of police

The article from 2010 is about the funeral of Stig Lennartson, chief of police in Ljungslöv from 1981 to 2006. It is illustrated with two pictures: one of Lennartson himself, a bald man with heavy bags under his eyes, and one of a large group of mourners leaving the church. Thea immediately recognises her in-laws, followed by Arne Backe, Dr Andersson, Erik and Per Nyberg, and various other people she's seen around the village.

So Lennartson is dead. Was he the one who tried to hide Elita's pregnancy in the autopsy report? Judging by Bexell's account, that seems entirely possible – but why? Lennartson had no personal connection to the case, as far as she can see. According to the article, he didn't even live in Tornaby, but out in the country on the other side of Ljungslöv.

If Lennartson didn't tamper with the report of his own initiative, then who had enough power and influence to make a senior police officer alter the information in a case file?

Thea looks at the funeral photo again. Her in-laws are almost right at the front. Ingrid looks the same as usual, the same determination in her eyes, chin carried a little too high. Bertil, on the other hand, looks quite different. The gentleness she is accustomed to isn't there; instead his gaze is fixed, his expression grim.

In 2010 Thea and David hadn't met. And Bertil wasn't diagnosed with dementia until two years later. Was he caught at an unfortunate moment, or does the picture show the real Bertil, the man he was before he began to slip into oblivion?

She googles him, finds some photos from roughly the same period. Meetings at the sports club, some celebratory dinner. He looks more cheerful at these occasions, but it's very clear that the gentleness she likes so much is something that he's acquired in later years.

Ingrid is there too, standing slightly behind Bertil, her hand tucked under his arm, as if she is deliberately staying in his shadow.

Thea thinks about the strange visit from her mother-in-law the other day. The effort Ingrid has made to help her and David get here. Ingrid's concerns over what people will think if Thea goes around talking about Elita Svart. Or is Ingrid actually worried about something else? Is she afraid that Thea will find something? A crack in the perfect façade, which will allow the dampness to start spreading, allow secrets to slip out.

She and David have breakfast together. He got home late, long after she'd gone to bed. He looks exhausted; he's spending every waking moment getting ready for the dinner.

She's finding it difficult to let go of what Kurt Bexell said: that David might have influenced the other children to identify Leo. She'd like to ask him about it, but he's already made it very clear that he doesn't want to talk about Elita Svart. Bringing it up now would definitely lead to a row.

Another thought has struck her. If Bexell was right, if Leo's confession was false and he was actually innocent, then the murderer is still out there. A murderer who has got away with it for over thirty years.

Is that what the warnings were about? The cellar, the Green Man on her car – is she in danger?

'I have to go.' David pulls on his jacket as he finishes his sandwich. 'I've got my hands full all day. See you tonight.'

She nods. Forces a smile.

Thea has three patient visits planned for her morning rounds. The first two are in Tornaby, and the GPS finds them without difficulty. The third is some distance outside the village.

During the drive she catches herself glancing frequently in the rear-view mirror, keeping any eye out for cars that might be following her. Everything seems normal, at least on the surface, yet she can't shake off the feeling of being watched. Emee whimpers nervously, as if she's picked up on Thea's mood.

As they pass the common she sees that the effigy of the Green Man is in position on top of the bonfire. It looks almost exactly the same as the old photographs in the Folk Museum: a shapeless mass of leaves and branches, the head and arms the only parts that make it vaguely human.

The GPS guides her to four identical houses by the side of the road, so close together that they look as if they're seeking shelter from the wind. The façades are dirty brown, the tiled roofs covered in moss. A TV aerial is perched on one, slightly askew. She can't see any numbers, and doesn't know which house she's supposed to be visiting, so she knocks on the first door. There's a rusty little van outside, but she doesn't realise who it belongs to until the door opens.

'What do you want?' Jan-Olof mutters, without returning her greeting.

'I'm looking for Böketoftavägen 23.'

'That's Mother.' He points to the neighbouring house. 'I'd better come with you – she doesn't always hear the bell.'

He unlocks the door with his key and shouts from the porch.

'Mother! The doctor's here!'

He goes in, beckons Thea to follow him. The air is rank. The kitchen is littered with packs of medication and empty spirit bottles.

'Mother!'

A reply comes from upstairs.

'Mother doesn't like doctors,' he says, sounding a little embarrassed. 'She can be a bit . . .' he hesitates, searching for the right word '. . . difficult, if you know what I mean.'

Thea nods. She read the notes before she came out, but hadn't realised that the patient was Jan-Olof's mother. They climb the narrow stairs and he taps on the bedroom door.

'The doctor's here.'

'I told you I don't want to see a fucking doctor. Is it that fat cow Sigbritt Andersson?'

'No, we've got a new doctor. I did tell you.'

Thea enters the room. It's small, the ceiling and walls slope so much that she has to fight the impulse to bend her head. Jan-Olof's mother is in bed. She's a big woman with lank grey hair; her cheeks and nose are covered in a network of broken capillaries. The air is filled with a sweet yet acrid smell of alcohol and urine. Thea blinks a couple of times.

'Oh, so you're the new one, are you?'

'Yes – Thea Lind.' She holds out her hand. 'And you must be Gertrud.'

The woman looks her up and down.

'Well, aren't you the little china doll. Are you sure you're a doctor?'

'You'll soon find out.' Thea opens her bag.

Gertrud glares at her. 'I don't like doctors. Bigheads, the lot of them.'

'That's true. You have to be a bighead, otherwise you don't get into medical school.'

Gertrud gives a start. 'Is she trying to be funny, Jan?'

Jan-Olof mumbles something from a corner. He seems to be making every effort to avoid eye contact with both Thea and his mother.

Thea pulls on her Latex gloves.

'Shall we take a look at that pressure sore?'

Gertrud continues to glare for a few more seconds, then she folds back the covers and allows Thea to examine her.

'You're Ingrid Nordin's daughter-in-law, aren't you?'

'That's right.'

'Ingrid's a stuck-up bitch who—'

'Mother!'

'What? It's true. Ingrid thinks she's better than everybody else, thinks she's got the right to have a finger in every pie just because her family has lived in Tornaby for seven generations or whatever it is. She drags poor Bertil around as if he's an oily rag. Once upon a time people were afraid of him, can you imagine that?'

She nudges Thea with an elbow.

'So I've heard.' Thea tries to sound as if the topic doesn't really interest her.

'Do you know why? Because Bertil was in charge of the bank. He knew who was short of money, who was about to get divorced, who was tucking away cash instead of paying the tax man. Bertil knew everyone's secrets. Even the count had to kowtow to him and Ingrid. People still kiss their arses out of pure fear, although these days it's mostly Ingrid, since she took over as the chair of the Bokelund Foundation. She's ruthless, your mother-in-law. Never forgets an injustice.'

'Mother!'

'Yes, yes.' Gertrud waves a dismissive hand at her son. 'I'm sure the doctor knows what I mean.'

Thea straightens up, removes her gloves.

'There, you've got a nice fresh dressing. I'll come back and take another look next week.'

Gertrud looks disappointed, as if she'd expected Thea to be shocked by what she'd said. She mutters something in response, then pulls up the covers and turns away.

Jan-Olof follows Thea down the stairs.

'I must apologise,' he says when they reach the porch. 'She doesn't mean what she said. Father died in '91; Bertil helped her to hold onto the house and sorted out a job for her. Without Bertil and Ingrid . . .' He glances anxiously up the stairs. 'You won't mention this to them, will you? Or to David?'

Thea shakes her head. 'I never discuss my patients with anyone outside the practice. That would be a breach of patient confidentiality.'

Jan-Olof gives a smile that manages to be both worried and grateful.

'You must have known David pretty well back then,' Thea goes on. 'I'm guessing he was pretty cocky in those days.'

Jan-Olof looks uncomfortable, then smiles.

'He was. David was always the most confident of us all.'

'And Nettan was the centre of attention?'

He nods, apparently enjoying the topic of conversation now. 'What about Sebastian?'

'He was more cautious. Wanted to think through everything.'

'Aha, so he was the planner. And who were you?'

Jan-Olof thinks for a moment.

'I guess I was the one who followed. Did what the others told me to do. That's probably why I never got away from here. Plus I had Mother, of course.'

Thea decides to seize the opportunity.

'Elita Svart,' she says. Jan-Olof's expression darkens immediately. 'You were there the night she died.'

She takes the Polaroid out of her inside pocket.

'That's the four of you, isn't it? David, Nettan, Sebastian and you. With Elita.'

Jan-Olof half-turns away, but can't help turning back to look at the photograph.

Thea holds it a little closer to him. 'Which of the animals are you?'

'The fox. I was the fox. I've always liked foxes.'

'And what did you see that night?'

He shrugs. 'I saw a horse, and a rider dressed up. We thought he was the Green Man, so we ran for our lives. Why do you ask?'

'Are you absolutely certain it was Leo you saw?'

He shakes his head. 'It was so many years ago – I don't remember.'

A lie, she's sure of it. Something about this slightly scruffy man tells her that he remembers every single second, but how is she going to persuade him to talk.

'Why do you ask?' he says again.

'I . . .' She takes a deep breath. 'I was involved in an incident in Syria about twelve months ago. The hospital where I was working was bombed.'

Jan-Olof seems to be listening carefully.

'People around me were killed, injured.' She pauses. The story makes her feel sick, but she has to continue.

'I still have nightmares about it. Down to the last detail. The sights, the sounds, the smells, even the taste of my own fear. At the same time I feel guilty because I survived when others didn't.'

Jan-Olof nods, as if he understands exactly what she means.

'I hadn't heard the story of the spring sacrifice until we moved here. David's never mentioned it, and he refuses to talk about it. He says he's put the whole thing behind him. Is it really possible . . .' She swallows, starts again. 'Is it really possible to forget something like that?'

Jan-Olof looks at her for a long time. The sadness in his eyes answers her question before he opens his mouth.

'No,' he says softly. 'You never forget. Even if you spend your whole life trying to do just that.'

'And you haven't forgotten that it was Leo you saw?'

He doesn't speak for a moment.

'Leo confessed to the police,' he says quietly.

'He did. But now he's changed his mind.'

She doesn't know why the words came out like that. Maybe it's because she was thinking about what Leo said on the phone to Kurt Bexell. Whatever the reason, they have a noticeable effect on Jan-Olof. He gives a start, the colour drains from his face. His lower lip is moving. Thea holds her breath, waiting for him to say something.

A shout from upstairs interrupts them.

'Jan! Jaaan!'

Jan-Olof presses his lips together. He nods to Thea, then slowly turns and goes back up the stairs. His shoulders are drooping, hands hanging loosely by his sides.

We all have our ghosts, Margaux whispers in her ear. *Who do you think his might be?*

64

S he eats her lunch and is back at the surgery at ten to one to be sure of opening on time. There's already a patient waiting – Philippe, the Canadian who injured his hand.

'*Bonjour, docteur Lind!* You told me to come back and have the wound re-dressed. I happened to be in the village today, so if it's convenient . . .' He holds up his bandaged hand.

'No problem – come on in.' She unlocks the door, lets Emee in and gestures to Philippe to sit down on the bed.

'Nice dog,' he says, holding out his uninjured hand. But Emee keeps her distance. Flattens her ears and growls.

When Thea tells her to go and lie down, she reluctantly obeys. Settles on her blanket, but keeps a close eye on the man.

'OK, let's take a look.' Thea pulls on her Latex gloves and removes the dressing. Notices that Philippe is observing both her movements and her face.

'What mineral was it you were prospecting for again?'

'Vanadium.'

'What's that used for?'

'Mobile phone batteries, mainly.'

'And you think there's some here, in the Tornaby area?'

He nods. 'The question is whether there's enough to make it worthwhile extracting. That's why we're doing test drilling.'

She cleans the wound; it has healed very well. The edges are pink, and the stitches have held.

'And how do you extract vanadium?'

'Open-cast mining.'

'How do the landowners feel about that? Do they really want gaping holes in their land?'

He shrugs. 'According to the law, they own only the surface layer. The bedrock is the property of the state, and if the state thinks a mine is a good idea, then the landowner doesn't have much say in the matter.'

'But why here?' She's seen open-cast mines in Africa, huge gaping sores in the landscape, machinery spewing out diesel fumes.

Another shrug. 'Because this is where the resources are.'

The answer irritates her – or maybe it's his nonchalant attitude. She places a fresh dressing on the wound.

'I'm guessing that the locals aren't too keen on your plans,' she says.

Philippe clenches and opens his hand a couple of times to test the movement.

'People want a new phone every year. Better and lighter batteries for each new model. But nobody wants a mineral mine near where they live. As long as the extraction is done in Africa or somewhere else far away, nobody cares how it happens. Even though most mines out there are environmental disasters.'

He's beginning to sound pompous, and Thea is getting tired of his mansplaining.

'We, on the other hand, can extract natural resources with minimum impact on the environment. We restore the landscape when we've finished . . .'

'Really?' she interrupts him. 'Isn't that what all the big companies claim? BP, Shell, and all the other friends of the environment. Maximum profit, minimum environmental impact. But that's not the way things usually turn out, is it?'

He gets to his feet. Glares at her for a few seconds as if he's trying to work out if she's serious.

'Are we done here, Doctor?'

'We are. That will be two hundred kronor. You can pay by Swish.' She points to the poster with the QR code. 'If your phone battery is charged, of course.'

He fiddles irritably with his phone for a few seconds. Stops on his way out and taps the little sign on the door.

'Is this surgery funded by the Bokelund Foundation?'

'Yes – why?'

'No reason – I was just curious. The foundation seems to be involved in most things around here, big and small. I believe your mother-in-law is the chair?'

A statement framed as a question. She doesn't answer.

'We have an information meeting in the community hall tomorrow evening. Why don't you come along? Who knows, we might even be able to convert you, Doctor.'

He smiles apologetically as if he's regretting his behaviour.

'By the way . . .' He reaches into his pocket and takes out an object which he places on the desk. 'This was on your windscreen in the car park. I noticed it on passing and I was curious. What is it?'

Thea freezes.

It's a Green Man figure, more or less identical to the one that was on her car after she'd been to Svartgården.

'Are you OK?' Philippe says. 'You've gone very pale.'

'I'm fine,' she murmurs, unable to take her eyes off the little figure.

65

Thea heads home just after four. Walks around the car before she gets in, carefully checks out the car park. She scrutinises every vehicle she meets on the drive back to the coach house; the steering wheel feels sticky against her palms.

She's been given another warning. Someone knows she hasn't listened, that she's carried on digging into the story of the spring sacrifice.

There's a group of people chatting on a corner; she thinks they fall silent and stare after her as she passes by. The GPS flashes and she is reminded that Dr Andersson told her the digital driving log is somehow linked to the foundation. Can they trace her movements? Is that how someone knew she'd parked by the old entrance to Svartgården? Have they tracked her journey to see Ronny, and her father in prison?

The thought turns her blood to ice.

Who has access to the log? Dr Andersson? Erik Nyberg, the foundation's treasurer? Her own mother-in-law?

As she approaches the castle she sees Per Nyberg's pick-up in front of the main entrance, next to her in-laws' car. Per and Erik are with Nettan, David and his parents.

She pulls up and goes over to them. Ingrid's hand is tucked under Bertil's arm. He looks bright, and is clearly having a good day.

'Hi Thea – we were just talking about you,' Per says.

'Oh yes?'

'David and Ingrid were telling us that you'd been through some tough times in Syria. That you'd lost a close friend.'

Thea tries not to glare at David. He's got no right to bring that up, especially not in front of a group of people, as if her trauma were some kind of entertainment. She's definitely not in the mood for this conversation, and she doesn't like hearing that they were talking about her.

'It must be nice to come to a quiet place like Tornaby – nothing ever happens here,' Nettan pipes up, contradicting everything she said the other night.

Thea's irritation spills over.

'Really?' She raises her eyebrows. 'What about ritual murder, a ghostly rider and a missing family?'

Per frowns, Nettan's expression is hard to interpret, and both David and his mother look furious. Only Erik Nyberg and Bertil seem unconcerned.

At that moment they hear footsteps on the gravel and Hubert comes round the corner. He looks surprised, and seems to be considering whether to go back the way he came.

'Hubert!' Bertil calls out, a little too loudly. 'It's been a long time – how's your father?'

Hubert comes over, greets everyone with a nod.

'Rudolf's been dead for many years – you know that,' Ingrid says, tugging at her husband's arm.

'Of course I do,' he says crossly. 'I was the one who helped him with . . .' He falls silent.

'The foundation,' Ingrid supplies. 'You helped Rudolf to set up the Bokelund Foundation, for which we're all very grateful, aren't we?'

A collective murmur of agreement.

'Except for Hubert,' Thea points out.

The murmur stops abruptly, but she sees one corner of Hubert's mouth turn up in a wry little smile directed at her.

'What the fuck was that all about?' David says as soon as they're alone. 'Ritual murder, the foundation, Hubert . . . Why the fuck did you say all that?'

'Why are you running around telling people about Syria? And Margaux?'

'I . . . I just want people to realise what you've been through.'

'Why?'

'I don't know. Because I want to help you.'

'By babbling on about what happened to me?'

'That's not what I meant.'

'You've helped me enough, David. I'm fine now, OK?'

'You're not though, are you? It's barely been a year. The psychologist said . . .'

'Fuck the psychologist. I don't need any help – not in that way.'

She's angry, furious, without really knowing why. David looks exhausted.

She takes a deep breath, makes an effort to soften her tone.

'I'm eternally grateful for everything you've done for me, but I can't be a victim all my life. I have to try to move on. Besides which, you've got other things to think about.'

He nods, manages a little smile.

He prefers you like that, Margaux whispers from nowhere. *Broken, cowed . . .*

Thea presses her lips together hard in order to shut her up.

66

'This puzzle gives me no peace, Margaux. I have to find answers to my questions. For my own sake. Who killed Elita Svart? What happened to her family? And who's watching me?'

The atmosphere is still a little strained at the breakfast table, but at least it's better than yesterday.

David is making an effort not to check his phone every thirty seconds, and Thea is doing her best to show an interest in the preview dinner.

'Two days to go until Walpurgis Night,' she says. 'How many of us will there be?'

'About fifty.'

'So many?'

'Yes, I've got people coming from the restaurant industry, a few journalists, then others it's useful to have on side – wedding and party planners, influencers and so on. It's important that we get off to a good start.'

He's attempting to sound relaxed, but he can't fool Thea.

'Fantastic,' she says, trying to shut out the sound of her father's voice.

One well-aimed Facebook post is all it would take.

She thinks about the conversation with Sebastian. Wonders whether to leave it, or whether it's better to tackle the issue now.

'Sebastian came to see me yesterday. He and Nettan are worried about the finances.'

David stiffens. 'He's spoken to you?'

'Yes, but with the best of intentions,' she adds unnecessarily.

David shakes his head, and Thea already regrets bringing up the subject.

'Those two have no fucking clue about anything. Never have, never will.'

He knocks back the rest of his coffee and stands up.

'Don't worry, Thea. I've got everything under control. It's going to be a fantastic evening, and afterwards nobody will be whining about money anymore.'

He manages a rigid smile, kisses her and heads out of the door.

Thea takes Emee for a walk. She looks for Hubert, but his car isn't in its usual place, so she assumes he isn't home.

She crosses the bridge to the forest. It's rained overnight, everything is wet. The birds are singing for all they're worth. From time to time the sun peeps out from between the clouds, and she should be full of the joys of spring, but there's too much going on in her head. She has to forget about Elita Svart and about whoever is watching her and concentrate on a more pressing problem, one that threatens not only her, but also David and their entire future.

It's only a matter of time before her father contacts her again, threatens her again. She even gave him her phone number.

After all these years, she's on the point of being sucked back into his universe. Is she really going to write a petition for his reprieve? After all, there is a reason why he's in jail. The people who've fallen victim to his crimes, not to mention Ronny and herself. What would have happened if she hadn't taken Mum's money and run? She would probably have been dead, sitting in that car with Jocke when he tried to get away from the police. Or behind bars, because she'd already been involved in her father's 'business affairs' back then.

He must have been terrified when she disappeared. Wondered if she'd gone to the police. If she was intending to tell them everything she knew, as Lasse had done with Leo.

She has reached the Gallows Oak. The lightning strike doesn't seem to have killed it; the leaves have unfurled beautifully, but the face looks even more alarming, with the fresh scar running down the trunk. It is staring almost accusingly at her, as if the strike was somehow her fault.

She keeps going, follows the path all the way to the point where the canal separates the forest from the marsh. She stops from time to time to make sure she really is alone.

In spite of her efforts, the thoughts come crowding in. It's all such a mess, but she can't let go of Elita's fate now; she's come too far.

Suddenly she realises that she's made a rookie error. She's been in too much of a hurry, allowed herself to be distracted by the sheer number of pieces in the puzzle instead of starting at one corner and methodically working her way forward.

So, what are her corners? What does she know for certain? Somehow she suspects that the key is the child Elita was carrying, so she ought to start there. Try to find out who altered the autopsy report, and why it was so important to hide Elita's pregnancy.

Lennartson, the chief of police, is a prime candidate. He led the investigation, and must have had the opportunity to appropriate the autopsy report, and to make sure there was no further contact between the forensic pathologist and the other officers on the case.

But why would Lennartson have done that? On whose instructions?

Lennartson is dead, so there's really only one person who can help her with that line of inquiry.

The same man who threatened to beat up Kurt Bexell if he didn't stop asking awkward questions.

Uncle Arne.

Thea pushes the case file into her bag, settles Emee in the car, then drives to Tornaby and on to Ljungslöv. Once again she passes the effigy of the Green Man on the bonfire on the common.

References to the Green Man recur throughout the investigation. The Green Man took her – that's what Lola said in her interview. The children saw him ride into the glade.

Elita had packed her suitcase. The time for her metamorphosis had arrived. The Green Man was supposed to collect her, and frighten the children away at the same time. The stories fit together up to that point – but what went wrong?

If Leo wasn't the Green Man, then who was?

She switches on the car radio, finds a station playing Eighties hits. Duran Duran, 'A View to a Kill'. She thinks of the poster in Elita's room, imagines her miming to this very song in front of the mirror, and she realises that something else doesn't make sense. Something to do with music, Svartgården, and the children's testimony.

She pulls over by a bus stop and takes out her phone. Scrolls through the photographs she took in Elita's room. Her clothes, the contents of her desk, the biology textbook, the cassettes labelled in someone else's handwriting. Cassettes, but no tape player. She consults the case file, turning first to the interviews with the children, then to the list of items held as evidence.

The children say that they'd recorded drumming and a rhyme on Elita's tape machine, and that the same machine was there in the stone circle.

But no tape player was found at the scene of the crime. Nor were the animal masks from the Polaroid. The children said they dropped the masks in the forest as they ran away, but no masks are listed among the evidence from the scene.

Why not? Maybe Arne can help to answer those questions too.

The police station in Ljungslöv is housed in a red-brick building opposite the bus and train station. Reception is open only one day a week, and the door is locked. Thea presses the intercom button.

'Police,' says a female voice.

'Hi, my name is Thea Lind. I'd like to speak to Arne Backe.'

A brief silence, then a buzzing sound as the door is unlocked.

Thea hesitates for a second. Is this a good idea? But Ingrid told her to speak to Arne if she had any more questions, which she does. And surely she'll be safe inside the police station?

A female officer meets her in the foyer. She can't be more than twenty-five, yet she already has the slightly weary look of someone who has seen too much of the worst aspects of humanity.

'Arne's not on duty today,' she says rather brusquely.

'Oh, that's a shame.' Thea realises she should have called first to check.

'Is that your car?' The officer nods in the direction of the easily recognisable vehicle, with the name of the local car dealer emblazoned on the side.

'Yes.'

'Oh, so you're the one who lives at Bokelund castle. You're married to Arne's nephew. You're opening a restaurant – Arne talks about it all the time.'

'That's right.' This information surprises Thea.

'He only lives around the corner, if it was something important you wanted?'

'Does he?'

'Algatan 14. It's no more than five minutes' drive. I'll show you.'

67

Arne's house is a large white bungalow with a double garage. A robot mower is buzzing around the lawn. The BMW in which he picked up her and Bertil is parked on the drive, next to another that is almost identical.

She still isn't sure whether this is a good idea. Calling in to see Arne at the station is one thing, but seeking him out at home is another. A lot more risky. On the other hand, she doesn't think she can get much further without his help. After all, they're family, and she's here now.

She gets out of the car and rings the doorbell. A grey tabby cat appears from nowhere and starts rubbing around her legs. It slips inside as soon as Arne opens the door.

He's in his pyjamas and dressing gown. Square reading glasses perched on the end of his nose.

'Thea, what a nice surprise,' he says, sounding as if he means it. 'Come on in – would you like a coffee?'

He steps aside to let her in. She hangs up her jacket; it occurs to her that she knows very little about Arne, except that he's a police officer, was more or less brought up by Ingrid and Bertil, and used to be married to a woman from Thailand. Apparently, he's a cat person too, which surprises her.

The house is clean and tidy. The oil paintings on the walls look as if they were bought on holiday overseas – paddy fields, sunsets, bamboo forests. Asian kitsch.

'Nice artwork,' she says as he shows her into the kitchen.

'My wife's. Ex-wife's, I mean.'

He nods towards a photograph. He is about ten years younger, standing beside a small woman dressed in white, wearing a little too much make-up. She's holding a bridal bouquet and smiling stiffly at the camera. Arne looks considerably more cheerful.

'Sweden was too cold for her. Take a seat,' he says, pointing to a kitchen chair before going over to a cupboard and getting out coffee cups. She sees him quickly hide a bottle of schnapps.

The kitchen smells of coffee and toast. There are several photographs on the walls, probably taken in Thailand. Arne and the woman again, often with a child – a boy aged about ten.

'Sammy,' Arne says when he sees her looking. 'My stepson. We're still in touch; I'm going to visit them in a couple of weeks. I try to get over there at least once a year.'

'Lovely.'

'Milk and sugar?'

'Please.'

He passes her a cup and brings out half a sponge cake, which she assumed he baked himself.

'It was your colleague who gave me your address.'

'Which one? There are four of us at the station.'

'A young woman.'

'Jönsson. Of course, it's Wednesday today.' He shakes his head. 'Ljungslöv used to have a real police station, fully staffed, and a patrol car that was out and about twenty-four/seven.' He takes a sip of coffee as if to wash away the bitterness in his voice. 'So to what do I owe the honour, Thea?'

'I have some questions about Elita Svart. I know it's all a bit sensitive, but Ingrid said you'd be able to help me.'

Arne raises his eyebrows. 'No problem. What do you want to know?'

'Were you involved in the investigation?'

He leans back on his chair, takes a moment to compose himself.

'Yes and no. I was pretty new to the job back then; I'd only qualified a few months earlier. The district CID team took on the case, but because I was from Tornaby, I got to help out – drive them around, explain who was who in the village, keep an eye on cordoned-off areas and so on.'

'Were you present at the interviews?'

'No. I didn't have enough experience, but of course I heard all about it afterwards. Lennartson, the chief of police back then, held daily briefings where everyone was brought up to date. It was a big thing, a local murder. The first and only one in all the years I've worked here.'

Arne is being much more helpful than Thea had expected. He's nowhere near as cautious or reticent as everyone else she's spoken to. She regrets not turning to him earlier, and tries to curb her enthusiasm.

'Who interviewed Leo?'

'Two colleagues from CID. One of them was called Bure, but I've forgotten the name of the other one. They were good, though.' Arne looks amused, as if he's trying to work out where she's going with this.

'And there was no doubt about Leo's guilt? No suggestion that his confession might have been obtained under duress?'

Arne leans back even further, making the chair creak under his weight. He stares at her for a few seconds over the rim of his coffee cup, then breaks into a broad grin.

'You must have read that book – *False Confessions*.'

'I have – you're familiar with it?'

'Of course. The author actually came down here. He asked for and was given the whole case file, but when he wanted to speak to the detectives who'd interviewed Leo, that was a step too far. Lennartson asked me to explain as clearly as possible to the little hack that it would be best if he got the hell out of here.'

Arne laughs, as if the memory appeals to him.

'Lennartson was a hard bastard, but the fact is that Bexell was on a fishing expedition. As I said, Bure and his colleague were good – very experienced. Old-school cops, admittedly, but they stuck to the rule book. More or less. Little Leo admitted everything. Told them exactly what he'd done to his stepsister and wept crocodile tears. There was also plenty of forensic evidence, so I can guarantee that Leo Rasmussen wasn't unjustly convicted, if that's what's bothering you.'

'You mean the cap badge and the hoof prints?'

'Exactly.' Arne nods, then frowns.

'The children – David and the others – were interviewed together. Was that accepted practice?'

'To be honest, I don't remember. I think Lennartson interviewed them.'

He puts down his cup, digs out a tin of tobacco and tucks a plug beneath his upper lip. Pushes it into place with the tip of his tongue. The frown lines have deepened.

'Lasse Svart changed his statement the day after Erik Nyberg found the cap badge,' Thea says. 'Why do you think he did that? Surely people like Lasse didn't usually talk to the police?'

Arne shrugs. 'I've no idea. I guess he was suffering from a guilty conscience. Didn't want to protect his daughter's killer. That business of honour among thieves is often overstated, in my experience.'

'And then he disappeared. Left Svartgården in a hurry and took Lola and Eva-Britt with him.'

'Exactly.'

'Didn't anyone look for him?'

'Of course they did. Lasse was called as a witness at the trial and didn't turn up, so we spent a while trying to find him, but then the judge decided his testimony wasn't crucial. Leo had already admitted that the information Lasse had given was true. I think they might have gone to Finland; both Lasse and Eva-Britt had family there. The two of them were actually distantly related – typical gypsies.'

The word makes Thea lose most of the warmth she was feeling towards him.

'You seem to know a hell of a lot about the case,' he goes on. 'Details that can't have been in the book.'

She considers lying, but decides against it. 'I've read the case file.'

'Have you now.' Arne's eyes narrow a fraction. 'And why, if I may ask? Why are you interested in a thirty-year-old murder case?'

'Because it's about David. Because I don't think he's ever really got over what happened. What he witnessed.'

She's been expecting the question, and has had time to prepare her answer. Plus it's true, or at least it was to begin with.

'Did you know that Elita was pregnant?' she asks in order to regain the initiative.

Arne remains silent for a few seconds too long.

'What gives you that idea?'

'I think the information was in the case file, but someone removed it. There's a page missing from the autopsy report. Someone took it out and altered the page numbers.'

He is very still for a moment, then he bursts out laughing. His reaction surprises her.

'So just because there's one page missing from the records, you know for sure that Elita was pregnant and that someone was trying to hide it? Don't you think those are big conclusions to draw from one missing piece of paper, Sherlock?'

'Her medical records are also gone. They're not in the county archive.'

'Do forgive me. Two missing pieces of paper.'

Arne has a point, she reluctantly admits to herself. She'd really like to show him the case file, the shadows of the Tippex and the thin line across the page, but she doubts if that would be enough to convince him. Instead she presses on.

'There's something else that's been bothering me. David and the other children talked about dancing to music they'd recorded, and Elita had cassette tapes in her desk – but there's no mention of a tape player being found at the crime scene.'

Arne's expression doesn't change, but a slight twitch of his upper lip gives him away. He quickly rubs his fingers over his moustache as if to hide his reaction.

'I don't remember. It's a very long time ago.'

A lie, she's almost sure of it. Arne clears his throat, leans across the kitchen table and adopts a warm, fatherly tone.

'This is what happened, Thea. Elita took the kids to the stone circle. She got them to dance and sing. Then Leo turned up on his horse and scared the shit out of them. He smashed Elita's skull with a rock and left the body on the sacrificial stone, probably because she'd asked him to do it. I assume you've read her letter.'

She nods, is about to say that the letter could be interpreted in more than one way, but Arne hasn't finished.

'And as far as evidence goes, apart from the fact that David and his friends unanimously identified Leo, we know that he rode there on a horse from Svartgården. Lasse found it in the forest, muddy and exhausted, and the technicians matched its hoof prints with those at the scene. It was Leo who killed Elita – I have no doubt about that whatsoever.'

'You're not concerned about inconsistencies in the story? Items that weren't found? The tape player, the masks . . .'

'The masks?'

'Yes, the children said they were wearing animal masks when they were dancing, but they're not listed among the evidence either.'

Arne shrugs. 'Maybe the forensic technicians didn't think it was worth including them. Maybe the kids took them home, how the fuck should I know. What I do know, however, is that if you pick out individual details from a bigger picture and put them back together, you can make strange patterns. That's how all conspiracy theories work.'

'And what about the family disappearing without a trace the day after the funeral? Don't you think that's weird?' Thea has the bit between her teeth now.

Arne sighs heavily.

'Listen to me. Lasse Svart was a nasty piece of work who'd been in and out of prison for half his life. We were taking a closer look at all his "business affairs", and he'd been given notice to quit Svartgården even before Leo killed Elita. It's hardly surprising that he took off as soon as she was in the ground.'

'Leaving everything behind? Clothes, medication . . .'

Arne leans back again. The chair makes its objections clear.

'You are well-informed, aren't you?' He stares at her in silence. 'Have you been out there? To Svartgården?'

She thinks about lying, but realises it's too late.

'Yes. I was there the other day.'

He slowly strokes his moustache. He doesn't even look surprised.

'A piece of good advice from Uncle Arne, Thea. Stop running around asking questions. David is like my kid brother. I care about him – about both of you. If you start digging, you never know what kind of shit you might find, if you understand me. Hang on.'

He leaves the room, and she hears him rummaging in a drawer before he returns with a thin black folder, which he places on the table in front of her.

'Your identity details are protected.'

A statement, not a question. For a second he reminds Thea of Ingrid, his big sister.

'So?' Her turn to play it cool.

'So I'm wondering why.' He sits down. Closer this time – close enough for her to smell tobacco and schnapps on his breath. 'Most people who have protected ID are either police officers, abused women, or criminals. Which of those categories do you fall into?'

'None of them.'

'No?' He leans even closer. The smell of schnapps is stronger now.

Arne has clearly looked her up in the police database, but her protected ID has stopped him, effectively blocking anything that would lead to Jenny Boman. She tells him exactly what she told Dr Andersson. Her work for Doctors Without Borders, travelling to war zones, the risk of repercussions.

'I thought you'd left? After that business in Syria? The hospital that was bombed?'

'That's right.' Thea swears to herself. The whole village seems to know what she's been through.

'But you've still chosen to keep your ID protected?'

'For the time being. Just to be on the safe side.'

Arne nods, seems to accept her explanation, which enables her to relax a little.

'When did you start working for Doctors Without Borders?'

'Two thousand and five.'

'Right.' He opens the folder, takes out a sheet of paper. Brings his glasses down from the top of his head.

Suddenly she realises where he's going, and her blood turns to ice.

'But you applied for ID protection in 1990. Fifteen years earlier. How old were you then? Nineteen?'

She nods slowly, trying to keep the mask in place.

Arne taps the piece of paper.

'Why does a nineteen-year-old need a protected ID? That's what this experienced old cop is wondering. What happened to her? Why does she need to become invisible? Impossible to find in any records.'

Her mind is whirling. She searches for an answer, an explanation that isn't too close to the truth, but comes up with nothing.

Arne smiles sympathetically.

'You know what, Thea? Maybe this is nothing to do with me. Rooting around in the past isn't always a good idea – what do you think?'

The phone rings before she can respond, playing a shrill version of 'Für Elise' that makes it impossible to carry on talking.

'Excuse me!' Arne gets up, grabs the cordless phone and takes it into the hallway. 'Hi, Sammy,' she hears him say. 'Good to hear from you! No, no, you're not disturbing me.'

He walks into another room, talking a little too loudly.

Should she take the opportunity to get out of here? Their conversation is definitely over. Arne has warned her against asking any more questions about Elita Svart, hinted that if she does, he'll be only too happy to dig into Thea's past.

She stands up and goes into the hallway. Arne must be at the far end of the house; she can hear him laughing.

Curiosity takes over and she pushes open the door on her left. It leads to a large parlour with dark wooden furniture. It's cool and smells faintly of dust. Presumably it's not a room Arne uses much.

She closes the door. Past the bathroom there is a little corridor and a step, then the living room with an enormous flatscreen TV on one wall, surrounded by a home cinema system. Four big leather armchairs – three look untouched, but there is a small towel on the fourth, as if to protect the leather from wear and tear.

There is plenty more tech on the shelves and walls – a hi-fi system, the expensive brand David has always wanted. Older items like a reel-to-reel tape recorder and a cine film projector. It's like a journey through time from the late Seventies to the present day.

A scratched little box catches her attention. It says POLAROID on the side. She opens it and finds a Polaroid camera – not one of the new models that became popular a couple of years ago, but an old one.

There was no camera in Elita's room, and nor was it mentioned in the case file. She picks it up and turns it over. PROPERTY OF ARNE BACKE, TORNABY is etched on the back.

How long has he had it?

There's an instruction booklet in the case. She takes it out; it was printed in 1984.

She can see something else in the case, something that makes her heart beat faster. Three photographs.

The first two show a young Arne in his police uniform, tall and gangly with a downy moustache. In one his eyes are closed, in the other he's smiling too broadly in a way that borders on unpleasant.

She's seen the third picture before – many times by this stage. Four children in animal masks standing around Elita Svart, holding the ribbons attached to her wrists. The note is written in Elita's rounded handwriting.

To Arne, Walpurgis Night 1986. Come to the stone circle at midnight. The spring sacrifice.

'What the fuck are you doing?'

Arne is standing in the doorway with the phone in his hand. Thea was so absorbed in the camera that she didn't hear him coming.

'Who gave you this?' she says, holding up the photo.

He doesn't answer, he merely stares at her, his expression grim. His lip is twitching, but this time he doesn't try to hide it.

He is blocking the route to the hallway and the front door. Thea looks for another way out, but she is trapped. She holds her breath, feels every muscle in her body tense.

Arne takes a step forward, clenches his fists. Unclenches them and moves to one side.

'I'd like you to leave now, Thea. Put those things down and get out of my house.'

68

'I'm getting closer and closer, Margaux. Closer to the truth about Elita. At the same time I'm finding it harder and harder to shake off the feeling of an approaching disaster.'

Thea stops in the pub car park and opens the car door to get some fresh air. The adrenaline rush is subsiding and she feels sick.

Clearly Arne knew Elita well enough to lend her an expensive camera. Well enough to be invited to the ceremony in the stone circle.

She tries to rewind, go over everything he told her. *I can guarantee that Leo Rasmussen wasn't unjustly convicted.*

That was what he said, wasn't it? Guarantee, not promise.

Had Arne actually been at the stone circle? Seen Leo come riding into the glade? Is that why he's so sure Leo was the Green Man? Whatever the reason, it was strange and careless of him to keep that photo.

She gets out of the car and stretches. Takes several deep breaths to try and quell the nausea. She hears footsteps behind her and spins around.

'Oh sorry – I didn't mean to scare you.' It's the young woman she met in the church. 'Hi – do you remember me? Tanya from the churchyard committee. I'm the one who was playing the organ.'

'Absolutely – hi.'

'I spotted your car as we pulled up. Simon and I usually eat here once a week. Tornaby doesn't have much to offer. Anyway . . . I've got something to tell you. Simon was in the church yesterday morning; he'd forgotten some sheet music he needed, so he was there before six thirty. He saw the back view of someone over by the mystery grave.'

'Was it a man or a woman?'

'He couldn't tell. At first he didn't realise which grave it was, so he didn't give it much thought. When he came back out the penny dropped, but by then the person was gone. However, there was a beautiful fresh rose by the gravestone. Simon thinks it's because it's almost Walpurgis Night – the anniversary of Elita's death. We'll keep an eye out – sooner or later we should be able to find out who it is. Would you like to join us for lunch, by the way?'

Thea shakes her head. 'That's very kind of you, but I'm not hungry.'

Tanya looks disappointed. 'OK – I'll be in touch if we see anything else. Are you coming along this afternoon?' She notices Thea's hesitation. 'The information meeting with the mining company in the community centre. Everybody's going – it should be pretty lively.'

'I'll be there.'

'Good – see you later then.'

Tanya walks away and a blond young man with his hair in a ponytail comes to meet her. He glances in Thea's direction, nods and smiles.

Thea lets Emee spend a few minutes on the lawn in front of the pub before heading back to Tornaby to open the surgery. It's quiet, with only a few patients. She's still shaken by her visit to Arne, and has to force herself to tackle some admin.

As soon as she's finished she takes out Elita's case file. She reads the interviews with the children again, but none of them mentions Arne. As far as she can see, he doesn't come up in the investigation at all, and yet she's convinced he was there that night. Why else would he be so sure of Leo's guilt?

Or could Arne have had something to do with Elita's death? He was in his twenties when she died, a man with a job and a car, which could make him a possible father of the child she was expecting – but Thea can't see the awkward young man in the photographs being with Elita Svart. Everything she's heard about Arne from David and Dr Andersson suggests that he was a little odd. Would Elita really have fallen for him?

She turns to Elita's letter, tries to read it with fresh eyes.

My name is Elita Svart. I am sixteen years old. I live deep in the forest outside Tornaby.

By the time you read this, I will already be dead.

She is still certain that the letter is not about death, but about change. Elita was on her way, ready to leave with her unborn child – but someone stopped her. Was it Arne?

She hears voices in the corridor, the outside door opening and closing. People arriving for the information meeting, presumably. She's about to go and take a look when her phone rings. Unknown number.

'Hi Jenny, it's your father.'

The voice makes her inhale sharply. She locks the door, returns to her desk.

'Hi.'

'How are you?'

She doesn't know what to say. The idea of her father calling her from prison to ask how she is seems so absurd that she's having difficulty processing it. She's kept away from him for so long, and now they're making small talk on the phone.

'Fine, thanks.'

'Aren't you going to ask how I am? Isn't politeness the glue that holds society together, in spite of everything? Isn't that what proves we're human and . . .'

'How are you, Leif?' She closes her eyes, pinches the bridge of her nose.

'I'm dying of lung cancer, how the fuck do you think I am?' His laughter is interrupted by a fit of coughing. 'How's the reprieve petition going? Have you looked up what to do?'

'Not yet.'

'Not yet. What the fuck are you waiting for? Are you hoping I'll die so that the problem will solve itself? In which case I can tell you that I've arranged an interview with a newspaper after the weekend. It'll be a real sob story about a hardened criminal on his deathbed who regrets what he's done. There might be a few lines about you too – my angry daughter who refuses to write my reprieve petition, when all I really want is for her to forgive me . . .'

'Is it?'

'What?'

'Is that what you want? For me to forgive you? Is it important to you?'

'Don't be stupid.'

'So the answer to the question is no?'

There is silence for a few seconds; she can almost hear him thinking on the other end of the line.

'Just do as I ask, Jenny.'

The call ends abruptly, and she sits there with the phone in her hand, anger pounding behind her eyes. She massages one temple, trying to ease the pressure. In the end she opens the drugs cabinet and takes two painkillers. There are other options – stronger, more effective. For a brief moment she considers taking something else, something that will stop her mind from racing, just for a few hours.

She closes and locks the cabinet before the impulse becomes too hard to resist.

The hum of conversation from the corridor is louder now.

'Stay here, sweetheart,' she says to Emee. She hangs the BACK SOON sign on the door.

The hall is so full that people are standing along the walls. The double doors to the corridor are open, as are the windows. Thea stays in the background, craning her neck to see over those standing in the doorway.

Three men are sitting on the podium. One of them is Philippe. Behind them, on a white screen, a PowerPoint slide says: *Nordic Vanadium. A mining company for the 2020s.*

Thea stays for a while, listening to the presentation. The image on the screen changes, showing electric cars, forests, rivers, cheerful workers in hi-vis jackets and yellow hard hats. Key words are superimposed on the pictures: *responsibility, humility, resource extraction, environmental awareness, switch to green technology.*

It's just a longer variation of what Philippe has already told her. They're test drilling to see if the find is worth an investment in large-scale mining.

As Thea expected, the audience's attitude is extremely negative, and the longer the presentation goes on, the more often it's interrupted by angry comments.

Philippe's two Swedish colleagues repeatedly stress that the project will bring job opportunities and generate tax revenue. They emphasise the same argument as Philippe: they will extract natural resources with minimum impact on the environment, they will restore the landscape when they've finished. The villagers, however, are not convinced.

'You're just coming here to plunder our resources,' says a familiar voice from the front row. 'You'll take what you want, ruin our land and our waterways, then you'll leave. We've seen it before.'

This elicits a long round of applause.

The men on the podium try to respond to Ingrid, but are drowned out by booing and more angry remarks. They do their best, but after a few minutes they thank the audience and end the meeting.

As soon as they step down, all three of them are surrounded by a group of irate villagers. They patiently answer questions for a few minutes, then begin to move towards the exit.

Philippe spots Thea, and his serious expression gives way to a smile.

'*Docteur Lind*, how nice to see you here. Did we manage to convert you to our cause?'

Thea smiles and shakes her head. People push past behind Philippe, giving them both dirty looks.

'How's your hand?'

'Better, thank you. When do you think the stitches can come out?'

'Call in early next week – there's no rush.'

'Will do. *Au revoir, docteur!*'

He waves goodbye with his bandaged hand and disappears through the door with his colleagues.

Someone grabs Thea's arm. It's her mother-in-law.

'Do you know him?'

'He's one of my patients.'

'He's a thief. The whole company is a collection of villains.' Ingrid is white-faced; Thea has never seen her so agitated. 'They want to destroy the whole area, fill it with huge, dusty open-cast mines. Trucks and excavators working day and night. He's got no business here.'

'I'm well aware of what he does, but I can't refuse anyone medical treatment.'

Ingrid doesn't look happy with her answer, but someone calls her name and she walks away without saying goodbye.

On the way back to the surgery, Thea stops and looks out of one of the front windows. The car park is full, and there are lots of people chatting in small groups. There are many familiar faces: Per and Erik Nyberg, Dr Andersson, Little Stefan, Tanya and her husband.

Thea turns away and almost bumps into Jan-Olof. He gives her a brief nod, then slides past, heading for the door.

Emee jumps up at her when she gets back to the surgery. The dog is pleased to see her, yet at the same time she seems anxious, as if she didn't appreciate being left alone.

Thea gathers up her things, puts Emee on the lead and locks up for the day. The car park is quieter now. She settles Emee in the boot; only when she gets into the driver's seat does she see something tucked under the windscreen wiper.

A third Green Man figure, maybe twenty centimetres high. Unlike the others, someone has ripped off all the leaves, so that the thorns are clearly visible.

69

S he drives home as fast as she can, constantly checking the rear-view mirror. Arne must have put the Green Man on her windscreen. The reason is crystal clear: she has found out his secret. If she had any doubts, they've been swept away. Arne was at the stone circle when Elita was killed. Maybe he was the one who killed her. In which case how far is he prepared to go to keep Thea quiet?

She has to talk to David, has to do something – but there is no sign of David's car by the castle or the coach house.

She lets Emee out of the car, drags her towards the house. The dog resists, plants all four paws firmly in the gravel. She's had enough of being locked up and kept on the lead.

'Inside!' Thea snaps. She notices too late that Emee has managed to wriggle out of her collar. Emee turns and races off in the direction of the bridge.

'Shit!' Thea tries the whistle, but to no avail. She runs into the house. Her suitcase is still standing by the wardrobe, and for a second she toys with the idea of disappearing. Leaving Tornaby, the spring sacrifice and her father far, far behind her.

But Margaux would never forgive her if anything happened to Emee.

She changes into her old wellingtons and sets off. As soon as she reaches the forest she turns left, aiming for the deer enclosure. She keeps calling Emee's name and blowing the whistle.

She tries not to think about the dead deer or the fact that Emee is a predator.

After about five minutes she hears rustling in the under-growth, and to her relief Emee appears. The dog seems tired; her head is drooping and she doesn't object to being put on the lead. Thea doesn't tell her off. She's in a hurry to get back to the coach house. She's put it off for too long, but now she has to talk to David. Tell him what she found at his uncle's house, what she suspects.

David doesn't arrive home until gone eight o'clock, and she can sense his irritation the second he walks in. She's made dinner, poured them each a glass of wine, but one look at his face tells her that's not going to work.

'Mum called me,' he says without even taking off his jacket or sitting down. 'Apparently, you've been round to Arne's, asking questions about Elita Svart. What the hell are you doing, Thea?'

'She was the one who told me to go and see Arne if I had any questions.'

'Did she tell you to snoop around his house? Poke about among his things?'

'It was Arne's Polaroid camera that was used to photo-graph the four of you and Elita in the stone circle. He knew Elita, and he was there that night. Maybe he was the one who killed her.'

David stares at her. She hadn't planned on blurting every-thing out like this, especially not the last bit, and she can see from his expression that she's made a mistake.

'Arne was there,' she says again. 'He's threatened me. Left little Green Man figures on my car.'

David shakes his head.

'*I* was there, Thea. Have you forgotten that? And I didn't see Arne. Or do you think I'm lying?'

'No . . .' She pauses, playing for time. 'He might have been hiding. Maybe he came out after you'd all run away.'

David shakes his head again.

'I went back. I saw Leo bending over the sacrificial stone. Leo, who later confessed to having murdered Elita.'

Thea doesn't know what to say.

'I'm in the middle of the most important project of our lives,' David goes on. 'I'm working around the clock to get everything sorted, keep everyone happy. And the best you can come up with to help me is to start digging up the past. Making people angry and suspicious.'

Rage takes over his voice, making his accent stronger, oddly enough.

'Plus you're hanging out with people from the mining company who want to destroy the whole area. Brilliant way of fitting in with the community, Thea – well done!'

'I'm not hanging out with him. He's my patient . . .'

'After everything I've done for you! Everything I've given up for your sake.'

The comment makes something that's been bubbling away inside her for a long time suddenly boil over.

'What the fuck have you given up, David? Your restaurants, your career? Are you seriously putting that on me?'

She gets to her feet, goes and stands in front of him.

'You were a crap chef, David. Your colleagues were scared of you. You slept with several of your female employees, and please don't bother denying it. The only thing that ruined your career was you, and the sooner you accept that, the better.'

She knows she's gone too far before she's finished the sentence. David has almost the same look in his eyes as when he was fighting with the builder the other day. He takes a step forward, clenches his fists. Emee stands up, growls loudly.

David freezes. He and the dog stare at each other for a few seconds.

'Lie down, you little fucker!' he snaps.

Emee doesn't obey him. Instead she moves forward and bares her teeth, still growling.

David backs away, then turns and disappears through the front door, slamming it behind him.

70

Thea gives David an hour or so to calm down before she calls him. He doesn't answer.

In the end she goes to bed. She tries to push aside all thoughts of Elita, David and Arne, but it's impossible. Everything is spinning around in her mind; it stays with her in her sleep.

She dreams of the Polaroid, Elita and the children around the sacrificial stone. The ghostly hawthorn trees behind them are swaying in the wind.

Come to the stone circle at midnight. The spring sacrifice.

'Wait a minute!' Elita shouts.

Thea realises that the girl is talking to her. She is the one holding the camera, peering through the little viewfinder. The children in the masks are shuffling uncomfortably. A hare, a fox, an owl and a deer.

'Pull harder!' Elita tells them, tugging at the silk ribbons.

The children do as they're told.

'Now!' Elita says to Thea. 'Take the picture now!'

The next moment everything has changed. It's night. A fire is burning in the stone circle. The sound of drumming and chanting reverberates from a tape player.

Elita is lying on her back on the sacrificial stone, looking up at her.

'He's on his way,' she whispers. 'Things have been set in motion, and the Green Man is riding through the forests. Can you hear him?'

Hoof beats are approaching in the darkness.

'Tell the truth,' Elita says. 'Tell them who did it. Who killed me. *The strongest love is unrequited love!*'

Thea is woken by a sound, and at first she thinks David has finally come home. But it's Emee, coughing.

She switches on the lamp. The dog is standing by the door; she is retching now, and before Thea can get out of bed Emee has thrown up on the floor.

'What's wrong, sweetheart?'

Emee tries to walk towards her; she wobbles and falls over. Thea is on her feet in a second. Emee gets up, seems confused. Whimpers loudly. Throws up again.

A sweetish, chemical smell spreads through the room, and Thea recognises it immediately. She's experienced it before, many times. She grabs Emee's jaws, forces them apart, sniffs.

Glycol – anti-freeze, no doubt about it. Emee has been poisoned by glycol, which means it's urgent.

She pulls on her clothes, shouting for David.

No reply.

His bedroom door is open. The room is empty, the bed untouched. She tries his mobile but it goes straight to voicemail. Emee vomits again; she's finding it difficult to stand.

Thea steers her towards the car and manages to put her on the back seat. She googles the nearest twenty-four-hour veterinary hospital; it's in Helsingborg, about forty minutes away.

Emee needs help, right now.

Thea jumps in the car, floors the accelerator. The castle is in darkness; David's car is parked by the east wing. The kitchen door is locked. She hammers on it as hard as she can, shouting his name. She quickly realises that he's probably sleeping in one of the upstairs rooms, and can't hear her.

She gets back in the car, drives around to the front. Keeps one hand on the horn, flashes the headlights repeatedly. No response. She calls David's name over and over again, pointlessly.

A faint whimper from the back seat; Emee can't wait any longer. They have to go.

Suddenly a silhouette appears from the west wing. It's Hubert, in his dressing gown and slippers, hair standing on end.

'What's going on?'

Thea opens the car door. 'Emee's been poisoned – glycol.'

'How?'

'I don't know. Something she ate.'

'Anything I can do?'

'Have you got any vodka?'

'Vodka?'

'I need alcohol – as pure as possible.'

'I've got a bottle of Absolut in the drinks cupboard.'

'Go and fetch it and get dressed. You have to drive us to the veterinary hospital.'

Hubert nods and runs back the way he came.

Thea takes her medical bag out of the boot and gets into the back seat. Emee lifts her head; she's been sick again, and the sweet smell fills the car.

Thea digs out a syringe, fits a cannula.

Hubert's back. He's put on trousers, his oilskin and wellingtons, but is still in his pyjama jacket. 'Here!' He hands her an unopened bottle of Absolut vodka.

'The veterinary hospital is in Helsingborg, on Bergavägen,' Thea tells him.

Hubert puts his foot down and the gravel sprays up around the tyres.

Thea opens the bottle, draws a few millilitres into the syringe. Emee weighs about thirty-five kilos; she tries to work out a suitable dose.

'What are you doing?' Hubert asks when they reach the main road.

'Glycol isn't poisonous until the body's broken it down. Ethanol prevents that process.'

She decides on the dose and runs her thumb over one of Emee's front legs, searching for a vein.

'Can you stop for a second and switch on the internal light so that I can give her an injection?'

Hubert does as she asks. Thea finds a vein, injects what she hopes will be just enough. Emee's eyelids are growing heavy.

'OK, go. We'll have to do this again in about ten minutes.'

Hubert speeds through the night.

'I'm guessing you've done this before,' he says over his shoulder.

'We had a few cases in Nigeria. A couple of men who'd bought adulterated moonshine, and a little boy who'd managed to open a bottle of anti-freeze in a garage. Glycol smells and tastes sweet, which is why animals and kids like it.'

'What happened to them?'

'The men recovered. They came to us in time, and a grown man is more resilient.'

'And the boy?'

She doesn't answer. Hubert understands, and drives even faster.

71

The journey takes just over half an hour. Hubert pulls up outside the emergency entrance and helps Thea to carry Emee inside.

The dog is barely conscious. She is showing the whites of her eyes, and her breathing is laboured. Thea has phoned ahead, explained the situation and told them what she's already done. Two nurses and a vet are waiting and immediately take over.

'She's in good hands,' one of the nurses reassures them. 'If you take a seat in the waiting room I'll come and speak to you as soon as I can.'

Hubert fetches coffee from a machine while Thea sinks down on a plastic chair.

How can Emee have ingested glycol? She goes through the previous day, trying to think of an opportunity when the dog could have eaten something she shouldn't.

Emee was only out of her sight on three occasions. The most likely scenario is that it happened when she ran off into the forest, but where would she find glycol in a forest, several kilometres from the nearest road and even further from a garage?

The other two occasions were when she locked Emee in the surgery during the information meeting, and after she fell asleep in the coach house. There is no source of glycol in either of those locations.

Could someone have deliberately poisoned Emee? She can't shake off the thought.

She tries calling David, leaves a message when he doesn't answer.

Hubert hands her a cup of coffee and sits down beside her.

'I used to have an animal I loved too,' he says after they've sat in silence for a while. 'Nelson. A pure-bred Arabian. He was wild and hard to handle, but I loved riding him. He made me feel strong, invincible.' He pauses, lost in his memories. Then he straightens up.

'Would you like another coffee? Something to eat? I can go and look for somewhere that's open.'

She shakes her head. 'What happened to Nelson?'

'Another time. It's not the right story to tell you just now.'

She places a hand on his arm. 'What happened?'

He sighs, gives in.

'Father sent me away to say with relatives in England. Just after I left, Nelson injured his leg. Father . . .' Hubert takes a deep breath, eyes shining with unshed tears. 'He shot him. Per Nyberg was there, he told me that Father did it himself. Led Nelson behind the stable and shot him in the forehead. Had the body collected and incinerated that same afternoon.'

Hubert shakes his head slowly.

'My father was a hard man. He had no patience with weakness.' He gives a wry smile. 'I warned you it wasn't the right story for tonight.'

'You did.'

Thea's body feels heavy. She closes her eyes, tries not to think about Emcc, fighting for her life along the corridor. About Margaux.

*How about calling her Emee? She can be our own little ghost.
Yours and mine, ma chère.*

'What was your father like?' Hubert asks.

'He was a complete bastard,' she murmurs.

'What did he do?'

She opens her eyes. Realises what she's said. 'Nothing. Forget it.'

The nurse reappears, her expression grave. An abyss opens
up in Thea's midriff. She gets to her feet, holding her breath.

'You were right, it was glycol poisoning,' the nurse says. 'We've
pumped her stomach and given her Fomepizol. At the moment it
seems to be working; that trick with the vodka probably saved her
life. However, I wouldn't recommend trying it.'

The relief is so great that Thea almost bursts into tears, but
she manages to compose herself.

'When can we take her home?'

'It's too early to say. Go home and get some sleep. Call in the
morning and we'll be able to give you more information.'

David calls when they're in the car. It's just after five; Hubert is
driving, because Thea still feels shaky.

'I just picked up your message – how is she?'

'OK. She's going to make it.'

'What was wrong with her?'

'Glycol poisoning.'

'What? How the hell did she get hold of glycol?'

'I don't know. Do we have any in the house or at the castle?'

'Not as far as I'm aware.'

They end the call with exaggerated warmth, as if neither of
them wants to acknowledge last night's quarrel.

'I have a question,' she says to Hubert after a little while. 'You
don't have to answer if you don't want to.'

'Go on.'

'Did you know Elita Svart?'

The silence is a fraction too long.

'Yes.'

'How?'

'We bumped into each other occasionally in the forest. Her father was one of our tenants.'

'What was she like?'

Another silence.

'Elita was . . . different.'

'In what way?'

Hubert shrugs. 'Hard to explain. She looked at life in her own particular way, if I can put it like that.'

'Do you believe it was Leo who killed her?'

'I don't know anything about that. I was in England when Elita . . .' He breaks off, as if the words won't come out.

'I've been to Svartgården,' Thea says.

'Why?'

'Because I was curious, I guess. I'm trying to understand what happened.'

'I thought it was all pretty clear?'

'Yes, but there are a few anomalies.'

'Like what?'

For a moment she considers telling him what she found at Arne's house, and her suspicions, but she decides to hold back. There is another aspect of the mystery that he might be able to help with. Three pieces of the puzzle that don't quite fit.

'Elita's family. They vanished without a trace, and your father had the house boarded up and the track destroyed the very next day.'

Hubert nods slowly.

'My father and Lasse Svart had been at loggerheads for years. Lasse had been given notice to quit before Elita died. My father made sure they couldn't come back.'

'That's a harsh way to treat a grieving family.'

Hubert shrugs. 'As I said, my father was a hard man.'

His tone indicates that he'd like to drop the subject. Thea waits, hoping he'll change his mind and go on, but the moment seems to have passed.

She gazes out of the window, then asks: 'Are you invited to the preview dinner?'

'Mm.'

'Are you coming?'

He shakes his head. 'I'm not very good with people. I prefer to keep myself to myself.'

Thea is disappointed. The dinner is David's project, and it would have been nice to have someone there who was more like a friend of hers.

When they reach the castle, he gets out of the car and she moves across to the driver's seat.

'Thank you so much, Hubert. If you hadn't helped me, Emee wouldn't have . . .'

He waves a dismissive hand.

'We Stanley Kunitz fans must stick together.'

He stops at the corner of the west wing and raises a hand in farewell before going inside.

Suddenly it's as if something clicks in Thea's mind. The sound of a piece of the puzzle falling into place.

72

Thea runs into the coach house, kicks off her boots and drops her jacket on the sofa. The poetry book is on her bedside table.

She picks it up, sits down at the desk, then finds Elita's letter in the case file. She follows the text with her index finger until she finds the right section.

> I'm sure you've heard about the other girls who died in the forest. Isabelle who drowned in the moat, and Eleonor who fell off her horse and broke her neck.
>
> Soon it will be Elita's turn.
>
> Beautiful women dead that by my side. Once lay.
>
> Isn't that lovely?
>
> There's something appealing about dying when you're at your most beautiful, don't you think?

She reads the awkward sentence once again.

Beautiful women dead that by my side. Once lay.

Thea leafs through the poetry book, finds a page with the corner turned down. The poem is called 'I Dreamed That I was Old'. She's read it a few times; it's sad. It's about a man dreaming of his old age, thinking of everything he's lost.

Almost at the bottom of the page she finds the lines she's looking for.

And cozy women dead that by my side / Once lay.

The wording is almost identical. She picks up her phone, brings up the pictures she took at Svartgården. Works backwards from the bloody handprint and the empty dressing packet until she reaches Elita's room. The space under the bed where Elita's suitcase had been stored. The pile of books next to it. She enlarges the image, her fingers trembling with excitement.

There it is, third from the bottom. The same title as the book in front of her on the desk. *Selected Poems* by Stanley Kunitz.

Elita has read it too; she even tried to translate one of the poems into Swedish. Where did a sixteen-year-old girl get a book of poems written in English by an American?

We bumped into each other in the forest occasionally.

Elita was . . . different.

She leans back, presses her fingertips against her eyelids.

Elita must have got the book from Hubert. She even mentions his relatives in the same section – Isabelle and Eleonor. The dead girls.

She opens the book again, reads the inscription.

The strongest love is unrequited love.

Is he talking about Elita? Was Hubert in love with Elita? The thought is dizzying; it puts everything in a new light.

At that moment her phone rings. Unknown number. Thea rejects the call, but whoever is trying to contact her refuses to give up, and in the end she answers.

'Hi, Jenny, it's your father.'

'I can't talk now – I'm afraid it's not convenient.'

Her head is all over the place, and she can't cope with his mind games right now.

'That's a shame. I actually called to apologise.' His voice is subdued, without the usual sarcastic undertone.

'Really?' She doesn't know what to think.

'Our last conversation didn't end well, so I thought I'd offer an olive branch. If you're interested.'

'I'm listening.'

'OK, so I asked around about Leo Rasmussen. A former colleague of mine has a nephew, Dejan, who was apparently Leo's cellmate in Stålboda in the late Eighties. Dejan is a bright guy with a fantastic memory for detail. It was his first stint inside, so it's not surprising that he remembers it.'

Thea picks up a pen.

'According to Dejan, Leo kept himself to himself. Behaved impeccably, was always polite to the guards, worked out every day. Dejan said he didn't exactly come across as a killer, whatever that means. In my humble opinion anyone can become a killer in the wrong circumstances.' He breaks off to cough.

'Did Leo talk about what he'd done?' Thea asks.

'No, apparently he preferred to avoid the topic. He didn't boast about it, but nor did he insist he was innocent.'

A fresh bout of coughing; she can hear his chest rattling.

'Anyway, Leo told Dejan that he was planning to go abroad as soon as he was released. He said there was money waiting for him – enough to make a fresh start.'

'Where was this money coming from?'

'I asked the same question, but Dejan didn't know. Leo seems to have said too much on one occasion, then closed up like a clam, so Dejan assumed there was something shady about the whole thing.'

'Did he know where Leo went?'

'They both enjoyed fishing, and talked about going on a fishing trip to Alaska. Typical prison plans, I'd say – a dream to keep you going from one day to the next.' He clears his throat. 'Although they both realised the Americans would never let them in with their criminal records. Leo thought they might be able to get into Canada.'

'Canada?'

'That's what Dejan said. Or rather, this is what he actually said: *If the guy's still alive and doesn't live in Sweden, I'd look for him in Canada.*'

Thea thinks for a moment. Kurt Bexell thought he'd called Leo on an American number, but she's pretty sure that Canada and the USA have the same international dialling code, so he could have been wrong.

'Did Dejan say anything else about Leo?'

'No, that was all. To be honest it was more than I'd hoped for. I also asked a contact in the police to do some checking, and Leo hasn't set foot in Sweden since he got out of jail – at least not under his own name. According to the tax office, he's listed as emigrated, address unknown.'

'OK.'

'OK? Is that all I get?'

She takes a deep breath.

'Thanks, Leif.'

'You're welcome.'

He ends the call and Thea sits there with the phone in her hand, his words echoing inside her head.

Leo was expecting money. Enough to enable him to leave the country, start afresh somewhere else.

Money from whom? For what?

73

'I'm sinking deeper and deeper into this story, Margaux. Being dragged down into the mud. Back to where I once came from.

'The question is – will I ever get out again?'

Just after nine she calls the veterinary hospital. Emee's condition is stable, but the vet wants to keep her in for a couple of days just to be on the safe side. He wonders whether Thea has any idea how Emee came to ingest glycol, but she doesn't have an answer. She's thought about it, but hasn't come up with anything. The forest is still the most likely location, but she remembers that Emee seemed anxious when she returned to the surgery after the information meeting. The door was locked, but she already knows she's not the only one who has a key.

Could someone really be so cruel as to try and kill her dog? She gives herself a mental shake and goes back to where she was before her father called.

Hubert Gordon was in love with Elita. He gave her his favourite poetry collection, in spite of the fact that Elita was four years younger than him, and came from a family that his father would never accept. Could Hubert have been the father of her unborn child? Thea finds that hard to believe. It seems more likely to have been something else – unrequited love, rejection, jealousy?

She has to find out more.

Thea takes the poetry book and heads for the castle. It's a complete circus over there, with at least a dozen cars and vans and twice as many people carrying supplies into the east wing.

David is in the middle of the kitchen, waving his hands and yelling orders in all directions. He stops as soon as he sees her.

'There you are – how's Emee?'

'Better, but they're keeping her in for a little while.'

'That's fantastic!' He spreads his arms wide in an exaggerated gesture. 'I'm sorry I didn't answer the phone last night – I didn't hear it.'

A lie. David sleeps with his phone virtually under his pillow.

'I was right outside the castle, sounding the horn and flashing the headlights.'

'Were you? I must have been in a really deep sleep.'

Another lie. In David's case they're pretty easy to spot, because he's better at lying than telling the truth.

'You weren't there, were you? You slept somewhere else.'

He moves closer, places a hand on her shoulder. Looks around, worried that someone will have heard her.

'We'll sort everything out as soon as the dinner is over,' he says quietly. 'No more secrets. You can ask me whatever you like, but please help me to get us through this first.'

He smiles, tries to make her do the same.

'OK.'

Through the window, almost opposite the stone steps, she sees a group of men building a Walpurgis Night bonfire. One of them is Little Stefan; he's erecting a familiar T-shaped frame in the middle of the bonfire.

'What's that?'

'It's Walpurgis Night – obviously we're having a bonfire.'

'And will you be burning the Green Man?'

'It was Mum's idea. She's got some local experts to make an effigy for us. It'll be here in a few hours – it's going to be brilliant!'

David is pretending that everything is fine. He almost succeeds, but not quite.

Walpurgis Night is here at last. Nature is hungry, and the Green Man is riding through the forests.

And nothing will ever be the same again.

Thea heads for the west wing and uses the heavy knocker on Hubert's door. He doesn't answer. The car is there, so she knows he's home. She tries again, knocks a little louder this time. She suddenly feels nervous. It's only a few hours since they were sitting in the same car, and yet it's as if the way she looks at him has changed.

She knocks again; he appears after the fourth attempt, an irritated furrow between his eyebrows. Maybe he was lying down, recovering from last night's adventures.

'Hi – sorry to disturb you. Were you sleeping?' She makes an effort to sound normal.

Hubert shakes his head.

Thea holds out the poetry book. 'I just wanted to return this. I think I've worked out which is your favourite.'

'Oh yes?'

'"I Dreamed That I was Old".'

'Good guess.'

She wants to ask about Elita, whether the unrequited love he wrote about in the inscription refers to her, but then she realises he still hasn't invited her in. He also seems uneasy, almost as if he's been caught out doing something he shouldn't.

She looks over his shoulder and up the stairs. The door of the chapel is open. He follows her gaze.

'If there's nothing else, I'm a little tired . . .' He begins to close the door, which piques her curiosity.

'I wanted to ask you . . .'

He stops.

'Won't you come to the dinner? Please? Give me a chance to thank you for your help with Emee?'

The frown disappears. 'Have you heard any more from the hospital?'

'I can bring her home in a couple of days.'

'That's great.' His relief seems genuine.

'So how about it? Will you come? Please say yes!'

She manages to coax a smile out of him.

'OK, I'll come.'

'Brilliant – see you there.'

The door closes with a heavy, metallic thud that echoes through the building.

74

'Things have been set in motion, Margaux. It's as if we're waiting for something. A spark that will ignite the bonfire.'

T hea is putting on her make-up in front of the bathroom mirror. She's picked out a dress that she knows David likes.

And yet it's not him she's thinking about. Her head is buzzing, there are more questions now, not fewer. The puzzle fills her mind.

Where did the money come from that Leo used to move overseas? Was it a bribe, or maybe some kind of compensation? What happened to the rest of his family? And where does Hubert Gordon fit into the picture?

She has no answers. Not yet. Which leads her to the next question: who is so afraid of Thea's digging that he or she locked her in the cellar at Svartgården, placed nasty little Green Man figures on her car, and maybe even tried to poison her dog?

Arne is the main suspect, especially after the discovery she made at his house. There is no statute of limitations for murder, which means that if Arne or someone else killed Elita, then he or she is still in danger of being sent to prison for life. A good reason to do whatever it takes to keep the past where it belongs.

The problem is that the conclusions in the case file appear to hold, in spite of all the question marks. Even if Leo's confession is discounted, a number of key facts remain.

The children all identified Leo as the rider disguised as the Green Man, and David insists that he clearly saw Leo bending over Elita on the sacrificial stone. The cap badge and Bill's hoof prints also tie Leo to the scene.

But what has happened to the missing items from that night – the tape player, the masks, Elita's suitcase?

Thea takes one last look in the mirror. There is one important piece of the puzzle somewhere, she's sure of it. A vital piece that will complete the picture.

Maybe there's a chance that she'll find it tonight.

The castle looks fantastic. Huge metal baskets of wood are blazing out at the front. A red carpet has been rolled out down the steps, and moving spotlights sweep across the façade. The bonfire is finished, the Green Man attached to his frame.

David is at the door ready to greet the guests. He looks good in his smoking jacket. He seems less tense, more like the David she once fell in love with.

'Wow!' Thea says as she joins him. 'You've really outdone yourselves – it's amazing!'

'Thanks!' His smile is warm and genuine.

David's parents arrive ten minutes early. Bertil also looks stylish in his smoking jacket, and Ingrid is wearing a dress that is a little too garish. Her attitude toward Thea is rather chilly, presumably because of their conversation after the information meeting. Bertil, however, is in an excellent mood.

'Darling Thea, what a fantastic evening. It's going to be so much fun!'

Nettan is the next to arrive, closely followed by Sebastian. They engage David in a quiet conversation while Thea is left to entertain Sebastian's girlfriend Bianca, who has lived in the USA and travelled all over the world.

'Tornaby is much cuter than the way Sebastian described it.'

'Is this your first visit?'

'Yes – weird, right? We've been together for almost three years, visited so many places – Singapore, Los Angeles, Moscow – but we've never been to his home village. Not until now.'

'How did you meet?'

'At something as boring as a technology fair. Not very romantic. How about you and David?'

'A charity event for Doctors Without Borders. David was doing the catering. After that we saw each other from time to time, when I wasn't away.'

She breaks off, doesn't want to talk about Idlib and Margaux, or to say any more about her relationship with David. Instead she asks questions about Sebastian and Bianca's travels.

She notices Arne, and makes an effort not to stare at him. He slaps David on the back, but sidles past Thea without even saying hello.

Per and Erik Nyberg are the next to show up.

'This looks wonderful, David,' Erik says. 'It reminds me of the way it was back in the count's day.'

Thea hasn't spoken to any of them since the little performance in the courtyard the other day, but neither Per nor his father refer to the incident. They greet her warmly and Per kisses her on the cheek.

David introduces a series of people to her – party planners, food and wine writers, a couple of influencers.

Kerstin Miller is accompanied by Jan-Olof.

'Lovely to see you, Thea. What a pretty dress!'

Jan-Olof is wearing an ill-fitting navy blue dinner jacket. He says hello without making eye contact, then grabs a glass of champagne. He doesn't look happy, and judging by his bloodshot eyes, he's had more than a couple of drinks to warm up in advance.

Dr Andersson arrives with a dried-up little man whom she introduces as her husband. Thea makes small talk with them for a few minutes while keeping an eye out for Hubert Gordon. Unfortunately there's no sign of him and she hopes he's just late, that he hasn't decided to follow the festivities in his former home from a distance.

The guests are still enjoying pre-dinner drinks out on the steps. The evening is mild, and the fire baskets provide extra warmth.

David gives a short, well-rehearsed speech, thanking the Bokelund Foundation and the residents of Tornaby for their help, and highlighting Sebastian and Nettan's contributions.

'Without you this project would never have come to fruition. And of course a big thank you to my wife Thea for putting up with me, especially over the past few weeks.'

All eyes turn to Thea. She raises her glass and summons up a smile.

David ends his speech by inviting everyone into the entrance hall. The doors to the dining room are thrown open and a big band begins to play. There are candles everywhere, the crystal chandeliers sparkle, their light reflected in the gold-panelled walls, and high up on the ceiling the creatures of the forest continue their revelry.

Thea glances up at the west wing, but the windows are in darkness. Hubert has obviously decided not to come.

They sit down; Per Nyberg is beside her.

'Don't say anything,' he whispers, 'but I swapped the place cards so I could sit next to you.'

He winks at her, and she's not sure if he's joking.

'How's the life of a musician these days?' she asks.

He smiles, shrugs.

'Well, it might not be the rock star career I dreamed of, but it'll do.'

Jan-Olof is also on their table, still knocking back everything in sight.

'Bloody hell!' Per suddenly exclaims.

Hubert Gordon is standing in the doorway. He looks a little lost, but Ingrid is there in a second to welcome him.

Per lets out a low whistle. 'The hermit has emerged from his cave. I wonder who managed to lure him here?'

'That would be me.'

'Well done – I'm impressed.'

Per raises his glass to her and they share a toast. When Thea lowers her glass, she sees that Hubert is watching them. He nods in greeting. He's been seated at the same table as David and his parents. Nettan is next to David, Thea notes.

'What's it like being newly married to David?'

'Good. Have you been married?'

Per laughs. 'No – I guess I've never met the right person. Tragic, wouldn't you say? A grown man still living at home with Daddy.' His tone is jocular, but Thea senses something else; a hint of sadness that surprises her.

The atmosphere in the dining room becomes more lively as the wine flows. Halfway through the main course, someone taps on a glass. It's Bertil. He gets to his feet, unfolds a sheet of paper and begins to read his speech.

'Dear David, what a fine job you and your friends have done here at Bokelund. To see you, Jeanette and Sebastian together again warms my heart. It seems like yesterday that you used to spend time at our home. I still don't know what you got up to, and I don't want to know either!'

He pauses, laps up the expected laughter.

'Another person we must thank is Rudolf Gordon. If the count hadn't set up the Bokelund Foundation, Tornaby wouldn't have been the village it is today. It's thanks to Rudolf's generosity and foresight that we're sitting here now.'

A brief burst of applause. Thea glances over at Hubert. His expression is completely neutral, showing no emotion at the mention of the generosity that robbed him of his inheritance.

Bertil goes on to talk about David's life, how he was interested in cooking from an early age. He gives a chronological summary of David's career, leaving out the ignominious departure from Stockholm, of course.

Bertil is having one of his most lucid days for a long time. It's clear that he's an experienced speaker; he's good at making contact with his audience, and stops in exactly the right places to elicit laughter and applause. Ingrid looks pleased. She nods in agreement after virtually every sentence, especially when David is the subject. The warmth in her eyes as she gazes up at Bertil is something Thea hasn't seen before.

Bertil glances down at her with equal affection, and for a moment it is possible to glimpse the two young people in the wedding photograph, so much in love. Thea realises that she finds it quite moving, and that she's not the only one.

After speaking for exactly the right number of minutes, Bertil raises his glass and is about to finish off with a toast that will raise the roof.

'You forgot something, Bertil,' Jan-Olof says, lumbering to his feet. He's obviously drunk. His table companion tugs at his sleeve, but he irritably shakes off her hand.

'You forgot to tell everyone what happened. With Elita and Leo.'

Several hands reach out to pull Jan-Olof down onto his chair, but he bats them away.

'Tell everyone what happened, Bertil. Tell them, for fuck's sake!'

Arne is suddenly at Jan-Olof's side. He grabs his arm like the police officer he is and hustles him out of the dining room.

Bertil remains standing, glass in hand. 'Well,' he says. 'There . . . isn't much more to say, really.'

He looks around at the guests as if he's searching for someone. Ingrid takes his hand, but he doesn't seem to notice.

'*Skål!*' someone calls out to help him.

'*Skål!*' everyone joins in.

Bertil gratefully raises his glass, empties it and sits down. There is no warmth in his eyes now.

75

David sends the waiting staff around to top up the glasses and the atmosphere soon recovers.

After a while Arne returns without Jan-Olof. Thea watches him closely. He stops by his sister's chair and they have a quiet conversation before he goes back to his own seat.

'What do you think happened to Jan-Olof?' Thea asks her companion.

Per shrugs. 'Presumably Arne straightened him out and put him in a taxi. He should never have been invited. Everyone knows Jan-Olof has problems with the booze.'

'So why was he invited?'

'Because Kerstin Miller will have put pressure on David. She's always looked out for Jan-Olof. His mother is a difficult woman, and David won't say no if Miss Miller asks him to do something.'

Thea is reminded of the invitation to coffee at Kerstin's, how David, Nettan and Sebastian seemed bothered by Jan-Olof's company. As if they hadn't expected him to be there.

Thea nips to the Ladies before pudding is served. She bumps into Arne in the hallway. He stops, pulls a face, but it's too late to pretend they haven't seen each other.

Thea stares at him, her mouth is suddenly as dry as dust. Is he the one who's threatened her, locked her in the cellar at Svartgården? Poisoned her dog? Is he the one who killed Elita Svart?

'What did you do with Jan-Olof?' she asks, mainly to hide what she's thinking.

'He's passed out in the bridal suite. The idiot was already pissed when he arrived, and it's not the first time.'

Arne takes a box of cigarillos out of his inside pocket.

'I'm going outside for a cheeky smoke,' he says. 'Coming?'

The suggestion is so unexpected that Thea doesn't know how to say no.

They find a corner at the bottom of the steps. Thea's eyes are drawn to the effigy of the Green Man on top of the bonfire – the empty face, the straggling arms.

Arne offers her a cigarillo. She takes one, waits while he lights it and his own. He takes a deep drag, leans against the stone balustrade and blows smoke up into the evening sky.

'After your visit I contacted a former colleague who now works for the state security police,' he says. 'I asked him to run some checks on you. Find out who you were before you got your protected ID.'

Thea goes cold all over. 'Oh yes,' she says hesitantly.

'Jenny Boman,' Arne goes on. 'Daughter of Leif Boman. Something of a drugs baron in his heyday, apparently.'

He doesn't sound particularly bothered.

'Who have you told?'

'No one – at least not yet.' He turns to face her. 'I thought if you were smart enough to get out of there, go to the trouble of changing your name and acquiring a protected ID, then you probably don't want anything to do with your father. Which means I don't need to worry about you either.'

He takes another deep drag.

'That's why I haven't mentioned this to my sister. Ingrid isn't nearly as understanding as I am. The apple doesn't fall far from the tree and so on . . .' He draws a circle in the air with his cigarillo. 'So now I know your secret, and I'm sure you suspect mine.'

Thea tries to work out what Arne is actually saying.

'Elita Svart?' She leaves the name hanging in the air like a question.

'Yes, I knew Elita. I was even a little bit in love with her. Or rather . . .' He frowns. 'Not in love, more . . .'

'Bewitched,' Thea suggests.

Arne nods slowly. 'I knew her father. I used to do the odd job for him, before Bertil got me into the police. Thank God. If you got dragged down into Lasse's crap it was hard to fight your way back up. I'm thinking you know what I mean?'

It's Thea's turn to nod. 'Walpurgis Night 1986. You got a photograph with an invitation written on it. Did you go?'

Arne picks a flake of tobacco off his tongue as he considers whether to answer.

'I was such an idiot. I went there in a patrol car, in uniform, even though I wasn't on duty. I wanted to impress her.' He snorts. 'I was young and stupid, that's all there is to it.'

Thea forces herself to hold back; she mustn't bombard him with questions. She is taken aback by his honesty, to say the least.

'So what happened?' she asks tentatively.

'It's all in the case file. Leo came riding into the glade dressed as the Green Man, the kids ran for their lives, and then . . .'

He breaks off, remains silent for a few seconds.

'Then Leo killed her.'

'Did you see him do it?'

'No. I'd climbed a tree to get a better view, but when Leo rode past I fell and knocked myself out. When I came round she was already lying dead on the sacrificial stone.' He shakes his head. 'I don't know why I'm telling you this when I've kept quiet for over thirty years.'

He chews his lower lip as if to stop any more words from escaping. His expression is anguished, and suddenly Thea understands why.

'You think you could have saved her,' she says quietly. 'If you hadn't lost consciousness, you could have saved her. Is that what you think?'

He looks away. She gives him time to compose himself.

'Did you go over to her?'

'Yes. She'd borrowed my ghetto blaster; it had my name on it. I had to go and get it; I was terrified of being dragged into the whole thing.'

Thea hears the sound of another piece of the puzzle falling into place.

'Her face was covered with a handkerchief,' Arne continues. 'I've always regretted lifting it up.' His expression is even more tortured now. 'What Leo did to her . . . Smashed her beautiful face to a pulp. Six years was way too lenient for that bastard.'

He falls silent, turns away again.

'What happened next?' Thea prompts him.

Arne looks at her. Takes a deep breath.

76

Walpurgis Night 1986

A rne tried to drive as steadily as he could. As if it was the most normal thing in the world to arrive at Ingrid and Bertil's house in a filthy patrol car in the middle of the night.

He knew where the spare key to the double garage was. He killed the headlights before he drove in. Their car was already there, the engine still ticking faintly, which meant they'd just got home.

He closed the doors from the inside, then went into the garden via the back way.

Just as he'd expected, the kids were in the bar. The lights were on and he could hear agitated voices, see several people moving around.

As he began to cut across the lawn, he heard a noise. He turned around, saw a dark figure and jumped, but it was only the Leanders' timid boy, presumably heading for the bar too.

When the boy saw him, he stopped dead. Arne could understand why; he must look like shit, with his uniform covered in dirt and mud.

'It's OK, Leander – it's me, Arne Backe. We're going to the same place. Why aren't you there already?'

The boy, whose name Arne couldn't remember, looked confused. Arne wasn't surprised; he wasn't the brightest kid in the village.

'Why are you late? The others are already here.'

'I . . . I got lost,' the boy stammered. 'I was a bit behind the rest of them.'

Jan-Olof, that was his name.

Arne gestured towards the bar. 'In you go. Let's get this mess sorted out.'

He followed Jan-Olof indoors. The resolve that had come over him after seeing that fucking horse was still there, and it grew stronger when he saw the pale faces of the three children. Bertil and Ingrid were standing opposite them, still in their fancy clothes from the party. Worried, anxious.

'What the hell happened to you?' Bertil said.

Arne waved a dismissive hand. 'Later. Elita Svart is dead.'

The three faces, four including Jan-Olof's, became even whiter. The children looked like little ghosts.

'Dead?' Ingrid snapped, her tone making it clear that she didn't believe him.

'She's lying in the middle of the stone circle with her skull smashed in. The kids were there, playing some kind of game – a spring sacrifice ritual. Then a horse came galloping into the glade, its rider dressed as the Green Man. The kids ran away and the rider killed Elita.'

The colour drained from Ingrid's face and she clutched Bertil's arm. Even Bertil, who was always so self-possessed, looked shocked.

Arne cleared his throat, tucked his thumbs into his belt and rocked back and forth on his heels.

'But I know who did it,' he said as calmly as he could. 'Who scared the kids and killed Elita. And I know how to get him. Provided we all work together.'

77

A rne drops the cigarillo butt on the ground and crushes it with his heel, then he spreads his arms wide.

'Now you know my secret, Thea. I was there, I saw what happened. With hindsight, of course I should have spoken to my colleagues, but I was terrified of losing my job. Plus there were already four witnesses who'd seen Leo on the horse; a fifth wasn't really important.'

'And you're sure it was Leo?' she asks, playing for time.

Is Arne lying? She can't see any signs; in fact, he seems relieved, as if the story has been chafing away at him for far too long.

'Absolutely certain. And I recognised the horse; I'd seen him earlier in the day in the paddock at Svartgården. Bill had a white sock on his right hind leg – there was no mistaking him.'

'And Elita's pregnancy? The fact that someone tampered with the autopsy report?'

He shakes his head. 'I don't know anything about that. I didn't have much of an insight into the investigation. Lennartson treated me like an errand boy. It was several years before he even looked me in the eye.'

The answer seems honest, just like the rest of his account.

The doors open at the top of the steps and several guests emerge.

'Maybe we should go back inside?' Arne suggests.

Thea nods. 'Thank you for telling me all this.'

'Thank you for listening. It was good to get it off my chest – but I'm sure you understand that our respective secrets must stay between us.'

'Of course.'

She follows him up the steps. Hubert is at the top, waiting for her.

'Hi,' she says. 'I'm so glad you came.'

She makes an effort to sound the same as always, but it's hard. Hubert looks serious, maybe a little annoyed.

'Are you enjoying Per's company?' he asks when Arne has gone indoors.

'Yes, I am.'

Hubert stares at her. 'Be careful with him,' he says quietly.

She wonders what he means, but more people are coming outside, and there's another question she has to ask.

'You knew Elita. You gave her a copy of the poetry book you lent to me.'

Hubert's expression doesn't change. They are surrounded by other guests now – Nettan, Sebastian, Bianca, and a few people that Thea doesn't know. Suddenly they've drawn her into a noisy conversation about the castle and David, and she can't get out of it. Hubert stands there watching her for a while, then turns and goes back inside.

It's a long time before Thea is able to re-join Per Nyberg.

'Good to see you – I thought you'd found someone else,' he says with a laugh.

'What have I missed?'

'Chocolate tart, coffee and cognac. But you haven't missed it – I got some for you.'

'That was kind of you – thanks.'

Hubert is also back in his seat. She can see that he is watching them again, even though he's trying to be discreet. She thinks about the poetry book once more, the words he wrote in it about love.

She lowers her voice, leans closer to Per.

'Did you know Elita Svart?'

'A little,' he says, frowning. 'Her stepbrother was in my class.'

'What was he like?'

'Leo? Pretty quiet. He was bullied for a while in the lower school, but once he filled out in puberty, nobody dared to mess with him.'

'And the rest of the family?'

Per shrugs. 'Why do you ask?'

'Elita and Hubert knew each other, didn't they?'

Per glances over at Hubert. 'Maybe. I don't really remember.'

His tone is suddenly evasive. He's lying, she's sure of it. Trying to protect his childhood friend – but why?

Per shuffles uncomfortably; the subject clearly bothers him, and Thea decides to back off. She clinks glasses with him as a diversionary tactic.

'By the way, how's it going with the deer? Any more attacks?'

Per pulls a face. 'We had another last night, unfortunately. That's the third.'

Thea feels an enormous sense of relief. Last night Emee was fighting for her life in the veterinary hospital. Her dog is innocent.

'I still think it's a lynx, but Dad won't have it. He insists that a lynx wouldn't attack a big animal like a deer. We'll see who's right.'

He nods in the direction of his father, who is deep in conversation with Bertil and Ingrid.

'Your father and Lasse Svart didn't get along,' Thea says, working her way back to Elita's story.

A bark of laughter. 'You could say that.' Per takes a deep breath, as if he's not too happy to be discussing the Svart family again. 'Lasse Svart was a terrible person. He was violent towards his women and Leo. Several times he beat them so badly that they had to jump in the car and flee for their lives.'

'Where did they go? To the police?'

'No, no – they wouldn't have dared.'

'So where did they go?'

Per lowers his voice. 'To Kerstin Miller. She was teaching Lola English.'

Thea nods, remembering that Kerstin had mentioned it.

'Lasse wasn't afraid of anything or anyone, but he did have some respect for Kerstin.'

'And your father – was he afraid of Lasse?'

Another mirthless laugh.

'I remember when the count sent us over to give Lasse notice to quit. Dad wasn't usually nervous, but he had an old-fashioned lead cosh at home, and he slipped it into his pocket when he thought I wasn't looking.'

'So how did it go?'

'It was a bit of an anti-climax in the end. Lasse yelled for a couple of minutes then drove off, so we served the papers to Eva-Britt. Then the count relented after Elita died, and said they could stay. I guess he didn't want to seem heartless.'

Thea is taken aback; she hasn't heard anything about this.

'But then they suddenly disappeared,' she says. 'And the count was very quick to board the place up and destroy the track.'

'Exactly. You seem to know most of the story already – you don't need me.' This time the laughter is slightly over the top.

'But why did the family take off if the count had rescinded the notice to quit? If they were allowed to stay at Svartgården?'

Per shrugs. 'I've no idea. As I said, Lasse Svart was a bastard. Nobody around here was sorry when he left, and nobody asked why. Anyway, it's time for dancing!'

The big band strikes up and Per immediately offers her his hand. He's a good dancer – very good, in fact. Occasionally he holds her a little too tightly, and she can feel Hubert's eyes on her again. Why is he watching her like that? And what did he mean by his comment about Per? *Be careful with him.* Was Hubert jealous, or was this about something else?

She sees David dancing with Nettan and Sebastian with Bianca. Dr Andersson is dancing with Bertil, Ingrid with Erik Nyberg.

Thea doesn't really like dancing, being so close to a stranger's body. After the two dances that politeness requires, she makes her excuses. Per is obviously disappointed, and makes her promise to come back soon.

She goes out into the hallway, steps over the rope with the STAFF ONLY sign and creeps upstairs. She needs some peace and quiet to think.

Arne's surprising confession definitely fills some of the gaps in the story, but there are still pieces of the puzzle missing. Why did the Svart family disappear? What happened to the animal masks the children were wearing? And the blue suitcase, into which she is convinced Elita had packed her best clothes?

She stops outside the bridal suite in the east wing, which was once Hubert Gordon's schoolroom. The lonely little boy in the castle. She remembers when they sat in his library drinking coffee; he told her he'd lost someone close. She'd assumed he meant his mother, but what if it was actually Elita?

The strongest love is unrequited love.

A sound from inside the room interrupts her train of thought. A thud, as if something has fallen on the floor.

She knocks on the door. 'Hello?'

No reply. She pushes down the handle; the door isn't locked.

Jan-Olof is lying face down on the bed, breathing heavily. His shoes are on the floor; presumably he's just kicked them off.

Tell everyone what happened, Bertil. Tell them, for fuck's sake!

She thinks about the words he yelled out during Bertil's speech, before Arne managed to get him out of the dining room.

After thirty years, Jan-Olof is still tormented by Elita's death. He's not the only one. David, Nettan and Sebastian can't shake off Elita's ghost either. Arne, who's kept a Polaroid photograph of her. Bertil, who wanders around in the forest by the stone circle. Erik Nyberg, who is worried about what Bertil might let slip. Not to mention the person who secretly donated money for the grave, and still lays flowers on it. And then there's Hubert and his poetry book.

Tell everyone what happened, Bertil.

Tell them what? What is it that hasn't come out? What secrets is Bertil keeping, and whose are they?

She recalls Hubert's strange behaviour this afternoon when she returned the poetry book. The open door of the old chapel. Hubert rarely leaves his wing, but tonight the hermit is out of his cave. Which means that the cave and any secrets it might hold are unguarded.

She glances up at the loft hatch. The ladder the builder was using has been left in a corner. She puts her handbag on the table and takes out her phone. Carries the ladder over, opens it out and places it beneath the hatch, then slips off her shoes.

78

'Everyone seems to be hiding something, Margaux. They're all stuck in a mire of lies and half-truths. And high above them floats Elita Svart.'

Thea has already begun to regret her impulse when she clambers into the loft. The darkness, the smell, the frightening thought of bats. She can still hear the music from the dining room, mingled with Jan-Olof's faint snores, which makes the whole thing feel even odder.

The torch on her phone illuminates only a few metres at a time, so she has to move cautiously. The wooden floor creaks beneath her feet, and she has to duck under thick beams that must have been here for centuries.

She glimpses a silhouette; she directs the beam at the figure and sees a chalk-white, distorted female face.

Thea gasps, then realises it's the statue of the saint that David mentioned. A woman with her hands clasped in front of her and two gaping holes where her eyes should be. It looks as if it's several hundred years old. The wood is cracked, the colours faded. It's about one and a half metres tall, and is standing on a square plinth. ST LUCIA, it says at the bottom. Not exactly the usual dressed-in-white-with-candles-in-her-hair version.

The statue is surrounded by a number of items which presumably come from the chapel. Two crosses, a couple of tall candlesticks and a large wooden chest. Beyond them she finds what she's looking for: a hatch just like the one she came up through. The bridal suite's position in the east wing matches that of the chapel in the west wing, which should mean that the hatch will lead her there.

She is right. The windows are covered and the torch on her phone isn't strong enough to enable her to see much more than the stone floor directly below the hatch, but it's obviously the chapel. The drop is around three metres, and if she hangs by her hands she should be able to jump down. She's not very heavy, her arms are strong and she's pretty fit. However, it will be considerably more difficult to get back up.

She turns the beam this way and that, hoping to spot something that she'll be able to stand on, but the darkness swallows the light and all she can see are silhouettes – presumably statues like the one in the attic. She must either take a chance and risk being locked in the chapel, or return to the dinner without having accomplished her mission.

Neither alternative appeals to her, but she might not get another opportunity. Hubert is hiding something, she's sure of it. Something that might be in the darkness below her.

She tucks her phone into her bra, then turns around, slides her legs over the edge and lowers herself slowly until her arms are fully extended. Ronny would be proud if he could see her now.

She takes a deep breath, lets go.

The drop is longer than she'd thought. Her bare feet hit the cold floor with such force that she tumbles over. She lies there for a few seconds to catch her breath, then gets up.

She glances at the dark rectangle above her and suddenly regrets the whole thing. How on earth is she going to get back up there?

Her phone has survived the fall, but reception is poor. She switches the torch on again.

The chapel doesn't look like a chapel at all. No pews, no altar. The only source of light is a faint strip beneath the door.

The silhouettes are indeed statues of saints, set out in the middle of the room in some kind of formation. She makes her way to the door; as expected it's locked, bolted from the outside, so whatever is in here, Hubert doesn't want it on display.

She finds a bank of switches, tries the top one.

Two spotlights come on, illuminating the centre of the room. Thea inhales sharply.

Five figures, almost in a row.

The one in the middle is on a plinth so that it's taller than the others. Silk ribbons run from this central figure to the other four, whose faces are covered by animal masks.

A hare, a fox, an owl and a deer.

79

Thea is finding it hard to breathe. It's as if she can hear her heartbeat bouncing off the stone walls. Hubert has removed all the religious trappings and staged his own version of the spring sacrifice.

She moves closer to the figures. On a table beside them is a record player with a black LP on the turntable, and propped up against one speaker is something she recognises only too well.

A Polaroid, virtually identical to the ones she found inside the Gallows Oak and at Arne's house.

Walpurgis Night 1986. To Hubert. Come to the stone circle at midnight. The spring sacrifice.

Hubert was also invited to the stone circle.

She picks up the photograph, compares the animal masks with the ones on the saints. They're the same. So how did they end up here, inside the Gordon family's private chapel?

She walks around the back of the tableau. There is something on the floor behind the figure representing Elita.

A blue suitcase.

Her heart begins to race. She sits down and opens the case. It contains two pairs of shoes, and neatly folded items of clothing. Two dresses, two pairs of jeans, a blouse, several tops, a passport. Right at the bottom is a soft toy, a little rabbit.

There is something very moving about it all. Elita Svart's most treasured possessions, the things she wanted to take with her as she floated high above Tornaby, never to return.

Can you see me, dear readers?

I can see you.

She flicks through the passport. It was issued in March 1986, only a month or so before Elita was killed. In the picture she looks happy. Expectant. As if she is waiting to take off. Instead she was beaten to death and left on a cold block of stone. With a child in her belly that no one must find out about.

Because no secret is greater than mine.

Thea gets to her feet, takes a few photos with her phone: the figures, the masks, Elita's suitcase.

More pieces of the puzzle have fallen into place, but the overall picture is still not clear.

The most logical conclusion is that Hubert must have been there that night, even though he claims to have been in England, and neither the children nor Arne mentioned him. Maybe he was hiding, watching everything from a distance, just like Arne. Waiting to see what would happen.

Why did Hubert take the masks and the suitcase, remove clear proof that Elita wasn't planning to die, as the police investigation assumed, but to run away? Leave Tornaby, possibly with the one she loved.

The strongest love is unrequited love.

As I said, the Gordons are terrible people.

Could a broken heart be reason enough for Hubert to commit murder?

A distant sound interrupts her train of thought, a door opening and closing somewhere in the building, followed by faint footsteps.

Thea tiptoes over to the door and puts her ear against it. The footsteps are coming closer. Someone is on their way up the stairs.

It must be Hubert. What will happen if he comes in? Catches her here, at the heart of a secret he's kept for over thirty years?

She has no intention of staying around to find out. Quickly she lifts the record player off the table. The album sleeve behind it falls on the floor – Stravinsky.

The table is heavy, it scrapes along the concrete as she drags it to the right spot. Whoever is outside must be able to hear the noise. She scrambles up and stretches her arms. There's a half-metre gap. She's going to have to jump.

Another sound, a bolt being drawn back, a key turning in a lock.

Thea takes a deep breath, bends her knees and pushes off with all her strength. Her fingers grip the edge of the hatch. For a second she thinks she won't be able to hold on, but then she manages to swing her body and press one foot against the ceiling, enabling her to crawl back into the loft.

Just as she draws her legs in, she hears the chapel door open.

80

Thea runs through the loft, keeping the beam of the torch on her phone in front of her. As soon as Hubert sees that the lights are on and that the table is beneath the hatch, he will know that someone has been there – but not who. Not yet, anyway.

She scrambles back down the ladder into the bridal suite. Jan-Olof is still snoring on the bed. Thea slips on her shoes, puts her phone in her bag and hurries into the bathroom. Her hair is standing on end, her hands and face are streaked with dirt, and the front of her dress is dusty from hauling herself back up into the loft.

She dampens a towel and rubs off the worst of it. Touches up her make-up and tidies her hair. She's heading for the door when someone grabs her shoulder.

For a second she's convinced that Hubert has somehow followed her, but it's Jan-Olof. He stares at her. His eyes are bloodshot, his face puffy.

'I know what you're up to,' he mutters. The alcohol fumes are so strong that she almost has to narrow her eyes.

'You're working for him, aren't you? For Leo. You gave it away the other day. You know him – go on, admit it!' He pushes his face closer to hers, his expression unpleasant to say the least.

'I . . .'

Thea searches for a good answer. Jan-Olof seems to have lost his grip on reality. He pokes her in the chest with one finger, shoves her backwards until she bumps into the wall.

She's getting scared now. The band is still playing downstairs, and she doubts if anyone would hear her if she screamed.

'Tell Leo . . .' he hisses. 'Tell . . .'

His eyes dart from side to side, and suddenly fill with tears. His arms drop to his sides.

'Tell him I'm sorry. Can you do that? Tell him Jan-Olof is sorry. Tell him I should have told the truth. Can you do that?'

The pleading tone takes her by surprise. He sounds like a little boy.

'Of course.' Thea edges towards the door, half-expecting his mood to change again, but Jan-Olof remains where he is, head down, arms dangling. He looks like a great big abandoned child.

She pushes down the door handle and slips out.

When she reaches the ground floor the music has stopped and the guests are moving into the hallway. She sees Per and goes over to him.

'Thea – there you are. What's this?'

He reaches out, touches her cheek and then her hair. Holds up a dust bunny between his thumb and forefinger.

She thinks fast.

'I've been helping David bring up some more wine from the cellar.'

He nods, seems to accept her explanation.

All around them people are putting on their outdoor clothes and going out onto the wide area at the top of the stone steps. Per offers Thea her coat. She doesn't ask what's going on, but simply pretends she's fully up to speed as they follow the other guests. When she sees David talking to Little Stefan and the other man who built the bonfire, she no longer needs to wonder. Little Stefan hands a burning torch to David.

A group of around twenty people, presumably from the village, have gathered on the far side of the courtyard.

The waiting staff circulate with glasses of champagne on silver trays. Thea takes one, shares a toast with Per and realises at the same time that Hubert is standing on the steps, watching her. She meets his gaze and raises her glass, gives him a smile that she hopes looks innocent. Hubert's expression doesn't change.

David walks up to the bonfire and pushes the torch deep inside. The fire catches so quickly that the wood must be drenched in some kind of accelerant. The Green Man stands motionless as the flames grow bigger.

'A fascinating ritual, don't you think?' Per says. 'Beneath the civilised surface we Tornaby residents are still pagans.'

Thea murmurs a response. She sees David go over to Nettan who takes his arm, holds onto it, caresses his elbow with her thumb.

The flames are leaping into the air now, licking at the Green Man's legs as they devour the wood.

Thea glances at Hubert. He is still staring at her.

'Nature is hungry and the Green Man is riding through the forests.'

'What did you say?'

Per gives a wry smile. 'It's something my dad used to say when I was little. He pretends to be a hard man, but he's actually very superstitious. We've got Green Man figures on both the house and the stables. He makes them himself every year.'

'Oh yes?'

Thea looks around for Per's father. Finds Ingrid and Dr Andersson, but no Erik Nyberg. Maybe he and Bertil decided to stay inside instead of facing the chilly evening air.

The fire has begun to consume the Green Man. The fresh leaves shrivel up, exposing the twigs beneath, black lines that show through the flames like a skeleton. Arms, legs, the loop forming the empty face. The crackling becomes a dull, alarming bass note. The people on the steps talk louder and louder, until Thea's ears are almost hurting, but the fire is louder still. Eventually the conversation dies away.

The Green Man is burning now, the flames reaching up into the sky. They are reflected in the eyes of the watchers on the far side of the courtyard. A loud bang from the bonfire sends a shower of sparks into the night.

Suddenly there is a scream. Thea turns towards the east wing. A window is open on the top floor, eight or maybe even ten metres above the ground. Jan-Olof is standing on the sill, clinging on with one hand as he leans out. One of the spotlights catches him as it sweeps across the façade.

'Fucking liars!' he roars. 'Fucking liars, the lot of you!'

A shocked murmur spreads through the crowd.

'Come down, Jan-Olof!' Several voices join in. Per and some of the others begin to run towards the main door.

Jan-Olof isn't listening. His face is ashen, his hair is standing on end. He is swaying alarmingly. Then he sees Thea. He stretches out his arm, points directly at her. She freezes at the top of the steps.

'Thea!' he yells. 'Tell Leo I'm sorry! Promise!'

She opens her mouth to reply. Say something, anything, to make him get down from the windowsill, but before she can speak, Jan-Olof's body jerks. He looks over his shoulder into the darkened room as if he's heard something. He turns, seems to be on the way back in. Then he wobbles. Falls backwards out of the window and lands on the paving below with a horrible thud.

81

Thea breaks into a run, pushing aside people on the steps to get through.

Jan-Olof is lying on his back. One leg is bent at an unnatural angle, and a pool of blood has begun to spread beneath his head. He's semi-conscious; his eyelids are fluttering and one arm is twitching. His breathing is rapid and shallow.

'I need something to stop the bleeding!' she shouts.

People crowd around her. She catches a glimpse of David and Nettan, with Sebastian and his girlfriend diagonally behind them.

'Give me something to stop the bleeding!' she yells again. 'And call an ambulance!'

Someone gives her a handkerchief. It's much too small, but it's better than nothing. She feels at the back of Jan-Olof's head, searching for the wound. Presses the handkerchief against it.

Jan-Olof's breathing is becoming more laboured. His chest rattles, he opens and closes his eyes. People are crowding in from all directions, Thea hardly has room to move.

'Stand back!' a man bellows in English. He pushes away those nearest to her and kneels down beside her. It's Philippe. Where has he come from? What's he doing here?

He hands her a scarf. 'What can I do?'

Thea gently lifts Jan-Olof's head, presses the scarf to the wound as hard as she dares.

'Hold this,' she instructs him. 'Try to keep the pressure even while I check if he has any more injuries.'

She gently runs her hands over Jan-Olof's chest and stomach.

'I've got emergency services on the phone,' someone says. Thea looks up; it's Sebastian's girlfriend, Bianca. 'What shall I tell them?'

'We have someone who's fallen from a height of between eight and ten metres. Severe head trauma, multiple fractures and possible internal bleeding.'

Jan-Olof's chest rattles again. His breathing becomes shallower.

'The ambulance is on its way,' Bianca says. 'There's one nearby.'

Jan-Olof's face is turning grey. Thea checks his pulse; it's faint and uneven. She lifts his chin, tips back his head and opens his mouth. Gently pinches his nose and blows two slow, long breaths into his lungs.

His chest rises and falls, then nothing.

'What shall we do?' Philippe asks.

At that moment the crowd parts to let Dr Andersson through.

'Head trauma, broken bones. Faint pulse, breathing compromised.'

The doctor kneels down beside Thea with some difficulty, then helps by holding Jan-Olof's head while Thea breathes into his lungs again, more deeply this time.

Jan-Olof's chest rises and falls as before, but suddenly he coughs, takes a deep, hacking breath, then another. His eyelids flutter, open.

He stares at Thea, then Dr Andersson.

'Can you hear me?' Thea asks. No response. 'Can you hear me, Jan-Olof?'

His eyes are wide open. He takes another shuddering breath. His lips move as if he's trying to say something.

'Tell Leo . . .'

Thea leans closer; Dr Andersson does the same.

'Not him,' Jan-Olof whispers.

'Not who?'

He half-closes his eyes; he looks as if he's fighting to remain conscious. He raises one hand and points over her shoulder. She hears the sound of fast-approaching sirens in the distance.

'Not him. It was me.'

Thea follows Jan-Olof's finger. Realises he's pointing straight at David.

82

Jan-Olof stops breathing again during the journey, but Thea and the paramedic manage to revive him.

The emergency team takes over when they reach the hospital in Helsingborg. Thea watches from the sidelines until his condition is stabilised, then she goes into the toilets and splashes her face with cold water. Her dress is spattered with Jan-Olof's blood. She finds an empty waiting room and tries to call David, but he doesn't answer.

Only now does she have the chance to think back over what happened. Was Jan-Olof's fall an accident? Impossible to say. He was very drunk, and could easily have lost his balance, but for a moment it looked as if he'd heard someone or something in the room behind him.

She tries to remember what he was rambling about up in the bridal suite. He seemed to think she was in cahoots with Leo, working for him. Where had that come from? After a while she realises that Jan-Olof must have misunderstood her at his mother's house the other day.

Whatever the reason, it's clear that the thought of Leo tormented him. Frightened him. What did he mean by the last words he managed to get out?

Not him. It was me.

He'd been pointing at David.

Not him. It was me.

Who did what?

She tries David again; still no answer. She finds Kerstin Miller's home number; the teacher answers right away.

'Thank you so much for calling – how's Jan-Olof?'

'He's in intensive care. One lung was punctured, but fortunately the head injury looked worse than it was. He has a broken leg and a number of other fractures, but if there are no further complications, he should make a full recovery.'

'Thank God you were there, Thea.' Kerstin's voice is both sad and warm at the same time.

'One more thing – could you let Jan-Olof's mother know what's happened? Maybe someone could go and see her tomorrow morning – I think she's pretty dependent on him.'

'No problem. And just give me a call if there's anything else I can do.'

'I will. Bye now.'

Thea closes her eyes and rests her head on the wall.

She is back in the stone circle. Hubert is holding the camera, she is standing beside him watching as Elita and the children pose. Hubert takes one photograph after another. He shakes them to make the colours and images appear more quickly. Elita runs to him, looks over his shoulder. Laughs and points.

Then everything changes.

It is night-time. Hubert and the children are gone. Elita stands alone by the sacrificial stone, the silk ribbons trailing from her wrists. She is waiting for someone. The person who is going to take her away.

The dream slowly dissolves, the colours fade away, then the contours, like a Polaroid in reverse, until all that remains is a little boy hiding among the trees.

Not him. It was me.

And suddenly she understands what Jan-Olof meant. What David and the others are hiding.

'Hello?'

Thea opens her eyes. How long has she been asleep? Half an hour, maybe.

A nurse is standing in front of her.

'Jan-Olof has regained consciousness – you can come and see him if you like.'

He is lying in a bed with tubes and wires all over the place. His head is bandaged, eyes closed. A ventilator is helping him to breathe.

'He squeezed my hand a little while ago,' the nurse tells her. 'So he can hear what you're saying.'

Thea goes up to the bed.

'Hi, Jan-Olof, it's Thea.' She takes his hand, hesitates briefly. It would probably be better to wait, but if she's right, this secret has haunted him for over thirty years, slowly eating him up from the inside, and it will continue to do so until the truth comes out.

'There's something I want to ask you. About the night Elita died.'

She bends down and whispers in his ear. Receives a faint but unmistakable squeeze of her hand in response.

83

The taxi drops Thea outside the castle. The courtyard is almost deserted, the fire baskets have burned out, and a pile of glowing embers is all that remains of the bonfire. There is broken glass on the steps.

She finds David in the dining room, sitting with his parents and Arne. He is leaning forward, his eyes are empty. There are still glasses and coffee cups on the table. Thea pauses in the doorway for a few seconds, then goes over to him.

'I tried to call you. Jan-Olof's going to be OK.' She stands behind David, places a hand on his shoulder.

He doesn't answer; he continues to stare blankly into space.

'What did Jan-Olof mean when he asked you to tell Leo he was sorry?' Ingrid demands.

Thea shrugs. 'I don't know. He's got it into his head that I know Leo. Which I don't,' she adds quickly.

'And how did he get that idea?'

'I haven't a clue.'

'When did you speak to Jan-Olof? Arne says he checked on him a couple of times in the bridal suite and he was out for the count.'

'I . . .' Thea searches for a reasonable explanation. 'I went up to see if he was all right, given how drunk he was. He woke up and started rambling about Leo. I'm not even sure he recognised me.'

Ingrid clearly doesn't believe her.

'And that guy from the mining company – where does he come into the picture?'

'Philippe? I really don't know. He just appeared out of nowhere. As I said before, he's a patient.'

Ingrid and Arne exchange a long look.

'You do realise this is all your fault,' her mother-in-law informs her.

'My fault?' Thea instinctively steps back.

'You've destroyed everything. The castle, the restaurant, David's reputation. Everything.' Ingrid shakes her head. Thea has no idea what she's supposed to say.

'We tried to warn you, Thea. Tried to stop you digging up the past. That wretched little gypsy girl . . .'

'Her name was Elita,' Thea says without thinking. 'Elita Svart.'

Ingrid raises her eyebrows.

'She was a little gypsy girl who's been dead for many years, and because of her you've thrown away everything we've worked for. Opened up old wounds. Driven poor Jan-Olof to try and take his own life.'

'That's not what happened. He didn't jump, he fell. Or—' She breaks off.

'We were all there. Don't try and get out of it,' Ingrid snaps.

'I'm not. Jan-Olof lost his balance – or someone pushed him.'

Ingrid holds up her hand.

'We don't want to hear any more of your lies. Enough, Thea. Or would you rather I called you Jenny? Jenny Boman?'

Thea's knees almost give way, but she reaches for the back of a chair and manages to stay on her feet. Arne avoids her gaze; their pact has obviously been broken.

'You lied to us,' Ingrid continues. 'Lied to me and Bertil. And to David.' She gestures towards her son, who is still staring into space. 'You deceived him, didn't tell him who you really are. What he was marrying into.'

'He wasn't marrying into anything,' Thea replies as calmly as she can. 'I've had no contact with my family since I was nineteen. The reason I changed my name and applied for a protected identity was to get away from them.'

Ingrid lets out a snort of derision.

'As if that makes any difference. You're still your father's daughter, regardless of whether you've changed your name or not. If we'd known from the start, we would never have let you into our family. Just look at what you've done!' She waves a hand around the messy, deserted room. 'Your lies have ruined everything!'

Thea has had enough.

'My lies? What about yours – claiming that Arne was at the stone circle when Elita died? Or the even bigger lie, the one David told the police when he said he was the one who ran back and saw Leo bending over Elita.'

David's body jerks as if someone has slapped him.

'It was Jan-Olof who went back, wasn't it, David? Not you.'

'I . . .' David's eyes dart from Thea to Ingrid and back again.

Ingrid reaches out and pats his arm. 'You don't need to say anything.'

'Your mother's right,' Thea goes on. 'You don't need to say anything. Jan-Olof has already told the truth. He was the one who saw someone bending over Elita, but he wasn't at all sure that it was Leo, which is why he didn't want to say anything when the four of you were interviewed by the police. He wasn't prepared to support the version you'd agreed on in the bar.'

She pauses, takes a deep breath.

'But since you were used to being the leader, you took over. You knew you were right. Arne had already told you that it was Leo who was riding the horse. Everyone agreed that it was him, so all you did was help out. But what if you were all wrong? What if it wasn't Leo?'

Arne shakes his head.

'It was. I saw him with my own eyes. I nearly ran into Bill when I drove away. Plus Leo confessed.'

'He was twenty years old. He was interviewed over and over again, deprived of sleep or contact with his family. He was more or less brainwashed.'

Arne shakes his head even more emphatically.

'Leo's lawyer was present at every interview. There were no irregularities. And his family took off, left him because they knew he was guilty. Because they didn't want to get dragged into his mess.'

'How come you're so invested in this story, Thea?' Ingrid asks. 'Explain it to me. Because the only reason I can think of is that you're in league with Leo. That he's somehow out for revenge.'

'Revenge for what?' Thea snaps back. 'For the fact that you framed him for a crime he didn't commit?'

'Stop it! Stop it, all of you!' David is on his feet. His face is chalk-white, his eyes black.

'I don't want to hear one more word about Elita Svart. Ever. And you,' he points to Thea, 'you can go to hell. Take your fucking theories and all the crap you own and get out of here.'

His voice breaks as he turns and runs towards the kitchen door.

'David!' his mother calls after him. 'David!'

There is total silence in the room for a few seconds, then Bertil says: 'Poor boy. That poor, poor child.'

84

'Is it over now? you're wondering. Is this how the story ends?
Will we never find out what really happened to Elita Svart?
    'Maybe not. Maybe this is a tale without a happy ending.
Rather like yours and mine, Margaux.'

The room in the guesthouse in Ljungslöv has heavy curtains and a thick fitted carpet. Thea isn't planning to stay here long-term, but it will take a few days to sort out a car and fetch the rest of her stuff from the coach house. The situation isn't made any easier by the fact that David refuses to answer when she calls him.

She understands why he's angry, understands that it's easier to take out his anger on her than admit that he was partly responsible for sending an innocent person to prison. Because she's now convinced that Leo is innocent, and that someone else was responsible for Elita's death. Unfortunately she can't prove it.

Leo is linked to the scene of the crime, and everything else is mere speculation. The photograph, the suitcase and the masks in the chapel suggest that Hubert was also at the stone circle. The poetry book shows that he and Elita knew each other. But none of it constitutes proof. Thea still doesn't know exactly what happened on Walpurgis Night, or what made Elita's family disappear. Or who gave Leo money when he got out of jail, and why.

Questions that may never be answered.

Dr Andersson called round to collect the keys to the Toyota and the surgery. They exchanged no more than a few words until she was leaving, when she looked Thea in the eye and said:

'You saved Jan-Olof's life. Thank you.'

Thea suspects those are the last friendly words she will hear in Tornaby. No doubt the Facebook group is already full of all kinds of rumour and gossip.

Her secret is out, the past has caught up with her at last, just as her father said it would.

Her phone rings. The man from the car rental company is waiting in reception. She signs the contract and is given the key. She spots a familiar face in the bar.

Philippe.

She goes over to him.

'*Docteur Lind*. Nice to see you again. How is the poor man?'

'I spoke to the hospital a little while ago; he's going to be fine, but it was a close thing. Thank you for your help.'

She says the last sentence in Swedish as a little test. Something Ingrid said stuck in her mind, a hint that Philippe is somehow involved in the whole story. He's from Canada, after all, and must be about the same age as Leo.

'You're welcome,' he says in heavily accented Swedish before reverting to French. 'Apologies – my Swedish isn't very good. Can I buy you a drink?'

He orders wine for her and beer for himself.

'What were you doing there anyway? At the castle?' she asks when they've raised their glasses to each other and taken the first sip.

Philippe shrugs. 'I missed the burning of the Green Man on the common; I got there just as it was all over. I'd intended to take some photographs and send them to my father. He's a history professor; he loves talking about the pagan Northerners.' He gives a wry smile. 'One of the villagers told me there was a bonfire at the castle too, so I drove over. Then things became a little more dramatic than I'd bargained for.'

Thea nods. 'Did you get any pictures?'

'Yes, enough to make my father happy. We don't speak very often. You could say I'm something of a disappointment, having chosen to work with my hands rather than my brain as he so eloquently puts it, especially after a couple of whiskies.' He shrugs. 'No matter how old you are, you remain a child in your parents' eyes.'

Thea thinks of her own father.

'True. Listen, I need to ask you something.'

'Go ahead.'

'Do you know someone called Leo Rasmussen? He's a Swede, about the same age as you, and he lives in Canada.'

'No. The only Swedes I know are the ones I've met through work.'

She studies his expression closely. If he's lying, he's doing it very well.

They chat for quarter of an hour or so before she makes her excuses and returns to her room. She managed to get the name of his father out of him, and googles it as soon as she gets through the door. Bruno Benoit is indeed a history professor. He lives in Quebec and has two children, a son and a daughter, which confirms what Philippe told her.

She takes Elita's case file out of her bag and drops it in the waste-paper bin. She feels a strange mixture of relief and disappointment. It's time to give up, accept that certain jigsaw puzzles just can't be completed.

Her phone rings; a withheld number.

'Hello?'

'It's your father.'

Thea sighs. She is on the point of asking what he wants, but can't face another argument about the importance of polite small talk.

'Hi, Leif, how are you?'

'Not bad, thank you for asking.'

He sounds calmer than before. Less angry.

'I haven't written that letter yet,' she says. 'There's been a lot going on here. The fact is . . .' She suddenly realises something. 'The fact is that David's family know who I am. They've thrown me out.'

There is a brief silence on the other end of the line.

'I'm sorry to hear that, Jenny. I hope you know it was nothing to do with me.'

Presumably the subdued tone of his voice is because he's just lost the hold he had over her.

'So what are you going to do now?'

'You mean, am I still going to write your petition?'

'No, that's not what I meant. I'm wondering what you're going to do now, with your life.'

The answer surprises her. 'I'm not sure, to be honest. David isn't speaking to me, so I assume we'll be getting a divorce. It's probably for the best.'

'Why? Don't you love him?'

The question is even more unexpected. 'No. No, I don't. Not in that way, anyhow.'

'So why did you marry him?'

'Because I owed it to him. He helped me after I lost someone I cared about very much.'

'I understand – but you can't build a relationship on obligation.'

'No.' She can't think of anything else to say. It feels weird, taking marital advice from her father. The person who frightened her more than anyone else. The person she's spent almost thirty years avoiding.

'I hope things work out for you, Jenny. There was something else I wanted to talk to you about, but we can leave it until another time.'

She shakes her head, even though he can't see her. 'No, now is fine. What is it?'

'Are you sure?'

'Absolutely.'

She's not sure how to handle this pleasant version of her father, but it fascinates her.

'I looked through that case file. What a terrible story. A sixteen-year-old girl with her whole life ahead of her shouldn't have to die like that. I can understand why it interests you – the similarities between you and her, me and her father . . .'

He falls silent for a moment. Thea hears the sound of a lighter, the hiss of burning paper and tobacco.

'The father, Lasse Svart, shopped his own stepson to the police. Did that seem strange to you?'

'It did.'

'In my experience, there are only two reasons why you'd do that to your own family. Neither is acceptable, but there you go.' He takes another drag. 'Either it's because you yourself are at risk of going down, or it's because you have something to gain. It's always about something big – a big risk or a big gain.'

'And which do you think it was in Lasse Svart's case?'

'I'm not sure, but the little I've read about Lasse suggests that it's the latter. Money. Or something else that was valuable to him.'

Thea thinks. 'He was about to lose his home. His forge and his means of making a living.'

She hears him blow out smoke.

'I'd say that's a pretty good motive.' He coughs, an unpleasant hacking cough that makes her hold the phone away from her ear. 'One more thing. Do you have the case file to hand?'

'I do.' She fishes it out of the bin.

'Look at the pictures on page fifty-six and fifty-seven. The hoof prints.'

She finds the right pages and sees the casts of the hoof prints in the mud at the stone circle, then a cast of Bill's hooves. The impressions are a ninety-five per cent match, according to a note added by the forensic technician.

'Yes?'

'Now turn to page twenty-six.'

She does as he says. Pictures from Svartgården: Elita's room, Leo's little cabin, Bill in his stall.

'Look at the horse,' her father says. 'Look at Bill. Do you see?'

Thea peers at the image. Bill appears to be sleeping. He's raised one hind leg as some horses do when they sleep. The lower part of the leg is white, just as Arne described it.

'Do you see?' her father asks again.

'See what?'

'The hoof. It's unshod.'

'And?' She still doesn't understand what he means.

'That photograph was taken the day after the murder. Bill is unshod – perfectly normal for a young horse in the process of being broken in. But the prints in the mud were made by a shod horse.'

Thea is stunned.

'So three days later, when the forensic technicians turn up at Svartgården to take casts of Bill's hooves, he's suddenly shod and the impressions match. And at about the same time—'

'Lasse Svart changes his statement and puts Leo in the frame,' Thea says. 'And the previous day Leo's cap badge was found by the stone circle.'

'Exactly. Do you understand what I'm getting at?'

Thea nods to herself. Gathers up the pieces of the puzzle. Leo's beret on the kitchen floor at Svartgården. The overturned chair. The empty dressing packet, the bloody handprint.

'Lasse was paid to frame Leo.'

'That's my conclusion too. If you can work out who paid him, then I think you're on the trail of a killer. But be careful, Jenny. Be very careful.'

85

'I think I know how it all fits together now, Margaux. What the spring sacrifice was really about. But in order to be completely sure I have to go there again. To the place where it all happened. And I have to talk to the person who has kept everyone's secrets all these years.'

Bertil opens the door after the second ring. The car isn't there, so presumably Ingrid is at the castle, helping David to salvage whatever he can after the disastrous end to the dinner.

'Thea – come in.' He looks bright today, which makes things easier.

'Thanks, but I was hoping you'd come out for a drive with me. I want to ask you a few questions. About Elita Svart.'

He nods slowly. 'I thought you might.' He remains standing in the doorway for a little while. 'Wait a minute – I just need to fetch a couple of things.'

The glade is completely still. Not a breath of wind, and the only sound is birdsong in the tall trees.

It is almost nine o'clock, and dusk is beginning to fall. Bertil and Thea stand in silence side by side. He collected two torches and a walking stick from the garage, then showed her the route that would enable them to get as close to the stone circle as possible. He is very different this evening. His posture is more erect, the look in his eyes more present. Yet at the same time there is tension in his expression, as if what he is doing requires a huge effort.

Thea switches on the torch he gave her. Directs the beam at the area in front of the sacrificial stone.

'Elita and the children were standing roughly there,' she says. 'They'd built a fire on the ground. David and his friends probably came along the same path as the one we've just used. Arne's ghetto blaster was on one of the stones, playing the recording of the drums.'

Bertil says nothing. He merely leans heavily on his stick while listening to her account.

Thea does her best to conjure images out of the darkness.

'The children are wearing their animal masks, Elita is dressed as the spring sacrifice. Silk ribbons are tied around her wrists, and each child is holding the end of one ribbon. They are drunk on the atmosphere and the music. Elita begins to dance, the children follow her lead.'

Thea closes her eyes; she can almost hear the drums. She turns towards the canal, shines her torch in among the trees.

'Arne is over there somewhere. He's been wandering around in the dark for a while and has lost his bearings. He has a pair of binoculars with him, and he is watching Elita.'

Bertil nods, but still he doesn't speak.

Thea enters the circle, imagining that she is holding the end of a long silk ribbon, murmuring to herself as she feels Elita's movements through the fabric.

'The dance grows wilder, the drums beat faster and faster. Then suddenly they hear the sound of approaching hooves.'

Thea's heart is also beating faster. She can hear the hooves, feel the fear the children must have felt. By this stage they are almost in a trance. They are tired, frightened, intoxicated. The masks cover their faces.

She realises that she has clasped her hands around the imaginary ribbon. The hooves come closer, and somewhere Arne falls out of his tree and knocks himself out.

The Green Man comes crashing through the trees and into the circle. The horse snorts, rears up.

Thea draws back her hands to protect herself. The children must have done the same, trapping Elita in the centre as the ribbons were pulled tight.

Then the screams. David and his friends let go of the ribbons and run back to the path in a panic, heading for their bicycles and safety.

Only Elita and the Green Man are left.

'I'm assuming you've worked it out,' Bertil says. 'What happened.'

'Almost. I don't think it was Bill the children saw. I think it was Nelson.'

Bertil pulls a face, then nods.

'Which means that Hubert was the Green Man.'

Another nod. 'The count did his best, but that boy has never been right,' Bertil says.

Thea shakes her head. 'So Leo came off Bill in the forest on the other side of the canal, just as he said in his early interviews. Bill ran away, down onto the road where Arne almost crashed into him.'

'Probably.'

'Arne assumed it was Bill, and therefore Leo, that he'd seen at the stone circle. He drove to your place, told you the story, and made the children believe the same thing.'

Bertil sighs. 'Arne didn't know any better. We were all shocked. No one knew what had actually happened. He only said what he thought was true.'

'But Jan-Olof wasn't quite so sure,' Thea continues. 'He'd seen someone bending over Elita, but that person wasn't as tall as Leo, and didn't have the same build. So when it was time for the children to be interviewed by the police, he hesitated. David stepped up and filled in the rest of the tale. He couldn't resist playing the leading role.'

Bertil's expression is melancholy now.

'But Lasse Svart knew that Bill hadn't come home covered in mud, and therefore he couldn't have floundered across the canal. Someone must have shown him the police photographs of the hoof prints, or he just came here to see for himself at some point. As soon as he saw the prints, he knew they weren't Bill's, and that there was only one other horse in the area that could have made them. A horse he'd shod himself. Nelson.'

Thea pauses, expecting Bertil to protest, to say that she's got it all wrong. But Bertil stands there in silence, looking as if he is trying very hard to stay sharp.

'So Lasse went to the count, asking for compensation in return for his silence. He wanted to keep Svartgården, which was why the count rescinded the notice to quit. Not out of sympathy, but because he had no choice.'

'Lasse wasn't satisfied with that,' Bertil says. 'The bastard demanded cash too. Fifty thousand.'

Thea can't hide her surprise.

'And that's where you came into the picture?'

'That's right. The count needed help to withdraw that amount of money from the bank. Lasse had also seen Arne's patrol car in the forest on Walpurgis Night, and he threatened to tell the police if we didn't pay up.'

'Was framing Leo part of the deal?'

Bertil shakes his head.

'Lasse did that of his own accord. He hated his stepson. He never regarded him as a member of the family. Arne said they'd had a fight on Walpurgis afternoon, and Lasse had pulled a knife. He was a vile person, but . . .'

Bertil pauses and his eyes cloud over for a moment, then he's back. Thea realises she doesn't have much time.

'Leo was already the main suspect,' she says. 'The children had identified him, and Elita's letter suggested that he might be involved. All Lasse had to do was change his statement slightly, claim that Bill had come home covered in mud, then shoe him so that the prints more or less matched Nelson's.'

'Something like that. But as I said, he did that off his own bat.'

'What about the cap badge? The one Erik Nyberg just happened to find?'

Bertil closes his eyes, as if he'd forgotten that detail.

'A bad decision. Nothing to do with me.'

'So Erik knew where to look? Knew where Lasse had planted evidence against Leo? And he and the count had no problem with Leo taking the blame?'

'The count and Erik did what they thought was best in order to protect Hubert.' Bertil's face has lost all its colour. 'I think I need to sit down.'

Thea helps him over to the sacrificial stone.

'How much do you actually remember, Bertil?'

'It comes in waves. I . . .' He breaks off, seems to be thinking.

'Have you talked about this to anyone outside the family before?'

He looks a little more present.

'No, and it's high time. Soon I won't be able to remember anything anymore, and I don't want to take the lies with me to the grave. They've already caused too much misery. Poor Jan-Olof, who has carried this for so long. David and the others too.'

'Do you think they had their doubts?'

'I'm sure they did – David definitely. Why do you think he stayed away for so many years? He knew he'd lied, both to the police and in court.'

'Did you tell him that he'd helped to frame an innocent man?'
Bertil shakes his head.

'No. We didn't tell him or Arne, but I think they had their suspicions. Particularly when . . .' He makes an irritated gesture as if he's forgotten what he was going to say.

'When the count set up the Bokelund Foundation with your help, and disinherited Hubert,' Thea says. 'Gave virtually his entire fortune to the community as a kind of recompense for what Hubert had done.'

'Yes.' Bertil sighs. The air seems to have gone out of him all of a sudden.

'Elita was pregnant. Who removed that information from the case file?'

'Lennartson, the chief of police. He and I played bridge together. We agreed that it was an unnecessary detail that would give rise to a whole lot of speculation. Make the situation worse.'

'I presume Lennartson owed a lot of money to your bank?'
Another sigh. 'He did.'

'Who was the child's father?'

'I've no idea.' Bertil shrugs; he looks as if he's telling the truth.

'And what happened to Hubert?'

'The count sent him to stay with relatives in England the very next day. Kept him away for years.'

'And the count had Nelson shot and the body incinerated as soon as possible to get rid of any evidence. With Erik Nyberg's help?'

'Yes.' Bertil leans heavily on his stick.

'And what about the Svart family?'

No response. She repeats the question, but Bertil doesn't look up or move.

'Bertil?' She touches his arm. His body jerks and he raises his head. The confusion is back.

'Kerstin?'

'No, it's me, Thea. Your daughter-in-law.'

Bertil frowns.

'Daughter-in-law? That can't be right. David's only . . .'

He loses the thread. Gets to his feet and gazes around.

'This is where it happened,' he murmurs. 'Poor girl.'

He takes a few steps, trips over something and falls head-long. Thea rushes over to him and helps him up. He's cut his forehead. She searches her pockets for something to staunch the bleeding, the moves on to his. Finds a white linen handkerchief and helps him to press it against the wound.

'We need to get back to the car, Bertil. That's going to need a stitch.'

'No, no. We'll go to Kerstin's . . .'

He points towards the hunting lodge, takes a couple of wobbly steps and almost falls again. Thea catches him just in time.

'Don't you think it would be better to go to the car and . . .'

'No!' he shouts. 'We'll go to Kerstin's. Dear, dear Kerstin. She'll help us.'

He sets off again with the handkerchief pressed to his forehead, and Thea realises she's not going to be able to steer him in any other direction.

She tucks her arm under his and lights the way with the torch.

86

It doesn't take too long to reach the hunting lodge. Bertil plods along determinedly. He doesn't say much, just concentrates on keeping the handkerchief in place.

Thea thinks about what he told her. Or rather confirmed.

Hubert murdered Elita, and Leo was sacrificed to save him. To save the reputation of the Gordon family, save the children who'd lied to the police, save Arne's career, and in the long term the whole community, since it is the Bokelund Foundation's money that keeps the village alive. All the pieces of the puzzle are in place – or almost all of them.

She still doesn't know what happened to the Svart family.

Once again she thinks about the beret she found in the kitchen at Svartgården. Had Eva-Britt and Lola somehow discovered what Lasse had done? Realised that he'd planted the cap badge, maybe even come across the blackmail money, or seen him shoeing Bill?

They arrive at the lodge before Thea has completed her train of thought. The grey tabby cat is sitting on the step, staring at them. Thea knocks on the door and Kerstin opens it almost immediately.

'Dear me, Bertil, did you get lost again?'

Bertil straightens up. 'No, not tonight. I've been talking to Thea. Telling her about the spring sacrifice . . .'

He shakes his head in frustration, as if to clear his mind.

'He's had a fall,' Thea says. 'Do you have a first aid kit?'

'Of course. Come into the kitchen and we'll fix you up, Bertil.'

They settle him on the kitchen sofa, just like last time. The bleeding has slowed.

Kerstin produces a surprisingly well-stocked first aid box, then makes tea while Thea tapes the wound.

'There you go – that'll do for now, but it would be best to get it stitched.' She turns to Kerstin. 'Can you call Ingrid? We're not on the best of terms at the moment, after what happened with Jan-Olof.'

Kerstin shakes her head.

'Poor Jan-Olof. He's had a difficult time for many years, both with his mother's health and his own. It was hardly your fault that he got drunk and fell – you saved his life!'

Thea feels a warmth spread through her chest, and it's not just from the tea. Kerstin glances at Bertil, who seems to have fallen asleep.

'Ingrid is very black and white. Empathy isn't her strong point. If you don't mind my saying so, I think it was a bad decision – throwing you out and giving you the sack just because you'd kept quiet about who your father was. I think a lot of people would have done the same in your situation.'

Thea sighs.

'I assume all this is on the Tornaby Facebook page? That the whole village knows about my family history?'

'I'm afraid so.'

Thea takes a gulp of her tea. It's one of Kerstin's own blends; it's slightly too bitter, but she can't bring herself to say so.

'Do you mind if I use the bathroom?'

'Go ahead. I'll give Ingrid a call.'

Thea sinks down on the toilet seat. Her body feels heavy.

She tries to gather her thoughts. Eva-Britt and Lola confront Lasse. They toss the beret on the table in front of him. Then what? No doubt there's a row. You don't demand answers from a man like Lasse Svart. Someone gets hurt, bleeds so much that he or she has to have the wound dressed in the bathroom. The print on the wall was made by a man with big hands. Is Lasse the one who's bleeding?

Thea's head feels heavy now. She stands up, splashes her face with cold water. Flops down again.

There are some magazines in a basket at her feet; the top one is *Bridge*. Another bridge player, like Bertil and the chief of police.

Suddenly another piece of the puzzle slots into place.

What was it Kerstin Miller said when Thea asked how she ended up in Tornaby?

Oh, the usual reason when someone moves halfway across the country – love. It didn't work out . . .

Dear, dear Kerstin – that was how Bertil referred to her. And Ingrid seems to do her best to stay away from the hunting lodge.

Thea returns to the kitchen. Bertil is fast asleep. Kerstin is sitting beside him on the sofa holding his hand. It could be a tender gesture, but Thea now realises it's much, much more than that.

'You love him,' she says. 'You moved down here because of him, in spite of the fact that he was married.'

Kerstin looks up, nods slowly.

'We met at the national bridge championship in Stockholm. I watched him win the title, then went and introduced myself afterwards. I told him how much I admired his game. As soon as our eyes met, I knew. He was ten years older than me, and married, but none of that mattered. It was Bertil I wanted to be with. When the post at Tornaby school came up I applied right away, even though I knew he'd never leave Ingrid. Love isn't something you can control.'

'You know what happened? The spring sacrifice, Elita, Hubert and Leo?'

'Yes. Bertil tried to do the right thing, but he was in an impossible situation. Someone had to do something, make a decision.'

'And that was what he did.' Thea sits down opposite them. 'Let Leo go to jail. Sacrificed him to save the village.'

Kerstin says nothing.

'How could he live with himself? An innocent young man going to jail while a murderer walked free?'

'He couldn't, really. Bertil is a man of great integrity. He was tortured by what he'd done, and together with the count he tried to make sure that as much as possible was put right afterwards.'

'Leo received money when he'd served his sentence,' Thea says. 'Hubert was sent away to England. The castle was given to the foundation, and the monastery received land as a penance for the count's sins.'

'Correct.'

'And the Svart family? What happened to Eva-Britt, Lola and Lasse?'

Kerstin doesn't answer.

'They'd quarrelled,' Thea says, a little too loudly although she doesn't know why. 'Lasse was injured. Lola and Eva-Britt ran to their car to drive to . . .'

Her brain feels like cotton wool, but suddenly she remembers something Per told her – about where the two women used to go when Lasse hit them. Not to the police, but to someone they trusted.

'They came here,' she says. 'Lola and Eva-Britt came here to get help that night. And Lasse followed them.'

Kerstin looks at her with sorrow in her eyes.

'It was the worst night of my life.'

87

18 May 1986

Kerstin and Bertil had just finished dinner. They were sitting on the sofa in front of the TV, her head resting on his shoulder, his arm around her.

On Wednesday and Sunday evenings Bertil said he had a lodge meeting in Lund, and his wife didn't ask any questions. However, in recent months Kerstin had begun to see small signs that Ingrid knew what was going on. That she tolerated their relationship even if she didn't approve of it. Ingrid was a strong woman. She loved Bertil just as much as Kerstin did, and was presumably prepared to sacrifice some of her pride in order to keep him.

That didn't matter. On Wednesdays and Sundays he was hers, and hers alone. They could be happy out here, away from everyone else. He parked his car on one of the logging tracks, then walked or cycled through the forest. She was happy with that; half a life was better than none. She knew she would never love anyone as much as she loved Bertil; she would do almost anything for him.

The noise made them both jump – a loud, metallic crash. Kerstin leaped up and ran over to the window. The rain was lashing down. She thought she could see car headlights among the trees.

'Someone's coming,' she said, which made Bertil get to his feet too.

But the lights were pointing in the wrong direction, down the slope towards the canal. An accident. Someone had come off the road.

'I need to go and find out what's happened.'

Bertil simply nodded; he knew he couldn't let anyone see him.

Kerstin pulled on her raincoat and boots, got in her car and drove along slowly with the windscreen wipers going full speed.

It was as she'd thought: a car had ploughed down the slope, churning up deep ruts in the sodden ground until it came to a halt only a metre or so from the slow-moving water, its wheels buried in the mud.

The engine was running, but the driver was making no attempt to free the vehicle. She recognised it, and as always it made her feel uncomfortable. Lasse Svart's red pick-up.

Kerstin briefly considered putting her car in reverse and going home. Cuddling up to Bertil and leaving Lasse to his own devices. But out here people helped their neighbours, even if they didn't like them – besides which, Lola or Eva-Britt might be in the car. She liked both women. They were good friends, and on a couple of occasions she'd let them sleep over when Lasse had gone too far.

She despised Lasse Svart, despised all men who thought they had the right to beat their women. Her father had been one of them. He'd allowed her mother to go off to work and come up with excuses for her bruises, even though everyone knew where they came from. He'd destroyed her pride, her dignity, until she barely existed. She moved around at home like a silent shadow.

Kerstin left the engine running and made her way down the slope. She was careful where she placed her feet; she didn't want to slip in the mud.

She shone the beam of her torch on the back window of the pick-up, but couldn't see the outline of the driver or passengers. When she reached the driver's door, she understood why. Lasse was slumped over the steering wheel, and beside him on the passenger seat lay a blue nylon bag with the words TORNABY SAVINGS BANK printed in white.

She knocked on the window, saw him stir. She knocked again, then opened the door.

Lasse looked up at her. He was as white as a sheet. His shirt was unbuttoned, and beneath it she could see a bandage that was dark red and shiny with blood. His boots and trousers were covered in mud.

Instinctively she took a step back.

'Don't move, Lasse. I'm going home to call an ambulance.'

She knew it was urgent. She would have to get Bertil to make the call while she hurried back with the first aid box to try and staunch the bleeding.

Lasse grinned at her.

'They got what they deserved,' he said in a thick voice, as if his throat was filled with blood.

'Who?'

'Those bitches. Those bitches who stabbed me and tried to steal my money.'

He pointed through the windscreen with a bloody finger. Kerstin adjusted the angle of the torch and saw something sticking up out of the water.

She froze. The torchlight was reflected in a bumper and a number plate, and she could see a half-open boot. She was looking at the back end of an old blue Ford. Eva-Britt's car, its nose buried deep in the muddy canal.

'Where are they?' she gasped. 'Where are Lola and Eva-Britt?'

Lasse pointed to the car again.

'Down there with the Green Man. Where no one will miss them.'

'What have you done, Lasse?'

Kerstin staggered backwards up the slope, slithering and sliding and landing on her bottom more than once, but keeping the beam of her torch on the Ford.

She didn't let herself cry until she was in her car reversing away. The same tears as when she was a little girl. Tears of anger, of impotence.

When she was only a hundred metres away from the hunting lodge, she stopped. She applied the handbrake, switched off the engine and sat in silence with the rain hammering on the roof. She wondered how long it would take for someone of Lasse's size to bleed to death. Ten minutes, maybe?

She checked her watch, closed her eyes and thought about her mother. She'd promised herself she would never be like that, never let anyone walk all over her as her mother had done. When twelve minutes had passed she started the car and slowly drove back to the lodge. Back to Bertil, to warmth and safety.

88

'L asse was dead when Bertil and I got down there.' Kerstin's voice is quiet, but the anger is clearly audible. 'Lasse murdered Lola and Eva-Britt. Pushed their car off the road and into the canal. They didn't have a chance in the muddy water. And as if that wasn't enough, Bertil worked out that he must have got out of the pick-up and opened the boot of the Ford, retrieved the bag of money without making any attempt to rescue the women. Lasse got what he deserved . . .'

She falls silent. Thea wants to ask a question, but the thought slides away. She takes another sip of her tea.

'What happened next?' she manages to ask.

'We didn't dare contact the police. Bertil was afraid they'd realise what had gone on, that the count, Erik and he himself would be dragged in, and the whole sorry story would come to light. So he called Erik and together they sank Lasse's pick-up next to the Ford. They made sure both vehicles ended up deep in the mud, where no one would find them.'

Thea thinks she knows the answer to her next question, but asks it anyway.

'And the money?'

'We agreed that it should go to Leo when he got out of jail. Anonymously, of course.'

Thea closes her eyes. Her mind is full of slow-moving thoughts.

'What . . .?' she begins, but can't get any further. Her mouth refuses to co-operate, her chin keeps dropping. 'What have you . . .?'

'Sleeping tablets. I ground them up and put them in your tea. I'm very sorry, but we need time to think things through. Work out what to do. Close your eyes and everything will be fine, I promise.'

The darkness closes in around Thea, sweeping in from the sides and swallowing her vision before finding its way into her head.

89

She is dreaming again, a horrible dream about dead women buried deep in the mud. Trapped, unable to get out. Elita, Lola, Eva-Britt. The two Gordon girls.

Beautiful women dead that by my side. Once lay.

Will she soon be lying next to them?

She is woken by loud voices. For a little while she lingers in the no-man's-land between sleep and wakefulness as her head slowly clears. She is sitting on a wooden chair in what is presumably Kerstin's pantry. Her arms and legs are secured to the chair with cable ties.

The voices are coming from the kitchen. There are three of them, and she recognises them all.

'We have no choice, Kerstin,' Ingrid says. 'If she starts talking, you and Bertil will be in real trouble. You might even end up in jail. Is that what you want?'

'Of course not, but isn't it high time the truth came out? Bertil seemed to think so too.'

'Bertil is no longer himself. You if anyone should realise that.'

'Not so loud – what if she wakes up and hears us?' The third voice belongs to Arne.

Someone switches on the radio. Music pours into the room, drowning out most of what is said. Thea tries to free herself, but the cable ties are immovable.

The conversation is becoming more heated, and she picks up the odd fragment through the music.

'We have no choice,' Ingrid repeats.

'. . . absolutely out of the question,' Kerstin counters. 'Bertil wouldn't have wanted . . .'

'What do you know about what Bertil would have wanted? You were nothing more than a diversion!'

'. . . for heaven's sake, Ingrid . . . other solutions.'

'There's only one way . . .'

This is followed by a crash as a piece of furniture falls over, then a loud thud. Murmuring voices. After a few minutes the music is switched off and the pantry door opens. Arne is standing there with a knife in his hand.

'Time for a little walk,' he says.

He cuts the cable ties and leads her into the kitchen, where Ingrid is picking up a chair.

'Where are Kerstin and Bertil?' Thea asks.

'They're having a little rest,' Ingrid answers, a fraction too quickly. Then she nods to Arne, jerks her head in the direction of the door.

'Are you really sure about this?' he asks her.

'Yes. You know what her type is like. Devious, untrustworthy.'

'What are you going to do to me?' Thea tries to hide her fear, but without success.

No response. Arne grabs her arm and hustles her out of the door. It's started raining.

'Head for the jetty,' he orders her.

She obeys, for a few metres at least. Then she stops dead.

'Keep going!'

She remains where she is. Turns to face him.

'No. If you want to kill me, then you're going to have to do it yourself. I have no intention of helping you.'

Arne pulls a face. Reaches into his pocket and produces a pistol. Her knees are trembling, she tenses her thighs as much as she can to stop them. She thinks about what Margaux would have done.

'Now move!'

Thea shakes her head.

Arne raises the gun. Thea takes a deep breath.

'Did you know that you sent the wrong person to jail? That Leo was innocent?'

'What?'

'It wasn't Leo and Bill you saw – not in the stone circle, anyway. It was Hubert, riding Nelson.'

'What the fuck are you talking about?' The hand holding the gun wavers.

'They've lied to you all these years, Arne. Bertil and your sister. Protected you because you persuaded the children to make a false statement.'

'Shut the fuck up!' His voice gives way.

'Somewhere deep down, I think you suspected. I think you knew something wasn't right about the investigation. Why else would Lennartson have told you to threaten that journalist? And why would the count, who was so passionate about the Gordon family history, disinherit his son? You had a feeling that a murderer had walked free while an innocent man ended up behind bars. And that Bertil, whom you so admired, was the brains behind it all. But neither you, David nor anyone else wanted to know the whole truth. You were happy for Bertil to keep the secret for you. It gave you the chance to pretend that you'd done the right thing.'

'Stop it!' Arne's voice has gone up in pitch, but Thea can see that her words have hit home.

'Drop the gun, Arne.'

The words come from the edge of the forest. Someone is standing there in the darkness. A short man in a yellow raincoat, holding a double-barrelled shotgun.

'Hubert?' Arne exclaims.

'Drop the gun, I said!' The man raises the shotgun and takes a couple of steps forward, into the glow of the outside lights.

Rain is pouring down onto Thea's face. She wipes her eyes so that she can see properly; it is indeed Hubert.

'What the fuck are you doing here?' Arne snaps.

'Kerstin called and told me what had happened. Please put down the gun, Arne.'

'I was only supposed to frighten her, for fuck's sake! Make her stop poking around and leave Tornaby for good.'

Arne lowers his arm, but keeps hold of the weapon.

'Is Thea right, Hubert? Was it you riding the horse?'

'Drop the gun, Arne.'

'Answer me!' He raises his arm, aiming at Hubert this time. The little man doesn't move; his shotgun is still trained on Arne.

'Come on, Hubert! Bertil's kept your secret all these years. I would never reveal something that would harm him.'

'And what secret is that?'

Arne wipes the rain from his face with his free hand as his brain tries to compute what Thea has told him.

'That it was you and not Leo who murdered Elita Svart.'

There is silence for a few seconds. Hubert's expression doesn't change, and all at once Thea knows why. She curses herself silently for not realising long ago, when she read the autopsy report.

Elita had died from a single powerful blow to the head. The ground all around her was covered in hoof prints, there was horse hair on her clothes.

Her hands were effectively bound by the ribbons. Nelson was difficult to handle, according to Hubert.

'It wasn't him,' she says loudly.

'What?' Arne gives a start.

'Hubert didn't kill Elita Svart. No one did.'

'What the fuck are you talking about?'

'Elita was kicked to death by Nelson. That's what happened, isn't it, Hubert?'

She turns to him.

'It wasn't Nelson's fault,' Hubert mumbles. 'The children started screaming, the drums, the fire – it was all too much. Nelson panicked and reared up. Elita was standing right in front of him and . . .'

'Shit!' Arne rubs his forehead. 'You mean the whole thing was an accident? Why the hell didn't you say anything?'

'I . . . I didn't dare.'

Thea sees Hubert's shoulders slump. The rain hammers down on his raincoat, trickling down in sad little rivulets.

'Shit,' Arne says again. 'So what do we do now?'

The question seems to be directed at Thea, but it is Ingrid who answers. She has silently appeared behind Arne.

'We protect the village,' she says. 'That's what Bertil and the count did, and we must do the same thing. For their sake.'

She places a hand on Arne's shoulder.

'Why didn't you tell me the truth?' he says. 'Didn't you trust me?'

'Bertil trusted you more than anyone else,' Ingrid assures her brother. 'You're like a son to him – he was so proud of you when you qualified as a police officer. He didn't want to see you get into trouble.'

She pats him gently.

'You did what you thought was right. We all did, especially Bertil. He realised that the truth was too costly, and that someone must be sacrificed for the good of everyone else. Just like now.'

'But we can't kill someone, can we?'

'We have no choice. If she talks, the whole thing collapses. Bertil could end up in jail and you'd probably lose your job. Think about David, the castle – everything we've built up would be taken away from us. That can't happen.'

Arne looks unsure, but he is still holding the pistol.

'You have to be strong now, Arne,' Ingrid continues. 'Do what Bertil would have done.'

'Enough.' Hubert raises the shotgun a fraction. 'I can't lie anymore.'

Ingrid tilts her head on one side.

'What do you think your father would have said about all this, Hubert? Wouldn't he have told you to protect the honour of the Gordon family, as he did? Do what's best for the village?'

She takes a couple of steps towards Hubert, whose shoulders slump even more.

Ingrid keeps walking, holds out her hand.

'Ingrid,' Arne says warningly.

Thea holds her breath.

'Give me the shotgun,' Ingrid says firmly.

Hubert's head droops.

'Well done, Hubert. Your father would have been proud of you. You're a true Gordon.'

Those words have an instant effect on Hubert. Without warning he sweeps the shotgun in a wide arc and fires.

The report is so loud and so deafening that Thea closes her eyes and covers her head with her arms. When she opens her eyes Ingrid is lying on the ground, and for a second she thinks Hubert has shot her. But Ingrid scrambles to her feet. Her face is ashen, but she appears to be unhurt. Hubert is looking in surprise at his stomach, where a small black-rimmed hole has appeared in his raincoat. Dark red blood is seeping out. Thea turns around. Arne is staring at Hubert, then suddenly he realises what he's done.

'No!' he gasps, and lowers the pistol.

Hubert drops the shotgun, his knees give way and he sinks to the ground. Thea rushes over to him. He is still conscious, and manages a strained smile.

'I'm sorry I haven't been completely honest with you, Thea.'

'Hush – not now.'

She unbuttons his raincoat. The wound is approximately ten centimetres diagonally above the navel. The right side to avoid the liver, but bullets often change direction inside the body. She rolls him over onto his side, finds the exit wound. There is blood here too, but not much. A good sign.

'No, no, no!'

Arne is walking around in circles. Ingrid still looks shocked.

Thea finds a handkerchief in Hubert's inside pocket, presses it against the entry wound.

Ingrid staggers over to Arne.

'We need to finish this, right now,' Thea hears her say.

Arne appears to have lost the plot completely, but he's still clutching the gun.

'Can you stand up?' Thea asks Hubert.

'I think so.'

She helps him up, drapes his arm over her shoulders and hobbles towards the edge of the forest as fast as she can.

Ingrid and Arne seem to be involved in a heated exchange of opinions, but Thea has no intention of sticking around to see who wins.

90

Thea tries to half-run through the forest, but it's impossible. Hubert is too heavy, and as soon as she's among the trees she loses the little path.

She will never be able to find her way back to the logging track where she left the car. They'll have to try and follow the canal as far as the moat, then cross the bridge to the castle. Lock themselves in the west wing and call the police.

She's far from sure that Hubert will be able to make it, but she can't see any other way. Hubert seems to understand, and keeps going as best he can. He doesn't complain, even though he must be in considerable pain.

'Forgive me,' he murmurs. 'All the trouble I've caused . . .'

She doesn't answer; she's fully occupied with trying to press on in the pouring rain. She looks back; the beams of two torches have appeared in the darkness behind them.

'We have to keep going,' she whispers, dragging Hubert to the left to get closer to the canal.

She smells the water before she sees it. It's impossible not to think about what's buried down there in the mud. A pick-up and a car with the remains of Lasse, Eva-Britt and Lola.

Hubert coughs, gasps for air. 'Sorry, sorry.'

The torches are getting closer.

'We can't stop now, Hubert.'

His legs can't carry him any longer. He is becoming heavier and heavier, and in the end she has to lay him down on the ground in a glade by the water's edge.

'Leave me here,' he whispers. 'Run – I'll delay them.'

Thea takes a couple of steps. Sees the blood on his raincoat. The handkerchief in his outstretched hand is more red than white. She goes back, sits down beside him. Helps him to press the handkerchief to the wound.

'Run, Thea.'

She shakes her head.

'You're my patient. I can't leave you.'

The torch beams have almost reached them. Thea thinks about curling up, but realises there's no point. There are reflective tags on Hubert's yellow raincoat that shine when the light hits them.

'Here!' Ingrid shouts. 'They're here!'

Ingrid and Arne enter the glade. Arne is still holding the gun. He clenches his jaw, a determined look in his eye.

Thea holds her breath. Margaux's face suddenly comes into her mind. Her smile, her voice.

Don't be afraid, ma chère.

At the same moment Thea hears a faint sound approaching through the night. At first she thinks she's imagining things, but then Arne lifts his head.

The sound comes closer, a rhythmic thumping. Hooves thundering on soft ground. A dazzling bright light blazes through the trees.

Arne shades his eyes with his hand, then staggers backwards.

The hoof beats and the light come closer and closer, illuminating Arne's face. Every scrap of colour has been replaced with ash-grey. His eyes are wide open, his mouth is gaping.

'Arne!' Ingrid yells, but he doesn't seem to hear her. He stands there as if he has been turned to stone, as if his worst nightmare has come true.

A big horse enters the glade; the blinding light is shining from the head of its rider.

'NOOO!' Arne screams. He drops the gun and turns around. The horse cannons into him and he falls into the thick, muddy water.

Horse and rider continue towards Ingrid, who begins to run. After only a couple of metres the horse knocks her down like a rag doll.

The rider reins in the animal, then circles around Ingrid to see if she's likely to get up. Ingrid lies there motionless. The horse comes to a halt and the rider switches off the powerful head torch.

'Did you think I wouldn't be able to get out of my own cellar?' Kerstin Miller says, without taking her eyes off Ingrid.

She turns to Thea.

'I really am so sorry about all this.' She jumps down, loops the reins over a branch. 'I've called emergency services. The police and an ambulance should be here in a few minutes. Let's see if we can get Hubert back to the house.'

91

The night is filled with blue lights, and Hubert is lying on a trolley. Thea and the paramedics have managed to stop the bleeding.

Arne was covered in mud when the police led him past, hands cuffed behind his back. He wept like a child as they put him in the patrol car. Ingrid was quieter.

It is Kerstin who talks to the police, explains what's happened. Thea has given only a brief summary, on the basis that she has to attend to her patient. She is standing beside Hubert holding his hand.

'You have to go now,' she says. 'You need to get to the hospital.'

'Not yet.' He gives her that smile she likes so much. 'I should have owned up long ago. Taken responsibility.'

She squeezes his hand.

'Don't think about that now. What's done is done.'

'I really wanted to confess, but I couldn't. We were young. We didn't have the courage.'

He returns the squeeze.

Another car arrives and Per Nyberg jumps out, looking worried. He goes over and speaks to one of the police officers, who points to Thea and Hubert.

Per hurries to join them.

'How is he?'

'He'll survive,' Thea reassures him. 'Hubert saved my life,' she adds, and sees the little man's face light up.

'I'm not surprised,' Per replies. 'Hubert is one of the most unselfish people I know.'

He reaches out and takes Hubert's other hand in a touchingly tender gesture.

One of the paramedics catches Thea's eye.

'Time we made a move.'

The men load the trolley onto the ambulance. Per holds onto Hubert's hand for a second before letting go. Thea remains standing beside him. She is exhausted, both physically and mentally.

She looks at Hubert. Sees how his eyes are fixed on Per. He raises a hand in farewell.

The strongest love is unrequited love.

And now, at long last, she finally understands how everything hangs together. The picture is complete.

Be careful with him, Hubert had said on the castle steps. She had interpreted it as a warning, but in fact it was an exhortation.

They stand in silence as the ambulance drives away.

'He loves you, doesn't he? *The strongest love is unrequited love* – that's what he wrote in his favourite book. It's you he's referring to.'

Per doesn't answer.

'You were riding Nelson that night,' she goes on quietly. 'You were dressed as the Green Man. You were the father of Elita's child.'

Eventually Per shakes his head slowly. 'I loved her, more than I've ever loved anyone else. But we were so young, all three of us. Hubert helped me to get dressed up, then he hid in the forest and watched. The plan was to scare the kids, pay them

463

back for all the crap Elita had had to put up with over the years. Hubert and I weren't too keen on the idea, but Elita insisted. She wanted to kill off her old self. We were going to fly away from here together, become something better.'

'You'd arranged to go to Paris, to Hubert's aunt. That's why Elita had her passport in her suitcase. The three of you were going to stay with her until Elita had had the baby. Maybe even longer.'

Per nods. 'We were dreamers, dreaming of something different. Something bigger. And for a few weeks it actually felt real, as if we could actually do it. A ridiculous dream, of course. Doomed to crash and burn.'

'So tell me about Walpurgis Night.'

'Nelson was nervous. Everything frightened him. He reared up, then took off. Galloped all the way home with me clinging to his back. I didn't know what had happened until Hubert showed up in the stable. He said Nelson had kicked Elita, and that she was dead. He'd laid her on the sacrificial stone. It was all over. I was in total shock, I couldn't speak. Hubert took care of the horse, then drove me home. Told me not to say a word to anyone. He said the whole thing was an accident, it wasn't my fault.'

He shakes his head again.

'I should have said no, but I was terrified of my father and the count. I didn't have the guts to look them in the eye and admit what I'd done. So I kept quiet, and suddenly Leo was in custody, Hubert was sent away to England, and I was alone with our secret. The children identified Leo, and I suppose I wanted to believe that he really had done it, that I wasn't responsible for her death. When he confessed, I felt a huge sense of relief. For a while, at least.'

He takes a deep breath.

'Deep down I knew the truth, but I chose to keep quiet like the pathetic coward I am.'

'And Hubert didn't say anything either,' Thea says. 'Because he didn't want to see you get into trouble. He never told his father that he wasn't a murderer, not even when the count took away the castle and the land.'

'As I said, Hubert is the most unselfish person I know. Time for me to try and be more like him, don't you think?'

He pats her arm, then turns and walks over to one of the police officers.

'There's something I need to tell you,' she hears him say. 'Something I've kept quiet about for far too long.'

92

'The story is almost over, Margaux. There is only one chapter left, and a confession. My own.'

Sister Aubert is sitting in the staffroom when she hears agitated voices in the corridor.

She has worked at the clinic for four years, and enjoys her job. She gets on well with the other nurses and the doctors, especially Dr Roland, who is unfortunately too shy to ask her out. She's decided to give him another two weeks before taking matters into her own hands.

The voices are coming closer. The door opens to reveal Sister Papin and Sister Ribot, her closest colleagues.

'Another message has arrived,' says Sister Ribot. 'From the Swede.'

Sister Aubert gets to her feet. Leaves her coffee and accompanies the two women to room fourteen.

The patient is a doctor, she knows that. The woman suffered a severe head trauma over a year ago during a bombing raid in Syria, and has been in a coma ever since. She will probably never regain consciousness, but her body hasn't given up. It continues to fight on, and as long as it does that, all they can do is wait and pray.

The patient has many visitors. Her family and friends are often here, sitting by her bed and chatting to her as the doctors have recommended. The family has even installed a telephone answering machine so that friends can leave little messages for her.

Every afternoon at four o'clock, Sister Aubert or one of her colleagues presses the button and plays the latest messages. They usually leave the room, but not when she has called. The Swede. That's what they call her, even though they know her name is Thea.

It is all Sister Papin's fault. She was the one who started listening to the Swede's story, then passed it on to the others.

A story about a castle and a dead girl.

As the days went by they all found a reason to be in room fourteen at four o'clock to hear the next instalment. Sat there in silence while the Swede told the tale of how she had slowly begun to untangle old secrets.

They have no idea whether the story is true. Maybe the Swede is making it up, maybe it's something she's read in a book, but they don't care. They simply sit there together and sometimes, although she knows it's impossible, Sister Aubert gets the feeling that the patient is listening as intently as they are.

They thought it was all over when the ambulance drove away with poor Hubert, and Per finally revealed what had happened on that Walpurgis Night so many years ago. Several weeks have passed since then – but now there is a new message.

They hurry along the corridor, close the door of room fourteen behind them. Settle down around the bed as usual, before Sister Ribot presses 'Play'.

'Hi, Margaux, it's me,' says the Swede. She doesn't sound quite as unhappy as she normally does. 'I'm sorry it's been so long; things have been a bit chaotic here. Ingrid and Arne

have been arrested and are waiting to go to court. The police dredged the canal and recovered the pick-up and the Ford with the remains of Lasse, Eva-Britt and Lola inside, just as Kerstin said. The women will probably be buried next to Elita. For some reason that feels like a kind of consolation, that she won't have to lie there alone anymore.

David has decided to sell the restaurant. He's not going to work for a while; he wants to take care of his father. Nettan and Sebastian have returned home. I think they, like David, are relieved that the truth has finally come out. Jan-Olof definitely feels that way. His fall was a pure accident, and he'll make a full recovery.

Hubert has promised to look after Emee for a while. The two convalescents will get better together, as he puts it. Neither he nor Per will face any charges. Elita's death was also an accident, after all.

It was a lynx that killed the deer. The glycol Emee ingested came from a bait trap set by Erik Nyberg. A stupid idea, according to Per. Hubert made Erik pay the vet's bill by way of an apology.

I also found out that it's Hubert and Per who pay for the upkeep of Elita's grave, and sometimes lay flowers upon it – but I'm sure you'd already worked that out, just as you'd worked out that it was Arne who locked me in the cellar at Svartgården, and who left the Green Man figures on my windscreen. As he said outside the hunting lodge, he was trying to scare me off so I'd stop digging.

I honestly don't think Arne is a bad person. None of them are, not even Ingrid. She loves Bertil, her family and Tornaby. She'd do anything to protect them. In that respect she has certain similarities with my father. I've written his reprieve petition, in case you're wondering. I might be angry with him, I might never be able to forgive him, but I can give him that.

You could call it grace.

I hope the others will also receive grace, especially David. He and I are talking again. We are friendly, almost affectionate, but we've agreed that divorce is the right course of action. Our journey together is finished. Just like yours and mine.

The story is almost over, Margaux. There is only one chapter left, and a confession. My own.

We will begin with the remaining chapter. I've asked a private detective to track down Leo in Canada. He deserves to know the truth. After all, he was the real spring sacrifice. I'm intending to go over there on my own. My first trip without you. It will feel very strange. At the same time, you are always with me, in my thoughts and in my heart.

And the confession. I've saved it until the end because it's the most difficult part. Maybe it was Hubert who gave me the strength to admit to myself who I am. Or maybe it was Elita Svart.

Thea Lind was a disguise. An alter ego I hid behind until I met you. I only wish I'd told you while there was still time. I almost did, on several occasions. And now I'm doing it. Confessing to you who I really am.

You are the person you want to be. And I only want to be your beloved.

I love you, Margaux. I always will. You are the great love of my life.

I miss you so much.'

The message ends. There is total silence in the room. And it might be her imagination, later Sister Aubert is almost certain that it is, but at that moment she could swear that the patient in the bed beside her smiles.

Epilogue

The log cabin lies deep in the forest. The private detective drops her off at the end of the drive.

'I'll wait here,' he says. 'Good luck.'

Thea picks up her bag and sets off towards the house. It is warm. The trees are dark green, the air is still. There is a boat on a trailer on the drive, and a rack of fishing rods on the veranda.

Two girls aged four or five are playing on the lawn.

'Hi!' one of them says. 'What do you want?' She has black hair, dark eyes and confident expression.

'I'm looking for John Swanson,' Thea says.

'He's my granddad!'

The front door opens and a tall man steps out. His beard and hair are peppered with grey, he has a slight stoop, and he's wearing jeans and a checked flannel shirt.

'Can I help you?' he asks in almost perfect English.

'I'm looking for Leo Rasmussen,' Thea says in Swedish. She sees him recoil, as if the name opens doors in his head that he would prefer to keep closed.

'I'm Thea Lind,' she adds quickly. 'I'm here to tell you what really happened on Walpurgis Night in 1986.'

The man stares at her, and for a few seconds she is convinced that he's going to tell her to leave. But then he gestures towards the veranda.

'Take a seat,' he replies in Swedish. 'Can I get you a drink?'

She sits down in a wicker armchair and he disappears into the house. He returns with two bottles of mineral water and sits down beside her.

Thea takes a deep breath, then tells him everything from beginning to end. He listens in silence.

'Here.'

She passes him her iPad, shows him a series of newspaper headlines from last spring. Pictures of the pick-up and the Ford being recovered from the canal. Of Leo and Elita when they were young. Of the Polaroid.

He scrolls through the images, still saying nothing. He lingers for a while on Elita's self-portrait. Touches her face with his index finger before moving on.

'Thank you,' he says when he's finished. 'Thank you for telling me all this.'

His eyes are shining with unshed tears, and it might be an illusion, but she thinks his back is suddenly a little straighter, as if a weight has been lifted from his shoulders.

She stays for a while and answers his questions, then gets up to say goodbye. She gives him a card with her phone number, then leaves him in peace with his thoughts.

On the way back to the car, the little dark-haired girl catches up with her. Takes her hand.

'What's your name?' the child asks.

'Thea. What's yours?'

'Elita.'

'What a lovely name,' Thea says.

For a brief moment she almost feels happy.

Author's note

Tornaby and Ljungslöv are both fictional places. Just like Reftinge in *End of Summer*, Nedanås in *Deeds of Autumn* and Vedarp in *Dead of Winter*, they are based on the area where I grew up in north-western Skåne.

Walpurgis Eve in Sweden falls on April 30th. Walpurgis, or *Valborgsmässoafton* ('Valborg' for short), is the night where bonfires are lit to celebrate spring. Traditionally the bonfires were believed to ward off evil spirits, and today people still gather together to light the fires and sing. On May Day there are parades and festivals held across the country as May 1st has been a public holiday in Sweden since 1939.

Keep reading for an exclusive extract from the next book in the
Seasons Quartet

End of Summer

You can always go home. But you can never go back . . .

Summer 1983: Four-year-old Billy chases a rabbit in the
fields behind his house. But when his mother goes to call him
in, Billy has disappeared. Never to be seen again.

Today: Veronica is a bereavement counsellor. She's never
fully come to terms with her mother's suicide after her brother
Billy's disappearance. When a young man walks into
her group, he looks familiar and talks about the trauma of
his friend's disappearance in 1983. Could Billy still be alive
after all this time?

Needing to know the truth, Veronica goes home – to the
place where her life started to fall apart.

Coming Summer 2021

Prologue

Summer 1983

The baby rabbit was crouching in the tall grass. Its coat was wet and shiny with the dew that had accompanied dusk into the garden.

He should really go in. His mum didn't like him being out on his own, especially not when it was getting dark. But he was a big boy now, he would be five in a few weeks, and he liked dusk a lot. Soon all the night animals would start to appear. Hedgehogs would peer out cautiously from beneath the big bushes, then set off across the grass in funny, zigzag paths. Bats would start to swirl about between the tall trees, and from the avenue of chestnuts on the other side of the house he could already hear the first cries of the owls.

It was the rabbits he wanted to see most. Having one of his own was right at the top of his wish list. A fluffy baby rabbit, just like the one sitting over there in the grass. The little creature looked at him, twitching its nose as if it wasn't sure about his smell. If he was dangerous or harmless. He took a couple of careful steps towards it. The rabbit stayed where it was, it didn't seem to have made up its mind.

He had been looking forward to his birthday for a couple of months already. He was hoping to get a kite from Mattias. He had watched his big brother spend hours making kites out in Dad's workshop. The way he carefully measured the canes for the frame, stretched twine between the ends and covered the whole thing with taut, shiny fabric that he had pinched from the boxes up in the attic. Clothes that had once belonged to their grandmother, that Mum hadn't got round to getting rid of.

Several times this summer he had watched as Mattias and his friends held competitions with their homemade creations. Mattias's kites always flew highest, every time. Hovering above the fields just like their feathered namesakes.

The rabbit in the grass was still looking at him, so he took a few more steps towards it. He stopped when the animal raised its head slightly. He felt like running straight at the rabbit to grab hold of it. But Uncle Harald always said that a good hunter didn't rush things, so he waited, standing perfectly still and thinking about his wish list.

He was hoping to get a red car he had seen in the shop in the village from his big sister. It had big flames on its sides, and if you pulled it backwards and then let go, it would race off on its own. It was probably expensive, but Vera was bound to buy it for him anyway. Dad would give her the money. If she asked for it. He didn't really know if she had forgiven him for the business with the hawk's eggs, but he didn't want to think about that. Mattias had forgiven him, but it was harder to tell with Vera.

The baby rabbit lowered its head again and started to nibble on a blade of grass. Its whiskers were twitching so cutely that he very nearly broke Uncle Harald's rules. But he needed to wait a bit longer. Wait for the moment the rabbit relaxed and was no longer looking in his direction.

He had asked for a bicycle from Mum and Dad. He had already started practising on Mattias's old one, even though he wasn't actually supposed to do that on his own. The other day he fell off and grazed his knee. Not badly, but enough to draw blood. He had started to cry, and went and hid in the treehouse. Uncle Harald had found him and gave him a telling off. 'What did your mum say? Don't you understand that she gets worried?'

Yes, he understood. His mum worried about him pretty much the whole time. 'Because you're my little mouse,' she always said. 'Because I can't bear the thought of anything happening to you.' That was why he had hidden himself away and didn't go back into the house. After telling him off, his uncle had put a plaster on his knee and told Mum that he had fallen over on the gravel path between the barn and the house. *Easily done if you're running in wooden-soled shoes.* The lie was for his mother's sake, not his. So she wouldn't worry. Since then he hadn't been allowed to wear wooden-soled shoes like Mattias and Vera. He thought that was unfair.

Suddenly the baby rabbit moved. It took a couple of short hops in his direction, in search of longer grass. Instead of running towards it he stood perfectly still. Waiting, just like Uncle Harald said.

Uncle Harald was the best hunter in the area, everyone knew that. There were almost always dead animals hanging from the roof of his boiler room. Pheasants, deer, hares, with empty eyes and stiff bodies. Uncle Harald had rough hands. He smelled of tobacco, oil, dogs and something he couldn't identify. But he guessed it was something dangerous. A lot of people were scared of Uncle Harald. Vera and Mattias were, even if Vera pretended not to be. She sometimes contradicted him, but you could hear the wobble in her voice. Mattias, on the other hand, didn't say anything, just stared down at the ground and did as he was told. Fetched Uncle Harald's pipe or fed his dogs. They weren't the sort of dogs you could play with. They lived outside in big pens and travelled on the back of the truck rather than inside it. Rough coats, anxious eyes that followed Uncle Harald's every movement. The other week he went to the swimming pool with Dad and Mattias. He had sat in the sauna listening to the old men talk. When Uncle Harald came in everyone moved out of the way, even Dad. Clearing the best space for him, right in the middle. Looking at him the same way the dogs did.

The only person who wasn't scared of Uncle Harald was Mum. Mum wasn't scared of anyone, except maybe God. Sometimes she and Uncle Harald had arguments. He had heard them say things to each other. Harsh words that he didn't really understand, but he knew they weren't nice.

All the same, Uncle Harald's birthday present was the one he had the highest hopes of. A little rabbit that would be his alone, that's what his uncle had promised. Maybe just like the one sitting a few metres away from him. If he could catch that one, he'd have two. And Uncle Harald would be proud of him. Proud of him for being a proper hunter.

He'd waited long enough now, so he took another careful step forward. The baby rabbit went on chewing the long grass, didn't even notice him getting closer. He took another step and slowly reached out his hands. It might just work.

'Billy, time to come in now!'

The rabbit raised its head, it seemed to be listening to the voice from the house. Then it turned and scampered away.

He felt disappointment tug at his chest. But then the rabbit stopped and looked back at him, as if it was wondering where he'd gone. He hesitated. Mum would be worried if he didn't go in. The owls were hooting louder now, and the outside lights had come on, making the shadows in the garden deeper. The rabbit was still looking at him. It seemed to be saying: *Are you coming?*

He took a couple of steps, then a few more.

'Billy!' his mum called. 'Billy, come inside now!'

The hunt was on. The rabbit scampered away from him, and if he was really lucky it would lead him to its burrow. Somewhere full of baby rabbits with big eyes and soft fur. Rabbits he could take home with him. Which could live in the çage Uncle Harald had promised him.

'Billy!' Mum's cry disappeared in the distance. The baby rabbit was still running ahead of him, and even though he was wearing his best running shoes it could probably easily outpace him if it wanted to. Perhaps the rabbit *wanted* him to catch it? Hug it, make it his.

He followed it through the rows of gnarled old fruit trees. Then in amongst the overgrown bushes. He didn't really like this furthest part of the garden. Earlier in the summer his friend Isak had found a jawbone on the ground under the dense branches, a white bone with four yellow molars attached. Uncle Harald had said that Grandfather used to bury things there. Things he wanted to get rid of for good. That the jawbone probably belonged to a pig, and that you had to bury some things very deep to stop the foxes finding them.

He had only ever seen one fox in his life. That was when Uncle Harald, Dad and the other men laid the results of their hunt out in the yard last autumn. Narrow eyes, a shimmering red coat, sharp teeth that stuck out beneath the bloodstained nose. The dogs kept their distance from it. They seemed unsettled, almost frightened. Uncle Harald had said that you always shot foxes if you got the chance. That it was the duty of every hunter, whenever the opportunity presented itself. Because foxes were cunning, just like in fairy tales. They knew how to move without leaving a trail.

'They've got incredible noses,' he said. 'And foxes love the smell of rabbits and little boys. So make sure you stay inside the fence, Billy!'

Then Uncle Harald had laughed, that rumbling laugh that sounded jolly and dangerous at the same time, and after a while he had started to laugh too. But he hadn't been able to stop thinking about foxes digging for skeletons in the garden. He even dreamed about them at night. Sharp teeth, paws digging in the soil, damp, shiny noses sniffing the air. Sniffing in the direction of the house for a little boy.

He had avoided that part of the garden since then, and hadn't protested when Isak wanted to take the pig's jaw-bone home with him, even though it should really have been his.

But right now neither skeletons nor foxes could stop him. The rabbit scampered round the dry bushes and he followed it deeper into the undergrowth. A low branch caught his sleeve and he had to stop for a couple of seconds. By the time he had pulled free the rabbit had disappeared.

He hesitated for a few moments, wondering if he should turn back and go up to the house. But he was still caught up in the thrill of the chase. That gave him the courage to go on. Further in amongst the bushes. Like a proper hunter.

More branches reached out towards him, feeling for his clothes with thorny fingers. Somewhere up ahead in the gloom he thought he could see a little white tail bobbing about. Perhaps he'd reached the burrow now? The thought made him speed up, and he almost ran straight into the tall fence that marked the end of the garden.

He stopped abruptly. Just a metre or so beyond the wire fence a dense crop of maize was growing. It wasn't going to be harvested for a while yet. Not until it had dried and turned yellow, Dad said.

Crickets were chirruping among the leaves, weaving their song into a crisp carpet of sound that almost drowned out his thoughts. The rabbit was on the other side. It was sitting right beneath the green wall of maize plants, watching him. Waiting for him.

The fence was tall. Maybe even taller than Uncle Harald, and certainly too tall for him to be able to climb over. The hunt was over. He wasn't going to see the rabbit's burrow. Even so, he couldn't help feeling a bit relieved. He had never been this far in the garden on his own before. There was only a thin streak of evening light left in the sky, and the shadows among the undergrowth had turned to dense darkness almost without him noticing.

He decided to go home, and was about to turn back when he caught sight of something. A small hollow had been dug out beneath the fence, just big enough for a small boy to crawl through. He looked over towards the rabbit. It was still sitting there.

A gust of wind blew through the field of maize, then the rusty links of the wire fence and the dark bushes behind him. He looked round, then got down on his knees, then his stomach. He wriggled carefully under the jagged wire fence, stood up and brushed the dirt from his hands and knees. He was tingling with excitement. He was out now, beyond the garden, for the first time on his own. He would tell Isak about it on Monday. Maybe Mattias and Vera too. Tell them how brave he was when he caught a rabbit of his very own, only they mustn't say anything to Mum.

There was a rustling sound among the maize and at first he thought it was the wind again. Then he saw the white tail disappear among the tall plants. The rabbit wasn't scampering anymore, it was running, fast. Its ears were tucked flat against its head and soil was flying up from its paws. It wasn't until the rabbit had disappeared from view that he realised what had happened. That the animal's sensitive nose had picked up a smell belonging to someone other than him. Someone who had burrowed under a fence. Someone with a red coat and sharp teeth who loved the smell of rabbits. And little boys . . .

His heart was beating fast, racing as if it belonged to a frightened little rabbit. The maize plants loomed above him like dark, swaying giants, pushing him back towards the fence. He felt a sob rise in his throat. From the corner of his eye he caught a glimpse of something moving, something red. He turned round and realised at the same moment that the crickets had fallen silent.

Mum! he had time to think. *Mum!*

DEAD OF WINTER

When fifteen-year-old Laura Aulin arrives to spend Christmas with her beloved aunt Hedda, she is also looking forward to spending time with Jack, Hedda's foster son.

But a lot has happened since last summer and Laura soon finds out that things are not what they first appear, as old faces and new seem to be keeping secrets from her. Tensions and jealousies come to an explosive finale at a party on the night of Lucia.

And when the smoke clears, all that is left is ash . . .

Coming Winter 2022